P9-EDJ-979

Praise for *Flights: Extreme Visions of Fantasy*

"*Flights* looks towards raising the bar for fantasy in terms of quality and imagination. . . . The authors represented within are some of the very best in the field. . . . If you love fantasy in any of its forms, and you enjoy short fiction, *Flights* may very well be the don't-miss collection of the year, sure to produce some award nominees and award winners, and maybe a few new classics. Miss this, and you'll be losing out on something rich and strange."   —*Chronicle*

"Taking the who's who of modern-day fantasy, worthy contributors provide powerful tales that run the genre's gamut and beyond. Each tale is well written, with some so good they may prove to be the opening act of a new series. Fans of anthologies will have a feast, for these are the grand masters in one collection and all provide a fine contribution that makes the realm and cast seem real. [A] quality offering."   —*Midwest Book Review*

"I love short fiction when it's presented in the form of an anthology like *Flights*. . . . There is very, very good fiction here. . . . One of the best anthologies I've ever read, bar none. . . . Everything here is superb. There's nothing less than a merely outstanding tale here. . . . What Al Sarrantonio has done is assemble a collection that should win awards by the armful if there's any justice in this world. Many of these tales would be well served by reading aloud to attentive readers on a cold winter's night in a room illuminated only by candlelight. They're that good. I've read, or at least skimmed, hundreds of fantasy anthologies over the past decades—some superb, some decidedly mixed, and more than a few that were terrible. *Flights* is among a mere handful that are truly great. If you like the various anthologies that Ellen Datlow and Terri Windling have done, you'll find this equally pleasing."   —*The Green Man Review*

"The authors here are at the top of their games. . . . This anthology succeeds in pointing the way to a new plateau for the genre."
        —*Science Fiction Weekly*

"All the work here has something to recommend it. . . . *Flights* would serve well as a course text. These authors represent a big slice of working genre writers, and the variety of stories provides a lot of opportunity for teachable moments. For general reading, this would make a great summer book—just enough in any one story to pass part of a warm afternoon, or perhaps to fine-tune one's tan."   —*SFRevu*

"Another sterling assemblage by a master anthologist." —*Booklist*

continued . . .

"The stories in this collection bear witness to the elegance and variety present in current fantasy." —*Library Journal*

"There are a good many treasures among the stories assembled here . . . a more than respectable percentage of excellent work by a terrifically eclectic selection of contributors." —*Locus*

Praise for *Redshift: Extreme Visions of Speculative Fiction*

"The best collection of new science fiction in recent memory."
—*Chicago Sun-Times*

"At least a dozen of the thirty stories in this anthology are high-water marks that will no doubt be short-listed for awards. . . . *Redshift* is filled with terrific stories." —*Milwaukee Journal Sentinel*

"A well-chosen, satisfyingly hefty anthology . . . by a who's who of SF and relative newcomers. . . . Humor is here in plenty . . . and many thoughtful pieces that will haunt your mental landscape for days." —*Booklist* (starred review)

"Excellent stories." —*Publishers Weekly*

"Exhibits a wide variety of styles and topics and aptly demonstrates the cutting edge of the genre." —*Library Journal*

"A large and high-quality field of SF stories. . . . *Redshift* delivers plenty of value." —*Locus*

"Absolutely first-rate . . . an extended and satisfying statement of what contemporary SF and fantasy have to offer."
—F. Brett Cox, Locus Online

"*Redshift* . . . may be the best anthology published in several years." —SciFi.com

"A fine collection of stories." —SF Site

"A great read." —Tangent Online

**DON'T FORGET TO CATCH *FLIGHTS* VOLUME II
COMING IN APRIL 2006**

FLIGHTS

EXTREME VISIONS OF FANTASY

VOLUME I

EDITED BY

AL SARRANTONIO

A ROC BOOK

ROC
Published by New American Library, a division of
Penguin Group (USA) Inc., 375 Hudson Street,
New York, New York 10014, USA
Penguin Group (Canada), 90 Eglinton Avenue East, Suite 700, Toronto,
Ontario, Canada M4P 2Y3 (a division of Pearson Penguin Canada Inc.)
Penguin Books Ltd., 80 Strand, London WC2R 0RL, England
Penguin Ireland, 25 St. Stephen's Green, Dublin 2,
Ireland (a division of Penguin Books Ltd.)
Penguin Group (Australia), 250 Camberwell Road, Camberwell, Victoria 3124,
Australia (a division of Pearson Australia Group Pty. Ltd.)
Penguin Books India Pvt. Ltd., 11 Community Centre, Panchsheel Park,
New Delhi - 110 017, India
Penguin Group (NZ), cnr Airborne and Rosedale Roads, Albany,
Auckland 1310, New Zealand (a division of Pearson New Zealand Ltd.)
Penguin Books (South Africa) (Pty.) Ltd., 24 Sturdee Avenue,
Rosebank, Johannesburg 2196, South Africa

Penguin Books Ltd., Registered Offices:
80 Strand, London WC2R 0RL, England

Published by Roc, an imprint of New American Library, a division of Penguin
Group (USA) Inc. Previously published in Roc hardcover and trade paperback
editions.

First Roc Mass Market Printing, February 2006
10 9 8 7 6 5 4 3 2 1

Copyright © Al Sarrantonio, 2004
Page 405 constitutes an extension of this copyright page.
All rights reserved

ROC REGISTERED TRADEMARK—MARCA REGISTRADA

Printed in the United States of America

Without limiting the rights under copyright reserved above, no part of this publication may be reproduced, stored in or introduced into a retrieval system, or
transmitted, in any form, or by any means (electronic, mechanical, photocopying, recording, or otherwise), without the prior written permission of both the
copyright owner and the above publisher of this book.

PUBLISHER'S NOTE
This is a work of fiction. Names, characters, places, and incidents either are the
product of the authors' imaginations or are used fictitiously, and any resemblance to actual persons, living or dead, business establishments, events, or locales is entirely coincidental.

The publisher does not have any control over and does not assume any responsibility for author or third-party Web sites or their content.

If you purchased this book without a cover you should be aware that this book
is stolen property. It was reported as "unsold and destroyed" to the publisher
and neither the author nor the publisher has received any payment for this
"stripped book."

The scanning, uploading and distribution of this book via the Internet or via any
other means without the permission of the publisher is illegal and punishable by
law. Please purchase only authorized electronic editions, and do not participate
in or encourage electronic piracy of copyrighted materials. Your support of the
authors' rights is appreciated.

To my sister, Marianne

ACKNOWLEDGMENTS

Every time I edit a book, I say the same thing on the acknowledgments page: No book is an island. It's no less true this time. My heartfelt thanks to:

Beth, always there, who put up with yet *another* one;

Laura Anne Gilman, editor supreme;

Kathleen Bellamy, whose gentle perseverance paid off;

Chris Lotts, for (lots of) help;

And, once more (and always), the editors, quiet linchpins of the field who, almost always without fanfare, got or get it done: Terry Carr, Damon Knight, Ellen Datlow, David G. Hartwell, Betsy Mitchell, Gordon Van Gelder, Gardner Dozois, Susan Allison, Ginjer Buchanan, Melissa Singer, Jennifer Brehl, John Douglas, Stan Schmidt, Scott Edelman, Patrick Nielsen Hayden, Shawna McCarthy . . .

Ever too many to name.

CONTENTS

In a way, it's comforting to start out a huge anthology like this with a familiar title. But there's nothing familiar about **Robert Silverberg**'s tale itself, which is exactly why it's leading off. It's beautifully told, visually picturesque, apt, thoroughly enjoyable—all attributes of Silverberg's long and distinguished career.

Not too long ago (and this is a sidebar) I plucked one of Bob's novels from the 1970s off my shelves, The Book of Skulls. I remembered it fondly, but was afraid that if I reread it, it would have lost the magic it wove from those long-ago late New Wave days. I was wrong. It was just as fresh as the day I first read it.

Silverberg's entire career has been like that: He's shown a restless and laser-sharp mind that transforms anything it focuses on into something special.

Like what follows, familiar title or no.

THE SORCERER'S APPRENTICE

Robert Silverberg

Gannin Thidrich was nearing the age of thirty and had come to Triggoin to study the art of sorcery, a profession for which he thought he had some aptitude, after failing at several others for which he had none. He was a native of the Free City of Stee, that splendid metropolis on the slopes of Castle Mount, and at the suggestion of his father, a wealthy merchant of that great city, he had gone first into meat-jobbing, and then, through the good offices of an uncle from Dundilmir, he had become a dealer in used leather. In neither of these occupations had he distinguished himself, nor in the desultory projects he had undertaken afterward. But from childhood on, he had pursued sorcery in an amateur way, first as a boyish hobby, and then as a young man's consolation for shortcomings in most of the other aspects of his life—helping out friends even unluckier than he with an uplifting spell or two, conjuring at parties, earning a little by reading palms in the marketplace—and at last, eager to attain more arcane skills, he had taken himself to Triggoin, the capital city of sorcerers, hoping to apprentice himself to some master in that craft.

Triggoin came as a jolt, after Stee. That great city, spreading out magnificently along both banks of the river of the same name, was distinguished for its huge parks and game preserves, its palatial homes, its towering riverfront buildings of reflective gray-pink marble. But Triggoin, far up in the north beyond the grim Valmambra Desert, was a closed, claustrophobic place, dark and unwelcoming, where Gannin Thidrich found himself confronted with a bewildering tangle of winding medieval streets lined by ancient mustard-colored buildings with blank facades and gabled roofs. It was winter here. The trees were leafless and the air was cold. That was a new thing for him, winter: Stee was seasonless, favored all the year round by the eternal springtime of Castle Mount. The sharp-edged air was harsh with the odors of stale cooking oil and unfamiliar spices; the faces of the few people he encountered in the streets just within the gate were guarded and unfriendly.

He spent his first night there in a public dormitory for wayfarers, where in a smoky, dimly lit room he slept, very poorly, on a tick-infested straw mat among fifty other footsore travelers. In the morning, waiting in a long line for the chance to rinse his face in icy water, he passed the time by scanning the announcements on a bulletin board in the corridor and saw this:

APPRENTICE WANTED

Fifth-level adept offers instruction for serious student, plus lodging. Ten crowns per week for room and lessons. Some

household work required, and assistance
in professional tasks.
APPLY TO V. HALABANT,
7 GAPELIGO BOULEVARD,
WEST TRIGGOIN.

That sounded promising. Gannin Thidrich gathered up
his suitcases and hired a street-carter to take him to West
Triggoin. The carter made a sour face when Gannin
Thidrich gave him the address, but it was illegal to refuse
a fare, and off they went. Soon Gannin Thidrich understood the sourness, for West Triggoin appeared to be very
far from the center of the city; a suburb, in fact, perhaps
even a slum, where the buildings were so old and dilapi-
dated, they might well have dated from Lord Stiamot's
time and a cold, dusty wind blew constantly down out of
a row of low, jagged hills. Number 7 Gapeligo Boulevard
proved to be a ramshackle lopsided structure, three
asymmetrical floors behind a weather-beaten stone wall
that showed sad signs of flaking and spalling. The ground
floor housed what seemed to be a tavern, not open at this
early hour; the floor above it greeted him with a pad-
locked door; Gannin Thidrich struggled upward with his
luggage and at the topmost landing was met with folded
arms and hostile glance by a tall, slender woman of about
his own age, auburn haired, dusky skinned, with keen, un-
wavering eyes and thin, savage-looking lips. Evidently
she had heard his bumpings and thumpings on the staircase and had come out to inspect the source of the com-
motion. He was struck at once, despite her chilly and
even forbidding aspect, with the despairing realization
that he found her immensely attractive.

"I'm looking for V. Halabant," Gannin Thidrich said,
gasping a little for breath after his climb.

"I am V. Halabant."

That stunned him. Sorcery was not a trade commonly practiced by women, though evidently there were some who did go in for it. "The apprenticeship—?" he managed to say.

"Still available," she said. "Give me these." In the manner of a porter she swiftly separated his bags from his grasp, hefting them as though they were weightless, and led him inside.

Her chambers were dark, cheerless, cluttered, and untidy. The small room to the left of the entrance was jammed with the apparatus and paraphernalia of the professional sorcerer: astrolabes and ammatepilas, alembics and crucibles, hexaphores, ambivials, rohillas and verilistias, an armillary sphere, beakers and retorts, trays and metal boxes holding blue powders and pink ointments and strange seeds, a collection of flasks containing mysterious colored fluids, and much more that he was unable to identify. A second room adjacent to it held an overflowing bookcase, a couple of chairs, and a swaybacked couch. No doubt this room was for consultations. There were cobwebs on the window, and he saw dust beneath the couch and even a few sandroaches, those ubiquitous nasty scuttering insects that infested the parched Valmambra and all territories adjacent to it, were roaming about. Down the hallway lay a small dirty kitchen, a tiny room with a toilet and tub in it, storeroom piled high with more books and pamphlets, and beyond it the closed door of what he supposed—correctly, as it turned out—to be her own bedroom. What he did not see was any space for a lodger.

"I can offer one hour of formal instruction per day, every day of the week, plus access to my library for your independent studies, and two hours a week of discus-

sion growing out of your own investigations," V. Halabant announced. "All of this in the morning; I will require you to be out of here for three hours every
afternoon, because I have private pupils during that
time. How you spend those hours is unimportant to me,
except that I will need you to go to the marketplace for
me two or three times a week, and you may as well do
that then. You'll also do sweeping, washing, and other
household chores, which, as you surely have seen, I have
very little time to deal with. And you'll help me in my
own work as required, assuming, of course, your skills
are up to it. Is this agreeable to you?"

"Absolutely," said Gannin Thidrich. He was lost in ad-
miration of her lustrous auburn hair, her finest feature,
which fell in a sparkling cascade to her shoulders.

"The fee is payable four weeks in advance. If you
leave after the first week, the rest is refundable, afterward not." He knew already that he was not going to
leave. She held out her hand. "Sixty crowns, that will
be."

"The notice I saw said it was ten crowns a week."

Her eyes were steely. "You must have seen an old notice. I raised my rates last year."

He would not quibble. As he gave her the money, he
said, "And where am I going to be sleeping?"

She gestured indifferently toward a rolled-up mat in
a corner of the room that contained all the apparatus.
He realized that that was going to be his bed. "You decide that. The laboratory, the study, the hallway, even.
Wherever you like."

His own choice would have been her bedroom, with
her, but he was wise enough not to say that, even as a
joke. He told her that he would sleep in the study, as she
seemed to call the room with the couch and books.

While he was unrolling the mat, she asked him what level of instruction in the arts he had attained, and he replied that he was a self-educated sorcerer, strictly a novice, but with some apparent gift for the craft. She appeared untroubled by that. Perhaps all that mattered to her was the rent; she would instruct anyone, even a novice, so long as he paid on time.

"Oh," he said as she turned away. "I am Gannin Thidrich. And your name is—?"

"Halabant," she said, disappearing down the hallway.

Her first name, he discovered from a diploma in the study, was Vinala, a lovely name to him, but if she wanted to be called Halabant, then Halabant was what he would call her. He would not take the risk of offending her in any way, not only because he very much craved the instruction that she could offer him, but also because of the troublesome and unwanted physical attraction that she held for him.

He could see right away that that attraction was in no way reciprocated. That disappointed him. One of the few areas of his life where he had generally met with success was in his dealings with women. But he knew that romance was inappropriate, anyway, between master and pupil, even if they were of differing sexes. Nor had he asked for it: it had simply smitten him at first glance, as had happened to him two or three times earlier in his life. Usually such smitings led only to messy difficulties, he had discovered. He wanted no such messes here. If these feelings of his for Halabant became a problem, he supposed, he could go into town and purchase whatever the opposite of a love-charm was called. If they sold love-charms here, and he had no doubt that they did, surely they would sell antidotes for love, as well. But he wanted to remain here, and so he would do whatever she asked of him, call her by whatever name she requested, and so forth, obeying her in all things. In this ugly, unfriendly city, she was the one spot of brightness and warmth for him, regardless of the complexities of the situation.

But his desire for her did not cause any problems, at first, aside from the effort he had to make in suppressing it, which was considerable but not insuperable.

On the first day he unpacked, spent the afternoon wandering around the unprepossessing streets of West Triggoin during the stipulated three hours for her other pupils, and, finding himself alone in the flat when he returned, he occupied himself by browsing through her extensive collection of texts on sorcery until dinnertime. Halabant had told him that he was free to use her little kitchen, and so he had purchased a few things at the corner market to cook for himself. Afterward, suddenly very weary, he lay down on his mat in the study and fell instantly asleep. He was vaguely aware, sometime later in the night, that she had come home and had gone down the hallway to her room.

In the morning, after they had eaten, she began his course of instruction in the mantic arts.

Briskly she interrogated him about the existing state of his knowledge. He explained what he could and could not do, a little surprised himself at how much he knew, and she did not seem displeased by it either. Still, after ten minutes or so, she interrupted him and set about an introductory discourse of the most elementary sort, beginning with a lecture on the three classes of demons, the untamable valisteroi, the frequently useful kalisteroi, and the dangerous and unpredictable irgalisteroi. Gannin Thidrich had long ago encompassed the knowledge of the invisible beings, or at least thought he had; but he listened intently, taking copious notes, exactly as though all this were new to him, and after a while he discovered that what he thought he knew was shallow indeed, that it touched only on the superficialities.

Each day's lesson was different. One day it dealt with amulets and talismans, another with mechanical conjuring devices, another with herbal remedies and the making of potions, another with interpreting the movements of the stars and how to cast spells. His mind was awhirl with new knowledge. Gannin Thidrich drank it all in greedily, memorizing dozens of spells a day. ("To establish a relationship with the demon Ginitiis: *Iimea abrasax iabe iarbatha chramne*" . . . "To invoke protection against aquatic creatures: *Loma zath aioin acthase balamaon*" . . . "Request for knowledge of the Red Lamp: *Imantou lantou anchomach*" . . .) After each hour-long lesson, he flung himself into avid exploration of her library, searching out additional aspects of what he had just been taught. He saw, ruefully, that while he had wasted his life in foolish and abortive business ventures, she had devoted her years, approximately the same number as his, to a profound and comprehensive study of the magical arts, and he admired the breadth and depth of her mastery.

On the other hand, Halabant did not have much in the way of a paying practice, skillful though she obviously was. During Gannin Thidrich's first week with her, she gave just two brief consultations: one to a shopkeeper who had been put under a geas by a commercial rival, one to an elderly man who lusted after a youthful niece and wished to be cured of his obsession. He as-

sisted her in both instances, fetching equipment from
the laboratory as requested. The fees she received in
both cases, he noticed, were minimal: a mere handful of
coppers. No wonder she lived in such dismal quarters
and was reduced to taking in private pupils like himself
and whoever it was who came to see her in the afternoons while he was away. It puzzled him that she remained here in Triggoin, where sorcerers swarmed
everywhere by the hundreds or the thousands and com-
petition had to be brutal, when she plainly would be
much better off setting up in business for herself in one
of the prosperous cities of the Mount, where a handsome young sorceress with skill in the art would quickly
build a large clientele.

It was an exciting time for him. Gannin Thidrich felt
his mind opening outward day by day, new knowledge
flooding in, the mastery of the mysteries beginning to
come within his grasp.

His days were so full that it did not bother him at all
to pass his nights on a thin mat on the floor of a room
crammed with ancient, acrid-smelling books. He needed
only to close his eyes, and sleep would come up and
seize him as though he had been drugged. The winter
wind howled outside, and cold drafts broke through into
his room, and sandroaches danced all around him, making sandroach music with their little scraping claws, but
nothing broke his sleep until dawn's first blast of light
came through the library's uncovered window. Halabant was always awake, washed and dressed, when he
emerged from his room. It was as if she did not need
sleep at all. In these early hours of the morning, she
would hold her consultations with her clients in the
study, if she had any that day, or else retire to her laboratory and putter about with her mechanisms and her

potions. He would breakfast alone—Halabant never touched food before noon—and set about his household chores, the dusting and scrubbing and all the rest, and then would come his morning lesson and after that, until lunch, his time to prowl in the library. Often he and she took lunch at the same time, though she maintained silence throughout and ignored him when he stole the occasional quick glance at her across the table from him.

The afternoons were the worst part, when the private pupils came and he was forced to wander the streets. He begrudged them, whoever they were, the time they had with her, and he hated the grimy taverns and bleak gaming-halls where he spent these winter days when the weather was too grim to allow him simply to walk about. But then he would return to the flat, and if he found her there, which was not always the case, she would allow him an hour or so of free discourse about matters magical, not a lesson but simply a conversation, in which he brought up issues that fascinated or perplexed him and she helped him toward an understanding of them. These were wonderful hours, during which Gannin Thidrich was constantly conscious not just of her knowledge of the arts but also of Halabant's physical presence, her strange off-center beauty, the warmth of her body, the oddly pleasing fragrance of it. He kept himself in check, of course. But inwardly he imagined himself taking her in his arms, touching his lips to hers, running his fingertips down her lean, lithe back, drawing her down to his miserable thin mat on the library floor, and all the while some other part of his mind was concentrating on the technical arcana of sorcery that she was offering him.

In the evenings, she was usually out again—he had no

idea where—and he studied until sleep overtook him, or, if his head was throbbing too fiercely with newly acquired knowledge, he would apply himself to the unending backlog of housekeeping tasks, gathering up what seemed like the dust of decades from under the furniture, beating the rugs, oiling the kitchen pots, tidying the books, scrubbing the stained porcelain of the sink, and on and on, all for her, for her, for love of her.

It was a wonderful time.

But then in the second week came the catastrophic moment when he awoke too early, went out into the hallway, and blundered upon her as she was heading into the bathroom for her morning bath. She was naked. He saw her from the rear, first, the long lean back and the narrow waist and the flat, almost boyish buttocks, and then, as a gasp of shock escaped his lips and she became aware that he was there, she turned and faced him squarely, staring at him as coolly and unconcernedly as though he were a cat, or a piece of furniture. He was overwhelmed by the sight of her breasts, so full and close-set that they almost seemed out of proportion on such a slender frame, and of her flaring sharp-boned hips, and of the startlingly fire-hued triangle between them, tapering down to the slim thighs. She remained that way just long enough for the imprint of her nakedness to burn its way fiercely into Gannin Thidrich's soul, setting loose a conflagration that he knew would be impossible for him to douse. Hastily he shut his eyes as though he had accidentally stared into the sun; and when he opened them again, a desperate moment later, she was gone and the bathroom door was closed.

The last time Gannin Thidrich had experienced such an impact, he had been fourteen. The circumstances had been somewhat similar. Now, dizzied and dazed as a tremendous swirl of adolescent emotion roared through his adult mind, he braced himself against the hallway wall and gulped for breath like a drowning man.

For two days, though neither of them referred to the incident at all, he remained in its grip. He could hardly believe that something as trivial as a momentary glimpse of a naked woman, at his age, could affect him so deeply. But of course there were other factors—the instantaneous attraction to her that had afflicted him at the moment of meeting her; and their proximity in this little flat, where her bedroom door was only twenty paces from his; and the whole potent master-pupil entanglement that had given her such a powerful role in his lonely life here in the city of the sorcerers. He began to wonder whether she had worked some sorcery on him herself as a sort of amusement, capriciously casting a little lust-spell over him so that she could watch him squirm, and then deliberately flaunting her nakedness at him that way. He doubted it, but, then, he knew very little about what she was really like, and perhaps—how could he say?—there was some component of malice in her character, something in her that drew pleasure from tormenting a poor fish like Gannin Thidrich, who had been cast upon her shore. He doubted it, but he had encountered such women before, and the possibility always was there.

He was making great progress in his studies. He had learned now how to summon minor demons, how to prepare tinctures that enhanced virility, how to employ the eyebrow of the sun, how to test for the purity of gold and silver by the laying on of hands, how to interpret weather omens, and much more. His head was swim-

ming with his new knowledge. But also he remained
dazzled by the curious sort of beauty that he saw in her,
by the closeness in which they lived in the little flat, by
the memory of that one luminous encounter in the
dawn. And when in the fourth week it seemed to him
that her usual coolness toward him was softening—she
smiled at him once in a while now, she showed obvious
delight at his growing skill in the art, she even asked him
a thing or two about his life before coming to Triggoin—
he finally mistook diminished indifference for actual
warmth and, at the end of one morning's lesson,
abruptly blurted out a confession of his love for her.

An ominous red glow appeared on her pale cheeks.
Her dark eyes flashed tempestuously. "Don't ruin
everything," she warned him. "It is all going very well as
it is. I advise you to forget that you ever said such a
thing to me."

"How can I? Thoughts of you possess me day and
night!"

"Control them, then. I don't want to hear any more
about them. And if you try to lay a finger on me, I'll turn
you into a sandroach, believe me."

He doubted that she really meant that. But he abided
by her warning for the next eight days, not wanting to
jeopardize the continuation of his course of studies.
Then, in the course of carrying out an assignment she
had given him in the casting of auguries, Gannin
Thidrich inscribed her name and his in the proper
places in the spell, inquired as to the likelihood of a sat-
isfactory consummation of desire, and received what he
understood to be a positive prognostication. This inflamed him so intensely with joy that when Halabant
came into the room a moment later, Gannin Thidrich
impulsively seized her and pulled her close to him,

pressed his cheek against hers, and frantically fondled her from shoulder to thigh.

She muttered six brief, harsh words of a spell unknown to him in his ear and bit his earlobe. In an instant he found himself scrabbling around amidst gigantic dust grains on the floor. Jagged glittering motes floated about him like planets in the void. His vision had become eerily precise down almost to the microscopic level, but all color had drained from the world. When he put his hand to his cheek in shock, he discovered it to be an insect's feathery claw, and the cheek itself was a hard thing of chitin. She had indeed transformed him into a sandroach.

Numb, he considered his situation. From this perspective, he could no longer see her—she was somewhere miles above him, in the upper reaches of the atmosphere—nor could he make out the geography of the room, the familiar chairs and the couch, or anything else except the terrifyingly amplified details of the immensely small. Perhaps in another moment her foot would come down on him, and that would be that for Gannin Thidrich. Yet he did not truly believe that he had become a sandroach. He had mastered enough sorcery by this time to understand that that was technically impossible, that one could not pack all the neurons and synapses, the total intelligence of a human mind, into the tiny compass of an insect's head. And all those things were here with him inside the sandroach, his entire human personality, the hopes and fears and memories and fantasies of Gannin Thidrich of the Free City of Stee, who had come to Triggoin to study sorcery and was a pupil of the woman V. Halabant. So this was all an illusion. He was not really a sandroach; she had merely made him *believe* that he was. He was certain of that.

That certainty was all that preserved his sanity in those first appalling moments.

Still, on an operational level, there was no effective difference between thinking you were a six-legged chitin-covered creature one finger-joint in length and actually *being* such a creature. Either way, it was a horrifying condition. Gannin Thidrich could not speak out to protest against her treatment of him. He could not restore himself to human shape and height. He could not do anything at all except the things that sandroaches did. The best he could manage was to scutter in his new six-legged fashion to the safety to be found underneath the couch, where he discovered other sandroaches already in residence. He glared at them balefully, warning them to keep their distance, but their only response was an incomprehensible twitching of their feelers. Whether that was a gesture of sympathy or one of animosity, he could not tell.

The least she could have done for me, he thought, was to provide me with some way of communicating with the others of my kind, if this is to be my kind from now on.

He had never known such terror and misery. But the transformation was only temporary. Two hours later—it seemed like decades to him, sandroach time, all of it spent hiding under the couch and contemplating how he was going to pursue the purposes of his life as an insect—Gannin Thidrich was swept by a nauseating burst of dizziness and a sense that he was exploding from the thorax outward, and then he found himself restored to his previous form, lying in a clumsy sprawl in the middle of the floor. Halabant was nowhere to be seen. Cautiously he rose and moved about the room, reawakening in himself the technique of two-legged locomotion, holding his outspread fingers up before his eyes for the delight of seeing fingers again, prodding his cheeks and arms and abdomen to confirm that he was once again a creature of flesh. He was. He felt chastened and immensely relieved, even grateful to her for having relented.

They did not discuss the episode the next day, and all reverted to as it had been between them, distant, formal, a relationship of pure pedagogy and nothing more. He remained wary of her. When, now and then, his hand would brush against hers in the course of handling some piece of apparatus, he would pull it back as if he had touched a glowing coal.

Spring now began to arrive in Triggoin. The air was softer, the trees grew green. Gannin Thidrich's desire for his instructor did not subside, in truth it grew more maddeningly acute with the warming of the season, but he permitted himself no expression of it. There were further occasions when he accidentally encountered her going to and fro, naked, in the hall in earliest morning. His response each time was instantly to close his eyes and turn away, but her image lingered on his retinas and burrowed down into his brain. He could not help thinking that there was something intentional about these provocative episodes, something flirtatious, even. But he was too frightened of her to act on that supposition.

A new form of obsession now came over him, that the visitors she received every afternoon while he was away were not private pupils at all, but a lover, rather, or perhaps several lovers. Since she took care not to have her afternoon visitors arrive until he was gone, he had no way of knowing whether this was so, and it plagued him terribly to think that others, in his absence, were caressing her lovely body and enjoying her passionate kisses while he was denied everything on pain of being turned into a sandroach again.

But of course he *did* have a way of knowing what took place during those afternoons of hers. He had progressed far enough in his studies to have acquired some skill with the device known as the Far-Seeing Bowl, which allows an adept to spy from a distance. Over the span of three days, he removed from Halabant's flat one of her bowls, a supply of the pink fluid that it required, and a pinch of the grayish activating powder. Also he helped himself to a small undergarment of Halabant's—its fragrance was a torment to him—from the laundry basket. These things he stored in a locker he rented in the nearby marketplace. On the fourth day, after giving himself a refresher course in the five-word spell that operated the bowl, he collected his apparatus from the locker, repaired to a tavern where he knew no one would intrude on him, set the bowl atop the garment, filled it with the pink fluid, sprinkled it with the activating powder, and uttered the five words

It occurred to him that he might see scenes now that would shatter him forever. No matter: he had to know.

The surface of the fluid in the bowl rippled, stirred, cleared. The image of V. Halabant appeared. Gannin Thidrich caught his breath. A visitor was indeed with her: a young man, a boy, even, no more than twelve or fifteen years old. They sat chastely apart in the study. Together they pored over one of Halabant's books of sorcery. It was an utterly innocent hour. The second student came soon after: a short, squat fellow wearing coarse clothing of a provincial cut. For half an hour Halabant delivered what was probably a lecture—the bowl did not provide Gannin Thidrich with sound—while the pupil, constantly biting his lip, scribbled notes as quickly as he could. Then he left, and after a time was replaced by a sad, dreamy-looking fellow with long shaggy hair, who had brought some sort of essay or thesis for Halabant to examine. She leafed quickly through it, frequently offering what no doubt were pungent comments.

No lovers, then. Legitimate pupils, all three. Gannin Thidrich felt bitterly ashamed of having spied on her, and aghast at the possibility that she might have perceived, by means of some household surveillance spell of whose existence he knew nothing, that he had done so. But she betrayed no sign of that when he returned to the flat.

A week later, desperate once again, he purchased a love-potion in the sorcerers' marketplace—not a spell to free himself from desire, though he knew that was what he should be getting, but one that would deliver her into his arms. Halabant had sent him to the marketplace with a long list of professional supplies to buy for her—such things as elecamp, golden rue, quicksilver, brimstone, goblin-sugar, mastic, and thekka ammoniaca. The last item on the list was maltabar, and the same dealer, he knew, offered potions for the lovelorn. Rashly Gannin Thidrich purchased one. He hid it among his bundles and tried to smuggle it into the flat, but Halabant, under the pretext of offering to help him unpack, went straight to the sack that contained it and pulled it forth. "This was nothing that I requested," she said.

"True," he said, chagrined.

"Is it what I think it is?"

Hanging his head, he admitted that it was. She tossed it angrily aside. "I'll be merciful and let myself believe that you bought this to use on someone else. But if I was the one you had in mind for it—"

"No. Never."

"Liar. Idiot."

"What can I do, Halabant? Love strikes like a thunderbolt."

"I don't remember advertising for a lover. Only for an apprentice, an assistant, a tenant."

"It's not my fault that I feel this way about you."

"Nor mine," said Halabant. "Put all such thoughts out of your mind, if you want to continue here." Then, softening, obviously moved by the dumbly adoring way in which he was staring at her, she smiled and pulled him toward her and brushed his cheek lightly with her lips. "Idiot," she said again. "Poor hopeless fool." But it seemed to him that she said it with affection.

Matters stayed strictly business between them. He hung upon every word of her lessons as though his continued survival depended on committing every syllable of her teachings to memory, filled notebook after notebook with details of spells, talismans, conjurations, and illusions, and spent endless hours rummaging through her books for amplifying detail, sometimes staying up far into the night to pursue some course of study that an incidental word or two from her had touched off. He was becoming so adept, now, that he was able to be of great service to her with her outside clientele, the perfect assistant, always knowing which devices or potions to bring her for the circumstances at hand; and he noticed that clients were coming to her more frequently now, too. He hoped that Halabant gave him at least a little credit for that.

He was still aflame with yearning for her, of course—there was no reason for that to go away—but he tried to burn it off with heroic outpourings of energy in his role as her housekeeper. Before coming to Triggoin, Gannin Thidrich had bothered himself no more about household work than any normal bachelor did, doing simply enough to fend off utter squalor and not going beyond that, but he cared for her little flat as he had never cared for any dwelling of his own, polishing and dusting and sweeping and scrubbing, until the place took on an astonishing glow of charm and comfort. Even the sandroaches were intimidated by his work and fled to some other apartment. It was his goal to exhaust himself so thoroughly between the intensity of his studies and the intensity of his housework that he would have no shred of vitality left over for further lustful fantasies. This did not prove to be so. Often, curling up on his mat at night after a day of virtually unending toil, he would be assailed by dazzling visions of V. Halabant, entering his weary mind like an intruding succubus, capering wantonly in his throbbing brain, gesturing lewdly to him, beckoning, offering herself, and Gannin Thidrich would lie there sobbing, soaked in sweat, praying to every demon whose invocations he knew that he be spared such agonizing visitations.

The pain became so great that he thought of seeking another teacher. He thought occasionally of suicide, too, for he knew that this was the great love of his life, doomed never to be fulfilled, and that if he went away from Halabant, he was destined to roam forever celibate through the vastness of the world, finding all other women unsatisfactory after her. Some segment of his mind recognized this to be puerile romantic nonsense, but he was not able to make that the dominant segment, and he began to fear that he might actually be capable of taking his own life in some feverish attack of nonsensical frustration.

The worst of it was that she had become intermittently quite friendly toward him by this time, giving him, intentionally or otherwise, encouragement that he had become too timid to accept as genuine. Perhaps his pathetic gesture of buying that love-potion had touched something in her spirit. She smiled at him frequently now, even winked, or poked him playfully in the shoulder with a finger to underscore some point in her lesson. She was shockingly casual, sometimes, about how she dressed, often choosing revealingly flimsy gowns that drove him into paroxysms of throttled desire. And yet at other times she was as cold and aloof as she had been at the beginning, criticizing him cruelly when he bungled a spell or spilled an alembic, skewering him with icy glances when he said something that struck her as foolish, reminding him over and over that he was still just a blundering novice who had years to go before he attained anything like the threshold of mastery.

So there always were limits. He was her prisoner. She could touch him whenever she chose, but he feared becoming a sandroach again should he touch her, even accidentally. She could smile and wink at him, but he dared not do the same. In no way did she grant him any substantial status. When he asked her to instruct him in the great spell known as the Sublime Arcanum, which held the key to many gates, her reply was simply, "That is not something for fools to play with."

There was one truly miraculous day when, after he had recited an intricate series of spells with complete accuracy and had brought off one of the most difficult effects she had ever asked him to attempt, she seized him in a sudden joyful congratulatory embrace and levitated them both to the rafters of the study. There they hovered, face-to-face, bosom against bosom, her eyes flashing jubilantly before him. "That was wonderful!" she cried. "How marvelously you did that! How proud I am of you!"

This is it, he thought, the delirious moment of surrender at last, and slipped his hand between their bodies to clasp her firm round breast, and pressed his lips against hers and drove his tongue deep into her mouth. Instantly she voided the spell of levitation and sent him crashing miserably to the floor, where he landed in a crumpled heap with his left leg folded up beneath him in a way that sent the fiercest pain through his entire body.

She floated gently down beside him.

"You will always be an idiot," she said, and spat, and strode out of the room.

Gannin Thidrich was determined now to put an end to his life. He understood completely that to do such a thing would be a preposterous overreaction to his situation, but he was determined not to allow mere rationality to have a voice in the decision. His existence had become unbearable, and he saw no other way of winning his freedom from this impossible woman.

He brooded for days about how to go about it, whether to swallow some potion from her storeroom or to split himself open with one of the kitchen knives or simply to fling himself from the study window, but all of these seemed disagreeable to him on the aesthetic level and fraught with drawbacks besides. Mainly what troubled him was the possibility that he might not fully succeed in his aim with any of them, which seemed even worse than succeeding would be.

In the end he decided to cast himself into the dark,

turbulent river that ran past the edge of West Triggoin on its northern flank. He had often explored it, now that winter was over, in the course of his afternoon walks. It was wide and probably fairly deep, its flow during this period of springtime spate was rapid, and an examination of a map revealed that it would carry his body northward and westward into the grim uninhabited lands that sloped toward the distant sea. Since he was unable to swim—one did not swim in the gigantic River Stee of his native city, whose swift current swept everything and everyone willy-nilly downstream along the mighty slopes of Castle Mount—Gannin Thidrich supposed that he would sink quickly and could expect a relatively painless death.

Just to be certain, he borrowed a rope from Halabant's storeroom to tie around his legs before he threw himself in. Slinging it over his shoulder, he set out along the footpath that bordered the river's course, searching for a likely place from which to jump. The day was warm, the air sweet, the new leaves yellowish green on every tree, springtime at its finest—what better season for saying farewell to the world?

He came to an overlook where no one else seemed to be around, knotted the rope about his ankles and, without a moment's pause for regret, sentimental thoughts, or final statements of any sort, hurled himself down headlong into the water.

It was colder than he expected it to be, even on this mild day. His plummeting body cut sharply below the surface, so that his mouth and nostrils filled with water and he felt himself in the imminent presence of death, but then the natural buoyancy of the body asserted itself, and despite his wishes, Gannin Thidrich turned upward again, breaching the surface, emerging into the air, spluttering and gagging. An instant later he heard a splashing sound close beside him and realized that someone else had jumped in, a would-be rescuer, perhaps.

"Lunatic! Moron! What do you think you're doing?"

He knew that voice, of course. Apparently V. Halabant had followed him as he made his doleful way along the riverbank and was determined not to let him die. That realization filled him with a confused mixture of ecstasy and fury.

She was bobbing beside him. She caught him by the shoulder, spun him around to face her. There was a kind of madness in her eyes, Gannin Thidrich thought. The woman leaned close and in a tone of voice that stung like vitriol, she said, *"Iaho ariaha . . . aho ariaha . . . bakaksikhekh! Ianian! Thatlat! Hish!"*

Gannin Thidrich felt a sense of sudden forward movement and became aware that he was swimming, actually swimming, moving downstream with powerful strokes of his entire body. Of course that was impossible. Not only were his legs tied together, but he had no idea of how to swim. And yet he was definitely in motion: he could see the riverbank changing from moment to moment, the trees lining the footpath traveling upstream as he went the other way.

There was a river otter swimming beside him, a smooth sleek beautiful creature, graceful and sinuous and strong. It took Gannin Thidrich another moment to realize that the animal was V. Halabant, and that in fact he was an otter also, that she had worked a spell on them both when she had jumped in beside them, and had turned them into a pair of magnificent aquatic beasts. His legs were gone—he had only flippers down there now, culminating in small webbed feet—and gone, too, was the rope with which he had hobbled himself. And he could swim. He could swim like an otter.

Ask no questions, Gannin Thidrich told himself. Swim! Swim!

Side by side they swam for what must have been miles, spurting along splendidly on the breast of the current. He had never known such joy. As a human, he would have drowned long ago, but as an otter he was a superb swimmer, tireless, wondrously strong. And with Halabant next to him, he was willing to swim forever: to the sea itself, even. Head down, nose foremost, narrow body fully extended, he drilled his way through the water like some animate projectile. And the otter who had been V. Halabant kept pace with him as he moved along.

Time passed and he lost all sense of who or what he was, or where, or what he was doing. He even ceased to perceive the presence of his companion. His universe was only motion, constant forward motion. He was truly a river otter now, nothing but a river otter, joyously hurling himself through the cosmos.

But then his otter senses detected a sound to his left that no otter would be concerned with, and whatever was still human in him registered the fact that it was a cry of panic, a sharp little gasp of fear, coming from a member of his former species. He pivoted to look and saw that V. Halabant had reverted to human form and was thrashing about in what seemed to be the last stages of exhaustion. Her arms beat the air, her head tossed wildly, her eyes were rolled back in her head. She was trying to make her way to the riverbank, but she did not appear to have the strength to do it.

Gannin Thidrich understood that in his jubilant onward progress, he had led her too far down the river, pulling her along beyond her endurance, that as an otter he was far stronger than she and by following him she had exceeded her otter abilities and could go no farther. Perhaps she was in danger of drowning, even. Could an otter drown? But she was no longer an otter. He knew that he had to get her ashore. He swam to her side and pushed futilely against her with his river otter nose, trying in vain to clasp her with the tiny otter flippers that had replaced his arms. Her eyes fluttered open and she stared into his and smiled, and spoke two words, the counterspell, and Gannin Thidrich discovered that he, too, was in human form again. They were both naked. He found that they were close enough now to the shore that his feet were able to touch the bottom. Slipping his arm around her, just below her breasts, he tugged her along, steadily, easily, toward the nearby riverbank. He scrambled ashore, pulling her with him, and they dropped down gasping for breath at the river's edge under the warm spring sunshine.

They were far out of town, he realized, all alone in the empty but not desolate countryside. The bank was soft with mosses. Gannin Thidrich recovered his breath almost at once; Halabant took longer, but before long she, too, was breathing normally. Her face was flushed and mottled with signs of strain, though, and she was biting down on her lip as though trying to hold something back, something that Gannin Thidrich understood, a moment later, to be tears. Abruptly she was furiously sobbing. He held her, tried to comfort her, but she shook him off. She would not or could not look at him.

"To be so weak—" she muttered. "I was going under. I almost drowned. And to have you see it—you—*you*—"

So she was angry with herself for having shown herself, at least in this, to be inferior to him. That was ridiculous, he thought. She might be a master sorcerer and he only a novice, yes, but he was a man, nevertheless, and she a woman, and men tended to be physically stronger than women, on the average, and probably that was true among otters, too. If she had displayed weakness during their wild swim, it was a forgivable weakness, which only exacerbated his love for her. He murmured words of comfort to her and was so bold to put his arm about her shoulders, and then, suddenly, astonishingly, everything changed—she pressed her bare body against him, she clung to him, she sought his lips with a hunger that was almost frightening, she opened her legs to him, she opened everything to him, she drew him down into her body and her soul.

Afterward, when it seemed appropriate to return to the city, it was necessary to call on her resources of sorcery once more. They both were naked, and many miles downstream from where they needed to be. She seemed not to want to risk returning to the otter form again, but there were other spells of transportation at her command, and she used one that brought them instantly back to West Triggoin, where their clothing and even the rope with which Gannin Thidrich had bound himself were lying in damp heaps near the place where he had thrown himself into the river. They dressed in silence and in silence they made their way, walking several feet apart, back to her flat.

He had no idea what would happen now. Already she appeared to be retreating behind that wall of untouchability that had surrounded her since the beginning. What had taken place between them on the riverbank was irreversible, but it would not transform their strange relationship unless she permitted it to do so,

Gannin Thidrich knew, and he wondered whether she would. He did not intend to make any new aggressive moves without some sort of guidance from her.

And indeed it appeared that she intended to pretend that nothing had occurred at all, neither his absurd suicide attempt nor her foiling of it by following him to the river and turning them into otters nor the frenzied, frenetic, almost insane coupling that had been the unexpected climax of their long swim. All was back to normal between them as soon as they were at the flat: she was the master, he was the drudge, they slept in their separate rooms, and when during the following day's lessons he bungled a spell, as even now he still sometimes did, she berated him in the usual cruel, cutting way that was the verbal equivalent of transforming him once again into a sandroach. What, then, was he left with? The taste of her on his lips, the sound of her passionate outcries in his ears, the feel of the firm ripe swells of her breasts against the palms of his hands?

On occasions over the next few days, though, he caught sight of her studying him surreptitiously out of the corner of her eye, and he was the recipient of a few not-so-surreptitious smiles that struck him as having genuine warmth in them, and when he ventured a smile of his own in her direction, it was met with another smile instead of a scowl. But he hesitated to try any sort of follow-up maneuver. Matters still struck him as too precariously balanced between them.

Then, a week later, during their morning lesson, she said briskly, "Take down these words: *Psakerba enphnoun orgogorgoniotrian phorbai.* Do you recognize them?"

"No," said Gannin Thidrich, baffled.

"They are the opening incantation of the spell known as the Sublime Arcanum," said Halabant.

A thrill rocketed down his spine. The Sublime Arcanum at last! So she had decided to trust him with the master spell, finally, the great opener of so many gates! She no longer thought of him as a fool who could not be permitted knowledge of it.

It was a good sign, he thought. Something was changing.

Perhaps she was still trying to pretend even now that none of it had ever happened, the event by the riverbank. But it had, it had, and it was having its effect on her, however hard she might be battling against it, and he knew now that he would go on searching, forever if necessary, for the key that would unlock her a second time.

I love this story.
And can I tell you why, exactly?
No.

A lot of **Kit Reed**'s *work is like that—there's some mojo subtext working on you while you're reading the tale that you're really not aware of: clockwork just out of your peripheral vision, strange tugs and whispers that you don't understand even as you read the words so cleanly laid out on the page.*

Her stuff is special, has always been special, and will always be special.

Kit was having trouble coming up with something for this book early on. If I remember what she told me correctly, she was on a train either coming from or going to New York City, when something began to click (or cluck?).

Lucky us.

PERPETUA

Kit Reed

We are happy to be traveling together in the alligator. To survive the crisis in the city outside, we have had ourselves made *very small*.

To make our trip more pleasant, the alligator herself has been equipped with many windows, cleverly fitted between the armor plates so we can look out at the disaster as we ride along. The lounge where we are riding is paneled in mahogany and fitted with soft leather sofas and beautifully sculpted leather chairs where we recline until seven, when the chef Father engaged calls us to a sit-down dinner in the galley lodged at the base of our alligator's skull. Our vehicle is such a technical masterpiece that our saurian hostess zooms along unhampered, apparently at home in the increasingly treacherous terrain. If she knows we're in here, and if she guesses that tonight we will be dining on Boeuf Wellington and asparagus terrine with Scotch salmon and capers while she has to forage, she rushes along as though she doesn't care. We hear occasional growls and sounds of rending and gnashing over the Vivaldi track

Father has chosen as background for this first phase of our journey; she seems to be finding plenty to eat outside.

Inside, everything is arranged for our comfort and happiness, perhaps because Father knows we have reservations about being here. My sisters and I can count on individualized snack trays, drugs of choice and our favorite drinks, which vary from day to day. Over our uniform jumpsuits, we wear monogrammed warm-up jackets in our favorite colors—a genteel lavender for Lily, which Ella apes because she's too young to have her own ideas; jade for Stephanie and, it figures, my aggressively girlish sister Anna is in Passive Pink; Father doesn't like it, but I have chosen black.

"Molly, that color doesn't become you."

"Nobody's going to see me, what difference does it make?"

"I like my girls to look nice."

I resent this because we all struggled to escape the family and made it, too. We'd still be out there if it wasn't for this. "Your girls, your girls—we haven't been your girls in years."

Father: "You will always be my girls." That smile.

OK, I am the family gadfly. "This crisis. Is there something funny going on that we don't know about?"

"Molly," he thunders. "Look out the windows. Then tell me if you think there's anything funny about this."

"I mean, is this a trick to get us back?"

"If you think I made this up, send a goddamn e-mail. Search the Web or turn on the goddamn TV!"

The chairs are fitted with wireless connections so we can download music and e-mail our loved ones, although we never hear back, and at our fingertips are multimedia remotes. We want for nothing here in the alligator. Nothing material, that is. I check my sources, and Father is right. It is a charnel house out there while in here with Father, we are pampered and well fed and snug.

It is a velvet prison, but look at the alternative! Exposure to thunderstorms and fires in collision, vulnerability to mudslides and flooding of undetermined origin; our alligator slithers through rivers of bloody swash, and our vision is obscured by the occasional collision with a severed limb. We can't comprehend the nature or the scope of the catastrophe, only that it's all around us, while here inside the alligator, we are safe.

Her name is Perpetua. Weird, right? Me knowing? But I do.

So we are safe inside Perpetua, and I guess we have Father to thank. Where others ignored the cosmic warnings, he took them to heart. Got ready. Spared no expense. I suppose we should be glad.

If it weren't for the absence of certain key loved ones from our table and from our sumptuous beds in the staterooms aft of the spiny ridge, we probably would.

It's Father's fault. Like a king summoning his subjects, he brought us back from the corners of the earth, where we strayed after we grew up and escaped the house. He brought us in from West Hollywood (Stephanie) and Machu Picchu (Lily) and (fluffy Anna) Biarritz and Farmington, for our baby sister Ella attends the exclusive Miss Porter's School. And Father reached me . . . where? When Father wants you, it doesn't matter how far you run, you will come back.

Emergency, the message said, *Don't ask. Just come,* and being loyal daughters, we did. With enormous gravity, he sat us down in the penthouse.

"My wandering daughters." He beamed. Then he explained. He even had charts. The catastrophe would start here, he said, pointing to the heart of the city. Then it would blossom, expanding until it blanketed the nation and finally, the world. Faced with destruction, would you dare take your chances outside? Would we?

He was not asking. "You will come."

"Of course, Father," we said, although even then I was not sure.

Anna the brownnose gilded the lily with that bright giggle. "Anything you say, Father. Anything to survive."

Mother frowned. "What makes you think you'll survive?"

"Erna!"

"What if this is the Last Judgment?" she had Father's Gutenberg Bible in her lap.

He shouted: "Put that thing down!"

She looked down at the book and then up at him. "What makes you think anybody will survive?"

"That's enough!"

"More than enough, Richard." She raked him with a smile. "I think I'll take my chances here."

He and Mother have never been close. He shrugged. "As you wish. But, you girls . . ."

Anna said, "Daddy, can we bring our jewelry?"

Stephanie laid her fingertip in the hollow of Father's throat. "I'm fresh out of outfits—can I go to Prada and pick up a few things?"

I said, "It's not like we'll be going out to clubs."

"Daddy?"

"Molly, watch your tone." Stephanie is Father's favorite. He told her, "Anything you want, sweet, but be back by four."

Little Ella asked if she could bring all her pets—a litter of kittens and a basset hound. The cat is the natural enemy of the alligator, Father explained; even in miniature—and we were about to be miniaturized—the cats would be an incipient danger, but the dog's all right. Ella burst into tears.

"Can I bring my boyfriend?" Lily said.

Our baby sister punched her in the breast so hard, she yelled. "Not if I can't take Mittens."

"Boyfriends?" We girls chorused, "Of course."

Father shook his head.

You see, because we are traveling in elegant but close quarters, there's no room for anybody else. This meant no boyfriends, which strikes me as thoughtless if not a little small. When we protested, Father reminded us of our choices: death in the disaster or life in luxury with concomitant reknotting of family ties. He slammed his fist on the hunt table his decorator brought from Colonial Williamsburg at great expense. "Cheap at the price."

I was thinking of my boyfriend, whom I had left sleeping in Rangoon. Never guessing I was leaving forever, I stroked his cheek and slipped out. "But Derek!"

"Don't give it another thought."

"Daddy, what's going to happen to Derek?"

"He'll keep."

Stephanie, Anna and Lily said, "What's going to happen to Jimmy/David/Phil!"

"Oh, they'll keep," he said. Perceiving that he had given the wrong answer, he added, "Trust me. It's being taken care of."

"But, Daddy!"

Perceiving that he still hadn't said enough, he explained that although we were being miniaturized, his technicians would see to it that all our parts would match when we and our boyfriends were reunited, although he did not make clear whether we would be restored to normal size or the men we loved would be made extremely small. He said whatever it took to make us do what he wanted, patting us each with that fond, abstracted smile.

"I've got my best people on it. Don't worry. They'll be fine."

Anna did her loving princess act. "Promise?"

Now Father became impatient. "Girls, I am sparing no expense on this. Don't you think I have covered every little thing?"

None of us dares ask him what this all cost. Unlike most people in the city outside, we are, after all, still alive, but the money! How much will be left for us when Father dies?

Of course in normal times, the brass fixtures, the ceiling treatment and luxurious carpeting that line our temporary home would be expensive, but the cost of miniaturizing all these priceless objects and embedding them in our alligator? Who can guess!

One of us began to cry.

"Stop that," Father roared. "Enough is enough."

It probably is enough for him, riding along in luxury with his five daughters, but what about Stephanie and Anna and Lily and Ella and me?

The first few days, I will admit, passed pleasantly as we settled into our quarters and slipped into our routines. Sleep as late as we like and if we miss breakfast Chef leaves it outside our doors in special trays that keep the croissants moist, the juice cold and the coffee hot. There's even a flower on the tray. Late mornings in the dayroom, working puzzles or reading or doing needlework, a skill Father insisted we learn when we were small. Looking at what he's made of us, I have to wonder: five daughters at his beck and call, making a fuss over him and doing calligraphy that would have pleased blind old Milton; we all nap after lunch. We spend our afternoons in the music room followed by cocktails in the lounge and in the evening we say grace over a delicious meal at the long table, with Father like the Almighty at the head. Is this what he had in mind for us from the first?

I have never seen him happier.

This poses a terrible problem. Is the catastrophe outside a real unknitting of society and the city as we know it and, perhaps, the universe, or is it something Father manufactured to keep us in his thrall?

My sisters may be happy, but I am uncertain. I'm bored and dubious. I'm bored and suspicious and lonely as hell.

The others are in the music room with Father at the piano, preparing a Donizetti quartet. I looked in and saw them together in the warm light; with his white hair sparkling in the halogen glow of the piano lamp, he looked exalted. As if there were a halo around his head. Now, I love Father, but I was never his favorite. There's no part in the Donizetti piece for me. Why should I go in there and play along? Instead I have retreated to the lounge, where I strain at the window in hope. For hours I look out, staring in a passion of concentration because Derek is out there somewhere, whereas I . . . If I keep at this, I think, if I press my face to the glass and stare intently, if I can *just keep my mind on what I want,* then maybe I can become part of the glass or pass through it and find Derek.

With my head pressed against the fabric of our rushing host, I whisper:

"Oh, please."

Outside it is quite simply desolate. Mud and worse things splash on my window as the giant beast that hosts us lunges over something huge, snaps at some adversary in her path, worries the corpse and takes a few bites before she rushes on. God, I wish she'd slow down. I wish she would stop! I want her to lurch onto a peak and let me out!

Can't. On autopilot.

Odd. The glass is buzzing. Vibration or what? I brush my face, checking for bees. If I knew how, I'd run to the galley at the base of her skull and thump on the brushed steel walls until she got my message. Crucial question: Do alligators know Morse code?

No need.

"What?"

My God. She and I are in communication.

"Lady!"

The windowpane grows warm, as though I have made her blush. *It's Perpetua.*

"I know!"

I thought you did.

"Oh, lady, can you tell me what's going on?"

Either more or less than you think.

In a flash I understand the following: We are not, as I suspected—hoped!—being duped. Father has his girls back, all right—he has us at his fingertips in a tight space where he has complete control—but this is his response to the warnings, not something he made up. Although my best-case scenario would confirm my suspicions and make it easy to escape, we are not captive inside a submarine in perfectly normal New York City, witlessly doing his bidding while our vehicle sloshes around in a total immersion tank.

There really is a real disaster out there.

Soon enough, tidal waves will come crashing in our direction, to be followed by meteorite showers, with volcanic eruptions pending and worse to come. As for Father's contrivances, I am correct about one thing: the cablevision we watch and the Web we surf aren't coming in from the world outside; they are the product of the database deep in the server located behind our alligator's left eye.

"But what about Derek?"

I don't know.

"Can you find out?"

You have to promise to do what I want.

I whisper into the window set into her flank: "What do you want?"

Promise?

"Of course I promise!"

Then all that matters is your promise. It doesn't matter what I want.

"I need to know what's happening! Maybe Mother is right—maybe it really is the hand of God. Wouldn't you get sick of people like us and want to clean house?"

Not clear.

"Whether God is sick of us?"

Any of it. The only clear thing is what we have to do.

"What? What!"

She lets me know that although I left him in Rangoon, Derek is adrift somewhere in New York. Don't ask me whether he flew or came by boat or what I'm going to do. Just ask me what I think, and then ask me how I know.

You have to help me.

"You have to stop and let me out!"

I know what's out there because, my God, Perpetua is showing me. Images spill into my head and cloud my eyes: explosions mushrooming, tornadoes, volcanic geysers, what? In seconds I understand how bad it is, although Perpetua can't tell me whether we are in the grip of terrorists or space aliens or a concatenation of natural disasters or what; she shows me Derek standing in the ruins of our old building with his hand raised as if to knock on the skeletal door, I see looters and carnivores and all the predictable detritus of a disaster right down to the truck with the CNN remote, and I see that they won't be standing there much longer because the roiling clouds are opening for a fresh hailstorm unless it's a firestorm or a tremendous belching of volcanic ash.

You won't last a minute out there, not the way you are.

She's right. To survive the crisis in the city outside, we have had ourselves made very small.

You got it. You don't stand a chance.

"Oh God," I cry.

Not God, not by a long shot.

"Oh, lady!" I hear Father and the others chattering as they come in from the music room. I whisper into the glass. My mouth leaves a wet lip print frosted by my own breath. "What am I going to do?"

Our saurian hostess exits my consciousness so quickly that I have to wonder whether she was ever there. My only proof? I have her last words imprinted; *Find out how.*

Chef brings our afternoon snack trays, and my sisters and I graze, browsing contentedly, like farm animals. Father nods, and he and Chef exchange looks before Chef bows and backs out of the room.

It comes to me like a gift.

Passionately, I press my lips to the glass. "It's in the food."

Find the antidote. Take it when you get out.

"Are you? Are you, Perpetua?" I am wild with it. "Are you really going to stop and let me out?"

She doesn't answer. The whole vehicle that encloses our family begins to thrash. I hear magnified snarling and terrible rending noises as she snaps some enemy's spine and over Vivaldi I hear her giant teeth clash as she worries it to death.

We bide our time then, Perpetua and I, at least I do. What choice do I have?

But while I am waiting, her history is delivered to me whole. It is not so much discovered as remembered, as though it happened to me. Sleeping or waking, I can't say when or how she reaches me; her story seeps into my mind, and as it unfolds I understand why she and I are bonded. Rather, why she chose me. Rushing along through the night while Father plots and my sisters sleep, our alligator somehow drops me into the tremendous ferny landscape of some remote, prehistoric dawn, where I watch, astonished, as her early life unfolds under a virgin sun that turns the morning sky pink. Although I am not clear whether it is her past or a universal past that Perpetua is drawing, at some level I understand. She shows me the serpentine tangle of clashing reptiles and the emergence of a king, and she takes me beyond that to deliver me at the inevitable: that all fathers of daughters are kings. I see Perpetua's gigantic, armored father with his flaming jaws and his great teeth, and I join his delicate, scaly daughters as they slither here and there in the universe, apparently free but always under his power.

So you see.

I have the context, if not the necessity.

Then over the next few days while we float along in

our comfortable dream world, she encourages me to explore.

While the others nap, I feel my way along the flexible vinyl corridors that snake through Perpetua's sinuous body, connecting the chambers where we sleep and the rooms where we eat and the ones where we entertain ourselves. The tubing is transparent, and I see Perpetua's vitals pulsing wherever I flash my light. Finally I make my way to the galley—quietly, because Chef sleeps nearby. It's a hop, skip and a jump to the medicine chest, where I find unmarked glass capsules sealed in a case. I slip one into my pocket, in case. From the galley, I discover, there are fixed passageways leading up and a flexible one leading down. I open the hatch and descend.

Yes, Perpetua says inside my head and as I get closer to her destination, repeating like an orgasmic lover, *Yes, yes, yes!*

I have found the Destruct button.

It is located at the bottom of the long stairway that circumvents her epiglottis; opening the last hatch I find my way into the control center, which is lodged in her craw. And here it is. Underneath there is a neatly printed plate put there by Father's engineers: IN CASE OF EMERGENCY, BREAK GLASS.

Perpetua's great body convulses. *Yes.*

Trembling, I press my mouth to the wall: "Is this what you want?" I can't afford to wait for an answer. "It would be suicide!"

We have a deal.

"But what about me?"

When it's time, you'll see.

The next few days are extremely hard. Perpetua rushes on without regard for me while Chef bombards

us with new delicacies and Father and my sisters re-
hearse Gilbert and Sullivan in the music room. I can't
help but think of Mother, alone in the ruins of our penthouse. Is she all right, is she maybe in some safe place
with my lover Derek, or did she die holding the Gutenberg Bible in an eternal *I told you so?* Mother! Is that
the Last Judgment shaping up out there, or is it simply
the end of the world? Whatever it is, I think, she and
Derek are better off than I am, trapped in here.

Father asks, "What's the matter with you?"

"Nothing. I'm fine."

My sisters say, "Is it Derek? Are you worried about
Derek? This is only the beginning, so get over it."

"I'm fine."

"Of course you are—we're terribly lucky," they say.
Father has given them jewels to match their eyes.
"We're lucky as hell, and everything's going to be fine."

I can hardly bear to be with them. "Whatever you
want," I whisper to Perpetua, "Let's do it."

When it's time.

Relief comes when you least expect it, probably because you aren't expecting it. Perpetua and I are of the
Zen Archer school of life. She summons me out of a
stone sleep.

It's time.

The alligator and I aren't one now, but we are thinking as one. Bending to her will, I pad along the corridors
to the galley and descend to the control room. She
doesn't have to explain. Predictably, the Destruct button is red. At the moment, it is glowing. I use the hammer to break the glass.

Now.

I push the button that sets the timer. The bottom falls
out of the control room, spilling me into her throat, and

she vomits me out. I crunch down on the breakable capsule that will bring me back to normal size.

My God, I'm back in the world! I'm back in the world, and it is terrible.

As I land in the muck, Perpetua rushes on like an express train roaring over me while I huddle on the tracks or the Concorde thundering close above as I lie on my back on the runway, counting the plates in its giant belly as it takes off. I have pushed the Destruct button. Is the timer working? Did it abort? Our alligator hostess is traveling at tremendous speeds, and as she slithers on, she whips her tail and opens her throat in a tremendous cry of grief that comes out of her in a huge, reptilian groan: *Noooooooo.*

Rolling out of her wake, I see the stars spiraling into the Hudson; in that second I think I see the proliferation and complexity of all creation dividing into gold and dross, unless it is light and dark, but which is which I cannot tell. A black shape on the horizon advances at tremendous speeds; it resolves into a monstrous reptile crushing everything in its path. The great mouth cracks wide as the huge beast approaches, blazing with red light that pours out from deep inside, and all at once I understand. This vast, dark shape is the one being Perpetua hates most, but she is helpless and rushing toward it all the same, and the terror is that she has no choice.

This is by no means God jerking her along; it is a stupendous alligator with its greedy jaws rimmed with blood, summoning Perpetua and its thousand other daughters into its path, preparing to devour them.

The thought trails after her like a pennant of fire. *The father is gathering us in.*

So I understand why the alligator helped me.

And I understand as well the scope of her gift to me:

in another minute, I will become an orphan, as the monster alligator lunges for Perpetua and she stops it in its tracks, destructing in an explosion that lights up the apocalyptic skies. And because I am about to be free, and free of Father forever. . . .

I understand why I had to help her die.

Scared now.

It's OK.

I'll be fine.

Catherine Asaro is, as I write this in the summer of 2003, now the president of the Science Fiction and Fantasy Writers of America. Her work has been nominated for Hugo and Nebula Awards and has earned many other honors, including the Analog *readers' poll and the National Readers Choice Award.*

She writes both space adventure and SF romantic thrillers. Her story for Flights *is neither, a strange and wonderful hybrid of fantasy and weird science.*

The Edges of Never-Haven

Catherine Asaro

Straight edges could take your soul.

The city of Never-Haven encircled a central plaza, where a circular fountain spewed up arches of water. Orb-houses filled the city, all round. Tonight, three moons lit the sky, as white as bone, casting ghostly light over the city of curves. Denric Windward Valdoria ran hard, gasping, his feet pounding on a path that spiraled from the outskirts of the city to its center.

He ran to stay alive.

Edger-demons pursued him, flitting from shadow to shadow. From edge to edge. In this city, straight edges brought the spells of cruelty, but only if they appeared in inanimate objects or drawings. A chance straight edge on a rock, a vertical cliff face, a stately tree trunk: none caused a threat. But build a house with straight walls or a road without turns and twists, and you invited the demons of Never-Haven.

Denric had been far from the city, wandering in the flats, or so he had thought. He hadn't realized he had reached the city outskirts. He had done no more than draw a line in the sand with his toe. Just a line. Always absentminded, he hadn't even realized what he had done—until it was too late.

His hosts in the sand flats had warned him: Avoid the city. If he was imprudent enough to enter, he must create no straight edges. Never-Haven offered a better life than the harsh sand flats where he had come to live a few days ago. The inhabitants of a long-vanished civilization had raised the original city. Its purpose: to cage Edgers. The demons were forever confined within its limits, never able to leave. They hadn't been able to stop humans from settling their city, but they made sure the trespassers lived on the edge of fear. As long as the humans created no straight lines, they remained free, but if ever they made a mistake—as had Denric tonight—they became prey to the Edgers.

So now he ran.

Denric gulped in breaths, his hand clamped over the stitch in his side. He was no athlete; he couldn't keep this pace much longer. His fear roiled. He had no idea how many Edgers were chasing him. Their wings rustled behind him. He didn't know what kept them from overtaking him; perhaps the curves in this path he followed. But they were drawing nearer. Their breath rasped, and their razor-claws clacked in the night.

"Help! Someone!" His yell echoed through the city— and the words bounced back to him like solid objects. The spell-enhanced echoes rained over him, buffeting his body until he stumbled. Catching his balance, he clamped his mouth shut, terrified by the unnatural echoes.

And he ran in silence, while Edgers pursued.

Desperate for a refuge, Denric veered toward a plaza on his left. No water arched out of its round fountain.

Infuriated hisses erupted from the Edgers close on his heels, and he redoubled his efforts, running even harder. The fountain loomed before him, one and a half times his height. Jumping up, he grabbed its upper edge, hauled himself over, and tumbled into the bowl. He hit the bottom with a jarring thump.

Wails arose in the plaza, accompanied by frenzied clicking. He squeezed his eyes shut as if that could hold off his tormentors, but a grating noise immediately spurred him to open them. Silhouetted against the night sky, thorny heads appeared around the rim of the bowl, human-size but triangular. Edgers peered down at him, glinting in the moonlight, each with three glittering eyes. Huddled in the bottom of the fountain, Denric wrapped his arms around his knees and shivered.

The bowl was too deep for them to reach him even with their long arms. They might have slid down, if they could have endured the fountain. But his hope proved sound; they seemed unable to tolerate its curved bowl.

"Go away," he said in a low voice, afraid to speak louder and restart the echoes. He traced curves in the air, on the fountain, even on himself, but nothing warded away the Edgers.

His heart was beating fast from his run. He hadn't realized how out of shape he had become at the university, where he had earned his doctorate in literature. Although he was healthy and hale, he no longer regularly exercised. All highborn youths among his people learned to use a sword and bow; as a prince, even the seventh of ten children, he had been no exception. But he had always preferred reading to swordplay, and he had stopped training years ago.

Unfortunately, books wouldn't help him now. How long would his pursuers wait up there? Edgers slept during the day, shunning the sunlight that bedeviled their translucent eyes and gnarly skin. They and the humans of Never-Haven maintained an uneasy truce; at night, humans stayed within their round houses while Edgers left their straight-edged dunes and prowled the city. But surely by morning, people would be out and about. Whether or not they would help him, if he survived until then, was another question altogether.

He had known, in theory, that people sometimes lived in places where they would never willingly stay if they had other prospects or a means to leave. But it had never seemed real before he came here, to Sandstorm, which included the sand flats, Never-Haven, the deserts, and the stark mountains beyond, a region with few resources, industries, or jobs. He had wanted to establish a school, teaching children to read and write.

Denric shivered, wondering if he would ever meet his students now. He loved teaching. After his graduation last year, several universities had offered him professorships, mostly because of his credentials, though his title as a Ruby Prince hadn't hurt. He had come here instead, for almost no pay, because he wanted to make a difference with his life, which until now had been one of privileges he had inherited rather than earned.

He had just meant to explore Sandstorm. But as often happened, he had become preoccupied with his thoughts, and so he hadn't realized he had crossed the invisible boundary around Never-Haven. Now he was trapped in a bowl, with Edgers after his absentminded royal hide.

The clank of metal awoke Denric. He wouldn't have believed he could sleep now, yet here he was, waking up, groggy and disoriented. The moons were gone from

overhead, but he could make out Edgers around the rim
of the bowl above him. More silhouettes had gathered.

Metal hit stone again—and something struck his leg,
what felt like a heavy chain. He jumped to his feet, holding in his yell. Another chain whacked his knee.

"No!" Backing away, he came up against the side of
the bowl. When a chain swung into his shoulder, he put
up his arm to ward it off—and a link caught his hand.

A square.

By the time Denric comprehended the shape, it was
too late; his direct contact with the chain had counter-
acted the bowl's protective spell. The link snapped
around his wrist, and he gasped at the shock of cold
iron. Nausea surged in him.

The Edgers pulled on the chain, yanking him against
the bowl, stretching his arm over his head. As he struggled, close to panic, they dragged him up the fountain.
But the longer he slid on its curving surface, the more
the link around his wrist weakened. His hope surged; if
he could just work free—

Then a second chain swung into him. He tried to twist
away, but he couldn't manage it. One of its square links
caught his other wrist, and the Edgers pulled his arm
above his head, towing him by both wrists now.

So they hauled him out of the fountain.

Denric had a sudden memory from years ago: climbing in the mountains with his older brothers Vyrl and
Del-Kurj. He had fallen into a hollow and broken his
leg. Only ten years old at the time, he had been terrified.
Then Vyrl had scrambled down to him while Del ran for
help. Their presence and concern had pushed back his
fear. He had help: he would survive. He wished fiercely
now for such assurance, but no rescue was coming
tonight.

When Denric reached the top of the bowl, he was ready to scream. Edgers loomed around him like giant praying mantises, their skin glistening darkly. Each had three triangular nostrils below three eyes, and a hexagonal mouth with teeth hanging over the lips. Instead of forearms, razor-claws extended from their elbows, two blades like a double sword. The metal glinted as his captors hauled him over the edge of the bowl.

"No!" Denric whispered. Those claws could slice him into pieces. None of his hosts had been able to tell him what happened to a person captured by Edgers; apparently no one had returned to offer the story.

But instead of cutting him, an Edger used its long arm like a rope, wrapping the upper part around Denric's torso, leaving the razor-claw free.

Then it jumped.

Denric grunted when they hit the ground. He lost his balance and would have fallen, but the Edger caught him. With a groan, Denric doubled over its arm. The Edger yanked him upright, wrenching his chained arms in front of his body. The links around his wrists opened, but before he could react, the Edger pulled his arms behind his back and chained him again. He felt shell-shocked, unable to absorb it all. The thought of dying terrified him.

An Edger planted its elbow against Denric's back and shoved. He stumbled forward, his hair swinging around his face. The Edger pushed again, driving him in a straight line.

So they took him away.

No light filtered into the cellar. The blackness had an oppressive quality, like a blanket of nothing. The Edgers had pushed Denric on his knees with his back to a large pipe, then pulled his arms back and shackled his wrists behind the pipe. His muscles ached, and cold seeped from the floor through his trousers. Whispers tugged at the edges of his hearing.

Denric fought his dismay. He was a scholar, ill suited to the escapes of an adventurer, but he couldn't just wait here. He yanked on his chains, gauging their strength. They felt unbreakable. The pipe rose up against his back, straight and hard, and the stone floor was flat under his knees. Nor did he doubt this room had straight walls.

A rustle came from the darkness.

"Who is it?" Denric hated the tremor in his voice. Steeling himself, he spoke more firmly. "Who walks there?"

Another rustle.

"Who is it?" The words escaped before he could stop them.

A creak came in front of him, like the bending of a rusty hinge. He pressed into the pole against his back, straining to pull his hands up or down, anything to free himself.

A cough.

"Gods, no." He tried to slide around the pole, but a rectangular duct blocked his way.

Light flared.

Denric jerked back and hit his head on the pipe. His vision swam, making it hard to focus on the glowing blur in front of him. As his sight cleared, he realized he was staring into a face—a human face—eerily lit from below by a boxy lamp. The man had gaunt features, with skin that stretched too tightly over his skull. His eyes, shadowed and dark, were deeply set and overhung by his eyebrows, giving his gaze a hooded aspect. Only a few feet away, he was crouching so his gaze was level with his prisoner's. Darkness hid his body.

He spoke in a shadowed voice. "My greetings, Teacher."

Denric hunched his shoulders. "How did you know I teach?"

"All here know. You are new to Sandstorm." He lifted his lamp, causing the sleeve of his robe to fall back.

Denric knew then that his first impression had been wrong. This creature had a man's face, yes, but instead of a forearm, two blades extended from his elbow, glinting in the light of his lamp.

"What do you want with me?" Denric asked hoarsely.

"Only this." The Edger-man reached forward with his razor-claw. Denric tried to duck, but he could go nowhere. The blades reached to his neck, closer, closer—

And snapped.

A scream caught in Denric's throat. It took him several moments to comprehend that the Edger-man hadn't just sliced open his jugular vein. Instead, he had cut Denric's . . . *hair?* It was true: a curl of gold hair lay balanced on the man's claw.

"So." The man studied the curl. "I wonder if you could calculate an equation for this."

Denric swallowed the bile in his throat. "I've no idea."

"Your hair protects you."

He gave a shaky laugh. "The ol' hair trick, eh?"

"Don't make fun of me, human."

Denric shut his mouth, fast.

The man's voice grated. "Were it my choice, you would die miserably for violating Never-Haven with your straight line. But your curls have stopped whatever I might have done."

Denric had no idea what he meant; he had thought only inanimate curves countered the Edger spells. And if they could cut off one of his curls, why not all of them? He didn't ask, lest he misspeak again and stir his captor's anger. He could feel the man's simmering rage like a tangible presence.

"No matter." The stranger stood, holding up his light. He traced lines in the air, speaking an arcane language Denric had never heard. But he recognized one phrase in the spell: *Prince Denricson Windward Valdoria.*

"What is that?" Denric's voice cracked. "What are you doing?"

The Edger-man didn't answer; he just continued his incantation. Shadows overcame Denric, shrouding his mind.

Silence. No whispers. Denric groggily opened his eyes into a white blur. Brightness surrounded him. He had been in a cellar; now he was . . .

Lying on a bed?

He squinted, confused. It was true. He lay sprawled facedown on a white quilt. Gauzy white curtains hung from ceiling to floor on all sides, enclosing the bed. The drapes were translucent, but they hung in many layers, enough so he couldn't see through them.

He pushed up on his hands, relieved to find himself mobile. But when he tried to pull his legs under him, he discovered his left ankle was chained to a squared bedpost. Gritting his teeth, he slid over to the bedpost and sat up, his ankle pulling the chain tight as his legs hung off the bed. He tried to push aside the curtains, but instead of cloth, they felt like a solid wall. The vertical drapes penned him as securely as any prison.

"Awake, I see," a woman said.

He turned with a start. Across the bed, a woman stood in the narrow space between the mattress and the curtains. Tall, with shimmering black hair, she had slanted eyes and a porcelain face that gave her an eerie, exotic beauty. A dark robe covered her from shoulder to wrist to ankle. Her hand showed beneath the hem of one sleeve, but the blades of a razor-claw glinted in her other sleeve.

"Who—?" Denric would have finished his sentence, except *Who are you?* sounded so trite.

She didn't answer. Instead, she sat at the head of the bed and stretched out her razor-claw. Even knowing she was too far away to reach him, he jerked back. This felt like another of his dreams, the one where he found himself armed with a sword much too heavy to use, facing opponents who handled theirs with ease, faceless creatures who could destroy him with barely a thought.

Those fears had stalked Denric throughout his youth, living as he did in a world that valued a man's prowess in battle far more than book learning. He just wanted to teach. He had never been strong enough to wield a sword well or interested enough to learn strategies that would compensate for his lack of muscle. Nor was his perpetually tousled mop of hair and his face, which too many people called "angelic," likely to inspire dread in his enemies. He was only a little less than average height, and in reasonably good shape, but compared with his brawny, towering brothers and their natural skill at weapons, he had always felt lacking.

"Ruby Prince." The woman had a voice like whiskey,

smooth and husky. If he listened too long, it would inebriate him.

"What do you want?" He tried to ignore her bladed arm.

"What do you think, hmm?" Leaning forward, she brought her claw arm to within a finger-span of his face. Sweat beaded on his forehead, but he didn't back down.

She touched his curls with the tip of a blade. "These do seem to protect you."

"How?" He hadn't meant to speak, but the word came out before he could stop it.

A smile, cool and perfect, touched her cultured lips. "Because I find them too attractive to destroy." She sat back, her lashes lowering over her tilted eyes. Then she crooked the finger of her human hand. "Come here, pretty human."

Ah, hell. Being a demon's plaything ranked about as high on his list of preferred activities as catching pneumonia.

"No," he said.

"I think yes." She traced a straight line in the air, from high to low, and a shudder went through Denric. When she drew a line from left to right, he felt pulled forward. He resisted, leaning back. Then she made a line from low to high, and he couldn't stop from tilting toward her. When she completed her rectangle in the air, with a line from right to left, he began to slide toward her despite his efforts to hold back.

Ironically, the chain came to his rescue, pulling him up short as it stretched his leg out behind him. With her spell drawing him, he had to brace his hands on the bed so he wouldn't keel over onto his face. The awkward position annoyed him so much, he momentarily forgot to be terrified. Instead, he scowled. "Are you done playing?"

"Should I be?" As she traced a curve in the air, the pulling sensation stopped, and he jerked back in compensation. With no warning, she slashed the bed with her claw, cutting the quilt in a line. Clinks rattled behind Denric, and he swung around to see the chain fall apart. He pulled his leg under him fast, before the chain could catch it again. Then he turned back to the woman, afraid to ask what she planned next.

"Come here," she murmured.

Alarmed, he tried to back away. It did no good; against his will, he slid forward those last few handspans to where she sat. When he raised his arm to defend himself, she caught it in her human hand. In reflex, he jerked back his other fist, ready to strike. She reacted just as fast, opening her razor-claw around his wrist.

Denric froze, staring at the blades. Light glinted on their edges. If she snapped the claw, she would slice his fist off at the wrist. Slowly, and ever so carefully, he drew his hand back and lowered his arm.

"What do you want with me?" he asked.

"Your children are heirs to an empire, eh?"

He felt as if his stomach had dropped. Of course she knew. A memory jumped in his mind from several years ago, a processional of the Imperialate nobility, the wealthy and powerful, those with lives such as most people never witnessed, except at such parades meant to entertain a weary public. Members of each noble House had walked down a great concourse, going to their seats in an amphitheatre, where they would watch the day's entertainment, plays and such.

Denric's family had entered last, as befitted their royal status, with lesser members coming first, then those with higher rank. The parade ended with his aunt, the Ruby Pharaoh. As the seventh child of the

Pharaoh's sister, Denric had gone before most of his other kin. But it still placed him higher in rank than the most powerful nobles. Unlike many of his siblings, who took their status for granted, it troubled him that he inherited rather than earned his standing. He wanted his achievements to arise from hard work. Regardless, one fact remained: Any legitimate child he fathered would have the rights, privileges, and power of a Ruby Dynasty heir.

"So quiet," the Edger-woman said.

"You can't have my child," Denric said.

Never taking her gaze from him, she traced her claw on the curtains. The spell that made them rigid walls to Denric had no effect on her blades. She neatly sliced the cloth into a hexagon, and a six-sided piece of gauze drifted onto the bed.

Denric blinked. "How did you do that?" He pressed the curtains nearest to him, but they remained solid.

She indicated her human hand. "Once I was all like this. No longer."

"You deliberately changed into an Edger?" What would possess a person to such insanity?

"For the spells. They are the reward of transformation."

"How could you?"

Her voice hardened. "You've never needed for anything, princeling. Never lived the edges of life, only its sweet fullness. Here we have nothing but edges. *Nothing.*" With deadly calm, she added, "Now you learn the other side."

Her words plucked a wire within him, one drawn tight by his fear that she spoke the truth, that he had no right to his life. He knew how his aunt, the pharaoh, would respond: *Our privileges are small compensation for the responsibilities we carry.* By the Ruby Dynasty, an empire rose or fell; if they faltered, untold populations could suffer.

At times Denric felt the weight of those duties crushing him, and he carried less than many members of his family. He couldn't defend the Imperialate as an officer; he lacked the military brilliance of his siblings. But he could teach, perhaps an even more effective defense for an empire. Educate her people. Help them learn to help themselves. Or so he had believed. Now, faced with someone who had given up her humanity just to survive, his idealistic views seemed hollow.

The Edger-woman was scrutinizing him as if trying to read his thoughts from his face. When she touched the hexagon of gauze on the bed, a shudder went through Denric, starting in his shoulders and shaking down his torso into his legs. Pushed by this new spell, he drew her into his arms. Inside he was shouting, fighting the compulsion she laid on him. The muscles in his arms and legs spasmed. Yet still he held her.

Her body felt human in his embrace. *Curved.* She put her human arm around his waist and laid her head on his shoulder. "I am pleased."

Unwilling but unable to stop, he leaned his head against hers. "Why are you doing this? No child I have with you would be legitimate." She threatened to scorch his heart. He came from a close, devoted family; they were his world. Over the years he had begun to long for his own. In that, legitimacy made no difference; he would acknowledge and love any offspring he sired. One of his deepest fears was that he would become a father but lose his child. It would kill him.

"By the time of its birth," she murmured, "it will be legitimate."

Denric stiffened. Good gods, could they force his

marriage? Surely not. A vow made under duress wasn't valid. "My family would never believe I consented to such a union."

She pressed her lips against his cheek. "What do you think they would do to have you back? And your baby, hmmm? But the child could stay here. That would be messy for you."

His panic sparked. *No.* Clenching his fists, he made circles on her back, pressing with his knuckles. It didn't help counter her spell; he continued to hold her as if they were lovers.

Denric drew in a deep breath. Damn it all, he wouldn't let the Edgers terrorize him. If the worst happened, he would deal with it, somehow. Some way.

He spoke in a quieter voice. "I don't understand how you could give up being human."

"Surely you see." She released him from her spell enough so she could lean back to look at him. "I have powers I could only imagine before."

"How much of you has changed?"

She hesitated, then seemed to make a decision. Pulling aside her robe, she revealed her leg where it hung off the bed. It was also a razor-claw, longer and deadlier than her arm, ending in a metal pad that would allow her to walk.

Denric touched the metal knee. "What transformed you?"

"The Edgers."

He looked up at her. "How?"

"They know spells."

"What spells?"

"Equations."

He grimaced. "Lots of people know equations." It didn't make the infernal things any more palatable.

"Edgers use them in ways humans cannot." She drew a line in the air. "Linear equations, those that make lines, are Edger spells. The equation of a curve can counter such spells because it is of a higher order. Nonlinear."

He didn't recall enough mathematics to understand fully, but he did remember what "higher order" meant. Linear equations had their variables raised only to the first power; curves had their variables raised to higher powers.

He tilted his head, curious despite himself. "Why would only linear spells do magic?" He wasn't convinced Edger spells really were the magic of demons rather than the ancient technology of a vanished alien race.

"Straight lines are unyielding." She shrugged. "Curves are softer."

It didn't tell him much. He wondered if she was thinking of herself more than the spells. He was almost certain curves were stronger than straight lines. Wasn't that why chain links were round instead of square? Edger chains needed spells to strengthen them. But her comment made sense in another way; in giving up part of her humanity, she had gained the unyielding edges she needed to survive.

She was watching him closely. "You are a complicated man, I think. Too complex for simple straight edges."

"Most people are." He shifted his weight, wanting to move away but unable to counter the remnants of her spell. He had never been good at equations. He wished he had the ability of his teenaged brother, Kelric, his youngest sibling. Kelric would have been a superb theorist, except he had been talked into attending a military academy instead. He would also marry in a few years, a dynastic union arranged with a noblewoman, an officer in the Imperial Fleet. Denric had almost ended up betrothed to her himself, but in the end she had chosen Kelric, whose military interests more closely matched her own.

An idea came to him. "You and I can't marry. I already have a wife."

She frowned. "We know you don't."

"It's a betrothal."

"You're lying."

"Check. Kelricson Valdoria is to wed Corey Majda, the Matriarch of Majda."

"Your name is Denric."

"That's a nickname." If she investigated, she would find references to both his and Kelric's possible betrothals, and it might not be immediately obvious he and his brother weren't the same person.

Her scowl deepened. "We will check this lie."

"Good." Perhaps it would buy him time.

"Even if it is true, you are still a valuable hostage." She studied him. "Perhaps even more so, if a powerful matriarch wants her golden-haired prince back."

Damn. "What is it you want from me?"

"You will see."

Concentrating on her, Denric realized the truth: They would never let him go. They had too much to lose. As soon as his family knew he was free, they would seek vengeance against his kidnappers. He had far more use as a hostage; his parents would give much to ensure his safety, all the more so because war, assassination, and politics had so often torn his family apart. He had been able to come here to teach only because he was the seventh child of the Pharaoh's sister; had he been closer to the throne, the government would have forbidden him this post. His parents worried for him regardless. He hated knowing he had fulfilled their worst fears.

Stop it, Denric thought. He had to live his own life. Yes, danger existed. But he had to face it, not hide in the protected shadow of his heredity.

"What deal did you make with the demons?" he asked. "What did you trade to them for this power of spells?"

Her shoulders hunched. "You ask too much."

"It's me, isn't it?" He watched for her reaction. "You promised to increase their sway over humans. Right now they have Never-Haven. But the more of us they control, the more their influence extends into human realms. Perhaps someday they will escape Never-Haven, yes? Those of you who have transformed must bring them valuable humans."

She clenched her fist. "We do as we please."

"I don't believe you. I think you have no choice."

Her voice was low. "Nor do you."

"No! I would never transform."

"Perhaps." She slid her arm around his neck and brushed her lips across his.

Clamping his mouth shut, he thought of circles, waves, parabolas, anything curved. Nothing helped: She continued to kiss him, and he continued to let her.

But then she drew back, her expression pensive. "Before the Edgers took me in, I had no home. Nowhere to go." Tightly, she added, "Men took advantage of that."

Denric felt ill, understanding her implication. "And now?"

Her eyes glinted. "No one touches me unless I allow it." Then she added, "It seems I cannot make myself force another."

Although she said no more, he sensed her inner

struggle. The Edgers hadn't taken all her humanity: She had a conscience. "Then surely you see you must let me go."

"The time will come, Ruby Prince, when you want me of your own free will." She flicked her fingers in a curve through the air, and the force holding him released. "The spells work on your mind as well as your body. It just takes longer."

With that, she rose to her feet, her robe falling over her leg, hiding the blades. Then she left, easily pushing aside the curtains. He tried to grab them, but they billowed away from his hand and fell into place, once again becoming a solid wall.

Denric sat cross-legged on the bed, thinking. The people of Never-Haven paid a devastating price to escape their harsh existence. It was true, Edgers offered them better lives, but only if the humans indentured themselves. They were still trapped, now by a pact with demons rather than by poverty. He had a responsibility here, but his becoming an Edger wasn't the solution. He wanted to help, not constrain these people in a life worse than what they already suffered.

He wondered, too, if Edger-humans had to remain in Never-Haven. If Edgers left, they faded away into nothing. But transformed humans weren't fully Edgers, at least not those he had seen. Did they have more freedom? The prospect of their leaving to prey on their untransformed brethren chilled Denric.

Edger motivations were alien to him. What would they do, alter every human in Never-Haven? Yes, apparently, if they could. And then? He was beginning to see the answer. They would lure in more humans. No wonder they wanted him as a hostage. He would draw people here: would-be rescuers, covert agents, and the curious, come to see the city that ensorcelled a Ruby Prince. Humans were safe as long as they avoided straight edges, but no one could keep that up forever. One by one, the Edgers would transform them. It was a bizarre scenario, a city packed with demons. If they reached a critical number, they could push out the boundaries of Never-Haven, making it larger and larger until it overran all Sandstorm.

Denric shuddered. He had to escape. The Edger-woman claimed he couldn't use their magic—if it really was magic and not an esoteric, ancient technology his people no longer understood. He wasn't even sure the two possibilities were that different. This had started when he drew a line in the sand, so obviously he could have an effect, if only he knew how. It all centered on equations. They did indeed seem like arcane spells to him, an unknowable language only its acolytes could comprehend. His drawing curves hadn't countered any spells, but perhaps that was because he didn't understand the math.

Denric struggled to remember the equation for a curve, *any* curve. He recalled only one, a parabola. Visualizing it in his mind, he imagined the curtains giving way to his push. But when he pushed, they still felt solid. What was he missing? Scowling, he slashed his hand across the drapes in a parabola.

They gave along the curve.

"Hey!" Denric grinned. Pushing the cloth, he dented its surface. No matter how hard he tried, though, he could achieve nothing more. Within seconds, the dent vanished. Disappointed, he concentrated and drew a bigger parabola. The drapes gave again, but no more than before.

His elation faded. He needed something more. What? A more complicated equation perhaps. Years ago he had known the formula for a circle, but he no longer remembered, besides which, he had never understood it anyway.

Try, he thought. He guessed at the equation and drew a circle on the curtains. Nothing happened. He changed the math in his mind and tried again, still with no luck. On his third try, the cloth gave a little, but no more than for the parabola.

Denric exhaled. Scanning his prison, he pondered what he could do. The hexagon the Edger-woman had cut from the drapes lay close to where he was sitting. With a frown, he scooted across the bed and tried his counterspell on the curtains farthest from the hexagon. The drapes dented—

And billowed out from his hand. Caught off guard, he froze. By the time he had gathered his wits enough to touch the curtains, they had settled down and become rigid again.

With his heart beating hard, Denric stood up between the bed and drapes. He repeated his spell, and this time when the drapes billowed, he shoved them aside and ran out—

Into darkness.

Cold.

Denric shivered. Darkness surrounded him. He reached out, but found nothing. Nor did he see any sign of his prison, no light, nothing.

Turning in a circle, he thought of the equation that had led him here—and light flickered in the distance. He stopped, blinking. He hadn't been trying a spell, but apparently the procedure worked regardless. Or more accurately, it negated a spell, in this case one of darkness.

He headed for the light, crossing his arms against the cold, rubbing his palms on his elbows for warmth. Soon he was walking down a rough-hewn tunnel of old stone blocks. Up ahead, an archway framed the corridor, coming to a triangular point high overhead. Light poured through it, so bright he could see nothing within the brilliance. Rattles, cracks, and clinks came from beyond the arch.

He stopped at the opening and bit his lip. This could be a gate to freedom or a path deeper into captivity. What to do: Enter the light or retreat into the dark? His inclination was to think of light as good, but that instinct might have little basis here.

Well, he had to do something, and he really, really didn't want to stay in the dark. Steeling himself, he walked forward. Light poured everywhere, blinding him. A voice keened, a lament of grief so great, it threatened to break his heart.

Gradually the light dimmed, until he could make out the surroundings. He was in a room of a castle.

His room.

Denric shook his head, trying to clear the vision. But it persisted. He recognized everything: the fresh atmosphere of home, so unlike the dusty air of Never-Haven; the distant voices of the castle waking in the morning; the aromas of breakfast. He also knew the person standing by the window alcove across the room, staring out at the Plains of Dalavador.

His mother.

When he realized she was crying, he strode over to her. "Mother? What is wrong? Why are you sad?"

She gave no sign she heard, only continued to gaze out the window, her face streaked with tears, her hair tumbling down her back in a gold mane, a much longer version of his own curls. She had a shawl around her shoulders and was wearing a long robe. Dawn was just lighting the sky outside.

"Mother?" He stopped next to her, reaching out—and his hand went through her arm.

Denric stared at his hand. "No, it can't be."

She continued to cry, oblivious of him. He spun around, intent on a counterspell—and froze. His body was laid out on the bed in a shroud of mourning. His mother was weeping for him. For his death.

"It's not true." He raised his voice. "Do you hear me?" He didn't know who he was challenging: the Edgers, fate, himself? "I'm *alive!*"

He turned back to his mother, the queen of Skyfall. It tore at him, seeing her grieve. Family, home, hearth—they mattered to him more than anything else. He was just a simple man who wanted to sit by the fire with a wife and children. His passing would be inauspicious, mourned by only a few, for unlike his brothers he was no great hero. His sister, Soz, had also entered the military, distinguishing herself far better than he ever could.

Denric mentally shook himself. No he wasn't a great officer. That didn't make him any less. He spoke gently to his mother, even knowing she couldn't hear. "If I truly have died, or soon will, please know I love you, Father, and the family. Remember that, feel it somehow, even if you never know I was here."

Unexpectedly, her lips formed a word: *Denric?* His heart leapt, but he had no chance to ask if she heard him. A mist was rising around them. It thickened until the world became formless and dim, with nothing but the ground beneath his feet. He called to her, but the fog muffled his words into silence.

Denric pushed his hands through his hair, his arms shaking. Had he died? He clenched his fists, pressing them against his head. "I won't give in." Then he shouted, "Do you hear me? I won't become an Edger."

Silence.

Denric lowered his arms, his muscles so tense he couldn't unclench his hands. He wanted to run, but he didn't dare, lest he become lost. He tried his counterspells, but nothing worked. His universe remained formless.

"It doesn't matter what you do," he told the mist, the spells, anyone who could hear. "It doesn't matter what you show me. I won't consent to become an Edger."

"Bravado," a voice hissed.

Denric swung around. "Who is that?"

"Mother," it whispered. "Father. Brother. Sister. Transform them."

"You're lying." It couldn't be true. They couldn't have brought his family here.

"No lie," the voice murmured.

The sibilant words lifted the hairs on Denric's neck. He opened his mouth to shout another denial. Then he stopped. Yelling at a formless voice wouldn't achieve anything.

Suddenly the Edger-woman spoke out of the mist. "Pretty boy. Will you die?"

"If I do, it will be as a human. I won't transform."

Silence.

Sweat beaded on Denric's forehead. "Is anyone there?"

No answer.

It took a conscious effort for him to stay put, to keep from calling in a panic. He had always thought of himself as an unruffled sort, but waiting now, in this nothingness, took every bit of control he could muster. Inside, he was terrified. But somehow he managed to keep from running like a maniac.

After a while, he realized the mist was thinning. As his surroundings became clearer, puzzlement set in. He was outside Never-Haven, farther out in the sand flats even than when he had traced a line in the ground with his toe.

Denric stepped back, away from the city. From the direction of Never-Haven, a dark figure was approaching, forming out of the thinning mist. It took a moment for him to recognize her as the Edger-woman. She stopped a few paces away, the wind blowing her hair around her face.

"I won't go back," Denric said.

Her voice came like gusts over a distant plain. "Not many escape."

"Escape?" He wasn't certain he had heard correctly.

She indicated the sand flats around them. "You are outside the boundaries of Never-Haven."

"You're letting me go?"

"No. You have left despite us."

He didn't believe it. "How?"

"Do you not wonder how someone as untutored in mathematics as yourself could evade our spells? If you can, surely anyone can manage it."

So much for her confidence in his intellect. "And can they?"

"No."

"Then why me?"

"Equations are only a framework. Fear makes the

spell." Her voice was a chill wind. "The only way to escape Never-Haven is to face your fears."

"That's it?" He couldn't hold back his incredulity.

She raised her eyebrow. "You consider it easy?"

He thought of what he had been through. "No, not easy."

"You are one of only a few to escape."

"What happened to the others?"

Her hair blew across her face. "They became like us."

Denric shuddered. "I should go now."

"Don't return, beautiful prince. I would take you before any other." Her voice was barely audible now, as her body began to thin, like mist. "I cannot follow you outside the city; I must stay in Never-Haven now that I am transformed. But if ever you become trapped here again, I will find a spell to hold you forever."

Denric spoke softly. "I cannot change what made your life hell. But perhaps I can help others."

"Perhaps."

He swallowed. "Good-bye."

"Good-bye," she whispered.

Then she faded from sight.

Grit blew across the sand flats. Denric stood alone, outside his rounded house. The fates willing, he would build a home here.

He looked toward Never-Haven in the distance, with its curved towers. *Fierce, beautiful city.* It demanded an abysmal price of its people, that they lose their humanity to survive. He thought of the woman, terrible in her beauty. Forever trapped. Denric knew he would live every moment in the shadow of Never-Haven, aware of its presence. It would never let him forget he owed these people a debt.

And yet—in dealing with the Edgers, he had found an inner core of his character, one that would help him survive. He would offer what he could to the children here, that they might find a better way to escape their crushing lives than the path chosen by their kin in the city.

Perhaps he could give them hope.

*Until he clued me in, I had no idea **Tim Powers** was born in New York (Buffalo), but I did know he was born in a leap year the same calendar year as me, which makes me in my fifties and Tim just into his teens. He is the author of many wonderful novels, among them the award-winners* **The Anubis Gates** *(Philip K. Dick Award and Prix Apollo),* **Dinner at Deviant's Palace** *(another Phil Dick award),* **Last Call** *(World Fantasy Award), and* **Declare** *(ditto).*

PAT MOORE

Tim Powers

"**I**s it okay if you're one of the ten people I send the letter to," said the voice on the telephone, "or is that redundant? I don't want to screw this up. 'Ear repair' sounds horrible."

Moore exhaled smoke and put out his Marlboro in the half-inch of cold coffee in his cup. "No, Rick, don't send it to me. In fact, you're screwed—it says you have to have ten friends."

He picked up the copy he had got in the mail yesterday, spread the single sheet out flat on the kitchen table and weighted two corners with the dusty salt and pepper shakers. It had clearly been photocopied from a photocopy, and originally composed on a typewriter.

This has been sent to you for good luck. The original is in San Fransisco. You must send it on to ten friend's, who, you think need good luck, within 24 hrs of receiving it.

"I could use some luck," Rick went on. "Can you loan me a couple of thousand? My wife's in the hospital, and we've got no insurance."

Moore paused for a moment before going on with the old joke; then, "Sure," he said, "so we won't see you at the lowball game tomorrow?"

"Oh, I've got money for *that*." Rick might have caught Moore's hesitation, for he went on quickly, without waiting for a dutiful laugh, "Mark 'n' Howard mentioned it this morning on the radio. You're famous."

The luck is now sent to you—you will receive Good Luck within three days of receiving this, provided you send it on. Do not send money, since luck has no price.

On a Wednesday dawn five months ago now, Moore had poured a tumbler of Popov Vodka at this table, after sitting most of the night in the emergency room at— what had been the name of the hospital in San Mateo, not Saint Lazarus, for sure—and then he had carefully lit a Virginia Slims from the orphaned pack on the counter and laid the smoldering cigarette in an ashtray beside the glass. When the untouched cigarette had burned down to the filter and gone out, he had carried the full glass and the ashtray to the back door and set them in the trash can, and then washed his hands in the kitchen sink, wondering if the little ritual had been a sufficient good-bye. Later he had thrown out the bottle of vodka and the pack of Virginia Slims too.

A young man in Florida got the letter, it was very faded, and he resolved to type it again, but he forgot. He had many troubles, including expensive ear repair. But then he typed ten copy's and mailed them, and he got a better job.

"Where you playing today?" Rick asked.

"The Garden City in San Jose, probably," Moore said, "the six- and twelve-dollar Hold 'Em. I was just about to leave when you called."

"For sure? I could meet you there. I was going to play at the Bay on Bering, but if we were going to meet there, you'd have to shave—"

"And find a clean shirt, I know. But I'll see you at Larry's game tomorrow, and we shouldn't play at the same table anyway. Go to the Bay."

"Naw, I wanted to ask you about something. So you'll be at the Garden City. You take the 280, right?"

Pat Moore put off mailing the letter and died, but later found it again and passed it on, and received threescore and ten.

"Right."

"If that crapped-out Dodge of yours can get up to freeway speed."

"It'll still be cranking along when your Saturn is a planter somewhere."

"Great, so I'll see you there," Rick said. "Hey," he added with forced joviality, "you're famous!"

Do not ignore this letter
ST LAZARUS

"Type up ten copies with your name in it, you can be famous too," Moore said, standing up and crumpling the letter. "Send one to Mark 'n' Howard. See you."

He hung up the phone and fetched his car keys from the cluttered table by the front door. The chilly sea breeze outside was a reproach after the musty staleness of the apartment, and he was glad he'd brought his denim jacket.

He combed his hair in the rearview mirror while the old slant-six engine of the Dodge idled in the carport, and he wondered if he would see the day when his brown hair might turn gray. He was still thirty years short of threescore and ten, and he wasn't envying the Pat Moore in the chain letter.

The first half hour of the drive down the 280 was quiet, with a Gershwin CD playing the *Concerto in F* and the pines and green meadows of the Fish and Game Refuge wheeling past on his left under the gray sky, while the pastel houses of Hillsborough and Redwood City marched across the eastern hills. The car smelled familiarly of Marlboros and Doublemint gum and engine exhaust.

Just over those hills, on the 101 overlooking the Bay, Trish had driven her Ford Grenada over an unrailed embankment at midnight, after a Saint Patrick's Day party at the Bayshore Meadows. Moore was objectively sure he would drive on the 101 one day, but not yet.

Traffic was light on the 280 this morning, and in his rearview mirror he saw the little white car surging from side to side in the lanes as it passed other vehicles. Like most modern cars, it looked to Moore like a computer mouse. He clicked up his turn signal lever and drifted over the lane-divider bumps and into the right lane.

The white car—he could see the blue Chevy cross on its hood now—swooped up in the lane Moore had just left, but instead of rocketing on past him, it slowed, pacing Moore's old Dodge at sixty miles an hour.

Moore glanced to his left, wondering if he knew the driver of the Chevy—but it was a lean-faced stranger in sunglasses, looking straight at him. In the moment before Moore recognized the thing as a shotgun viewed muzzle-on, he thought the man was holding up a microphone; but instantly another person in the white car had blocked the driver—Moore glimpsed only a purple shirt and long dark hair—and then with squealing tires the car veered sharply away to the left.

Moore gripped the hard green plastic of his steering wheel and looked straight ahead; he was braced for the sound of the Chevy hitting the center-divider fence, and so he didn't jump when he heard the crash—even though the seat rocked under him and someone was now sitting in the car with him, on the passenger side against the door. For one unthinking moment he thought someone had been thrown from the Chevrolet and had landed in his car.

He focused on the lane ahead and on holding the Dodge Dart steady between the white lines. Nobody could have come through the roof, or the windows or the doors. Must have been hiding in the backseat all this time, he thought, and only now jumped over into the front. What timing. He was panting shallowly, and his ribs tingled, and he made himself take a deep breath and let it out.

He looked to his right. A dark-haired woman in a purple dress was grinning at him. Her hair hung in a neat pageboy cut, and she wasn't panting.

"I'm your guardian angel," she said. "And guess what my name is."

Moore carefully lifted his foot from the accelerator—he didn't trust himself with the brake yet—and steered the Dodge onto the dirt shoulder. When it had slowed to the point where he could hear gravel popping under the tires, he pressed the brake; the abrupt stop rocked him forward, though the woman beside him didn't shift on the old green upholstery.

"And guess what my name is," she said again.

The sweat rolling down his chest under his shirt was a sharp tang in his nostrils. "Hmm," he said, to test his voice; then he said, "You can get out of the car now."

In the front pocket of his jeans was a roll of hundred-dollar bills, but his left hand was only inches away from the .38 revolver tucked into the open seam at the side of the seat. But both the woman's hands were visible on her lap, and empty.

The engine was still running, shaking the car, and he could smell the hot exhaust fumes seeping up through the floor. He sighed, then reluctantly reached forward and switched off the ignition.

"I shouldn't be talking to you," the woman said in the sudden silence. "*She* told me not to. But I just now saved your life. So don't tell me to get out of the car."

It had been a purple shirt or something, and dark hair. But this was obviously not the person he'd glimpsed in the Chevy. A team, twins?

"What's your name?" he asked absently. A van whipped past on the left, and the car rocked on its shock absorbers.

"Pat Moore, same as yours," she said with evident satisfaction. He noticed that every time he glanced at her, she looked away from something else to meet his eyes; as if whenever he wasn't watching her, she was studying the interior of the car, or his shirt, or the freeway lanes.

"Did you—get threescore and ten?" he asked. Something more like a nervous tic than a smile was twitching his lips. "When you sent out the letter?"

"That wasn't me, that was *her*. And she hasn't got it yet. And she won't, either, if her disciples kill all the available Pat Moores. You're in trouble every which way, but I like you."

"Listen, when did you get into my car?"

"About ten seconds ago. What if he had backup, another car following him? You should get moving again."

Moore called up the instant's glimpse he had got of the thing in front of the driver's hand—the ring had definitely been the muzzle of a shotgun, twelve-gauge, probably a pistol grip. And he seized on her remark about a backup car because the thought was manageable and complete. He clanked the gearshift into Park, and the Dodge started at the first twist of the key, and he levered it into Drive and gunned along the shoulder in a cloud of dust until he had got up enough speed to swing into the right lane between two yellow Stater Bros. trucks.

He concentrated on working his way over to the fast lane, and then when he got there, his engine roaring, he just watched the rearview mirror and the oncoming exit signs until he found a chance to make a sharp right turn across all the lanes and straight into the exit lane that swept toward the southbound 85. A couple of cars behind him honked.

He was going too fast for the curving interchange lane, his tires chirruping on the pavement, and he wrestled with the wheel and stroked the brake.

"Who's getting off behind us?" he asked sharply.

"I can't see," she said.

He darted a glance at the rearview mirror and was pleased to see only a slow-moving old station wagon, far back.

"A station wagon," she said, though she still hadn't

looked around. Maybe she had looked in the passenger-side door mirror.

He had got the car back under control by the time he merged with the southbound lanes, and then he braked, for the 85 was ending ahead, at a traffic signal by the grounds of some college.

"Is your neck hurt?" he asked. "Can't twist your head around?"

"It's not that. I can't see anything you don't see."

He tried to frame an answer to that, or a question about it, and finally just said, "I bet we could find a bar fairly readily. Around here."

"I can't drink. I don't have any ID."

"You can have a Virgin Mary," he said absently, catching a green light and turning right just short of the college. "Celery stick to stir it with." Raindrops began spotting the dust on the windshield.

"I'm not so good at touching things," she said. "I'm not actually a living person."

"Okay, see, that means what? You're a *dead* person, a ghost?"

"Yes."

Already disoriented, Moore flexed his mind to see if anything in his experience or philosophies might let him believe this; and there was nothing that did. This woman, probably a neighbor, simply knew who he was, and she had hidden in the back of his car back at the apartment parking lot. She was probably insane. It would be a mistake to get further involved with her.

"Here's a place," he said, swinging the car into a strip-mall parking lot to the right. "Pirate's Cove. We can see how well you handle popcorn before you try a drink."

* * *

He parked around behind the row of stores, and the back door of the Pirate's Cove led them down a hallway stacked with boxes before they stepped through an arch into the dim bar. There were no other customers in the place at this early hour, and the long room smelled more like bleach than like beer; the teenaged-looking bartender barely gave them a glance and a nod as Moore led the woman across the worn carpet and the parquet square to a table under a football poster. There were four low stools instead of chairs.

The woman couldn't remember any movies she'd ever seen, and claimed not to have heard about the war in Iraq, so when Moore walked to the bar and came back with a glass of Budweiser and a bowl of popcorn, he sat down and just stared at her. She was easier to see in the dim light from the jukebox and the neon bar signs than she had been out in the gray daylight. He would guess that she was about thirty—though her face had no wrinkles at all, as if she had never laughed or frowned.

"You want to try the popcorn?" he asked as he unsnapped the front of his denim jacket.

"Look at it so I know where it is."

He glanced down at the bowl, and then back at her. As always, her eyes fixed on his as soon as he was looking at her. Either her pupils were fully dilated, or else her irises were black.

But he glanced down again when something thumped the table and a puff of hot salty air flicked his hair, and some popcorn kernels spun away through the air.

The popcorn still in the bowl had been flattened into little white jigsaw-puzzle pieces. The orange plastic bowl was cracked.

Her hands were still in her lap, and she was still looking at him. "I guess not, thanks."

Slowly he lifted his glass of beer and took a sip. That was a powerful raise, he thought, forcing himself not to show any astonishment—though you should have suspected a strong hand. Play carefully here.

He glanced toward the bar; but the bartender, if he had looked toward their table at all, had returned his attention to his newspaper.

"Tom Cruise," the woman said.

Moore looked back at her and after a moment raised his eyebrows.

She said, "That was a movie, wasn't it?"

"In a way." *Play carefully here.* "What did you—? Is something wrong with your vision?"

"I don't have any vision. No retinas. I have to use yours. I'm a ghost."

"Ah. I've never met a ghost before." He remembered a line from a Robert Frost poem: *There's something the dead are keeping back.*

"Well, not that you could see. You can see me only because . . . I'm like the stamp you get on the back of your hand at Disneyland; you can't see me unless there's a black light shining on me. *She's* the black light."

"You're in her field of influence, like."

"Sure. There's probably dozens of Pat Moore ghosts in the outfield, and *she's* the whole infield. I'm the shortstop."

"Why doesn't . . . *she* want you to talk to me?" He never drank on days he intended to play, but he lifted his glass again.

"She doesn't want me to tell you what's going to happen." She smiled, and the smile stayed on her smooth face like the expression on a porcelain doll. "If it were up to me, I'd tell you."

He swallowed a mouthful of beer. "But."

She nodded, and at last let her smile relax. "It's not up to me. She'd kill me if I told you."

He opened his mouth to point out a logic problem with that, then sighed and said instead, "Would she know?" She just blinked at him, so he went on, "Would she know it, if you told me?"

"*Oh* yeah."

"How would she know?"

"You'd be doing things. You wouldn't be sitting here drinking, for sure."

"What would I be doing?"

"I think you'd be driving to San Francisco. If I told you—if you asked—" For an instant she was gone, and then he could see her again; but she seemed two-dimensional now, like a projection on a screen—he had the feeling that if he moved to the side, he would just see this image of her get narrower, not see around the other side of her.

"What's in San Francisco?" he asked quickly.

"Well, if you asked me about Maxwell's Demon-n-n-n—"

She was perfectly motionless, and the drone of the last consonant slowly deepened in pitch to silence. Then the popcorn in the cracked bowl rattled in the same instant that she silently disappeared like the picture on a switched-off television set, leaving Moore alone at the table, his face suddenly chilly in the bar's air-conditioning. For a moment *air-conditioning* seemed to remind him of something, but he forgot it when he looked down at the popcorn—the bowl was full of brown BBs, unpopped dried corn. As he watched, each kernel slowly opened in white curls and blobs until all the popcorn was as fresh looking and uncrushed as it had been when he had carried it to the table. There hadn't been a sound, though he caught a strong whiff of gasoline. The bowl wasn't cracked anymore.

He stood up and kicked his stool aside as he backed away from the table. She was definitely gone.

The bartender was looking at him now, but Moore hurried past him and back through the hallway to the stormy gray daylight.

What if she had backup? he thought as he fumbled the keys out of his pocket; and, *She doesn't want me to tell you what's going to happen.*

He realized that he'd been sprinting only when he scuffed to a halt on the wet asphalt beside the old white Dodge, and he was panting as he unlocked the door and yanked it open. Rain on the pavement was a steady textured hiss. He climbed in and pulled the door closed, and had rammed the key into the ignition—

—when the drumming of rain on the car roof abruptly went silent, and a voice spoke in his head: *Relax. I'm you. You're me.*

And then his mouth had opened and the words were coming out of his mouth: "We're Pat Moore, there's nothing to be afraid of." His voice belonged to someone else in this muffled silence.

His eyes were watering with the useless effort to breathe for himself.

He knew this wasn't the Pat Moore he had been in the bar with. This was the *her* she had spoken of. A moment later the thoughts had been wiped away, leaving nothing but an insistent pressure of *all-is-well.*

Though nothing grabbed him, he found that his head was turning to the right, and with dimming vision he saw that his right hand was moving toward his face.

But *all-is-well* had for some time been a feeling that was alien to him, and he managed to resist it long

enough to make his infiltrated mind form a thought—
she's crowding me out.

And he managed to think too: Alive or dead, stay
whole. He reached down to the open seam in the seat
before he could lose his left arm too, and he snatched up
the revolver and stabbed the barrel into his open
mouth. A moment later he felt the click through the
steel against his teeth when he cocked the hammer
back. His belly coiled icily, as if he were standing on the
coping of a very high wall and looking up.

The intrusion in his mind paused, and he sensed con-
fusion, and so he threw at it the thought, *One more step,
and I blow my head off.* He added, *Go ahead and call
this bet, please. I've been meaning to drive the 101 for a
while now.*

His throat was working to form words that he could
only guess at, and then he was in control of his own
breathing again, panting and huffing spit into the gun
barrel. Beyond the hammer of the gun, he could see the
rapid distortions of rain hitting the windshield, but he
still couldn't hear anything from outside the car.

The voice in his head was muted now: *I mean to help
you.*

He let himself pull the gun away from his mouth,
though he kept it pointed at his face, and he spoke into
the wet barrel as if it were a microphone. "I don't want
help," he said hoarsely.

I'm Pat Moore, and I want help.

"You want to . . . take over, possess me."

I want to protect you. A man tried to kill you.

"That's your pals," he said, remembering what the
ghost woman had told him in the car. "Your disciples,
trying to kill all the Pat Moores—to keep you from taking one over, I bet. Don't joggle me now." Staring down

the rifled barrel, he cautiously hooked his thumb over the hammer and then pulled the trigger and eased the hammer down. "I can still do it with one pull of the trigger," he told her as he lifted his thumb away. "So you— what, you put off mailing the letter, and died?"

The letter is just my chain mail. The only important thing about it is my name, and the likelihood that people will reproduce it and pass it on. Bombers evade radar by throwing clouds of tinfoil. The chain mail is my name, scattered everywhere so that any blow directed at me is dissipated.

"So you're a ghost too."

A prepared ghost. I know how to get outside of time.

"Fine, get outside of time. What do you need me for?"

You're alive, and your name is mine, which is to say your identity is mine. I've used too much of my energy saving you, holding you. And you're the most compatible of them all—you're a Pat Moore identity squared, by marriage.

"Squared by—" He closed his eyes and nearly lowered the gun. "Everybody called her Trish," he whispered. "Only her mother called her Pat." He couldn't feel the seat under him, and he was afraid that if he let go of the gun, it would fall to the car's roof.

Her mother called her Pat.

"You can't have me." He was holding his voice steady with an effort. "I'm driving away now."

You're Pat Moore's only hope.

"You need an exorcist, not a poker player." He could move his right arm again, and he started the engine and then switched on the windshield wipers.

Abruptly the drumming of the rain came back on, sounding loud after the long silence. She was gone.

His hands were shaking as he tucked the gun back

into its pocket, but he was confident that he could get back onto the 280, even with his worn-out windshield wipers blurring everything, and he had no intention of getting on the 101 any time soon; he had been almost entirely bluffing when he told her, *I've been meaning to drive the 101 for a while now.* But like an alcoholic who tries one drink after long abstinence, he was remembering the taste of the gun barrel in his mouth: *That was easier than I thought it would be,* he thought.

He fumbled a pack of Marlboros out of his jacket pocket and shook one out.

As soon as he had got onto the northbound 85, he became aware that the purple dress and the dark hair were blocking the passenger-side window again, and he didn't jump at all. He had wondered which way to turn on the 280, and now he steered the car into the lane that would take him back north, toward San Francisco. The grooved interchange lane gleamed with fresh rain, and he kept his speed down to forty.

"One big U-turn," he said finally, speaking around his lit cigarette. He glanced at her; she looked three-dimensional again, and she was smiling at him as cheerfully as ever.

"I'm your guardian angel," she said.

"Right, I remember. And your name's Pat Moore, same as mine. Same as everybody's, lately." He realized that he was optimistic, which surprised him; it was something like the happy confidence he had felt in dreams in which he had discovered that he could fly and leave behind all earthbound reproaches. "I met *her,* you know. She's dead too, and she needs a living body, and so she tried to possess me."

"Yes," said Pat Moore. "That's what's going to happen. I couldn't tell you before."

He frowned. "I scared her off, by threatening to shoot myself." Reluctantly he asked, "Will she try again, do you think?"

"Sure. When you're asleep, probably, since this didn't work. She can wait a few hours—a few days, even, in a pinch. It was just because I talked to you that she switched me off and tried to do it right away, while you were still awake. *Jumped the gun,*" she added, with the first laugh he had heard from her. It sounded as if she were trying to chant in a language she didn't understand.

"Ah," he said softly. "That raises the ante." He took a deep breath and let it out. "When did you . . . die?"

"I don't know. Some time besides now. Could you put out the cigarette? The smoke messes up my reception; I'm still partly seeing that bar, and partly a hilltop in a park somewhere."

He rolled the window down an inch and flicked the cigarette out. "Is this how you looked, when you were alive?"

She touched her hair as he glanced at her. "I don't know."

"When you were alive—did you know about movies, and current news? I mean, you don't seem to know about them now."

"I suppose I did. Don't most people?"

He was gripping the wheel hard now. "Did your mother call you Pat?"

"I suppose she did. It's my name."

"Did your . . . friends, call you Trish?"

"I suppose they did."

I suppose, I suppose! He forced himself not to shout

at her. She's dead, he reminded himself, she's probably doing the best she can.

But again he thought of the Frost line: *There's something the dead are keeping back.*

They had passed under two gray concrete bridges, and now he switched on his left turn signal to merge with the northbound 280. The pavement ahead of him glittered with reflected red brake lights.

"See, my wife's name was Patricia Moore," he said, trying to sound reasonable. "She died in a car crash five months ago. Well, a single-car accident. Drove off a freeway embankment. She was drunk." He remembered that the popcorn in the Pirate's Cove had momentarily smelled like spilled gasoline.

"I've been drunk."

"So has everybody. But—you might be her."

"Who?"

"My wife. Trish."

"I might be your wife."

"Tell me about Maxwell's Demon."

"I would have been married to you, you mean. We'd *really* have been Pat Moore then. Like mirrors reflecting each other."

"That's why *she* wants me, right. So what's Maxwell's Demon?"

"It's . . . She's dead, so she's like a smoke ring somebody puffed out in the air, if they were smoking. Maxwell's Demon keeps her from disappearing like a smoke ring would, it keeps her . . ."

"Distinct," Moore said when she didn't go on. "Even though she's got no right to be distinct anymore."

"And me. Through her."

"Can I kill him? Or make him stop sustaining her?"

And you, he thought; it would stop him sustaining you. Did I stop sustaining you before? Well, obviously.

Earthbound reproaches.

"It's not a *him,* really. It looks like a sprinkler you'd screw onto a hose, to water your yard, if it would spin. It's in her house, hooked up to the air-conditioning."

"A sprinkler." He was nodding repeatedly, and he made himself stop. "Okay. Can you show me where her house is? I'm going to have to sleep sometime."

"She'd kill me."

"Pat—Trish—" Instantly he despised himself for calling her by that name. "—you're already dead."

"She can get outside of time. Ghosts aren't really in time anyway. I'm wrecking the popcorn in that bar in the future as much as in the past, it's all just cards in a circle on a table, none in front. None of it's really now or not-now. She could make me not ever—she could take my thread out of the carpet—you'd never have met me, even like this."

"Make you never have existed."

"Right. Never was any me at all."

"She wouldn't dare—Pat." Just from self-respect, he couldn't bring himself to call her Trish again. "Think about it. If you never existed, then I wouldn't have married you, and so I wouldn't be the Pat Moore squared that she needs."

"If you *did* marry me. *Me,* I mean. I can't remember. Do you think you did?"

She'll take me there, if I say yes, he thought. She'll believe me if I say it. And what's to become of me, if she doesn't? That woman very nearly crowded me right out of the world five minutes ago, and I was wide awake.

The memory nauseated him.

What becomes of a soul that's pushed out of its body,

he thought, as *she* means to do to me? Would there be *anything* left of *me,* even a half-wit ghost like poor Pat here?

Against his will came the thought, You always did lie to her.

"I don't know," he said finally. "The odds are against it."

There's always the 101, he told himself, and somehow the thought wasn't entirely bleak. Six chambers of it, hollow-point .38s. Fly away.

"It's possible, though, isn't it?"

He exhaled, and nodded. "It's possible, yes."

"I think I owe it to you. Some Pat Moore does. We left you alone."

"It was my fault." In a rush he added, "I was even glad you didn't leave a note." It's true, he thought. I was grateful.

"I'm glad she didn't leave a note," this Pat Moore said.

He needed to change the subject. "*You're* a ghost," he said. "Can't you make *her* never have existed?"

"No. I can't get far from real places or I'd blur away, out of focus, but she can go way up high, where you can look down on the whole carpet, and—twist out strands of it; bend somebody at right angles to *everything,* which means you're gone without a trace. And anyway, she and her students are all blocked against that kind of attack, they've got ConfigSafe."

He laughed at the analogy. "You know about computers?"

"No," she said emptily. "Did I?"

He sighed. "No, not a lot." He thought of the revolver in the seat, and then thought of something better. "You mentioned a park. You used to like Buena Vista Park. Let's stop there on the way."

*   *   *

Moore drove clockwise around the tall, darkly wooded hill that was the park, while the peaked roofs and cylindrical towers of the old Victorian houses were teeth on a saw passing across the gray sky on his left. He found a parking space on the eastern curve of Buena Vista Avenue, and he got out of the car quickly to keep the Pat Moore ghost from having to open the door on her side; he remembered what she had done to the bowl of popcorn.

But she was already standing on the splashing pavement in the rain, without having opened the door. In the ashy daylight, her purple dress seemed to have lost all its color, and her face was indistinct and pale; he peered at her, and he was sure the heavy raindrops were falling right through her.

He could imagine her simply dissolving on the hike up to the meadow. "Would you rather wait in the car?" he said. "I won't be long."

"Do you have a pair of binoculars?" she asked. Her voice too was frail out here in the cold.

"Yes, in the glove compartment." Cold rain was soaking his hair and leaking down inside his jacket collar, and he wanted to get moving. "Can you . . . *hold* them?"

"I can't hold anything. But if you take out the lens in the middle you can catch me in it, and carry me."

He stepped past her to open the passenger-side door and bent over to pop open the glove compartment, and then he knelt on the seat and dragged out his old leather-sleeved binoculars and turned them this way and that in the wobbly gray light that filtered through the windshield.

"How do I get the lens out?" he called over his shoulder.

"A screwdriver, I guess," came her voice, barely audible above the thrashing of the rain. "See the tiny screw by the eyepiece?"

"Oh. Right." He used the small blade from his pocketknife on the screw in the back of the left barrel, and then had to do the same with a similar screw on the forward side of it. The eyepiece stayed where it was, but the big forward lens fell out, exposing a metal cross on the inside; it was held down with a screw that he managed to rotate with the knife tip—and then a triangular block of polished glass fell out into his palm.

"That's it—that's the lens," she called from outside the car.

Moore's cell phone buzzed as he was stepping backward to the pavement, and he fumbled it out of his jacket pocket and flipped it open. "Moore here," he said. He pushed the car door closed and leaned over the phone to keep the rain off it.

"Hey Pat," came Rick's voice, "I'm sitting here in your Garden City Club in San Jose, and I could be at the Bay. Where are you, man?"

The Pat Moore ghost was moving her head, and Moore looked up at her. With evident effort, she was making her head swivel back and forth in a clear *no* gesture.

The warning chilled Moore. Into the phone he said, "I'm—not far, I'm at a bar off the 85. Place called the Pirate's Cove."

"Well, don't chug your beer on my account. But come over here when you can."

"You bet. I'll be out of here in five minutes." He closed the phone and dropped it back into his pocket.

"They made him call again," said the ghost. "They lost track of your car after I killed the guy with the shotgun." She smiled, and her teeth seemed to be gone. "That was good, saying you were at that bar. They can tell truth from lies, and that's only twenty minutes from being true."

Guardian angel, he thought. "You killed him?"

"I think so." Her image faded, then solidified again. "Yes."

"Ah. Well—good." With his free hand he pushed the wet hair back from his forehead. "So what do I do with this?" he asked, holding up the lens.

"Hold it by the frosted sides, with the long edge of the triangle pointed at me; then look at me through the two other edges."

The glass thing was a blocky right-triangle, frosted on the sides but polished smooth and clear on the thick edges; obediently he held it up to his eye and peered through the two slanted faces of clear glass.

He could see her clearly through the lens—possibly more clearly than when he looked at her directly—but this was a mirror image: the dark slope of the park appeared to be to the left of her.

"Now roll it over a quarter turn, like from noon to three," she said.

He rotated the lens ninety degrees—but her image in it rotated a full 180 degrees, so that instead of seeing her horizontal, he saw her upside down.

He jumped then, for her voice was right in his ear. "Close your eyes, and put the lens in your pocket."

He did as she said, and when he opened his eyes again, she was gone—the wet pavement stretched empty to the curbstones and green lawns of the old houses.

"You've got me in your pocket," her voice said in his ear. "When you want me, look through the lens again and turn it back the other way."

It occurred to him that he believed her. "Okay," he said, and sprinted across the street to the narrow stone stairs that led up into the park.

His leather shoes splashed in the mud as he took the path to the left. The city was gone now, hidden behind the dense overhanging boughs of pine and eucalyptus, and the rain echoed under the canopy of green leaves. The cold air was musky with the smells of mulch and pine and wet loam.

Up at the level playground lawn, the swing sets were of course empty, and in fact he seemed to be the only living soul in the park today. Through gaps between the trees, he could see San Francisco spread out below him on all sides, as still as a photograph under the heavy clouds.

He splashed through the gutters that were made of fragments of old marble headstones—keeping his head down, he glimpsed an incised cross filled with mud in the face of one stone, and the lone phrase IN LOVING MEMORY on another—and then he had come to the meadow with the big old oak trees he remembered.

He looked around, but there was still nobody to be seen in the cathedral space, and he hurried to the side and crouched to step in under the shaggy foliage and catch his breath.

"It's beautiful," said the voice in his ear.

"Yes," he said, and he took the lens out of his pocket. He held it up and squinted through the right-angle panels, and there was the image of her, upside down. He rotated it counterclockwise ninety degrees, and the image was upright, and when he moved the lens away from his eye, she was standing out in the clearing.

"Look at the city some more," she said, and her voice now seemed to come from several yards away. "So I can see it again."

One last time, he thought. Maybe for both of us; it's nice that we can do it together.

"Sure." He stepped out from under the oak tree and walked back out into the rain to the middle of the clearing and looked around.

A line of trees to the north was the panhandle of Golden Gate Park, and past that he could see the stepped levels of Alta Vista Park; more distantly to the left he could just make out the green band that was the hills of the Presidio, though the two big piers of the Golden Gate Bridge were lost behind miles of rain; he turned to look southwest, where the Twin Peaks and the TV tower on Mount Sutro were vivid above the misty streets; and then far away to the east the white spike of the Transamerica Pyramid stood up from the skyline at the very edge of visibility.

"It's beautiful," she said again. "Did you come here to look at it?"

"No," he said, and he lowered his gaze to the dark mulch under the trees. Cypress, eucalyptus, pine, oak— even from out here he could see that mushrooms were clustered in patches and rings on the carpet of wet black leaves, and he walked back to the trees and then shuffled in a crouch into the aromatic dimness under the boughs.

After a couple of minutes, "Here's one," he said, stooping to pick a mushroom. Its tan cap was about two inches across, covered with a patch of white veil. He unsnapped his denim jacket and tucked the mushroom carefully into his shirt pocket.

"What is it?" asked Pat Moore.

"I don't know," he said. "My wife was never able to tell, so she never picked it. It's either *Amanita lanei,* which is edible, or it's *Amanita phalloides,* which is fatally poisonous. You'd need a real expert to know which this is."

"What are you going to do with it?"

"I think I'm going to sandbag *her*. You want to hop back into the lens for the hike down the hill?"

He had parked the old Dodge at an alarming slant on Jones Street on the south slope of Russian Hill, and then the two of them had walked steeply uphill past close-set gates and balconies under tall sidewalk trees that grew straight up from the slanted pavements. Headlights of cars descending Jones Street reflected in white glitter on the wet trunks and curbstones, and in the wakes of the cars the tire tracks blurred away slowly in the continuing rain.

"How are we going to get into her house?" he asked quietly.

"It'll be unlocked," said the ghost. "She's expecting you now."

He shivered. "Is she. Well, I hope I'm playing a better hand than she guesses."

"Down here," said Pat, pointing at a brick paved alley that led away to the right between the Victorian-gingerbread porches of two narrow houses.

They were in a little alley now, overhung with rose-bushes and rosemary, with white-painted fences on either side. Columns of fog billowed in the breeze, and then he noticed that they were human forms—female torsos twisting transparently in the air, blank-faced children running in slow motion, hunched figures swaying heads that changed shape like water balloons.

"The outfielders," said the Pat Moore ghost.

Now Moore could hear their voices: *Goddam car—I*

got yer unconditional right here—Excuse me, you got a problem?—He was never there for me—So I told him, you want it, you come over here and take it—Bless me, Father, I have died—

The acid smell of wet stone was lost in the scents of to-bacco and jasmine perfume and liquor and old, old sweat.

Moore bit his lip and tried to focus on the solid pave-ment and the fences. "Where the hell's her place?" he asked tightly.

"This gate," she said. "Maybe you'd better—"

He nodded and stepped past her; the gate latch had no padlock, and he flipped up the catch. The hinges squeaked as he swung the gate inward over flagstones and low-cut grass.

He looked up at the house the path led to. It was a one-story 1920s bungalow, painted white or gray, with green wicker chairs on the narrow porch. Lights were on behind stained glass panels in the two windows and the porch door.

"It's unlocked," said the ghost.

He turned back toward her. "Stand over by the roses there," he told her, "away from the . . . the outfielders. I want to take you in in my pocket, okay?"

"Okay."

She drifted to the roses, and he fished the lens out of his pocket and found her image in the right-angle faces, then twisted the lens and put it back into his pocket.

He walked slowly up the path, stepping on the grass rather than on the flagstones, and stepped up to the porch.

"It's not locked, Patrick," came a woman's loud voice from inside.

He turned the purple-glass knob and walked several paces into a high-ceilinged kitchen with a black-and-white tiled floor; a blond woman in jeans and a sweat-shirt sat at a Formica table by the big old refrigerator. From the next room, beyond an arch in the white-painted plaster, a steady whistling hiss provided an irritating background noise, as if a tea kettle were boiling.

The woman at the table was much more clearly visible than his guardian angel had been, almost aggressively three-dimensional—her breasts under the sweatshirt were prominent and pointed, and her nose and chin stood out perceptibly too far from her high cheekbones, and her lips were so full that they looked distinctly swollen.

A bottle of Wild Turkey bourbon stood beside three *Flintstones* glasses on the table, and she took it in one hand and twisted out the cork with the other. "Have a drink," she said, speaking loudly, perhaps in order to be heard over the hiss in the next room.

"I don't think I will, thanks," he said. "You're good with your hands." His jacket was dripping on the tiles, but he didn't take it off.

"I'm the solidest ghost you'll ever see."

Abruptly she stood up, knocking her chair against the refrigerator, and then she rushed past him, her Reeboks beating on the floor—and her body seemed to rotate as she went by him, as if she were swerving away from him, though her course to the door was straight. She reached out one lumpy hand and slammed the door.

She faced him again and held out her right hand. "I'm Pat Moore," she said, "and I want help."

He flexed his fingers, then cautiously held out his own hand. "I'm Pat Moore too," he said.

Her palm touched his, and though it was moving very slowly, his own hand was slapped away when they touched.

"I want us to become partners," she said. Her thick

lips moved in ostentatious synchronization with her words.

"Okay," he said.

Her outlines blurred for just an instant; then she said, in the same booming tone, "I want us to become one person. You'll be immortal, and—"

"Let's do it," he said.

She blinked her black eyes. "You're—agreeing to it," she said. "You're accepting it, now?"

"Yes." He cleared his throat. "That's correct."

He became aware that a figure was sitting at the table. He looked past her and saw that it was a transparent old man in an overcoat, hardly more visible than a puff of smoke.

"Is he Maxwell's Demon?" Moore asked.

The woman smiled, baring huge teeth. "No, that's . . . a soliton. A poor little soliton who's lost its way. I'll show you Maxwell's Demon."

She lunged and clattered into the next room, and Moore followed her, trying simultaneously not to slip on the floor and to keep an eye on her and on the misty old man.

He stepped into a parlor, and the hissing noise was louder in here. Carved dark wood tables and chairs and a modern exercise bicycle had been pushed against a curtained bay window in the far wall, and a vast carpet had been rolled back from the dusty hardwood floor and humped against the chair legs. In the high corners of the room and along the fluted top of the window frame, things like translucent cheerleaders' pom-poms grimaced and waved tentacles or locks of hair in the agitated air. Moore warily took a step away from them.

"Look over here," said the alarming woman.

In the near wall, an air-conditioning panel had been

taken apart, and a red rubber hose hung from its machinery and was connected into the side of a length of steel pipe that lay on a TV table. Nozzles on either end of the pipe were making the loud whistling sound.

Moore looked more closely at it. It was apparently two sections of pipe, one about eight inches long and the other about four, connected together by a blocky fitting where the hose was attached, and a stove stopcock stood half-open near the end of the longer pipe.

"Feel the air," the woman said.

Moore cupped a hand near the end of the longer pipe and then yanked it back—the air blasting out of it felt hot enough to light a cigar. More cautiously he waved his fingers over the nozzle at the end of the short pipe; and then he rolled his hand in the air jet, for it was icy cold.

"*It's* not supernatural," she boomed, "even though the air conditioner's set for seventy. A spiral washer in the connector housing sends air spinning up the long pipe; the hot molecules spin out to the sides of the little whirlwind in there, and it's them that the stopcock lets out. The cold molecules fall into a smaller whirlwind inside the big one, and they move the opposite way and come out at the end of the short pipe. Room-temperature air is a mix of hot and cold molecules, and this device separates them out."

"Okay," said Moore. He spoke levelly, but he was wishing he had brought his gun along from the car. It occurred to him that it was a rifled pipe that things usually come spinning out of, but which he had been ready to dive into. He wondered if the gills under the cap of the mushroom in his pocket were curved in a spiral.

"But this is counterentropy," she said, smiling again.

"A Scottish physicist named Maxwell p-postulay-postul—guessed that a Demon would be needed to sort the hot molecules from the cold ones. If the Demon is present, the effect occurs, and vice versa—if you can make the effect occur, you've summoned the Demon. Get the effect, and the cause has no choice but to be present." She thumped her chest, though her peculiar breasts didn't move at all. "And once the Demon is present, he—he—"

She paused, so Moore said, "Maintains distinctions that wouldn't ordinarily stay distinct." His heart was pounding, but he was pleased with how steady his voice was.

Something like an invisible hand struck him solidly in the chest, and he stepped back.

"You don't touch it," she said. Again there was an invisible thump against his chest. "Back to the kitchen."

The soliton old man, hardly visible in the bright overhead light, was still nodding in one of the chairs at the table.

The blond woman was slapping the wall, and then a white-painted cabinet, but when Moore looked toward her, she grabbed the knob on one of the cabinet drawers and yanked it open.

"You need to come over here," she said, "and look in the drawer."

After the things he'd seen in the high corners of the parlor, Moore was cautious; he leaned over and peered into the drawer—but it contained only a stack of typing paper, a felt-tip laundry-marking pen, and half a dozen yo-yos.

As he watched, she reached past him and snatched out a sheet of paper and the laundry marker; and it occurred to him that she hadn't been able to see the contents of the drawer until he was looking at them.

I don't have any vision, his guardian angel had said. *No retinas. I have to use yours.*

The woman had stepped away from the cabinet now. "I was prepared, see," she said loudly enough to be heard out on Jones Street, "for my stupid students killing me. I knew they might. We were all working to learn how to transcend time, but I got there first, and they were afraid of what I would do. So *boom-boom-boom* for Mistress Moore. But I had already set up the Demon, and I had Xeroxed my chain mail and put it in addressed envelopes. Bales of them, the stamps cost me a fortune. I came back strong. And I'm going to merge with you now and get a real body again. You accepted the proposal—you said 'Yes, that's correct'—you didn't put out another bet this time to chase me away."

The cap flew off the laundry marker, and then she had slapped the paper down on the table next to the Wild Turkey bottle. "Watch me!" she said, and when he looked at the piece of paper, she began vigorously writing on it. Soon she had written *Pat* in big sprawling letters and was embarked on *Moore.*

She straightened up when it was finished. "Now," she said, her black eyes glittering with hunger, "you cut your hand and write with your blood, tracing over the letters. Our name is us, and we'll merge. Smooth as silk through a goose."

Moore slowly dug the pocketknife out of his pants pocket. "This is new," he said. "you didn't do this name-in-blood business when you tried to take me in the car."

She waved one big hand dismissively. "I thought I could sneak up on you. You resisted me, though—you'd probably have tried to resist me even in your sleep. But since you're accepting the inevitable now, we can do a proper contract, in ink and blood. Cut, cut!"

"Okay," he said, and unfolded the short blade and cut a nick in his right forefinger. "*You've* made a new bet now, though, and it's to me." Blood was dripping from the cut, and he dragged his finger over the *P* in her crude signature.

He had to pause halfway through and probe again with the blade tip to get more freely flowing blood; and as he was painfully tracing the *R* in *Moore,* he began to feel another will helping his hand to push his finger along, and he heard a faint drone like a radio carrier wave starting up in his head. Somewhere he was crouched on his toes on a narrow, outward-tilting ledge with no handholds anywhere, with vast volumes of emptiness below him—and his toes were sliding—

So he added quickly, "And I raise back at you."

By touch alone, looking up at the high ceiling, he pulled the mushroom out of his shirt pocket and popped it into his mouth and bit down on it. Check and raise, he thought. Sandbagged. Then he lowered his eyes, and in an instant her gaze was locked on to his.

"What happened?" she demanded, and Moore could hear the three syllables of it chug in his own throat. "What did you do?"

"*Amanita,*" said the smoky old man at the table. His voice sounded like nothing organic—more like sandpaper on metal. "It was time to eat the mushroom."

Moore had resolutely chewed the thing up, his teeth grating on bits of dirt. It had the cold-water taste of ordinary mushrooms, and as he forced himself to swallow it, he forlornly hoped, in spite of all his bravura thoughts about the 101 freeway, that it might be the *lanei* rather than the deadly *phalloides.*

"He ate a mushroom?" the woman demanded of the

old man. "You never told me about any mushroom! Is it a poisonous mushroom?"

"I don't know," came the rasping voice again. "It's either poisonous or not, though, I remember that much."

Moore was dizzy with the first twinges of comprehension of what he had done. "Fifty-fifty chance," he said tightly. "The death-cap *Amanita* looks just like another one that's harmless, both grown locally. I picked this one today, and I don't know which it was. If it's the poison one, we won't know for about twenty-four hours, maybe longer."

The drone in Moore's head grew suddenly louder, then faded until it was imperceptible. "You're telling the truth," she said. She flung out an arm toward the back porch, and for a moment her bony forefinger was a foot long. "Go vomit it up, now!"

He twitched, like someone mistaking the green left-turn arrow for the green light. No, he told himself, clenching his fists to conceal any trembling. Fifty-fifty is better than zero. You've clocked the odds and placed your bet. Trust yourself.

"No good," he said. "The smallest particle will do the job, if it's the poisonous one. Enough's probably been absorbed already. That's why I chose it." This was a bluff, or a guess, anyway, but this time she didn't scan his mind.

He was tense, but a grin was twitching at his lips. He nodded toward the old man and asked her, "Who *is* the lost sultan, anyway?"

"Soliton," she snapped. "He's you, you—dumbbrain." She stamped one foot, shaking the house. "How can I take you now? And I can't wait twenty-four hours just to see if I *can* take you!"

"Me? How is he me?"

"My name's Pat Moore," said the gray silhouette at the table.

"Ghosts are solitons," she said impatiently, "waves that keep moving all-in-a-piece after the living push has stopped. Forward or backward doesn't matter to them."

"I'm from the *future*," said the soliton, perhaps grinning.

Moore stared at the indistinct thing, and he had to repress an urge to run over there and tear it apart, try to set fire to it, stuff it in a drawer. And he realized that the sudden chill on his forehead wasn't from fright, as he had at first assumed, but from profound embarrassment at the thing's presence here.

"I've blown it all on you," the blond woman said, perhaps to herself even though her voice boomed in the tall kitchen. "I don't have the . . . sounds like *courses* . . . I don't have the energy reserves to go after another living Pat Moore *now*. You were perfect, Pat Moore squared—why did you have to be a die-hard suicide fan?"

Moore actually laughed at that—and she glared at him in the same instant that he was punched backward off his feet by the hardest invisible blow yet.

He sat down hard and slid, and his back collided with the stove; and then, though he could still see the walls and the old man's smoky legs under the table across the room and the glittering rippled glass of the windows, he was somewhere else. He could feel the square tiles under his palms, but in this other place he had no body.

In the now-remote kitchen, the blond woman said, "Drape him," and the soliton got up and drifted across the floor toward Moore, shrinking as it came so that its face was on a level with Moore's.

Its face was indistinct—pouches under the empty

eyes, drink-wrinkles spilling diagonally across the
cheekbones, petulant lines around the mouth—and
Moore did not try to recognize himself in it.

The force that had knocked Moore down was holding
him pressed against the floor and the stove, unable to
crawl away, and all he could do was hold his breath as
the soliton ghost swept over him like a spiderweb.

You've got a girl in your pocket, came the thing's
raspy old voice in his ear.

Get away from me, Moore thought, nearly gagging.

Who get away from who?

"I can get another living Pat Moore," the blond
woman was saying, "if I never wasted any effort on you
in the first place, if there was never a *you* for me to notice." He heard her take a deep breath. "I can do this."

Her knee touched his cheek, slamming his head
against the oven door. She was leaning over the top of
the stove, banging blindly at the burners and the knobs,
and then Moore heard the triple click of one of the
knobs turning, and the faint thump of the flame coming
on. He peered up and saw that she was holding the
sheet of paper with the ink and blood on it, and then he
could smell the paper burning.

Moore became aware that there was still the faintest
drone in his head only a moment before it ceased.

"Up," she said, and the ghost was a net surrounding
Moore, lifting him up off the floor and through the in-
tangible roof and far away from the rainy shadowed
hills of San Francisco.

He was aware that his body was still in the house, still
slumped against the stove in the kitchen, but his soul, in-
distinguishable now from his ghost, was in some vast region where *in front* and *behind* had no meaning, where
the once-apparent dichotomy between *here* and *there*

was a discarded optical illusion, where comprehension was total but didn't depend on light or sight or perspective, and where even *ago* and *to come* were just compass points; everything was in stasis, for motion had been left far behind with sequential time.

He knew that the long braids or vapor trails that he encompassed and that surrounded him were lifelines, stretching from births in that direction to deaths in the other—some linked to others for varying intervals, some curving alone through the non-sky—but they were more like long electrical arcs than anything substantial even by analogy; they were stretched across time and space, but at the same time, they were coils too infinitesimally small to be perceived, if his perception had been by means of sight; and they were electrons in standing waves surrounding an unimaginable nucleus, which also surrounded them—the universe, apprehended here in its full volume of past and future, was one enormous and eternal atom.

But he could feel the tiles of the kitchen floor beneath his fingertips. He dragged one hand up his hip to the side pocket of his jacket, and his fingers slipped inside and touched the triangular lens.

No, said the soliton ghost, a separate thing again.

Moore was still huddled on the floor, still touching the lens—but he and his ghost were sitting on the other side of the room at the kitchen table too, and the ghost was holding a deck of cards in one hand and spinning cards out with the other. It stopped when two cards lay in front of each of them. The Wild Turkey bottle was gone, and the glow from the ceiling lamp was a dimmer yellow than it had been.

"Hold 'Em," the ghost rasped. "Your whole lifeline is the buy-in, and I'm going to take it away from you.

You've got a tall stack there, birth to now, but I won't go all-in on you right away. I bet our first seven years— Fudgsicles, our dad flying kites in the spring sunsets, the star decals in constellations on our bedroom ceiling, our mom reading the Narnia books out loud to us. Push 'em out." The air in the kitchen was summery with the pink candy smell of Bazooka gum.

Hold 'Em, thought Moore. I'll raise.

Trish killed herself, he projected at his ghost, *rather than live with us anymore. Drove her Granada over the embankment off the 101. The police said she was doing ninety, with no touch of the brake.* Again he smelled spilled gasoline—

—and so, apparently, did his opponent; the pouchy-faced old ghost flickered but came back into focus. "I make it more," said the ghost. "The next seven. Bicycles, the Albert Payson Terhune books, hiking with Joe and Ken in the oil fields, the Valentine from Theresa What's-her-name. Push 'em out, or forfeit."

Neither of them had looked at their cards, and Moore hoped the game wouldn't proceed to the eventual arbitrary showdown—he hoped that the frail ghost wouldn't be able to keep sustaining raises.

I can't hold anything, his guardian angel had said.

It hurt Moore, but he projected another raise at the ghost: *When we admitted we had deleted her poetry files deliberately, she said "You're not a nice man." She was drunk, and we laughed at that when she said it, but one day after she was gone, we remembered it, and then we had to pull over to the side of the road because we couldn't see through the tears to drive.*

The ghost was just a smoky sketch of a midget or a monkey now, and Moore doubted it had enough substance even to deal the next three cards. In a faint bird-like voice it said, "The next seven. College, and our old motorcycle, and—"

And Trish at twenty, Moore finished, grinding his teeth and thinking about the mushroom dissolving in his stomach. *We talked her into taking her first drink. Pink gin, Tanqueray with Angostura bitters. And we were pleased when she said, "Where has this been all my life?"*

"All my life," whispered the ghost, and then it flicked away like a reflection in a dropped mirror.

The blond woman was sitting there instead. "What did you have?" she boomed, nodding toward his cards.

"The winning hand," said Moore. He touched his two facedown cards. "The pot's mine—the raises got too high for him." The cards blurred away like fragments left over from a dream.

Then he hunched forward and gripped the edge of the table, for the timeless vertiginous gulf, the infinite atom of the lifelines, was a sudden pressure from outside the world, and this artificial scene had momentarily lost its depth of field.

"I can twist your thread out, even without his help," she told him. She frowned, and a vein stood out on her curved forehead, and the kitchen table resumed its cubic dimensions and the light brightened. "Even dead, I'm more potent than you are."

She whirled her massive right arm up from below the table and clanked down her elbow, with her forearm upright; her hand was open.

Put me behind her, Pat, said the Pat Moore ghost's remembered voice in his ear.

He made himself feel the floor tiles under his hand and the stove at his back, and then he pulled the triangular lens out of his pocket; and when he held it up to his eye, he was able to see himself and the blond woman at the table across the room, and the Pat Moore ghost was visible upside down behind the woman. He rotated the glass a quarter turn, and she was now upright.

He moved the lens away and blinked, and then he was gripping the edge of the table and looking across it at the blond woman, and at her hand only a foot away from his face. The fingerprints were like comb-tracks in clay. Peripherally he could see the slim Pat Moore ghost, still in the purple dress, standing behind her.

"Arm wrestling?" he said, raising his eyebrows. He didn't want to let go of the table, or even move—this localized perspective seemed very frail.

The woman only glared at him out of her irisless eyes. At last he leaned back in the chair and unclamped the fingers of his right hand from the table edge; and then he shrugged and raised his right arm and set his elbow beside hers. With her free hand she picked up his pocketknife and hefted it. "When this thing hits the floor, we start." She clasped his hand, and his fingers were numbed as if with a hard impact.

Her free hand jerked, and the knife was glittering in a fantastic non-euclidean parabola through the air, and though he was braced all the way through his torso from his firmly planted feet, when the knife clanged against the tiles, the massive power of her arm hit his palm like a falling tree.

Sweat sprang out on his forehead, and his arm was steadily bending backward—and the whole world was rotating too, narrowing, tilting away from him to spill him, all the bets he and his ghost had made, into zero.

In the car, the Pat Moore ghost had told him, *She can bend somebody at right angles to* everything, *which means you're gone without a trace.*

We're not sitting at the kitchen table, he told himself;

we're still dispersed in that vaster comprehension of the universe.

And if she rotates me ninety degrees, he was suddenly certain, I'm gone.

And then the frail Pat Moore ghost leaned in from behind the woman and clasped her diaphanous hand around Moore's; and together they were Pat Moore squared, their lifelines linked still by their marriage, and he could feel her strong pulse in supporting counterpoint to his own.

His forearm moved like a counterclockwise second hand in front of his squinting eyes as the opposing pressure steadily weakened. The woman's face seemed in his straining sight to be a rubber mask with a frantic animal trapped inside it, and when only inches separated the back of her hand from the Formica tabletop, the resistance faded to nothing, and his hand was left poised empty in the air.

The world rocked back to solidity with such abruptness that he would have fallen down if he hadn't been sitting on the floor against the stove.

Over the sudden pressure-release ringing in his ears, he heard a scurrying across the tiles on the other side of the room, and a thumping on the hardwood planks in the parlor.

The Pat Moore ghost still stood across the room, beside the table; and the Wild Turkey bottle was on the table, and he was sure it had been there all along.

He reached out slowly and picked up his pocketknife. It was so cold that it stung his hand.

"Cut it," said the ghost of his wife.

"I can't cut it," he said. Barring hallucinations, his body had hardly moved for the past five or ten minutes, but he was panting. "You'll die."

"I'm dead already, Pat. This"—she waved a hand from her shoulder to her knee—"isn't any good. I should be gone." She smiled. "I think that was the *lanei* mushroom."

He knew she was guessing. "I'll know tomorrow."

He got to his feet, still holding the knife. The blade, he saw, was still folded out.

"Forgive me," he said awkwardly. "For everything."

She smiled, and it was almost a familiar smile. "I forgave you in midair. And you forgive me too."

"If you ever did anything wrong, yes."

"Oh, I did. I don't think you noticed. Cut it."

He walked back across the room to the arch that led into the parlor, and he paused when he was beside her.

"I won't come in with you," she said, "if you don't mind."

"No," he said. "I love you, Pat."

"Loved. I loved you too. That counts. Go."

He nodded and turned away from her.

Maxwell's Demon was still hissing on the TV table by the disassembled air conditioner, and he walked to it one step at a time, not looking at the forms that twisted and whispered urgently in the high corners. One seemed to be perceptibly more solid than the rest, but all of them flinched away from him.

He had to blink tears out of his eyes to see the air hose clearly, and when he did, he noticed a plain ON-OFF toggle switch hanging from wires that were still connected to the air-conditioning unit. He cut the hose and switched off the air conditioner, and the silence that fell then seemed to spill out of the house and across San Francisco and into the sky.

He was alone in the house.

He tried to remember the expanded, timeless perspective he had participated in, but his memory had already simplified it to a three-dimensional picture, with himself floating like a bubble in one particular place.

Which of the . . . jet trails or arcs or coils was mine? He wondered now. How long is it?

I'll be better able to guess tomorrow, he thought. At least I know it's there, forever—and even though I didn't see which one it was, I know it's linked to another.

If there's anything in the literary world that **Joyce Carol Oates** *hasn't done, I'd like to know what it is.*

Recent things of hers I've read, stumbled across, noted: We Were the Mulvaneys *(an* Oprah *selection);* The Tattooed Girl, *a new novel; an introduction to* The Best of the Kenyon Review; *another introduction to a paperback edition of Conrad's* The Heart of Darkness *and* The Secret Sharer. *Believe me, that's only a taste of what she's been up to.*

For us, though, she's in familiar territory, writing a Gothic with Lovecraftian overtones, a dark fantasy that made the hair on the back of my head stand up.

⸎⸎⸎: Six Hypotheses

Joyce Carol Oates

The child Fitzie was the first to succumb to what could not yet have been named the ⸎⸎⸎ contagion in the Loving household. It was therefore taken for granted that the ⸎⸎⸎ contagion began with Fitzie, or began in Fitzie. (The linguistic distinction *with/in* is crucial to our understanding of the tragedy.) Yet it's possible to think—and this theory is the most attractive as it is the most impersonal, absolving any individual member of the Loving family of wittingly or unwittingly introducing disaster into their household—it started in Fitzie's small room off the first-floor landing of the Lovings' eighteenth-century stone farmhouse on the Delaware River, Upper Black Eddy, Pennsylvania.

Sometime soon after the March thaw of 1999, when the child was seven years old.

HYPOTHESIS #1: *The Room*

Because, according to witnesses who'd entered Fitzie's room, during and after the time of the ▨▨▨ contagion, the room was *not right*. Just a sensation you had, a visceral sense something is *not right*. The room wasn't on the ground floor of the house, and it wasn't on the second floor with the other bedrooms. It was a dwarf room off the landing, at the rear of the house. Overlooking the bog.

Dwarf room! Why dwarf!

A crude pejorative with a sinister connotation. Dwarf!

The ceiling was at least two inches lower than the ceilings of the other bedrooms. And it was a beamed ceiling, so the beams made it appear even lower. The room used to be a servant's room. Long ago, in the years 1845 to 1863, it was (possibly) used as a stop on the legendary Underground Railway.* When you step through the doorway to enter the room, instinctively you duck your head. If you're an adult, you do. Big Fitzie bumped his head on the damned doorframe more than once, stumbling inside in the night to rescue Little Fitzie from one of the nightmares. Momma Kat, who wasn't nearly so tall as her six-foot-three husband, would instinctively stoop when she entered the room, flinching. Yet it was a cozy room. It was a hideaway kind of room that would appeal to a seven-year-old eager for a room of his own.

---

* A number of private residences in Bucks County have been authenticated as stops on the legendary Underground Railway, which provided runaway slaves of the antebellum South hiding places, provisions, and moral support on their way north. The property owned by the Lovings has been designated "historic" by the Bucks County Historical Preservation Society, and the "strong likelihood" is that it was a stop on the Underground Railway.

But there was something about its cramped dimensions that stole your breath like a cave in which oxygen is slowly and irrevocably being depleted.

Not a cave! Not a dwarf room, and not a cave.

Walls, beamed ceiling, woodplank floor, and a dormer window.

Overlooking the bog.

HYPOTHESIS #2: *The Bog*

Swampy rank-smelling profusion of cattails and tall snaky-sinuous rushes that sway, writhe, undulate in the wind as if stroked by a gigantic hand and those beautiful upright deep-purple cluster flowers that begin to bloom in midsummer and continue until the first frost—

Loosestrife.

In early spring coming alive with peepers—a frantic singing/mating of myriad tiny frogs. In summer, thrumming with bullfrogs, nocturnal insects of every species. In the muck in the fecundity of the rank-smelling bog a cascade, a waterfall, ceaseless trill of life seeking blindly to—

Reproduce!

The Lovings. Of whom it would be repeatedly said that they had been, before the disaster, the ideal American family. And that their name was "ironic."

Big Fitzie a.k.a. Dad-*dy*
Momma Kat a.k.a. Mom-*my*
Dee-Dee a.k.a. Grump
Ray-Ray a.k.a. Awesome Possum

Little Fitzie a.k.a. Tickle
Baby Ceci

More objectively, the Lovings would be identified in the media:

Fritz Loving, 39
Katherine Donahue Loving, 36
Deirdre Loving, 12
Raymond Loving, 10
Fritz Loving Jr., 7
Ceci Loving, 9 months

HYPOTHESIS #3: *Baby Ceci*

That it was not Fitzie but his infant sister who was the (unconscious, unwitting) agent of the contagion. For, who knows what dreams drift through an infant's soft brain? Who knows what (accidental, unrecorded) bumps to an infant's soft skull might provoke such dreams? According to all reports, this youngest and most vulnerable of the Lovings was a "colicky" baby who cried incessantly. Especially in the night. A bundle of frantic shorted-out neurons. Kicking and shrieking red-faced gasping for breath like a tiny pig being smothered and both parents exhausted and sleep-deprived staggering through their daytime lives like somnambulists. Only Momma Kat's heavy milk-filled breasts could quench Baby Ceci's ravenous hunger, temporarily.

Colic. A commonplace medical condition in infants, usually outgrown after three or four months.

*   *   *

Sometime after the March thaw, 1999. In the night, the otherwise healthy, normal seven-year-old began to feel what he called something—some things—that were "tight"—"tighttight"—pulse beats in his head coming "fastfast"—"fastfastfaster"—close to bursting. Nights in succession he whimpered in his sleep, sweated through his pajamas, dampening sheets and mattress. Poor Fitzie who had not wet his bed in years now began again to lose control of his bladder out of agitation. Poor Fitzie terrified by bad dreams. Deeply ashamed of being such a baby. Crying Mom-*my*! Dad-*dy*! in the night so that sleep-dazed Big Fitzie would bump his forehead entering, Momma Kat would stumble barefoot, stubbing a toe, hurrying to hug the frightened child in his bed, Fitzie sweetie it's only a bad dream, only a dream sweetie, your lamp hasn't been turned off, your lamp is on honey, nobody will turn it off, Daddy and Mommy are here now honey, the bad things can't get you, there are no bad things sweetie, nothing to be afraid of nothing trying to squeeze through the window, nothing in the ceiling, see sweetie nothing beneath your bed no alligator or crocodile or Gila monster Mommy and Daddy promise!

When Fitzie's nightmares first began, Momma Kat would remain with him for what remained of the night, cuddling beside the shaken child and dozing off, as sometimes, reassured by his mother, Fitzie would also. As the nightmares continued, Momma Kat had a harder time dozing off in Fitzie's bed, or anywhere.

The change in Fitzie. Fearful now of falling asleep anywhere, not just in his room. For the Up-and-Down Black Things as he'd begun to call them followed him anywhere. Overnight at Grandma's house, the Up-and-Down Things were waiting for him, and angry knowing he'd tried to escape them. Nasty Up-and-Down Things aiming for his eyes, his nostrils. Aiming for his opened mouth as he sucked for air.

Needle Things.

〰〰 Things.

Trying to explain to his parents how they were tight-tight things. Crowded together and going fastfastfaster so it was awful, like his head was on fire.

Fitzie, sweetie, can you draw them for me? Can you?

Momma Kat gave Fitzie a black Crayola and a sheet of construction paper.

Fitzie was frightened at first. Hunched over the paper, panting. As if running. Running uphill. Panting, perspiring. They could see the terror glistening in his eyes. Looking up at Momma Kat and saying finally the crayon was not right, he needed a pencil or a pen, so Momma Kat gave him a felt-tip pen. Fitzie, try!

〰〰〰

Momma Kat was astonished: *Musical notes?*

Dee-Dee had begun piano lessons a few months before. Momma Kat, who'd been a fairly serious piano student as a girl, often drifted to the spinet in the living room, battered old Chickering from another era, a few snatched minutes of piano-playing, just fooling around as Katherine called it. Often a child would clamber up on Mommy's lap or cuddle cozily beside her on the piano bench. At seven, Fitzie was a little too big for Momma Kat's lap, but he would cuddle beside her on the bench when she sat down to run her capable hands up and down the keyboard, making the living room windows vibrate and quiver as if with the passing of marching men, making whichever children were within earshot giggle in delight as Momma Kat shifted from one of her prissy-boring old Mozart rondos/Chopin études to boogie-woogie, "Chopsticks," "Battle Hymn of the Republic." For a spell when he was three or four, Fitzie was intrigued by the musical notes, always black, always upright like fishhooks or sea horses on the always-black staves for "treble" and "bass" that were always five lines each never six, never four, never ten, never one hundred and ten, *Why is that, Mommy?* and Mommy laughed saying as she did in reply to many of her children's unanswerable questions *Just is, honey.*

And a wet little kiss.

Having the distraught, sleep-deprived child draw the **✳✳✳** Things was a mistake. The first of several (unconscious, unwitting) parental mistakes made by the Lovings.

For now the **✳✳✳** Things acquired shape, visual identity. Once seen, they could not be forgotten. They'd acquired a way *in.*

A way into—what?

A way into Momma Kat.

Poor Dee-Dee!

A healthy pretty girl of twelve. One of the most popular girls in her seventh grade class at Upper Black Eddy Middle School. Always good-natured, smiling. (Calling Dee-Dee "Grump" was a Loving family joke begun when Dee-Dee was a toddler.) Always a good eater, a good sleeper. With her mother's serene disposition, hazel eyes, fair freckled skin. About two weeks after Fitzie began to have trouble sleeping, Dee-Dee began to wake from anxious shallow dreams in which needlelike things were jabbing at her: eyes, nostrils, ears, mouth. Insomnia struck Dee-Dee like a virulent strain of measles. Within a few nights she was desperate. Night fevers, sweating through her pajamas and bedclothes. For most of her young life, Dee-Dee had loved to read, sat up now in bed in the night trying to read but could not concentrate though knowing that the Needle Things were not really in the room with her (she'd checked, every square inch) but could not concentrate embarked upon her journey as Fitzie was embarked upon his unable to comprehend what had happened or was happening or would happen for if you don't sleep Dee-Dee was shortly to discover at home at school at friends' houses if you don't sleep the ▒▒▒ Things being to stalk you in daytime too if you don't sleep you begin to shatter into pieces at mealtimes in the Lovings' spacious country kitchen the ▒▒▒ Things pushing boldly near writhing, undulating turn your head and they leap back out of sight, you see just the afterimage not the ▒▒▒ Things themselves. Like her little brother Fitzie who gagged when he tried to eat, now Dee-Dee who'd always had a healthy appetite began to gag and vomit after a few mouthfuls, and Momma Kat and Big Fitzie were becoming desperate for what was happening to their happy family? What was happening to their happy lives? They had been such devoted parents! They were such devoted parents! Worse yet their insomniac children were not the children they knew. Dee-Dee who'd been such a sweet-natured child had changed by quick degrees into a short-tempered girl grimacing at her family as if she couldn't bear to see them let alone be loved by them, or approached—"Don't touch!" And there was Fitzie sullen and indifferent his teeth glistening with saliva as if he'd have liked to tear out somebody's throat. *These are not our beautiful children, what has happened to our beautiful children?*

Pediatricians, child psychiatrists, and psychotherapists. Some wished to prescribe tranquilizers, barbiturates; some cautioned against powerful psychotropic drugs especially for a seven-year-old. As for Baby Ceci—"She'll grow out of it."

HYPOTHESIS #4: *Demons*

Demons?
   There are none.

Ray-Ray, ten years old. For most of his life the "middle" child. Quiet, watchful. Even in his bassinet. With an air of something brooding and withheld. A slender boy, with an olive-pale complexion. Unlike his fair freckled parents who laughed that Ray-Ray was smarter than either of them, must be the emergence of "genius" genes from an obscure ancestor. Ten years old in sixth grade at Upper Black Eddy Elementary, Ray-Ray was allowed to take ninth grade math at the adjoining Middle School; his science teacher was encouraging him to work on a Time Travel project for the upcoming Bucks County School Science Fair, which Ray-Ray was doing with such concentration, you'd think that he believed in time travel. (Did he? Ray-Ray was evasive answering.) Precocious child, you could tell by the eyes. Dreamy theorizing, not very practical minded. Known as the Awesome Possum within the family the reason wasn't clear why, possibly Ray-Ray's dreamy slow-blinking

manner at mealtimes lost in his own thoughts while the
others are noisy, laughing and teasing one another and
in their midst there's Ray-Ray frowning calculating how
Time Travel might be achieved. And so when the 🖤🖤
Things began to invade Ray-Ray's sleep, he had difficulty waking, lacked the capacity to be jolted out of a
nightmare by sheer fright into wakefulness. Poor Ray-
Ray, only ten years old, enduring nightmares of
stress/tension/things-pulling-at-things/vertical things in-
tersecting with horizontal things producing static elec-
tricity and these things tightly impacted as if (was this
the explanation?) the linear medium of Time that pre-
vents all things from happening simultaneously had
begun to fray and buckle, and soon allthingswouldbe-
happeningatonceintheuniverse and a gigantic black hole
would swallow it all. Unlike the other children, Ray-
Ray seemed incapable of screaming for his parents to
come rescue him. Suffered soaring blood pressure, in
danger of blood vessels bursting in his brain. The pedia-
trician's nurse was stunned taking a reading of the child's
blood pressure so much higher than the blood pressure
of any child in her experience. Ray-Ray suffered from
migraine headaches, eyes leaking tears so he was nearly
blind. In school lapsing into a light doze so his teachers
despaired of him. A thousand pulses beating in his brain
he said as in halting speech tried to explain the emergence of the 🖤🖤 Things a door opens in the earth
swings upward like an old-fashioned cellar door built
slantwise across a flight of crumbling stone steps (like
the cellar door at the rear of the old part of the Lovings' house), at once you are drawn down, and inside.
At once! No choice but to OBEY! For such doors swing
upward opening a kind of vacuum (or BLACK HOLE to
use the commonplace metaphor) and always you are

swept inside a BLACK HOLE the definition of which is if there could be a single instant when you are conscious of the malevolent presence of a BLACK HOLE it would be the identical instant you are sucked inside the BLACK HOLE, to oblivion.

Ray-Ray began to laugh explaining. Ray-Ray was so much smarter than his bumbling parents. Well-intentioned dummies. In the crude jargon of middle-school assholes. But hey, Ray-Ray loved them. Certainly he loved them. Momma Kat he loved, Big Fitzie his daddy he loved. Drawing ██████ on a sheet of paper to show them the BLACK HOLE exerts such a powerful suction it drags into its (limitless, uncharted and unchartable) depths even the memory of an entity. Where/when the entity CEASES TO EXIST its history is simultaneously SUCKED INTO OBLIVION with it.

Ray-Ray was really laughing now. Wiping at his eyes that were looking gluey. The kid's old-young eyes, teachers at the middle school would speak of after his death. Refuting Ray-Ray's terror of forgetfulness, instant oblivion. Ray-Ray rocking with laughter as his anxious parents try to calm him.

Dee-Dee who'd been listening sucking her thumb standing barefoot in the middle of the kitchen smelling of scorched food saying Mom-*my*, Dad-*dy* it's what the ████ Things have come to tell us we will forget each other, too.

Third month of the ████ contagion. Humid midsummer. The bog is fraught with reptilian/insect life. Thrumming through the night and much of the day. A drunk-looking moon swings overhead. Big Fitzie isn't going to abandon his family, spends nights away in

Philly the two-hour commute to and from is treacherous when you're sleep-deprived, can't keep your fucking eyes open. Can't sleep at the Dream House but can't
sleep anywhere else, either. Shattering into pieces is Big
Fitzie. He'd begun to see the things, too. Awake-seeming
he has seen. Flying/pecking/jabbing/stabbing black fis-
sures in the air like tears in fabric. Can't focus on the
things directly only elliptically. Afterimage not the
things themselves. In the corner of Big Fitzie's disinte-
grating brain.

His doctor has prescribed a barbiturate. Taking this
barbiturate leaves Big Fitzie dehydrated and stunned
sleeping for nine, twelve, fourteen hours on weekends
sleep of the dead, delicious!

High blood pressure, though. Big Fitzie must take
beta blockers now, blood thinners, not yet forty years
old. One night realizing stone cold sober thinking is not
worth the terrible effort required like running through
a bog into ever deeper muck sucksucksucking at your
clumsy feet. Big Fitzie's secret is he blames himself for
the distress of his household. Blames blames himself!
For a husband and father may be unfaithful to his family in black moods of doubt hidden from others. In fact
since age fifteen Fritz Loving has been weak, vicious.
Finding in a culvert amid stinky semi-rotting things a
naked rubber doll-baby, at first he'd thought it might be
an actual baby but it was not, only a rubbery doll-baby
he'd kicked across the culvert *No life matters, no life
matters shit.* He'd been relieved. He'd been anxious before worrying about his soul but relieved now. The
memory swung at him like an elbow. Hey asshole it's
you. It ain't your children it's *you.*

Nobody knew. Kat certainly did not know. Pregnant
with Deirdre years ago unsuspecting gorgeous-glowing

Kat with the radiant skin and manelike red-gold hair
had not known. Her husband who adored her yet *If they
die it would be easier.* Not a thought Big Fitzie had actually "had" but a thought that sailed into his head like
a tune. Desperate with love for his wife and the baby-to-
be. Most adoring father after Dee-Dee was born. (He'd
assisted in the birth. He'd been there trying not to
faint.) Heart torn from his chest as in one of those Aztec
ceremonies, nearly. Love came so strong for that beautiful baby girl. Yet there was the next, Raymond. Thinking *Another baby! But I am her baby.* Crazy about his
son, though. An American dad requires a son. Catcher's
mitt, tossing a softball. Backyard. Bicycle with training
wheels, then without. Repeat when the next one was
born. What's-his-name: Fritzie Jr. Little Fitzie. (Ray-Ray
had trouble pronouncing *r* as in Fritzie so his baby
brother came to be, inside the family, Fitzie. Logical?)
This last baby another girl, forget the name, colic-baby,
no one's fault certainly not the baby's fault, who knows
what severe abdominal pains a colic-suffering baby en-
dures, unable to speak, able only to scream, kick, cry,
pierce her parents' hearts with stabbing needles, no
one's fault he wishes her frenzied little heartbeat would
simply cease, her lungs pumping away like a miniature
bellows would simply collapse, *Christ let me sleep.*

Momma Kat (Oh, she's come to hate that silly name:
Why did her husband start calling her that, when Dee-
Dee was a toddler grasping at speech) continues of
course to seek professional help. It's what you do if
you're an affluent American. So ashamed! Her family
so afflicted! You're the mommy, you must know it's
your fault. Certainly it's your fault. As "Katherine Lov-

ing" making an appointment with a psychiatrist on the staff of Penn medical school, older Caucasian male suggests that the entire Loving family seems to have succumbed to mass hysteria possibly provoked by some unconscious, unwitting remark/action of hers. Very likely. (But Katherine can't remember. Her memory has become a sieve, she's only thirty-six years old.) The psychiatrist prescribes a tranquilizer, a mood-elevator, a barbiturate. Momma Kat returns racked with guilt, she believes in holistic medicine, holistic healing, she and Dee-Dee both, now she's a hypocrite, takes the barbiturate just once dropping into a trancelike sleep that becomes a nightmare she can't wake from groaning and writhing in her sleep, has to sleep naked since she sweats through her nightgowns, assailed by ▓▓▓ Things like savage perforations in her optic nerves. Trapped in such a delirium in midafternoon her children come rushing to her Mom*my*! Mom*my*! Wake up Mom*my* but Mommy sleeps for fourteen hours.

HYPOTHESIS #5: "MASS HYSTERIA"

Mass is an extreme adjective applied to only six individuals of whom one is a baby less than a year old. "Mass hysteria" is a matter of *Whether God's archangels or only just wayward roaming demons the revelation received by the afflicted children's mother is she must not allow the ▓▓▓ Things to comprehend that she is aware of them for their mission is to destroy her through her children as her children are to be destroyed/cleansed through her.*

*   *   *

Mommy help me Dee-Dee begged. The shattered things
inside her head, hurting. Only when she splashed cold—
icy cold!—water onto her face were her eyes truly
awake. Then the vagueness sifted back.

Dee-Dee's seventh grade homeroom. She could manage to stay awake by pinching/poking/digging at herself
with her already broken nails. Yet at the back of the
room the beige rough-textured wall fell away into
depthless darkness no one else seemed to notice except
Dee-Dee Loving.

Her underarms were beginning to sprout hairs. Between her legs, too. And she was breathless, and hot.
Fever-hot. Sweaty. And there were thoughts careening
and stabbing like deranged knitting needles. So (she
knew) she could never be clean again. Never pure
again. She knew.

She'd read sixty-nine Nancy Drew novels (of which
she could not recall a single plot!) since she'd begun
reading the series at the age of ten.

Doomed not only to forget but also to be forgotten.

Big Fitzie was home often now. Did his work via e-mail,
fax, telephone. Spared himself the treacherous commute to and from Philly. Was Big Fitzie on sick leave
from the brokerage, or had Big Fitzie been "termi-
nated"? Momma Kat kept meaning to ask him but kept
forgetting.

In the bog amid the twittering cries of late summer,
slow unfurling coils of water snakes. Licorice black, with
creamy-pale bellies and eyes unperturbed as glass.

Big Fitzie understood that his place was at home.
Momma Kat had Baby Ceci, and Little Fitzie, and Ray-
Ray, and Dee-Dee, these children in their afflictions

were her responsibility but could not be hers alone. Big
Fitzie could not desert her in this time of crisis, and
would not. Momma Kat speaking in her cracked ruined
voice of God's archangels. Unless she was speaking to
God's archangels. Avengers of error and sin. Punishers.
Executioners.

It was possible to see, as Momma Kat was beginning
to see, that the ▦ Things were not a contagion after
all but a gift of God to those beloved of Him.

HYPOTHESIS #6: *Time Travel*

Through a tear in the fabric of time, precipitated by
Ray-Ray in all innocence, the ▦ contagion rushed
into the Loving family.

For Ray-Ray alone of the Lovings knew: the universe
is a four-dimensional nexus of (simultaneous) events
perceived and experienced as chronological. Already at
the age of ten, Ray-Ray understood what mathematics
would one day have assured him (had he lived just a few
years beyond September 30, 1999): Time moves at an
unvarying rate, Time is a warm current in a stream so
uniform as to be unnoticed so long as you are moved
along with the current you have no idea you are moving. "Clock time" can instruct you that you are in fact
moving—or being moved. But you are not conscious of
this movement, because it is so slow no consciousness of
the terrible stream moving you from "birth" to "death"
from the first burst of blinding daylight to the final oc-
cluded spasm of extinction.

Children! Breakfast!

*   *   *

Ray-Ray ignored his mother's call. Possibly, Ray-Ray did not hear his mother's call. Already with the clarity of hallucination he was stepping into his Time Machine. Already he'd constructed his Time Machine. No one was welcome to ride with Ray-Ray on his risky journey. He loved Dee-Dee; he loved poor Little Fitzie. He would not wish to endanger them. Ray-Ray was an explorer into the Unknown. The upright rods parted shivering, and Ray-Ray stepped through. Too late to put on his cyclist's crash helmet, Mommy would not know. Too late to say good-bye to her and Daddy. At first it wasn't clear in which direction Ray-Ray was traveling: Past? Future? (Since all events happen simultaneously, the distinction remained mysterious to him.) He shut his eyes, he was in sudden dizzying motion. Hurtling backward, against the current of Time therefore into the "past." Emerging exhausted and confused clawing his way out of the Time Machine and into a hallway it was the upstairs hallway he was just outside his room hadn't left the house blinking and dry-mouthed hearing footsteps on the back stairs and seeing his mirror reflection lurching toward him except it was no mirror *it was Ray-Ray himself.*

Quickly Ray-Ray stumbled into his parents' bedroom. He had made a terrible mistake, he'd journeyed only a few days into the past, nearly confronted his own self of the previous week, what an asshole! What a joke! Ray-Ray waited for his "younger" self to pass by the bedroom door, saw the "younger" self dreamy and preoccupied yawning/scratching at his head/at his crotch imagining no one could see him. Ray-Ray felt a sense of loss so profound, his heart seemed to turn to wet sand, so ashamed. He had assumed he'd travel back farther into the past before his own birth certainly, perhaps into

the previous century, instead he has traveled such a tri-
fling distance, as if his desire to time-travel has been
mocked, and now he must hide from his own "self" and
from the others in his family not wishing to astonish
and terrify them, makes his way down the back stairs
quietly as he can pushes out the screen door runs floating across the lawn crashing into cattails erect and
sharp as swords flailing at his face, he is determined to
hide in the bog until dark at least, must spare his family the shock of seeing a second Ray-Ray in their midst,
hurtled into the not-distant past by a crude miscalcula-
tion, in the bog the soft wet spongy earth begins to suck
at his feet, he loses his balance, falls and cuts his hands,
the six-foot rushes writhing and undulating in what
seems like agitation, unease, his face is being slapped,
slashed, he's down on hands and knees, struggling to
breathe, ▨▨▨ rushing at him as water snakes to their
prey that struggling desperately cannot struggle desperately enough.*

Not that Big Fitzie is so convinced as Momma Kat. The
news of the archangels. Revelation! Interior of Big
Fitzie's head isn't so sparkly as Momma Kat's. In Big
Fitzie's head confused clusters of ▨▨▨ dense as gnats
on a humid summer night in the vicinity of the bog.
▨▨▨ growing bolder each day. Moving freely about the
Dream House. As if the Dream House is their house.
Relatives of the family concerned about Fritz and

* In theory, Raymond Loving's body, which was not among the bodies recovered from the house fire, is somewhere in the bog. There is
also the slim possibility that somehow Ray-Ray escaped, and is still
alive somewhere, having wandered off amnesiac.

Katherine's "increasingly strange, uncommunicative" behavior over the summer will speak of coming to the house knocking at the door peeking through windows seeing no human figures but wraithlike sticks? Rods? Floating in the air of certain of the rooms careening in sunshine like motes so the assumption is that you are "seeing things" and not seeing "things" and so out of a natural fear of incipient madness you wish to see nothing further.

Big Fitzie wishes to see nothing further! Big Fitzie has seen enough. A man must protect his family against all danger but Big Fitzie cannot. Big Fitzie is shutting down. Breakfast! is the clarion call. Breakfast, my darlings! I love you calls Momma Kat forlorn and hopeful come to breakfast please *please*.

Except for Momma Kat's quivering voice the house is strangely quiet. Though no one has noticed, Baby Ceci has gradually ceased her terrible crying. She lies upstairs in her reeking bassinet, feebly kicking. For some days Dee-Dee has been changing the infant's soaked diapers, gingerly washing her and dabbing baby powder on her inflamed skin but now Dee-Dee too in her exhaustion has forgotten Baby Ceci.

More frantically now Momma Kat calls her family to breakfast. Slowly they obey her: Big Fitzie shirtless, in unironed khaki shorts and barefoot; Dee-Dee in a soiled nightgown, stumbling down the stairs; Little Fitzie drifting into the kitchen like a wraith. No one notices, or will notice, that Ray-Ray is not among them.

Ray-Ray come back, Ray-Ray we love you they would have called to the ten-year-old tears streaking their baffled faces but all memory of "Raymond Loving" seems to have faded from them.

Blueberry pancakes, scrambled eggs and little pork sausages and whole grain toast, luscious feast of a breakfast no one is hungry to eat not even Momma Kat nodding off, falling asleep open-eyed at the grill seeing Big Fitzie chewing sausage with slow-grinding jaws and forcing himself to swallow, Dee-Dee yawning pushing at her plate, Fitzie steeling himself trying not to gag as he lifts a forkful of scrambled eggs slowly tremulously to his mouth. Momma Kat has ground up each of her numerous barbiturate/tranquilizer/mood-elevator capsules and sprinkled the mixture into the food and into tall brimming-white glasses of milk set out for Big Fitzie and the children but she sees now that this phase of God's mission isn't going to work, no one will be eating more than a few desultory mouthfuls of their final meal together including Momma Kat herself in a dream nostalgic mood recalling the lavish Sunday brunches she'd prepared for herself and her young husband when they'd been newlyweds, in that long-ago years before the storm of fecundity burst upon them, how happy they'd been she is smiling to recall.

My darlings. I love you.

Momma Kat has prepared the next step. She has brought into the kitchen a two-gallon can of gasoline from the garage, gasoline used for Big Fitzie's tractor lawn mower, now she sprinkles it about her groggy family seated in the kitchen nook, Dee-Dee's sensitive nostrils twitch, Little Fitzie's eyelids quiver, Big Fitzie scratches at his fatty-muscled chest as if bewildered but it's too late, Momma Kat has drawn a deep breath, lighted a match, and tossed it.

Come to us! Sleep. We love you.

Elizabeth A. Lynn has two World Fantasy Awards to her credit, for *"The Woman Who Loved the Moon"* (*Best Short Story, 1980*) *and* Watchtower (*Best Novel, same year*). *She has published two story collections, as well as a bunch of novels besides* Watchtower (*which is the first book in a trilogy that also includes* The Dancers of Arun *and* The Northern Girl), *in both fantasy and SF. Her most recent novel is* Dragon's Treasure, *published by Ace in 2004.*

THE SILVER DRAGON

Elizabeth A. Lynn

This is a story of Iyadur Atani, who was master of Dragon Keep and lord of Dragon's Country a long, long time ago.

At this time, Ryoka was both the same as and different than it is today. In Issho, in the west, there was peace, for the mages of Ryoka had built the great wall, the Wizards' Wall, and defended it with spells. Though the wizards were long gone, the power of their magic lingered in the towers and ramparts of the wall. The Isojai feared it, and would not storm it.

In the east, there was no peace. Chuyo was not part of Ryoka, but a separate country. The Chuyokai lords were masters of the sea. They sailed the eastern seas in black-sailed ships, landing to plunder and loot and carry off the young boys and girls to make them slaves. All along the coast of Kameni, men feared the Chuyokai pirates.

In the north, the lords of Ippa prospered. Yet, having no enemies from beyond their borders to fight, they grew bored, and impatient, and quarrelsome. They quarreled with the lords of Issho, with the Talvelai, and the

Nyo, and they fought among themselves. Most quarrelsome among them was Martun Hal, lord of Serrenhold. Serrenhold, as all men know, is the smallest and most isolated of the domains of Ippa. For nothing is it praised: not for its tasty beer or its excellence of horseflesh, nor for the beauty of its women, nor the prowess of its men. Indeed, Serrenhold is notable for only one thing: its inhospitable climate. *Bitter as the winds of Serrenhold,* the folk of Ippa say.

No one knew what made Martun Hal so contentious. Perhaps it was the wind, or the will of the gods, or perhaps it was just his nature. In the ten years since he had inherited the lordship from his father Owen, he had killed one brother, exiled another, and picked fights with all his neighbors.

His greatest enmity was reserved for Roderico diCorsini of Derrenhold. There had not always been enmity between them. Indeed, he had once asked Olivia diCorsini, daughter of Roderico diCorsini, lord of Derrenhold, to marry him. But Olivia diCorsini turned him down.

"He is old. Besides, I do not love him," she told her father. "I will not wed a man I do not love."

"Love? What does love have to do with marriage?" Roderico glared at his child. She glared back. They were very alike: stubborn and proud of it. "Pah. I suppose you *love* someone else."

"I do," said Olivia.

"And who might that be, missy?"

"Jon Torneo of Galva."

"Jon Torneo?" Roderico scowled a formidable scowl. "Jon Torneo? He's a shepherd's son! He smells of sheep fat and hay!" This, as it happened, was not true. Jon Torneo's father, Federico Torneo of Galva, did own sheep. But he could hardly be called a shepherd: he was a wool merchant, and one of the wealthiest men in the domain, who had often come to Derrenhold as Roderico di-Corsini's guest.

"I don't care. I love him," Olivia said.

And the very next night she ran away from her father's house and rode east across the countryside to Galva. To tell you what happened then would be a whole other story. But since the wedding of Olivia di-Corsini and Jon Torneo, while of great import to them, is a small part of this story, suffice it to say that Olivia married Jon Torneo and went to live with him in Galva. Do I need to tell you they were happy? They were. They had four children. The eldest—a boy, called Federico after his grandfather—was a friendly, sturdy, biddable lad. The next two were girls. They were also charming and biddable children, like their brother.

The fourth was Joanna. She was very lovely, having inherited her mother's olive skin and black, thick hair. But she was in no way biddable. She fought with her nurses and bullied her brother. She preferred trousers to skirts, archery to sewing, and hunting dogs to dolls.

"I want to ride. I want to fight," she said.

"Women do not fight," her sisters said.

"I do," said Joanna.

And her mother, recognizing in her youngest daughter the indomitable stubbornness of her own nature, said, "Let her do as she will."

So Joanna learned to ride, and shoot, and wield a sword. By thirteen she could ride as well as any horseman in her grandfather's army. By fourteen she could outshoot all but his best archers.

"She has not the weight to make a swordsman," her father's arms-master said, "but she'll best anyone her own size in a fair fight."

"She's a hellion. No man will ever want to wed her," Roderico diCorsini said, so gloomily that it made his daughter smile. But Joanna Torneo laughed. She knew very well whom she would marry. She had seen him, shining brighter than the moon, soaring across the sky on his way to his castle in the mountains, and had vowed—this was a fourteen-year-old girl, remember— that Iyadur Atani, the Silver Dragon, would be her husband. That he was a changeling, older than she by twelve years, and that they had never met disturbed her not a whit.

Despite his age—he was nearly sixty—the rancor of the lord of Serrenhold toward his neighbors did not cool. The year Joanna turned five, his war band attacked and burned Ragnar Castle. The year she turned nine, he stormed Voiana, the eyrie of the Red Hawks, hoping for plunder. But he found there only empty chambers and the rushing of wind through stone.

The autumn Joanna turned fourteen, Roderico di-Corsini died: shot through the heart by one of Martun Hal's archers as he led his soldiers along the crest of the western hills. His son, Ege, inherited the domain. Ege di-Corsini, though not the warrior his father had been, was a capable man. His first act as lord was to send a large company of troops to patrol his western border. His next act was to invite his neighbors to a council. "For," he said, "it is past time to end this madness." Couriers were sent to Mirrinhold and Ragnar, to Voiana and to far Mako. A courier was even sent to Dragon Keep.

His councilors wondered at this. "Martun Hal has never attacked the Atani," they pointed out. "The Silver Dragon will not join us."

"I hope you are wrong," said Ege diCorsini. "We need him." He penned that invitation with his own hand. And, since Galva lay between Derrenhold and Dragon Keep, and because he loved his sister, he told the courier, whose name was Ullin March, to stop overnight at the home of Jon Torneo.

Ullin March did as he was told. He rode to Galva. He ate dinner that night with the family. After dinner, he spoke quietly with his hosts, apprising them of Ege diCorsini's plan.

"This could mean war," said Jon Torneo.

"It will mean war," Olivia diCorsini Torneo said.

The next day, Ullin March took his leave of the Torneo family and rode east. At dusk he reached the tall stone pillar that marked the border between the diCorsini's domain and Dragon's Country. He was about to pass the marker, when a slender form leaped from behind the pillar and seized his horse's bridle.

"Dismount," said a fierce young voice, "or I will kill your horse." Steel glinted against the great artery in the gray mare's neck.

Ullin March was no coward. But he valued his horse. He dismounted. The hood fell back from his assailant's face, and he saw that it was a young woman. She was lovely, with olive-colored skin and black hair, tied back behind her neck in a club.

"Who are you?" he said.

"Never mind. The letter you carry. Give it to me."

"No."

The sword tip moved from his horse's neck to his own throat. "I will kill you."

"Then kill me," Ullin March said. Then he dropped, and rolled into her legs. But she had moved. Something hard hit him on the crown of the head.

Dazed and astonished, he drew his sword and lunged at his attacker. She slipped the blow and thrust her blade without hesitation into his arm. He staggered, and slipped to one knee. Again he was hit on the head. The blow stunned him. Blood streamed from his scalp into his eyes. His sword was torn from his grasp. Small hands darted into his shirt, and removed his courier's badge and the letter.

"I am sorry," the girl said. "I had to do it. I will send someone to help you, I promise." He heard the noise of hoofbeats, two sets of them. Cursing, he staggered upright, knowing there was nothing he could do.

Joanna Torneo, granddaughter of Roderico diCorsini, carried her uncle's invitation to Dragon Keep. As it happened, the dragon-lord was at home when she arrived. He was in his hall when a page came running to tell him that a courier from Ege diCorsini was waiting at the gate.

"Put him in the downstairs chamber, and see to his comfort. I will come," said the lord.

"My lord, it's not a him. It's a girl."

"Indeed?" said Iyadur Atani. "See to her comfort, then." The oddity of the event roused his curiosity. In a very short time he was crossing the courtyard to the little chamber where he was wont to receive guests. Within the chamber he found a well-dressed, slightly grubby, very lovely young woman.

"My lord," she said calmly, "I am Joanna Torneo, Ege diCorsini's sister's daughter. I bear you his greetings and a letter." She took the letter from the pocket of her shirt and handed it to him.

Iyadur Atani read her uncle's letter.

"Do you know what this letter says?" he asked.

"It invites you to a council."

"And it assures me that the bearer, a man named Ullin March, can be trusted to answer truthfully any questions I might wish to put to him. You are not Ullin March."

"No. I took the letter from him at the border. Perhaps you would be so kind as to send someone to help him? I had to hit him."

"Why?"

"Had I not, he would not have let me take the letter."

"Why did you take the letter?"

"I wanted to meet you."

"Why?" asked Iyadur Atani.

Joanna took a deep breath. "I am going to marry you."

"Are you?" said Iyadur Atani. "Does your father know this?"

"My mother does," said Joanna. She gazed at him. He was a handsome man, fair, and very tall. His clothes, though rich, were simple; his only adornment, a golden ring on the third finger of his right hand. It was fashioned in the shape of a sleeping dragon. His gaze was very direct, and his eyes burned with a blue flame. Resolute men, men of uncompromising courage, feared that fiery gaze.

When they emerged, first the girl, radiant despite her mud-stained clothes, and then the lord of the Keep, it was evident to all his household that their habitually reserved lord was unusually, remarkably happy.

"This is the lady Joanna Torneo of Galva, soon to be my wife," he said. "Take care of her." He lifted the girl's hand to his lips.

That afternoon he wrote two letters. The first went to Olivia Torneo, assuring her that her beloved daughter was safe in Dragon Keep. The second was to Ege diCorsini. Both letters made their recipients very glad indeed. An exchange of letters followed: from Olivia Torneo to her headstrong daughter, and from Ege diCorsini to the lord of the Keep. Couriers wore ruts in the road from Dragon Keep to Galva, and from Dragon Keep to Derrenhold.

The council was held in the great hall of Derrenhold. Ferris Wulf, lord of Mirrinhold, a doughty warrior, was there, with his captains; so was Aurelio Ragnarin of Ragnar Castle and Rudolf diMako, whose cavalry was the finest in Ippa. Even Jamis Delamico, matriarch of the Red Hawk clan, had come, accompanied by six dark-haired, dark-eyed women who looked exactly like her. She did not introduce them: no one knew if they were her sisters, or her daughters. Iyadur Atani was not present.

Ege diCorsini spoke first.

"My lords, honored friends," he said, "for nineteen years, since the old lord of Serrenhold died, Martun Hal and his troops have prowled the borders of our territories, snapping and biting like a pack of hungry dogs. His people starve, and groan beneath their taxes. He has attacked Mirrinhold, and Ragnar, and Voiana. Two years ago, my lord of Mirrinhold, his archers killed your son. Last year they killed my father.

"My lords and captains, nineteen is too long. It is time to muzzle the dogs." The lesser captains shouted. Ege diCorsini went on. "Alone, no one of us has been able to prevail against Martun Hal's aggression. I suggest we unite our forces and attack him."

"How?" said Aurelio Ragnarin. "He hides behind his walls, and attacks only when he is sure of victory."

"We must go to him, and attack him where he lives."

The leaders looked at one another, and then at diCorsini as if he had lost his mind. Ferris Wulf said, "Serrenhold is unassailable."

"How do you know?" Ege diCorsini said. "For nineteen years no one has attacked it."

"You have a plan," said Jamis Delamico.

"I do." And Ege diCorsini explained to the lords of Ippa exactly how he planned to defeat Martun Hal.

At the end of his speech, Ferris Wulf said, "You are sure of this?"

"I am."

"I am with you."

"And I," said Aurelio Ragnarin.

"My sisters and my daughters will follow you," Jamis Delamico said.

Rudolf diMako stuck his thumbs in his belt. "Martun Hal has stayed well clear of my domain. But I see that he needs to be taught a lesson. My army is yours to command."

Solitary in his fortress, Martun Hal heard through his spies of his enemies' machinations. He summoned his captains to his side. "Gather the troops," he ordered. "We must prepare to defend our borders. Go," he told his spies. "Watch the highways. Tell me when they come."

Sooner than he expected, the spies returned. "My lord, they come."

"What are their forces?"

"They are a hundred mounted men, and six hundred foot."

"Archers?"

"About a hundred."

"Have they brought a ram?"

"Yes, my lord."

"Ladders? Ropes? Catapults?"

"They have ladders and ropes. No catapults, my lord."

"Pah. They are fools, and overconfident. Their horses will do them no good here. Do they think to leap over Serrenhold's walls? We have three hundred archers, and a thousand foot soldiers," Martun Hal said. His spirits rose. "Let them come. They will lose."

The morning of the battle was clear and cold. Frost hardened the ground. A bitter wind blew across the mountain peaks. The forces of the lords of Ippa advanced steadily upon Serrenhold castle. On the ramparts of the castle, archers strung their bows. They were unafraid, for their forces outnumbered the attackers, and besides, no one had ever besieged Serrenhold and won. Behind the castle gates, the Sererenhold army waited. The swordsmen drew their swords and taunted their foes: "Run, dogs! Run, rabbits! Run, little boys! Go home to your mothers!"

The attackers advanced. Ege diCorsini called to the defenders, "Surrender, and you will live. Fight, and you will die."

"We will not surrender," the guard captain said.

"As you wish," diCorsini said. He signaled to his trumpeter. The trumpeter lifted his horn to his lips and blew a sharp trill. Yelling, the attackers charged. Despite the rain of arrows coming from the castle walls, a valiant band of men from Ragnar Castle scaled the walls, and leaped into the courtyard. Back to back, they fought their way slowly toward the gates. Screaming out of the sky, a flock of hawks flew at the faces of the amazed archers. The rain of arrows faltered.

A second group of men smashed its way through a postern gate and battled in the courtyard with Martun Hal's men. Ferris Wulf said to Ege diCorsini, "They weaken. But still they outnumber us. We are losing too many men. Call him."

"Not yet," Ege diCorsini said. He signaled. Men brought the ram up. Again and again they hurled it at the gates. But the gates held. The men in the courtyard fought and died. The hawks attacked the archers, and the archers turned their bows against the birds and shot them out of the sky. A huge red hawk swooped to earth and became Jamis Delamico.

"They are killing my sisters," she said, and her eyes glittered with rage. "Why do you wait? Call him."

"Not yet," said Ege diCorsini. "Look. We are through." The ram broke through the gate. Shouting, the attackers flung themselves at the breach, clawing at the gate with their hands. Fighting with tremendous courage, the attackers moved them back from the gates, inch by inch.

But there were indeed many more defenders. They drove the diCorsini army back, and closed the gate, and braced it with barrels and wagons and lengths of wood.

"Now," said Ege diCorsini. He signaled the trumpeter. The trumpeter blew again.

Then the dragon came. Huge, silver, deadly, he swooped upon the men of Serrenhold. His silver claws cut the air like scythes. He stooped his head, and his eyes glowed like fire. Fire trickled from his nostrils. He breathed upon the castle walls, and the stone hissed and melted like snow in the sun. He roared. The sound filled the day, louder and more terrible than thunder. The archers' fingers opened, and their bows clattered to the ground. The swordsmen trembled, and their legs turned to jelly. Shouting, the men of Ippa stormed over the broken gates and into Serrenhold. They found the lord of the castle sitting in his hall, with his sword across his lap.

"Come on," he said, rising. "I am an old man. Come and kill me."

He charged them then, hoping to force them to kill him. But though he fought fiercely, killing two of them, and wounding three more, they finally disarmed him. Bruised and bloody, but whole, Martun Hal was bound and marched at swordpoint out of his hall to the court-yard where the lords of Ippa stood. He bowed mock-ingly into their unyielding faces.

"Well, my lords. I hope you are pleased with your vic-tory. All of you together, and still it took dragonfire to defeat me."

Ferris Wulf scowled. But Ege diCorsini said, "Why should more men of Ippa die for you? Even your own people are glad the war is over."

"Is it over?"

"It is," diCorsini said firmly.

Martun Hal smiled bleakly. "Yet I live."

"Not for long," someone cried. And Ferris Wulf's chief captain, whose home Martun Hal's men had burned, stepped forward and set the tip of his sword against the old man's breast.

"No," said Ege diCorsini.

"Why not?" said Ferris Wulf. "He killed your father."

"Whom would you put in his place?" Ege diCorsini said. "He is Serrenhold's rightful lord. His father had three sons, but one is dead, and the other gone, who knows where. He has no children to succeed him. *I* would not reign in Serrenhold. It is a dismal place. Let him keep it. We will set a guard about his border, and restrict the number of soldiers he may have, and watch him."

"And when he dies?" said Aurelio Ragnarin.

"Then we will name his successor."

Glaring, Ferris Wulf fingered the hilt of his sword. "He should die *now*. Then we could appoint a regent. One of our own captains, someone honorable and deserving of trust."

Ege diCorsini said, "We could do that. But that man would never have a moment's peace. *I* say, let us sct a watch upon this land, so that Martun Hal may never trouble our towns and people again, and let him rot in this lifeless place."

"The Red Hawk clan will watch him," Jamis Delamico said.

And so it came to pass. Martun Hal lived. His weapons were destroyed; his war band, all but thirty men, was disbanded and scattered. He was forbidden to travel more than two miles from his castle. The lords of Ippa, feeling reasonably secure in their victory, went home to their castles, to rest and rebuild and prepare for winter.

Ege diCorsini, riding east amid his rejoicing troops, made ready to attend a wedding. He was fond of his niece. His sister had assured him that the girl was absolutely determined to wed Iyadur Atani, and as for the flame-haired, flame-eyed dragon-lord, he seemed equally eager for the match. Remembering stories he had heard, Ege diCorsini admitted, though only to himself, that Joanna's husband was not the one he would have chosen for her. But no one had asked his opinion.

The wedding was held at Derrenhold and attended by all the lords of Ippa, except, of course, Martun Hal. Rudolf diMako attended, despite the distance, but no

one was surprised; there was strong friendship between
the diMako and the Atani. Jamis Delamico came. The
bride was pronounced to be astonishingly beautiful, and
the bride's mother almost as beautiful. The dragon-lord
presented the parents of his bride with gifts: a tapestry,
a mettlesome stallion and a breeding mare from the
Atani stables, a sapphire pendant, a cup of beaten gold.
The couple drank the wine. The priestess said the bless-
ings.

The following morning, Olivia diCorsini Torneo said
farewell to her daughter. "I will miss you. Your father
will miss you. You must visit often. He is older than he
was, you know."

"I will," Joanna promised. Olivia watched the last of
her children ride away into the bright autumnal day. The
two older girls were both wed, and Federico was not
only wed but twice a father, as well.

I don't feel like a grandmother, Olivia Torneo
thought. Then she laughed at herself and went inside to
find her husband.

And so there was peace in Ippa. The folk of Derrenhold
and Mirrinhold and Ragnar ceased to look over their
shoulders. They left their daggers sheathed and hung
their battle-axes on the walls. Men who had spent most
of their lives fighting put aside their shields and went
home, to towns and farms and wives they barely remembered. More babies were born the following summer than had been born in the previous three years put
together. The midwives were run ragged trying to attend the births. Many of the boys, even in Ragnar and
Mirrinhold, were named Ege or Roderico. A few of the
girls were even named Joanna.

Martun Hal heard the tidings of his enemies' good fortune, and his hatred of them deepened. Penned in his dreary fortress, he took count of his gold. Discreetly, he let it be known that the lord of Serrenhold, although beaten, was not without resources. Slowly, cautiously, some of those who had served him before his defeat crept across the border to his castle. He paid them and sent them out again to Derrenhold and Mirrinhold, and even—cautiously—into Iyadur Atani's country.

"Watch," he said, "and when something happens, send me word."

As for Joanna Torneo Atani, she was as happy as she had known she would be. She adored her husband and was unafraid of his changeling nature. The people of his domain had welcomed her. Her only disappointment, as the year moved from spring to summer and to the crisp cold nights of autumn again, was that she was childless.

"Every other woman in the world is having a baby," she complained to her husband. "Why can't I?"

He smiled and drew her into the warmth of his arms. "You will."

Nearly three years after the surrender of Martun Hal, with the Hunter's Moon waning in the autumn sky, Joanna Atani received a message from her mother.

Come, it said. *Your father needs you.* She left the next morning for Galva, accompanied by her maid and escorted by six of Dragon Keep's most experienced and competent soldiers.

"Send word if you need me," her husband said.

"I will."

The journey took two days. Outside the Galva gates,

a beggar warming his hands over a scrap of fire told Joanna what she most wanted to know.

"Your father still lives, my lady. I heard it from Viksa the fruit-seller an hour ago."

"Give him gold," Joanna said to her captain as she urged her horse through the gate. Word of her coming hurried before her. By the time Joanna reached her parents' home, the gate was open. Her brother stood before it.

She said, "Is he dead?"

"Not yet." He drew her inside.

Olivia diCorsini Torneo sat at her dying husband's bedside, in the chamber they had shared for twenty-nine years. She still looked young, nearly as young as the day she had left her father's house behind for good. Her dark eyes were clear, and her skin smooth. Only her lustrous thick hair was no longer dark; it was shot through with white, like lace.

She smiled at her youngest daughter and put up her face to be kissed. "I am glad you could come," she said. "Your sisters are here." She turned back to her husband.

Joanna bent over the bed. "Papa?" she whispered. But the man in the bed, so flat and still, did not respond. A plain white cloth wound around Jon Torneo's head was the only sign of injury; otherwise, he appeared to be asleep.

"What happened?"

"An accident, a week ago. He was bringing the herd down from the high pasture when something frightened the sheep; they ran. He fell among them and was trampled. His head was hurt. He has not woken since. The physician Phylla says there is nothing she can do."

Joanna said tremulously, "He always said sheep were stupid. Is he in pain?"

"Phylla says not."

That afternoon, Joanna wrote a letter to her husband, telling him what had happened. She gave it to a courier to take to Dragon Keep.

Do not come, she wrote. *There is nothing you can do. I will stay until he dies.*

One by one his children took their turns at Jon Torneo's bedside. Olivia ate her meals in the chamber and slept on a pallet laid by the bed. Once each day she walked outside the gates, to talk to the people who thronged day and night outside the house, for Jon Torneo was much beloved. Solemn strangers came up to her weeping. Olivia, despite her own grief, spoke kindly to them all.

Joanna marveled at her mother's strength. She could not match it: she found herself weeping at night and snapping by day at her sisters. She was even, to her shame, sick one morning.

A week after Joanna's arrival, Jon Torneo died. He was buried, as was proper, within three days. Ege di-Corsini was there, as were the husbands of Joanna's sisters, and all of Jon Torneo's family, and half Galva, or so it seemed.

The next morning, in the privacy of the garden, Olivia Torneo said quietly to her youngest daughter, "You should go home."

"Why?" Joanna said. She was dumbstruck. "Have I offended you?" Tears rose to her eyes. "Oh, Mother, I'm so sorry. . . ."

"Idiot child," Olivia said, and put her arms around her daughter. "My treasure, you and your sisters have been a great comfort to me. But you should be with your husband at this time." Her gaze narrowed. "Joanna? Do you not know that you are pregnant?"

Joanna blinked. "What makes you—? I feel fine," she said.

"Of course you do," said Olivia. "DiCorsini women never have trouble with babies."

Phylla confirmed that Joanna was indeed pregnant.

"You are sure?"

"Yes. Your baby will be born in the spring."

"Is it a boy or a girl?" Joanna asked.

But Phylla could not tell her that.

So Joanna Atani said farewell to her family, and, with her escort about her, departed Galva for the journey to Dragon Keep. As they rode toward the hills, she marked the drifts of leaves on the ground and the dull color on the hills, and rejoiced. The year was turning. Slipping a hand beneath her clothes, she laid her palm across her belly, hoping to feel the quickening of life in her womb. It seemed strange to be so happy, so soon after her father's untimely death.

Twenty-one days after the departure of his wife from Dragon Keep, Iyadur Atani called one of his men to his side.

"Go to Galva, to the house of Jon Torneo," he said. "Find out what is happening there."

The courier rode to Galva. A light snow fell as he rode through the gates. The steward of the house escorted him to Olivia Torneo's chamber.

"My lady," he said, "I am sent from Dragon Keep to inquire after the well-being of the lady Joanna. May I speak with her?"

Olivia Torneo's face slowly lost its color. She said, "My daughter Joanna left a week ago to return to Dragon Keep. Soldiers from Dragon Keep were with her."

The courier stared. Then he said, "Get me fresh horses."

He burst through the Galva gates as though the demons of hell were on his horse's heels. He rode through the night. He reached Dragon Keep at dawn.

"He's asleep," the page warned.

"Wake him," the courier said. But the page would not. So the courier himself pushed open the door. "My lord? I am back from Galva."

The torches lit in the bedchamber.

"Come," said Iyadur Atani from the curtained bed. He drew back the curtains. The courier knelt on the rug beside the bed. He was shaking with weariness, and hunger, and also with dread.

"My lord, I bear ill news. Your lady left Galva to return home eight days ago. Since then, no one has seen her."

Fire came into Iyadur Atani's eyes. The courier turned his head. Rising from the bed, the dragon-lord said, "Call my captains."

The captains came. Crisply their lord told them that their lady was missing somewhere between Galva and Dragon Keep, and that it was their task, their only task, to find her. "You *will* find her," he said, and his words seemed to burn the air like flames.

"Aye, my lord," they said.

They searched across the countryside, hunting through hamlet and hut and barn, through valley and cave and ravine. They did not find Joanna Atani.

But midway between Galva and the border between the diCorsini land and Dragon's Country, they found, piled in a ditch and rudely concealed with branches, the bodies of nine men and one woman.

"Six of them we know," Bran, second-in-command of Dragon Keep's archers, reported to his lord. He named them: they were the six men who Joanna Atani's escort had comprised. "The woman is my lady Joanna's maid. My lord, we have found the tracks of many men and horses, riding hard and fast. The trail leads west."

"We shall follow it," Iyadur Atani said. "Four of you shall ride with me. The rest shall return to Dragon Keep, to await my orders."

They followed that trail for nine long days across Ippa, through bleak and stony hills, through the high reaches of Derrenhold, into Serrenhold's wild, windswept country. As they crossed the borders, a red-winged hawk swept down upon them. It landed in the snow, and became a dark-eyed woman in a gray cloak.

She said, "I am Madelene of the Red Hawk sisters. I watch this land. Who are you, and what is your business here?"

The dragon-lord said, "I am Iyadur Atani. I am looking for my wife. I believe she came this way, accompanied by many men, perhaps a dozen of them, and their remounts. We have been tracking them for nine days."

"A band of ten men rode across the border from Derrenhold into Serrenhold twelve days ago," the watcher said. "They led ten spare horses. I saw no women among them."

Bran said, "Could she have been disguised? A woman with her hair cropped might look like a boy, and the lady Joanna rides as well as any man."

Madelene shrugged. "I did not see their faces."

"Then you see ill," Bran said angrily. "Is this how the Red Hawk sisters keep watch?" Hawk-changeling and archer glared at one another.

"Enough," Iyadur Atani said. He led them onto the path to the fortress. It wound upward through the rocks. Suddenly they heard the clop of horses' hooves against the stone. Four horsemen appeared on the path ahead of them.

Bran cupped his hands to his lips. "What do you want?" he shouted.

The lead rider shouted back, "It is for us to ask that! You are on our land!"

"Then speak," Bran said.

"Your badges proclaim that you come from Dragon Keep. I bear a message to Iyadur Atani from Martun Hal."

Bran waited for the dragon-lord to declare himself. When he did not, the captain said, "Tell me, and I will carry it to him."

"Tell Iyadur Atani," the lead rider said, "that his wife will be staying in Serrenhold for a time. If any attempt is made to find her, then she will die, slowly and in great pain. That is all." He and his fellows turned their horses and bolted up the path.

Iyadur Atani said not a word, but the dragon rage burned white hot upon his face. The men from Dragon Keep looked at him, once. Then they looked away, holding their breaths.

Finally he said, "Let us go."

When they reached the border, they found Ege diCorsini, with a large company of well-armed men, waiting for them.

"Olivia sent to me," he said to Iyadur Atani. "Have you found her?"

"Martun Hal has her," the dragon-lord said. "He says he will kill her if we try to get her back." His face was set. "He may kill her anyway."

"He won't kill her," Ege diCorsini said. "He'll use her to bargain with. He will want his weapons and his army back, and freedom to move about his land."

"Give it to him," Iyadur Atani said. "I want my wife."

So Ege diCorsini sent a delegation of his men to Martun Hal, offering to modify the terms of Serrenhold's surrender, if he would release Joanna Atani unharmed.

But Martun Hal did not release Joanna. As diCorsini had said, he used her welfare to bargain with, demanding first the freedom to move about his own country, and then the restoration of his war band, first to one hundred, then to three hundred men.

"We must know where she is. When we know where she is, we can rescue her," diCorsini said. And he sent spies into Serrenhold, with instructions to discover where in that bleak and barren country the lady of Ippa was. But Martun Hal, ever crafty, had anticipated this. He sent a message to Iyadur Atani, warning that payment for the trespass of strangers would be exacted upon Joanna's body. He detailed, with blunt and horrific cruelty, what that payment would be.

In truth, despite the threats, he did nothing to hurt his captive. For though years of war had scoured from him almost all human feeling save pride, ambition, and spite, he understood quite well that if Joanna died, and word of that death reached Dragon Keep, no power in or out of Ryoka could protect him.

As for Joanna, she had refused even to speak to him from the day his men had brought her, hair chopped like a boy's, wrapped in a soldier's cloak, into his castle. She did not weep. They put her in an inner chamber, and placed guards on the door, and assigned two women to care for her. They were both named Kate, and since one was large and one not, they were known as Big Kate and Small Kate. She did not rage, either. She ate the meals the women brought her and slept in the bed they gave her.

Winter came early, as it does in Serrenhold. The wind moaned about the castle walls, and snow covered the mountains. Weeks passed, and Joanna's belly swelled. When it became clear beyond any doubt that she was indeed pregnant, the women who served her went swiftly to tell their lord.

"Are you sure?" he demanded. "If this is a trick, I will have you both flayed!"

"We are sure," they told him. "Send a physician to her, if you question it."

So Martun Hal sent a physician to Joanna's room. But Joanna refused to let him touch her. "I am Iyadur Atani's wife," she said. "I will allow no other man to lay his hands on me."

"Pray that it is a changeling, a dragon-child," Martun Hal said to his captains. And he told the two Kates to give Joanna whatever she needed for her comfort, save freedom.

The women went to Joanna and asked what she wanted.

"I should like a window," Joanna said. The rooms in which they housed her had all been windowless. They moved her to a chamber in a tower. It was smaller than the room in which they had been keeping her, but it had a narrow window, through which she could see sky and clouds, and on clear nights, stars.

When her idleness began to weigh upon her, she said, "Bring me books." They brought her books. But reading soon bored her.

"Bring me a loom."

"A loom? Can you weave?" Big Kate asked.

"No," Joanna said. "Can you?"

"Of course."

"Then you can teach me." The women brought her the loom, and with it, a dozen skeins of bright wool. "Show me what to do." Big Kate showed her how to set up the threads, and how to cast the shuttle. The first thing she made was a yellow blanket, a small one.

Small Kate asked, "Who shall that be for?"

"For the babe," Joanna said.

Then she began another: a scarlet cloak, a large one, with a fine gold border.

"Who shall that be for?" Big Kate asked.

"For my lord, when he comes."

One gray afternoon, as Joanna sat at her loom, a red-winged hawk alighted on her windowsill.

"Good day," Joanna said to it. It cocked its head and stared at her sideways out of its left eye. "There is bread on the table." She pointed to the little table where she ate her food. She had left a slice of bread untouched from her midday meal, intending to eat it later. The hawk turned its beak and stared at her out of its right eye. Hopping to the table, it pecked at the bread.

Then it fluttered to the floor and became a dark-eyed, dark-haired woman wearing a gray cloak. Crossing swiftly to Joanna's seat, she whispered, "Leave the shutter ajar. I will come again tonight." Before Joanna could answer, she turned into a bird and was gone.

That evening Joanna could barely eat. Concerned, Big Kate fussed at her. "You have to eat. The babe grows swiftly now; it needs all the nourishment you can give it. Look, here is the cream you wanted, and here is soft ripe cheese, come all the way from Merigny in the south, where they say it snows once every hundred years."

"I don't want it." Big Kate reached to close the window shutter. "Leave it!"

"It's freezing."

"I am warm."

"You might be feverish." Small Kate reached to feel her forehead.

"I am not. I'm fine."

At last they left her. She heard the bar slide across the door. She lay down on her bed. As was their custom, they had left her but a single candle, but light came from the hearth log. The babe moved in her belly. "Little one, I feel you," she whispered. "Be patient. We shall not always be in this loathsome place."

Then she heard the rustle of wings. A human shadow sprang across the walls of the chamber. A woman's voice said softly, "My lady, do you know me? I am Madelene of the Red Hawk sisters. I was at your wedding."

"I remember." Tears—the first she had shed since the start of her captivity—welled into Joanna's eyes. She knuckled them away. "I am glad to see you."

"And I you," Madelene said. "Since first I knew you were here, I have looked for you. I feared you were in torment, or locked away in some dark dungeon, where I might never find you."

"Can you help me to escape this place?"

Madelene said sadly, "No, my lady. I have no power to do that."

"I thought not." She reached beneath her pillow and brought out a golden brooch shaped like a full-blown rose. It had been a gift from her husband on their wedding night. "Never mind. Here. Take this to my husband."

*   *   *

In Dragon Keep, Iyadur Atani's mood grew grimmer and more remote. Martun Hal's threats obsessed him: he imagined his wife alone, cold, hungry, confined to darkness, perhaps hurt. His appetite vanished; he ceased to eat, or nearly so.

At night he paced the castle corridors, silent as a ghost, cloakless despite the winter cold, his eyes like white flame. His soldiers and his servants began to fear him. One by one, they vanished from the castle.

But some, more resolute or more loyal, remained. Among them was Bran the archer, now captain of the archery wing, since Jarko, the former captain, had disappeared one moonless December night. When a strange woman appeared among them, claiming to bear a message to Iyadur Atani from his captive wife, it was to Bran the guards brought her.

He recognized her. Leading her to Iyadur Atani's chamber, he pounded on the closed door. The door opened. Iyadur Atani stood framed in the doorway. His face was gaunt.

Madelene held out the golden brooch.

Iyadur Atani knew it at once. The grief and rage and fear that had filled him for four months eased a little. Lifting the brooch from Madelene's palm, he touched it to his lips.

"Be welcome," he said. "Tell me how Joanna is. Is she well?"

"She bade me say that she is, my lord."

"And—the babe?"

"It thrives. It is your child, my lord. Your lady charged me to say that, and to tell you that no matter what rumors you might have heard, neither Martun Hal nor any of his men has touched her. Indeed, no torment has been offered her at all. Only she begs you to please, come quickly to succor her, for she is desperate to be home."

"Can you visit her easily?"

"I can."

"Then return to her, of your kindness. Tell her I love her. Tell her not to despair."

"She will not despair," Madelene said. "Despair is not in her nature. But I have a second message for you. This one is from my queen." She meant the matriarch of the Red Hawks, Jamis Delamico. "She said to tell you, where force will not prevail, seek magic. She says, go west, to Lake Urai. Find the sorcerer who lives beside the lake, and ask him how to get your wife back."

Iyadur Atani said, "I did not know there were still sorcerers in the west."

"There is one. The common folk know him as Viksa. But that is not his true name, my queen says."

"And does your queen know the true name of this reclusive wizard?" For everyone knows that unless you know a sorcerer's true name, he or she will not even speak with you.

"She does. And she told me to tell it to you," said Madelene. She leaned toward the dragon-lord and whispered in his ear. "And she also told me to tell you, be careful when you deal with him. For he is sly, and what he intends to do, he does not always reveal. But what he says he will do, he will do."

"Thank you," Iyadur Atani said, and he smiled, for the first time in a long time. "Cousin, I am in your debt." He told Bran to see to her comfort and to provide her with whatever she needed—food, a bath, a place to sleep. Summoning his servants, he asked them to bring him a meal and wine.

Then he called his officers together. "I am leaving,"

he said. "You must defend my people and hold the borders against outlaws and incursions. If you need help, ask for aid from Mako or Derrenhold."

"How long will you be gone, my lord?" they asked him.

"I do not know."

Then he flew to Galva.

"I should have come before," he said. "I am sorry." He assured Olivia that despite her captivity, Joanna was well, and unharmed. "I go now to get her," he said. "When I return, I shall bring her with me. I swear it."

Issho, the southeastern province of Ryoka, is a rugged place. Though not so grim as Ippa, it has none of the gentle domesticated peace of Nakase. Its plains are colder than those of Nakase, and its rivers are wilder. The greatest of those rivers is the Endor. It starts in the north, beneath that peak which men call the Lookout, Mirrin, and pours ceaselessly south, cutting like a knife through Issho's open spaces to the border where Chuyo and Issho and Nakase meet.

It ends in Lake Urai. Lake Urai is vast, and even on a fair day, the water is not blue, but pewter gray. In winter, it does not freeze. Contrary winds swirl about it; at dawn and at twilight gray mist obscures its contours, and at all times the chill bright water lies quiescent, untroubled by even the most violent wind. The land about it is sparsely inhabited. Its people are a hardy, silent folk, not particularly friendly to strangers. They respect the lake and do not willingly discuss its secrets. When the tall, fair-haired stranger appeared among them, having come, so he said, from Ippa, they were happy to prepare his food and take his money, but were inclined to answer his questions evasively, or not at all.

The lake is as you see it. The wizard of the lake? Never heard of him.

But the stranger was persistent. He took a room at The Red Deer in Jen, hired a horse—oddly, he seemed to have arrived without one—and roamed about the lake. The weather did not seem to trouble him. "We have winter in my country." His clothes were plain, but clearly of the highest quality, and beneath his quiet manner there was iron.

"His eyes are different," the innkeeper's wife said. "He's looking for a wizard. Maybe he's one himself, in disguise."

One gray March afternoon, when the lake lay shrouded in mist, Iyadur Atani came upon a figure sitting on a rock beside a small fire. It was dressed in rags and held what appeared to be a fishing pole.

The dragon-lord's heart quickened. He dismounted. Tying his horse to a tall reed, he walked toward the fisherman. As he approached, the hunched figure turned. Beneath the ragged hood he glimpsed white hair, and a visage so old and wrinkled that he could not tell if he was facing a man or a woman.

"Good day," he said. The ancient being nodded. "My name is Iyadur Atani. Men call me the Silver Dragon. I am looking for a wizard."

The ancient one shook its head and gestured, as if to say, Leave me alone. Iyadur Atani crouched.

"Old One, I don't believe you are as you appear," he said in a conversational tone. "I believe you are the one I seek. If you are indeed"—and then he said the name that Madelene of the Red Hawks had whispered in his ear—"I beg you to help me. For I have come a long way to look for you."

An aged hand swept the hood aside. Dark gray eyes stared out of a withered, wrinkled face.

A feeble voice said, "Who told you my name?"

"A friend."

"Huh. Whoever it was is no friend of *mine*. What does the Silver Dragon need a wizard for?"

"If you are truly wise," Iyadur Atani said, "you know."

The sorcerer laughed softly. The hunched figure straightened. The rags became a silken gown with glittering jewels at its hem and throat. Instead of an old man, the dragon-lord faced a man in his prime, of princely bearing, with luminous chestnut hair and eyes the color of a summer storm. The fishing pole became a tall staff. Its crook was carved like a serpent's head. The sorcerer pointed the staff at the ground and said three words.

A doorway seemed to open in the stony hillside. Joanna Torneo Atani stood within it. She wore furs and was visibly pregnant.

"Joanna!" The dragon-lord reached for her. But his hands gripped empty air.

"Illusion," said the sorcerer known as Viksa. "A simple spell, but effective, don't you think? You are correct, my lord. I know you lost your wife. I assume you want her back. Tell me, why do you not lead your war band to Serrenhold and rescue her?"

"Martun Hal will kill her if I do that."

"I see."

"Will you help me?"

"Perhaps," said the sorcerer. The serpent in his staff turned its head to stare at the dragon-lord. Its eyes were rubies. "What will you pay me if I help you?"

"I have gold."

Viksa yawned. "I have no interest in gold."

"Jewels," said the dragon-lord, "fine clothing, a horse to bear you wherever you might choose to go, a castle of your own to dwell in . . ."

"I have no use for those."

"Name your price, and I will pay it," Iyadur Atani said steadily. "I reserve only the life of my wife and my child."

"But not your own?" Viksa cocked his head. "You intrigue me. Indeed, you move me. I accept your offer, my lord. I will help you rescue your wife from Serrenhold. I shall teach you a spell, a very simple spell, I assure you. When you speak it, you will be able to hide within a shadow. In that way you may pass into Serrenhold unseen."

"And its price?"

Viksa smiled. "In payment, I will take—*you*. Not your life, but your service. It has been many years since I had someone to hunt for me, cook for me, build my fire, and launder my clothes. It will amuse me to have a dragon as my servant."

"For how long would I owe you service?"

"As long as I wish it."

"That seems *unfair*."

The wizard shrugged.

"When would this service start?"

The wizard shrugged again. "It may be next month, or next year. Or it may be twenty years from now. Do we have an agreement?"

Iyadur Atani considered. He did not like this wizard. But he could see no other way to get his wife back.

"We do," he said. "Teach me the spell."

So Viksa the sorcerer taught Iyadur Atani the spell which would enable him to hide in a shadow. It was not a difficult spell. Iyadur Atani rode his hired horse back to The Red Deer and paid the innkeeper what remained on his bill. Then he walked into the bare field beside the inn, and became the Silver Dragon. As the innkeeper and his wife watched openmouthed, he circled the inn once and then sped north.

"A dragon!" the innkeeper's wife said with intense satisfaction. "I wonder if he found the sorcerer. See, I told you his eyes were odd." The innkeeper agreed. Then he went up to the room Iyadur Atani had occupied and searched carefully in every cranny, in case the dragon-lord had chanced to leave some gold behind.

Now it was in Iyadur Atani's mind to fly immediately to Serrenhold Castle. But remembering Martun Hal's threats, he did not. He flew to a point just south of Serrenhold's southern border. And there, in a nondescript village, he bought a horse, a shaggy brown gelding. From there he proceeded to Serrenhold Castle. It was not so tedious a journey as he had thought it would be. The prickly stunted pine trees that grew along the slopes of the windswept hills showed new green along their branches. Birds sang. Foxes loped across the hills, hunting mice and quail and the occasional stray chicken. The journey took six days. At dawn on the seventh day, Iyadur Atani fed the brown gelding and left him in a farmer's yard. It was a fine spring morning. The sky was cloudless; the sun brilliant; the shadows sharp-edged as steel. Thorn-crowned hawthorn bushes lined the road to Serrenhold Castle. Their shadows webbed the ground. A wagon filled with lumber lumbered toward the castle. Its shadow rolled beneath it.

"Wizard," the dragon-lord said to the empty sky, "if

you have played me false, I will find you wherever you try to hide, and eat your heart."

In her prison in the tower, Joanna Torneo Atani walked from one side of her chamber to the other. Her hair had grown long again: it fell around her shoulders. Her belly was round and high under the soft thick drape of her gown. The coming of spring had made her restless. She had asked to be allowed to walk on the ramparts, but this Martun Hal had refused.

Below her window, the castle seethed like a cauldron. The place was never still; the smells and sounds of war continued day and night. The air was thick with soot. Soldiers drilled in the courtyard. Martun Hal was planning an attack on Ege diCorsini. He had told her all about it, including his intention to destroy Galva. *I will burn it to the ground. I will kill your uncle and take your mother prisoner,* he had said. *Or perhaps not. Perhaps I will just have her killed.*

She glanced toward the patch of sky that was her window. If Madelene would only come, she could get word to Galva, or to her uncle in Derrenhold. . . . But Madelene would not come in daylight; it was too dangerous.

She heard a hinge creak. The door to the outer chamber opened. "My lady," Big Kate called. She bustled in, bearing a tray. It held soup, bread, and a dish of thin sour pickles. "I brought your lunch."

"I'm not hungry."

Kate said, troubled, "My lady, you have to eat. For the baby."

"Leave it," Joanna said. "I will eat." Kate set the tray on the table and left.

Joanna nibbled at a pickle. She rubbed her back, which ached. The baby's heel thudded against the inside of her womb. "My precious, my little one, be still," she said. For it was her greatest fear that her babe, Iyadur Atani's child, might in its haste to be born arrive early, before her husband arrived to rescue them. That he would come, despite Martun Hal's threats, she had no doubt. "Be still."

Silently, Iyadur Atani materialized from the shadows.

"Joanna," he said. He put his arms about her. She reached her hands up. Her fingertips brushed his face. She leaned against him, trembling.

She whispered into his shirt, "How did you—?"

"Magic." He touched the high mound of her belly. "Are you well? Have they mistreated you?"

"I am very well. The babe is well." She seized his hand and pressed his palm over the mound. The baby kicked strongly. "Do you feel?"

"Yes." Iyadur Atani stroked her hair. A scarlet cloak with an ornate gold border hung on a peg. He reached for it and wrapped it about her. "Now, my love, we go. Shut your eyes, and keep them shut until I tell you to open them." He bent and lifted her into his arms. Her heart thundered against his chest.

She breathed into his ear, "I am sorry. I am heavy."

"You weigh nothing," he said. His human shape dissolved. The walls of the tower shuddered and burst apart. Blocks of stone and splintered planks of wood toppled into the courtyard. Women screamed. Arching his great neck, the Silver Dragon spread his wings and rose into the sky. The soldiers on the ramparts threw their spears at him and fled. Joanna heard the screaming and felt the hot wind. The scent of burning filled her nostrils. She knew what must have happened. But the arms about her were her husband's, and human. She did not know how this could be, yet it was. Eyes tight shut, she buried her face against her husband's shoulder.

Martun Hal stood with a courier in the castle hall. The crash of stone and the screaming interrupted him. A violent gust of heat swept through the room. The windows of the hall shattered. Racing from the hall, he looked up and saw the dragon circling. His men crouched, sobbing in fear. Consumed with rage, he looked about for a bow, a spear, a rock . . . Finally he drew his sword.

"Damn you!" he shouted impotently at his adversary.

Then the walls of his castle melted beneath a white-hot rain.

In Derrenhold, Ege diCorsini was wearily, reluctantly preparing for war. He did not want to fight Martun Hal, but he would, of course, if troops from Serrenhold took one step across his border. That an attack would be mounted he had no doubt. His spies had told him to expect it. Jamis of the Hawks had sent her daughters to warn him.

Part of his weariness was a fatigue of the spirit. *This is all my fault. I should have killed him when I had the opportunity. Ferris was right.* The other part of his weariness was physical. He was tired much of the time, and none of the tonics or herbal concoctions that the physicians prescribed seemed to help. His heart raced oddly. He could not sleep. Sometimes in the night he wondered if the Old One sleeping underground had dreamed of him. When the Old One dreams of you, you die. But he did not want to die and leave his domain and its people in danger, and so he planned a war, knowing all the while that he might die in the middle of it.

"My lord," a servant said, "you have visitors."

"Send them in," Ege diCorsini said. "No, wait." The physicians had said he needed to move about. Rising wearily, he went into the hall.

He found there his niece Joanna, big with child, and with her, her flame-haired, flame-eyed husband. A strong smell of burning hung about their clothes.

Ege diCorsini drew a long breath. He kissed Joanna on both cheeks. "I will let your mother know that you are safe."

"She needs to rest," Iyadur Atani said.

"I do not need to rest. I have been doing absolutely nothing for the last six months. I need to go home," Joanna said astringently. "Only I do not wish to ride. Uncle, would you lend us a litter and some steady beasts to draw it?"

"You may have anything I have," Ege diCorsini said. And for a moment he was not tired at all.

Couriers galloped throughout Ippa, bearing the news: Martun Hal was dead; Serrenhold Castle was ash, or nearly so. The threat of war was—after twenty years— truly over. Martun Hal's captains—most of them—had died with him. Those still alive hid, hoping to save their skins.

Two weeks after the rescue and the burning of Serrenhold, Ege diCorsini died.

In May, with her mother and sisters at her side, Joanna gave birth to a son. The baby had flame-colored hair and eyes like his father's. He was named Avahir. A year and a half later, a second son was born to Joanna Torneo Atani. He had dark hair, and eyes like his mother's. He was named Jon. Like the man whose name he bore, Jon Atani had a sweet disposition and a loving heart. He adored his brother, and Avahir loved his younger brother fiercely. Their loyalty to each other made their parents very happy.

Thirteen years almost to the day from the burning of Serrenhold, on a bright spring morning, a man dressed richly as a prince, carrying a white birch staff, appeared at the front gate of Atani Castle and requested audience with the dragon-lord. He refused to enter or even to give his name, saying only, "Tell him the fisherman has come for his catch."

His servants found Iyadur Atani in the great hall of his castle.

"My lord," they said, "a stranger stands at the front gate, who will not give his name. He says. 'The fisherman has come for his catch.' "

"I know who it is," their lord replied. He walked to the gate of his castle. The sorcerer stood there, leaning on his serpent-headed staff, entirely at ease.

"Good day," he said cheerfully. "Are you ready to travel?"

And so Iyadur Atani left his children and his kingdom to serve Viksa the wizard. I do not know—no one ever asked her, not even their sons—what Iyadur Atani and his wife said to one another that day. Avahir Atani, who at twelve was already full-grown, as changeling children are wont to be, inherited the lordship of Atani Castle. Like his father, he gained the reputation of being fierce but just.

Jon Atani married a granddaughter of Rudolf di-Mako and went to live in that city.

Joanna Atani remained in Dragon Keep. As time passed and Iyadur Atani did not return, her sisters and her brother, even her sons, urged her to remarry. She told them all not to be fools; she was wife to the Silver Dragon. Her husband was alive and might return at any time, and how would he feel to find another man warming her bed? She became her son's chief minister, and in that capacity could often be found riding across Dragon's Country, and elsewhere in Ippa, to Derrenhold and Mirrinhold and Ragnar, and even to far Voiana, where the Red Hawk sisters, one in particular, always welcomed her. She would not go to Serrenhold.

But always she returned to Dragon Keep.

As for Iyadur Atani: he traveled with the wizard throughout Ryoka, carrying his bags, preparing his oatcakes and his bathwater, scraping mud from his boots. Viksa's boots were often muddy, for he was a great traveler, who walked, rather than rode, to his many destinations. In the morning, when Iyadur Atani brought the sorcerer his breakfast, Viksa would say, "Today we go to Rotsa"—or Ruggio, or Towena. "They have need of magic." He never said how he knew this. And off they would go to Vipurri or Rotsa or Talvela, to Sorvino, Ruggio, or Rowena.

Sometimes the need to which he was responding had to do directly with magic, as when a curse needed to be lifted. Often it had to do with common disasters. A river had swollen in its banks and needed to be restrained. A landslide had fallen on a house or barn. Sometimes the one who needed them was noble, or rich. Sometimes not. It did not matter to Viksa. He could enchant a cornerstone, so that the wall it anchored would rise straight and true; he could spell a field, so that its crop would thrust from the soil no matter what the rainfall.

His greatest skill was with water. Some sorcerers draw a portion of their power from an element: wind, water, fire, or stone. Viksa could coax a spring out of earth that had known only drought for a hundred years. He could turn stagnant water sweet. He knew the names of every river, stream, brook, and waterfall in Issho.

In the first years of his servitude, Iyadur Atani thought often of nis sons, and especially Avahir, and of Joanna, but after a while his anxiety for them faded. After a longer while, he found he did not think of them so often—rarely at all, in fact. He even forgot their names. He had already relinquished his own. *Iyadur is too grand a name for a servant,* the sorcerer had remarked. *You need a different name.*

And so the tall, fair-haired man became known as Shadow. He carried the sorcerer's pack and cooked his food. He rarely spoke.

"Why is he so silent?" women, bolder and more curious than their men, asked the sorcerer.

Sometimes the sorcerer answered, "No reason. It's his nature." And sometimes he told a tale, a long, elaborate fantasy of spells and dragons and sorcerers, a gallant tale in which Shadow had been the hero, but from which he had emerged changed—broken. Shadow, listening, wondered if perhaps this tale was true. It might have been. It explained why his memory was so erratic, and so vague.

His dreams, by contrast, were vivid and intense. He dreamed often of a dark-walled castle flanked by white-capped mountains. Sometimes he dreamed that he was a bird, flying over the castle. The most adventurous of the women, attracted by Shadow's looks and, sometimes, by his silence, tried to talk with him. But their smiles and allusive glances only made him shy. He thought that he had had a wife, once. Maybe she had left him. He thought perhaps she had. But maybe not. Maybe she had died.

He had no interest in the women they met, though as far as he could tell, his body still worked as it should. He was a powerful man, well formed. Shadow wondered sometimes what his life had been before he had come to serve the wizard. He had skills: he could hunt and shoot a bow, and use a sword. Perhaps he had served in some noble's war band. He bore a knife now, a good one, with a bone hilt, but no sword. He did not need a sword. Viksa's reputation, and his magic, shielded them both.

Every night, before they slept, wherever they were, half speaking, half chanting in a language Shadow did not know, the sorcerer wove spells of protection about them and their dwelling. The spells were very powerful. They made Shadow's ears hurt.

Once, early in their association, he asked the sorcerer what the spell was for.

"Protection," Viksa replied. Shadow had been surprised. He had not realized Viksa had enemies.

But now, having traveled with the sorcerer as long as he had, he knew that even the lightest magic can have consequences, and Viksa's magic was not always light. He could make rain, but he could also make drought. He could lift curses or lay them. He was a man of power, and he had his vanity. He enjoyed being obeyed. Sometimes he enjoyed being feared.

Through spring, summer, and autumn, the wizard traveled wherever he was called to go. But in winter they returned to Lake Urai. He had a house beside the lake, a simple place, furnished with simple things: a pallet, a table, a chair, a shelf for books. But Viksa rarely looked at the books; it seemed he had no real love for study. Indeed, he seemed to have no passion for anything, save sorcery itself—and fishing. All through the Issho winter, despite the bitter winds, he took his little coracle out upon the lake and sat there with a pole. Sometimes he caught a fish, or two, or half a dozen. Sometimes he caught none.

"Enchant them," Shadow said to him one gray afternoon, when his master had returned to the house empty-handed. "Call them to your hook with magic."

The wizard shook his head. "I can't."

"Why not?"

"I was one of them once." Shadow looked at him, uncertain. "Before I was a sorcerer, I was a fish."

It was impossible to tell if he was joking or serious. It might have been true. It explained, at least, his affinity for water.

While Viksa fished, Shadow hunted. The country around the lake was rich with game; despite the winter, they did not lack for meat. Shadow hunted deer and badger and beaver. He saw wolves, but did not kill them. Nor would he kill birds, though birds there were; even in winter, geese came often to the lake. Their presence woke in him a wild, formless longing.

One day he saw a white bird, with wings as wide as he was tall, circling over the lake. It had a beak like a raptor. It called to him, an eerie sound. Something about it made his heart beat faster. When Viksa returned from his sojourn at the lake, Shadow described the strange bird to him, and asked what it was.

"A condor," the wizard said.

"Where does it come from?"

"From the north," the wizard said, frowning.

"It called to me. It looked—noble."

"It is not. It is scavenger, not predator." He continued to frown. That night he spent a long time over his nightly spells.

In spring, the kingfishers and guillemots returned to

the lake. And one April morning, when Shadow laid breakfast upon the table, Viksa said, "Today we go to Dale."

"Where is that?"

"In the White Mountains, in Kameni, far to the north." And so they went to Dale, where a petty lordling needed Viksa's help in deciphering the terms and conditions of an ancient prophecy, for within it lay the future of his kingdom.

From Dale they traveled to Secca, where a youthful hedge-witch, hoping to shatter a boulder, had used a spell too complex for her powers and had managed to summon a stone demon, which promptly ate her. It was an old, powerful demon. It took a day, a night, and another whole day until Viksa, using the strongest spells he knew, was able to send it back into the Void.

They rested that night at a roadside inn, south of Secca. Viksa, exhausted from his battle with the demon, went to bed right after his meal, so worn that he fell asleep without taking the time to make his customary incantations.

Shadow considered waking him to remind him of it, and decided not to. Instead, he, too, slept.

And there, in an inn south of Secca, Iyadur Atani woke.

He was not, he realized, in his bed, or even in his bedroom. He lay on the floor. The coverlet around his shoulders was rough, coarse wool, not the soft quilt he was used to. Also, he was wearing his boots.

He said, "Joanna?" No one answered. A candle sat on a plate at his elbow. He lit it without touching it.

Sitting up soundlessly, he gazed about the chamber, at the bed and its snoring occupant, at the packs he had packed himself, the birchwood staff athwart the doorway. . . . Memory flooded through him. The staff was Viksa's. The man sleeping in the bed was Viksa. And he—*he* was Iyadur Atani, lord of Dragon Keep.

His heart thundered. His skin coursed with heat. The ring on his hand glowed, but he could not feel the burning. Fire coursed beneath his skin. He rose.

How long had Viksa's magic kept him in thrall—five years? Ten years? More?

He took a step toward the bed. The serpent in the wizard's staff opened its eyes. Raising its carved head, it hissed at him.

The sound woke Viksa. Gazing up from his bed at the bright shimmering shape looming over him, he knew immediately what had happened. He had made a mistake. *Fool,* he thought, *Oh, you fool.*

It was too late now.

The guards on the walls of Secca saw a pillar of fire rise into the night. Out of it—so they swore, with such fervor that even the most skeptical did not doubt them—flew a silver dragon. It circled the flames, bellowing with such power and ferocity that all who heard it trembled.

Then it beat the air with its wings and leaped north.

In Dragon Keep, a light powdery snow covered the garden. It did not deter the rhubarb shoots breaking through the soil, or the fireweed, or the buds on the birches. A sparrow swung in the birch branches, singing. The clouds that had brought the snow had dissipated; the day was bright and fair, the shadows sharp as the angle of the sparrow's wing against the light.

Joanna Atani walked along the garden path. Her face was lined, and her hair, though still lustrous and thick, was streaked with silver. But her step was as vigorous, and her eyes as bright, as they had been when first she came to Atani Castle, over thirty years before.

Bending, she brushed a snowdrop free of snow. By midday, she judged, the snow would be gone. A clatter of pans arose in the kitchen. A clear voice, imperious and young, called from within. She smiled. It was Hikaru, Avahir's firstborn and heir. He was only two years old, but had the height and grace of a lad twice that age.

A woman answered him, her voice soft and firm. That was Geneva Tuolinnen, Hikaru's mother. She was an excellent mother, calm and unexcitable. She was a good seamstress, too, and a superb manager; far better at running the castle than Joanna had ever been. She could scarcely handle a bow, though, and thought swordplay was entirely men's work.

She and Joanna were as friendly as two strong-willed women can be.

A black, floppy-eared puppy bounded across Joanna's feet, nearly knocking her down. Rup the dog-boy scampered after it. They tore through the garden and raced past the kitchen door into the yard.

A man walked into the garden. Joanna shaded her eyes. He was quite tall. She did not recognize him. His hair was nearly white, but he did not move like an old man. Indeed, the height of him and the breadth of his shoulder reminded her of Avahir, but she knew it was not Avahir. He was hundreds of miles away, in Kameni.

She said, "Sir, who are you?"

The man came closer. "Joanna?"

She knew that voice. For a moment she ceased to breathe. Then she walked toward him.

It was her husband.

He looked exactly as he had the morning he had left

with the wizard, sixteen years before. His eyes were the same, and his scent, and the heat of his body against hers. She slid her palms beneath his shirt. His skin was warm. Their lips met.

I do not know—no one ever asked them—what Iyadur Atani and his wife said to one another that day. Surely there were questions, and answers. Surely there were tears, of sorrow and of joy.

He told her of his travels, of his captivity, and of his freedom. She told him of their sons, particularly of his heir, Avahir, who ruled Dragon's Country.

"He is a good lord, respected throughout Ryoka. His people fear him and love him. He is called the Azure Dragon. He married a girl from Issho. She is cousin to the Talvela; we are at peace with them, and with the Nyo. She and Avahir have a son, Hikaru. Jon, too, is wed. He and his wife live in Mako. They have three children, two boys and a girl. You are a grandfather."

He smiled at that. Then he said, "Where is my son?"

"In Kameni, at a council called by Rowan Imorin, the king's war leader, who wished to lead an army against the Chuyo pirates." She stroked his face. It was not true, as she had first thought, that he was unchanged. The years had marked him. Still, he looked astonishingly young. She wondered if she seemed old to him.

"Never leave me again," she said.

A shadow crossed his face. He lifted her hands to his lips and kissed them, front and back. Then he said, "My love, I would not. But I must go. I cannot stay here."

"What are you saying?"

"Avahir is lord of this land now. You know the dragon-nature. We are jealous of power, we dragons. It would go ill were I to stay."

Joanna's blood chilled. She did know. The history of the dragon-folk is filled with tales of rage and rivalry: sons strive against fathers, brothers against brothers, mothers against their children. They are bloody tales. For this reason, among others, the dragon kindred do not live very long.

She said steadily, "You cannot hurt your son."

"I would not," said Iyadur Atani. "Therefore I must leave."

"Where will you go?"

"I don't know. Will you come with me?"

She locked her fingers through his huge ones and smiled through tears. "I will go wherever you wish. Only give me time to kiss my grandchild and write a letter to my son. For he must know that I have gone of my own accord."

And so, Iyadur Atani and Joanna Torneo Atani left Atani Castle. They went quietly, without fuss, accompanied by neither man nor maidservant. They went first to Mako, where Iyadur Atani greeted his younger son and met his son's wife, and their children.

From there they went to Derrenhold, and from Derrenhold, west, to Voiana, the home of the Red Hawk sisters. From Voiana, letters came to Avahir Atani and to Jon Atani from their mother, assuring them, and particularly Avahir, that she was with her husband, and that she was well.

Avahir Atani, who truly loved his mother, flew to Voiana. But he arrived to find them gone.

"Where are they?" he asked Jamis Delamico, who was still matriarch of the Red Hawk clan. For the Red Hawk sisters live long.

"They left."

"Where did they go?"

Jamis Delamico shrugged. "They did not tell me their destination, and I did not ask."

There were no more letters. Over time, word trickled back to Dragon Keep that they had been seen in Rowena, or Sorvino, or Secca, or the mountains north of Dale.

"Where were they going?" Avahir Atani asked, when his servants came to him to tell him these stories. But no one could tell him that.

Time passed; Ippa prospered. In Dragon Keep, a daughter was born to Avahir and Geneva Atani. They named her Lucia. She was small and dark-haired and feisty. In Derrenhold and Mako and Mirrinhold, memories of conflict faded. In the windswept west, the folk of Serrenhold rebuilt their lord's tower.

In the east, Rowan Imorin, the war leader of Kameni, summoned the lords of all the provinces to unite against the Chuyo pirates. The lords of Ippa, instead of quarreling with each other, joined the lords of Nakase and Kameni. They fought many battles. They gained many victories.

But in one battle, not the greatest, an arrow shot by a Chuyo archer sliced into the throat of Avahir Atani, and killed him. Grimly, his mourning soldiers made a pyre and burned his body. For the dragon-kindred do not lie in earth.

Hikaru, the Shining Dragon, became lord of Dragon Keep. Like his father and his grandfather before him, he was feared and respected throughout Ippa.

One foggy autumn, a stranger arrived at the gates of Dragon Keep, requesting to see the lord. He was an old man with silver hair. His back was stooped, but they could see that he had once been powerful. He bore no sword, but only a knife with a bone hilt.

"Who are you?" the servants asked him.

"My name doesn't matter," he answered. "Tell him I have a gift for him."

They brought him to Hikaru. Hikaru said, "Old man, I am told you have a gift for me."

"It is so," the old man said. He extended his palm. On it sat a golden brooch, fashioned in the shape of a rose. "It is an heirloom of your house. It was given by your grandfather, Iyadur, to his wife Joanna, on their wedding night. She is dead now, and so it comes to you. You should give it to your wife, when you wed."

Frowning, Hikaru said, "How do you come by this thing? Who are you? Are you a sorcerer?"

"I am no one," the old man replied, "a shadow."

"That is not an answer," Hikaru said, and he signaled to his soldiers to seize the stranger.

But the men who stepped forward to hold the old man found their hands passing through empty air. They hunted through the castle for him, but he was gone. They decided that he was a sorcerer, or perhaps the sending of a sorcerer. Eventually they forgot him. When the shadow of the dragon first appeared in Atani Castle, rising like smoke out of the castle walls, few thought of the old man who had vanished into shadow one autumnal morning. Those who did kept it to themselves. But Hikaru Atani remembered. He kept the brooch and gave it to his wife upon their wedding night. And he told his soldiers to honor the shadow-dragon when it came, and not to speak lightly of it.

"For clearly," he said, "it belongs here."

The shadow of the dragon still lives in the walls of Atani Castle. It comes as it chooses, unsummoned. And still, in Dragon's Country, and throughout Ippa and Issho, and even into the east, the singers tell the story of Iyadur Atani, of his wife, Joanna, and of the burning of Serrenhold.

L. E. Modesitt *is equally at home in the worlds of fantasy and science fiction. Recent books include* Ecolitan Prime *and* The Ethos Effect. *His* Spellsong Cycle, *which numbered five books, concerned wizardry emerging from music.*

For the present project he contributes a nifty tale concerning . . . well, read the title.

FALLEN ANGEL

L. E. Modesitt, Jr.

Jaweau was sitting in the big white chair behind his desk when I walked in. The desk is white. Everything is, except for some of the chairs, and yet it's not blinding. "You are always welcome, Lucian, even if you never bother knocking. . . ."

"Stow it. You always know I'm coming."

He nodded in that phony sad manner of his, like he wanted to be the forgiving male counterpart of the Maid. "We know, Lucian."

I took the black oak chair, the one he kept for me. Two others were gray, the rest white. All sorts came to see Jaweau, but not many who weren't white. That was why I was there. "What's the job?"

"Real estate. We need an attraction spell for the new villas beyond the Elysian Gardens. Aesthetic and ecological balance, you know?"

"An attraction spell for what angels should want to do naturally?"

"Goodness does not equal wisdom, Lucian," he

pointed out. "Nor, as you have repeatedly proved, does wisdom equate to goodness."

"So you're calling me in?"

"I thought we should have something with depth and staying power. I even thought you might reconsider—"

"Never." Once had been enough. More than enough.

"Never is a long time."

I ignored that possibility. "An appeal to young angels, cherubim, mothers, that sort of thing?" I had to sneer. Even saints and angels retained some cupidity.

"No . . . the full spectrum. Draw in the seraphim, too." Jaweau shrugged as only an angel could shrug, resigned without being cynical.

"Muckin' Maid!" An attraction spell for cherubim and seraphim, and Jaweau and his crew of goody-goodies looked down on me?

"Don't swear. If I have to clean the place, it comes off your fee. I told you—"

I was still pissed. A full-spectrum attraction spell, for the dark's due! "You want to pay for that? Do you know what that means? You need a priestess—twice—stable holy water, a virgin singer, and I'll have to be celibate the whole time until I write the song. I can't do crap else if I take the job. That's a thousand golds, minimum."

"Well . . . that would just about take care of what you owe. . . ." Jaweau smiled sweetly, the white creep. "Besides, you're always celibate here, unless you do a resonance spell. What choice do you have?"

He was stating a fact, and I ignored it. "Owe! Maid be damned . . ."

He raised his right hand, and the light gathered at his fingertips. "I warned you."

"I'm sorry." The bastard had me. One dose of his goody-goodies, and I'd be worthless for days. I can't afford that much of what everyone else calls holiness, not and remain sane. How Jaweau does it is beyond me. I mean, how can a guy who looks like an angel, and *is* one, run both Ciudad Eternidad and the only ad agency in the city? Well, someone has to, and it has to be an angel. All they let us do is be consultants. There are some things they just can't do. Like disease-killing . . . they can't even destroy a tiny bacterium . . . or deep attraction spells.

I shifted my weight in the black chair and looked toward him. He was waiting for me to talk. Of course, I couldn't stare him down. That would have set the whole place on fire, and I couldn't afford to pay that off, either. And I'd have a headache for months, after I lost the job and woke up a month later. The opposites bit, again. "All right. How good does it have to be?"

"You do this one right, and we'll call it even. You can stay away from here forever, if you want."

"I occasionally like to come up here and look around. It's worth seeing to understand why I prefer Hel." I paused. "Besides, it upsets you. You really don't want me around, do you? Gets them asking questions."

Jaweau shrugged again. He didn't have to admit anything, but I could tell I was getting on his nerves. Maybe I reminded him of the old days too much.

"Give me a couple of days," I finally said. "I didn't plan on two songs."

"You can do the dark side in a couple of hours." Jaweau let a halo circle that golden hair. He always did have an eye for effects.

"That's the easy part. You think it's easy for me to write a virgin song, even for a fallen angel?"

"I always admitted you were an artist, Lucian de-Noir—"

"Don't say it."

"You comprehend the fallen. I still don't understand. . . ."

"You never will." I stood up. "You'll know when the songs are ready."

He nodded. "The skies will weep . . . again."

Such dragon crap, and he believes it. All the damned angels and saints do because he does.

I left as quickly as I could, and I sure as Hel didn't look in his eyes. Once I had trusted him, but you know where trusting an angel leads. I'm sure the bastard used his web of light to remove any traces of skepticism I'd left behind.

My villa was the same as always, the same low hill, the same as when—I try not to think about it, but I'm sure Jaweau leaves it that way just to remind me. The painting of the Maid still hangs over the couch in the workroom. The harps are gone, but I don't need them anyway. I poured a goblet of water—that's the one drink I can have in Ciudad Eternidad without risk. Then I sat down, the Maid looking over my shoulder.

Writing the song for the dark side of the resonance spell took a couple of hours. That was after it took me three days to write the piece for the singer, and the white song had to come first. With all the crap about grace, they have to turn to me to write a true white song. The Maid has a sense of irony, all right.

I have to finish on the dark side, or I'd start believing in all that crap about grace and forgiveness, and I don't ever want to believe that again.

It was cloudy when I finished, but that was my legacy. Jaweau can be a real bastard. At least it was done. I sealed both folios, one with white wax, the other with black, and made my way back to Jaweau's. I walked deliberately.

He met me outside the big chamber, and I suppose his eyes were sad, but I didn't look.

"Who's the singer?" Not that I really cared, though I'd have to before the spell was set and twisted.

"Name's Kyralyn. The blonde by the pentagram."

"All right." I didn't look at her or at the three angels who carried the harps. The singer carried her own. She had to, of course, since the strings were different.

The dark drummer was Khango. I'd worked with him before. Solid, but really didn't care much so long as he could work. He was naturally dark. Some are.

"Are you going to check her out?" Jaweau held the web between his hands, and the light cascaded along the strings.

I lifted a hand, and he stepped back.

"Keep your black hands off my webs, Lucian."

"Then don't tell me when to check out the singers." I grinned, but he didn't grin back. I took a deep breath and looked at the singer, really looked, and not through his web, either.

She stared back with eyes as blue and deep as Eden, blue over the tears of a fallen angel. I almost wanted to turn away, but, what the Hel, it was her choice. No one had made her do what she had, and, if she wanted to sing the spell, that was her choice, too.

Except it wasn't, and we both knew it. And neither of us could say so. In some ways, Jaweau is an angelic sadist.

One of the angels smiled sadly over a golden harp, and I wanted to paste him, not that it would have done any good, just would have confirmed his opinion of me.

People think working a resonance spell is like similarity or contagion. That's dragon crap, not that there've ever been dragons, but dark mages—that's what I think of myself as, anyway, no matter what the holies call me—are supposed to believe in the unbelievable. More crap.

A resonance spell is a lot trickier, because you've got to have a virgin song, sung by a virgin singer—not pure, but virgin—and then you've got to twist it so that it resonates. The twist's the thing, a betrayal of the first two. I didn't like it, but we all do things we don't like.

"Let's get on with it."

"As you wish." Jaweau moved the web, and a line of fire flared around the pentagram.

I stepped into the pentagram, and Jaweau closed the gap with the light web. Kyralyn stood at the focal point of the pentagram, on the lines, but not breaking them, and opened the folio. White wax crumpled to the floor. No one else had seen the song, and she couldn't even open the folder until I was held inside the pentagram, not if the spell were to resonate properly.

Khango sat on a black stool between the two base points of the pentagram. After Kyralyn broke the seal on her folder, he opened his. The black wax melted in dark flames. His black sticks hovered above the drums, waiting for Kyralyn to begin.

She studied at the notes, and time froze. Finally, her fingers touched the silver harp strings. The angels used gold, but Kyralyn was still a fallen angel and only a virgin technically, thanks to Jaweau. He'll bend the rules when he wants to, the sanctimonious bastard.

I waited behind the white lines of the pentagram.

Kyralyn began.

Hel, could she sing! I might have heard better in the

time since . . . but I didn't recall when. She was so good
that the faint cloak of darkness that had surrounded
her, the one that probably only Jaweau and I could see,
seemed to lighten as she sang, almost vanishing. As she
shimmered toward the white, Khango continued weaving the counterpoint, and the darkness gathered around
the base of the pentagram. Even before she finished, the
chamber was resonating.

Although I had written the notes and words, when
Kyralyn sang them, I forgot them, and that was as it
should be. No one else would remember them either,
nor the black counterpoint sung by the dark drummer.

As the song and countersong shivered to a close, I
wiped my forehead. It was hot in the pentagram,
damned hot, as always.

Outside the pentagram, Jaweau and the others
squirmed, as if the resonance were the beat of an unheard dance that picked at them. The whole chamber
echoed with the unheard songspell, the resonance lingering, waiting for the next phase, and for the priestess.
We all waited. I certainly couldn't do anything else.

The good mothers like to make you wait and squirm,
to realize exactly what you've done. That unset resonance even twisted my guts as I watched for the door to
open. Finally, the priestess stepped into the chamber.
Actually, it was a chapel, since you don't mess with
things like resonance spells in any other place, not if you
want to keep a whole soul in your body. I might belong
to the depths, but even I don't like the thought of spending eternity rent into burning fragments, and the Maid
has never been that merciful to those of us who harbor
darkness.

The priestess didn't waste any time, either, starting
right out with the familiar words. "Dearly beloved . . ."

When she got to the part about redemption through love, I looked down. After that, she avoided looking at me, and her eyes kept straying to Kyralyn.

I watched Kyralyn's eyes, too. They were a deep open blue, the honest kind you don't associate with fallen angels, and I wondered how exactly she had betrayed herself, not that what I was doing was any better, even if everyone knew it was necessary. I mean, you do have to set the spell, and no one was going to let me out of the pentagram unbound. The ceremony binds the power between us, and the twist locks it back into the rune rods that Jaweau had already placed out beyond the Elysian Gardens.

The good mother did the shortest ceremony possible, ending up with the traditional pronouncement about not putting asunder what the Maid hath joined, and once our hands touched across the pentagram, and the silver rings flared their linked fires, Jaweau opened the pentagram. I shivered. I couldn't help it.

Kyralyn didn't. Those open blue eyes held so much pain that I had to look away. Me . . . I had to look away. Figure that, and over a resonance spell.

I swallowed, and stepped across the pentagram. It still hurt, even after Jaweau erased the light.

Kyralyn turned to me. Tears should have been falling from those eyes, but they were as clear as old-time skies. She actually stepped toward me until we were perhaps three paces apart. She licked her lips, but her eyes met mine.

"You're Lucian—"

"Please don't say it. You don't have to."

"All right." Her speaking voice was a trace husky, unlike the silver tones that had set the spell.

I drew her to me, gently, with both hands. Her hands

touched my waist, and my fingers traced the fine line of her chin. In time, I looked her full in the face, and my eyes burned as they met hers. Even if she were just a singer, that made her, after all, a fallen angel, and that's hard. Especially for me, no matter what anyone says.

I took her arm, and we made our way from the chapel toward my villa. We had to walk, because nothing in Ciudad Eternidad would carry me.

Her eyes widened as we neared the open gate, and the villa beyond, far more graceful and beautiful, still, than any other structure in the city. "I didn't . . . realize. . . ."

"He was merciful . . ." I temporized.

"I wouldn't call it that." Her tone was thoughtful, but her steps matched mine as we crossed the line of black marble between the gateposts and walked to the low steps leading to the portico.

Once we reached the room with the balcony, I offered her water. That was all. I didn't want to tempt her, although it would have been technically fair. She could have refused, but I like to play it straight, unlike Jaweau.

She took the water, looked at it, and then slowly sipped it.

In time, she let me undress her, and I was gentle.

For a while, I even forgot.

Later, I told her, "I do love you."

"You can't." Her words were sad, even as her hands drew me closer. "You belong to . . ."

I forced myself to meet her eyes. "I can't lie here. Everything I say in Ciudad Eternidad must be true." That is absolutely true, so far as it goes. I cannot lie in any city of the saints or angels. And I did love her, absolutely, as those deep, innocent eyes cut through me. Not that it mattered. Nothing had changed, except for those moments when I held a fallen angel, and they came to an end too soon.

When she finally slept, I eased away from her crumpled form and watched the boreali. Then I went down to my workroom and looked at the Bucelli painting for a long time. Maybe there were other universes where it had turned out differently. Maybe.

Morning came, and eventually Kyralyn walked down the stairs, wearing the white gown. She deserved that, and it looked good on her.

I didn't let her say a word. "You can pick up the papers at the priestess's after the Sabbath. I even paid gold for an annulment, not a lousy twenty pieces of silver for a divorce." I had to be the one who paid for the betrayal, of course, or the resonance wouldn't stay set.

Her eyes glistened for a moment, like silver, I'd say . . . if I were the poetic sort. Then she looked at the painting of the Maid, the one by Bucelli that shows Her before the judges, just before they crucified Her. I had Merleno duplicate it. The spell cost a good ten golds, but it was worth it then, more so now. He captured the innocence in her eyes, the way no one else did. Sort of like Kyralyn's, I guess.

"You don't mean it." Kyralyn looked at me again, like the first time after the resonance set in us, and my eyes still burned.

"You were a great lay, Kyralyn, and we did one Hel of a resonance spell. But that's all I can give you." I looked down at the black tabletop—all the furniture got darker when I stayed at the villa for very long. She was already shimmering a bit, and the annulment hadn't even been entered. I knew I'd never do another resonance as good. Too bad the spell doesn't work unless there's betrayal.

"You don't mean it," she repeated. "You don't have to do this."

But I did. Or Jaweau would have everything. "Like I said, you were a great lay." I didn't meet her eyes. Instead I looked back at the copy of the Bucelli. Damn, Merleno had done a fine job.

The workroom was silent, but I refused to look into those eyes. If I had, I'd have been thinking about . . . never mind.

When I finally looked up, Kyralyn was gone.

You've redeemed your soul, Kyralyn. The saints will be pleased. I wasn't sure Jaweau would be, and that pleased me.

Business is business, I guess. But I even envied the pain in Kyralyn's eyes.

I sat down in the wooden chair at the oak table and looked at the portrait of the Maid for a long time. Perhaps I really looked at the Maid, but all I saw was Kyralyn. What else could I do? It was time to head back to Hel, until Jaweau or someone else needed me. Jaweau would, again, sooner or later.

He always does.

Trish Cacek has won both a Bram Stoker and a World Fantasy Award *for her short fiction, some of which has been collected in* Leavings, *as well as a mini-collection,* In the Spirit.

She is currently working on the second of four books called The New Hope Quartet, *set, she says,* "in the very real and very haunted township of New Hope, Pennsylvania."

THE FOLLOWING

P. D. Cacek

The stones moved.

The soft clatter of one stone tumbling over another was almost lost in the rustle of leaves. It was such an ordinary sound—the sound of feet walking on stone—and one she'd gotten used to over the years. So many years now that she didn't even bother to look back over her shoulder.

Besides, she knew what she'd see.

Nothing. The path would be empty, but the stones would still move as though shuffled by invisible feet.

It was amazing what a person could get used to, Lydia thought.

When they had to.

Crash. "Mitch!"

It was the tone of panic in her voice, more than the sound of shattering glass, that jerked Mitchell out of the last play of a doubleheader and sent him running toward the upstairs bedroom they'd shared for just over two months.

He'd been expecting something to happen. And hoping to God that it wouldn't.

The house had been quiet for almost four days—a new, all-time record—which was almost long enough to convince him that the thumps and moans and flickering lights, which couldn't be fixed no matter how many electricians checked the wiring, was just the house settling. Just the house getting used to being lived in again after standing empty for so long.

Thump—crash.

Just the house.

"Mitch!"

Mitchell bumped the doorjamb as he ran into the room, but the pain barely registered when he saw the remains of the antique-reproduction cheval mirror on the unmade bed. The rosewood frame was splintered in a half-dozen places and the glass shattered. Silvered fragments lay among the rumpled blankets like razor-sharp snowflakes.

"Damn," he whispered. He'd bought the mirror as a "Moving-In Day" present for the woman who was currently cowering in the narrow opening between the dresser and wall. "What did you do?"

He realized how stupid that question sounded right after he said it. She probably hadn't done anything.

Debra glared at him from over the top of her clasped, white-knuckled hands. The two Army Surplus duffle bags she'd moved in with were packed and sitting at her feet. There were shards of mirrored glass embedded in the faded olive-green canvas.

"I didn't touch it, Mitch," she said, anger replacing fear as she confirmed what he already suspected. "It just broke."

"Things just don't break, Debra. There's always a reason for everything that happens."

He tried to make himself believe that as he walked over to the bed and brushed the tips of his fingers lightly over a large shard of mirror that had remained in the frame. *Christ.* He wasn't aging well. Only thirty-seven, and he already looked like a man pushing fifty ... and a nondescript man of fifty at that—gaunt, medium build, slightly stooped at the shoulders. Gray of hair and face and eyes, as unremarkable as air. Mitchell still couldn't understand what Debra had ever seen in him, except equity and a solid line of credit at most of the stores in town.

Mitchell shook his head at the bitter old man in the broken glass. That wasn't fair—Debra had stayed with him longer than any of his other lovers.

Two months and almost three weeks.

Another record.

It just wasn't fair.

He pressed down on the glass and felt a sharp sting. There was a smear of blood on the mirror when he moved his hand away.

"You don't believe me?"

Mitchell blinked as he looked up. It was strange, but he'd almost forgotten she was still there.

"Yeah, sure I do. I'm sorry. Look, I really don't want you to go, okay? I mean, it's ... this, all of this has a reasonable explanation. Come on, I'll help you unpack."

She was about to say something poignant—they'd been together just long enough for him to be able to tell that by the way she sucked air into her mouth ... but the house beat her to it.

There was a low rumble in the walls and then a flutter of air through the old heating ducts sounded like laughter. Mitchell looked down at the broken mirror and watched his reflection go a little grayer.

"Mitch?"

He didn't look up.

"Oh God, Mitch. Don't tell me you didn't hear that."

His reflection shrugged.

"It's just a draft. Old houses are drafty, you know that."

"And was it a draft that yanked the mirror out of my hands when I tried to move it?"

That finally made him look up. Debra's face was still pale, but there were growing spots of color in both her cheeks.

"I thought you said you didn't touch it."

The spots of color spread rapidly across her face, deepening it to a ghastly shade of red. She looked like she was about to have a stroke. Mitchell knew he should be worried about that. God knows he didn't want her to die . . . not in the house anyway.

He didn't have a choice.

"Look, maybe you're right, we're both on edge, so maybe it would be better if you left." He looked down at the duffle bags so he wouldn't have to look at her. "For a while. I'll carry these out to the car for you."

He was careful not to get any blood on the canvas handles when he picked up the bags.

"There are some things in the bathroom," Mitchell said, daring a peek as she stood up. He shouldn't have, but he stared at the interplay of muscles in her calves and thighs and remembered how her legs had felt wrapped around the small of his back when they made love. Just last night. "Do you need a box for those, or do you want to leave them?"

He wanted to add *"for when you come back"* but couldn't make himself say it. He hadn't been able to say it to any of his other lovers when they left.

The house settled, without warning, and the framed Georgia O'Keeffe print over the bed crashed to the floor.

"There!" She screamed as she ran out of the bedroom and down the hall, her voice trailing behind her like a contrail. "You saw that! You can't tell me you didn't see that. This place is haunted, Mitch! I kept telling you it's haunted, but you wouldn't listen!"

Her voice already sounded so far away.

Mitchell picked up the bags and followed the trail of sound to the front hall. She was standing just outside the open door, a video clutched in her hands, her natural hemp bag slung over one shoulder. The look in her eyes was almost as far away as the sound of her voice.

"I don't know why you just won't admit it, Mitch, but you know as well as I do that there's . . . something in this house. You've lived here longer than I have, you must know that."

Mitchell stood in the front hall of his house and rolled his shoulders. They were beginning to ache from the weight of the bags, and he wondered what of his, if anything, she may have packed. One of his other fiancées had *accidentally* taken one of his old sweatshirts when she moved out, and the house had been upset . . . noisy for a week after.

"It's just an old house," he repeated, low enough for the house to hear, "and old houses make noises and settle and sometimes things fall down and break."

"Goddamn it, Mitch, when are you going to wake up? You're living in a haunted house!" She thrust the video toward him, and Mitchell jerked back, expecting a blow. "Here, I bought this at the shop a week ago and was meaning to give it to you before I . . ." The spots of color on her cheeks deepened again. "You need to watch it.

There's a number you can call at the end. Call her and then call me. I love you, Mitch, but I can't live like this."

He looked at the video's cover and chuckled. Done against a stark black-and-white background, the lurid red letters seemed to float a few inches above the plastic case: *A Step into the Unknown—Conversations with Lydia Light, Ghost Exterminator.* Mitchell tightened his grip on the handles so he wouldn't be tempted to take the video and toss it out the open door. Debra was always bringing things like this home from her job at the Crystalline Moon New Age Shoppe. Mitchell hadn't minded the scented candles or incense, and he was almost getting used to the mind-thawing tones she called music, but this was too much.

"You're kidding," he asked hopefully, "right?"

The color faded again, like someone throwing a switch, and she set the video down on the small hall table before walking out the front door and down the steps.

Mitchell followed, down the steps and out to her car, then stood there, bags in hand, and waited for her to unlock the trunk, waited for her to tell him she was kidding. When she didn't say anything, he hoisted the bags into the clutter of jumper cables, yellowed receipts and empty soda cans.

Debra's hand closed over his as he closed the trunk.

The front door of the house slammed shut. The wind was coming in the opposite direction. She pulled her hand away.

"Call me when it's gone," was all Debra said as she climbed into her dusty little economy car and drove away. Mitchell stood on the curb and watched until the taillights disappeared into the evening shadows. Like a ghost.

"Ghosts aren't real," he whispered.

And the air in the ducts laughed at him when he opened the door.

Lydia hadn't bothered to cut the grass at the edge of the path, hoping the hard, early frosts that had already reduced the tomato and pole bean vines to little more than tattered yellow scraps would do the job for her. And that had been a mistake.

With the stones, she could pretend it was just the wind, just errant gusts playing landscape designer. It was harder to pretend though, when the wall of autumn-dry grass was pushed aside, step by step by invisible step.

So many of them. There were so many of them.

For a moment as she climbed the stairs to the back porch, she thought she could almost see them. Almost recognize a face or two. Or twelve.

"I'm sorry," she whispered, letting the wind carry the words back to them. "I'm so sorry."

Mitchell jumped when the man answered the phone.

For some reason, even though he didn't know why, he thought she'd answer, saying: "Lydia Light, Ghost Exterminator." The first time he watched the video, he alternated between incredulous laughter and genuine bafflement that anyone could have actually believed any of the things the overly fawning host (*"—our favorite guest—wonderful woman—emissary of light in the world of darkness—"*) was saying about the flamboyant ebony-haired woman in flowing robes (*"—I don't know why I can do this, but I capture souls—have all my life—extermination is guaranteed—"*). After the second view he wasn't laughing as much. And when he finished watching the video a third time, Mitchell wrote down the out-of-state Help Line Number and listened to the house thump the walls around him.

"Hello?"

Mitchell had no memory of either walking to the phone or dialing up the number on the piece of paper in his hand. It was stupid; he didn't believe in things like that. He was too rational, too sensible and living in a house that was just too old. That's all. Old houses creaked and thumped and sometimes things fell off walls. That's all it was. To think it was anything else was . . . pathetic.

But he still jumped when the man answered.

"Um, hello?"

"I think—" Mitchell took a deep breath. *This was so stupid, why am I doing this?* "I think I . . . I mean . . ."

"Yes?"

"Nothing. Sorry. Wrong number." *Which it probably is . . . the video is from a show that aired almost twenty years ago. Lydia Light could be dead now for all I know.*

"No problem."

The line went dead, and Mitchell stood there, the handset still to his ear—listening to the white noise static while the house moaned and gibbered and settled in for the night.

It's stupid to think that it might be something else.
So stupid.

Keith looked up when she opened the back door, smiling from ear to ear as he nodded to the mound of potato peels on the kitchen table in front of him. A long russet-colored curl unwound from the edge of the paring knife as he worked. It was a little game he liked to play, seeing how long a peel he could cut without it breaking.

He enjoyed his small victories.

It was one of the things she loved most about him.

One of the things she loved least, however, was his inability to judge quantity. It looked like he'd already peeled almost all of the ten-pound sack she thought she'd hidden well enough in the pantry.

"Oh, you've started dinner."

She hoped she sounded more pleased than surprised as she stepped over the sea salt that was laid across the threshold. There were other salt barriers at the threshold of the front door and along the inner ledge of each window. For eighteen years, the length of their marriage, she'd told him that it stopped ants from getting into the house, and he'd believed her.

Never questioned her once about it.

That was another thing she loved about him.

"Shoot," he said, and the smile lines around his mouth suddenly changed directions. "I guess I forgot to tell you."

Lydia Terrell unwound the knitted scarf from around her neck and draped it over the back of one of the kitchen chairs. She didn't want to spend the rest of the evening mentally adding and subtracting his faults and virtues, so she made herself think of nothing as she slipped out of her barn coat and rubbed her hands together to warm them.

"So tell me now."

"I said we'd bring the potato salad for the Friends of the Library potluck tomorrow night."

We? she wanted to ask. Looking at the hillock of peeled potatoes that still had to be cut, boiled, and lovingly mixed into the concoction of mayonnaise, brown mustard, paprika, diced onions, celery and pickles that had won her blue ribbons at every county fair within driving distance, Lydia unconsciously began flexing the stiffness out of her fingers. The early frost had been as hard on her arthritis as it had been on the tomato vines.

"I thought that was Saturday night."

Keith's frown deepened between his hazel-green eyes as the russet-colored peel broke and fell to the table. "No, I'm pretty sure it was Friday. I think."

Lydia had worked most of the stiffness out of her fingers by the time she reached the phone in the hall.

"I'll call Bernice and double-check," she called over her shoulder. "One nice thing about potato salad, it can't go bad as long as you keep it cold—Oh."

She cocked her head and pressed the phone closer to her ear. The normal bumblebee hum was missing, and in its place was the soft, but recognizable sound of someone breathing.

"Hello?"

The steady breathing changed into a ragged gasp.

"Hello?" she repeated. "Is someone there?"

Silence now, not even the hint of breath. Lydia shook her head. Every one of her instincts told her to hang up, hang up now—hang up right now and start making that potato salad. All the real-life police shows Keith watched on TV said the same thing when it came to suspicious phone calls: Hang up. *Do it. Hang up.*

"Um," a man's voice said, "I'm looking for a Lydia Light? I got this number from an old video."

Lydia sat down on the chair next to the phone. *Too late.* There was a rawness to the man's voice like an open wound; she couldn't hang up without at least hearing him out.

"This is the Terrell household," she said, hoping the truth would set her free, then added softly, "I'm Lydia."

A sigh whispered through the lines, and Lydia closed her eyes.

"I—uh, first let me just say that I don't believe in ghosts."

"Then why did you call?"

When the line went silent again, she opened her eyes and looked down the hall to the kitchen. Keith was still peeling potatoes, whistling a song that had been popular back in the Summer of Love, when they were both kids and reality was something that could be toyed with and changed if you believed hard enough and toked the right controlled substance. Lydia smiled when he looked up to wink and grab another potato. For Keith, reality lay on the table in front of him—she'd be up most of the night making potato salad. For her, reality was the phone in her hand.

"I called," the man finally said, "because . . . a friend of mine thinks there may be something . . . otherworldly going on in my house and I thought . . . my friend thought that you might be able to help. She, my friend, gave me a video of a show you did a while back and—Damn . . . sorry."

"That's all right," Lydia said, getting to her feet. "Anger's a powerful emotion. Stay angry and keep your disbelief. Sometimes that helps."

"But—the host of the show, the man who interviewed you said you can . . . that *if* a house is haunted you can—"

"He died."

"What?"

"Alan Wineberg, the interviewer. He died a few years ago." Lydia shook the memory away. She'd known he was dead before she read about it in the paper. He'd tapped at the kitchen window while she was drying dishes. "I'm sorry, that's an old video, and I'll tell you what I tell everyone: I don't do that sort of thing anymore. Good-bye and good luck."

The man was starting to say something, something beyond the "No, wait, please," when she replaced the receiver and walked back to the kitchen. She'd done those shows almost twenty-five years ago, back when she thought her talent was a blessing instead of a curse, and hadn't thought about them since . . . until, five Halloweens ago when she started getting calls. Some video junkie had found the old tapes of the *A Step into the Unknown* series and remastered them for modern equipment. Since then, for a week each year around Halloween, Lydia was again bombarded by requests for *ghost exterminations,* radio interviews and personal appearances at horror conventions and metaphysical bookstore openings. Could she appear on talk shows devoted to the paranormal? Would she be interested in being in a documentary about real-life hauntings? Could she *please* help?

Even if the caller, like the man she'd just hung up on, didn't believe in ghosts.

Kevin stopped whistling as he tossed the last peeled potato into the clear glass bowl. The ones on the bottom were already beginning to go brown. She'd have to soak them in cold water before boiling them.

"Well," he asked with the air of a man who'd just accomplished a great thing, "is the potluck tomorrow or Saturday?"

Lydia frowned until she realized what he was talking about. The phone call—she was supposed to have been on the phone with Bernice. She gave him one of her well-rehearsed befuddled looks, and it worked like a charm.

As it always did.

"You forgot to ask."

She shrugged her shoulders.

"Just like a woman, you start talking about one thing and forget the other. That's why it's men who go to war." He winked and she chuckled. It was a good marriage, all things considered. "Want me to call her back?"

"No," Lydia said, turning back toward the phone. "I'll do it. You start running cold water on those potatoes."

"Me?" He seemed genuinely shocked that she'd ask him to help beyond the peeling stage.

"You. And if I'm on the phone longer than five minutes, you come rescue me."

That he could do and he nodded.

Lydia waited until she heard the water running in the sink before picking up the receiver. She didn't know what she'd say if the man was still on the phone—*Go away, leave me alone, the video is ancient history. I don't do that anymore. What? All right, I'll be right there, but I have to warn you*—and almost felt faint with relief when she heard the bumblebee hum of an unconnected line.

Thank God.

Bernice answered on the second ring. "Ya-ho?"

"Hi, Bernice, it's Lydia. Is the potluck Friday or Satur—"

"Oh, Lydia! Wow, talk about ESP—I was just thinking about you. I know Keith said you two would be bringing potato salad, but I was wondering—oh, it's Saturday, hon, I tried to push for Friday since I have Melanie's dance recital Saturday morning and I know I'll be an absolute wreck even before the dinner, but the committee voted for Saturday—and, like I was saying, I know you and Keith want to bring potato salad, but I was wondering if I could persuade you into bringing something else? See, Nell, Jean and Steffie are *all* bringing potato salad—talk about not coordinating, huh—and frankly that's two too many, if you get my meaning. Not that I don't *love* potato salad but—"

Lydia sat down hard enough to make the back of the chair knock against the wall, but not loud enough for Keith to hear over the sound of running water and come to the rescue. She was doomed, doomed.

"So, you wouldn't mind, would you? I thought maybe something along the lines of finger food. Oh, you know the sort of thing, small things people can just—"

"Eat with their fingers," Lydia slipped in quickly, "like potato pancakes."

"Yes, or something with a little less starch. I mean we have all that potato salad, and I wouldn't want people to think—"

Lydia closed her eyes and prayed for release.

Mitchell was afraid to close his eyes, even though he knew it was foolish.

It was all Debra's fault. If she hadn't put the idea of ghosts into his head, he wouldn't be standing there right now, wondering about it.

And he sure as hell wouldn't have made that stupid call.

But there was something about the woman's voice on the phone . . . something that made me almost want to believe in—

No! It is stupid. So stupid.

He realized that the moment he'd hung up the phone. But at the same time, the noises he'd always been able to rationally explain away—*air in the pipes, loose floor-boards, wind in the eaves*—had become louder, almost as if the house . . . or something inside the house had been listening to his side of the phone conversation and was angry at what he'd tried to do.

Even though he didn't believe in ghosts.

"There's nothing here," he said out loud to *the nothing* in the house. "It's just an old house and old houses settle."

Something, another picture or maybe the towel rack in the small downstairs half-bath crashed to the floor. Then, one by one, the lights downstairs began to blink out until only the desk lamp next to him remained on.

Mitchell didn't believe in ghosts, never had, but he leaned back in his chair and pressed his elbows hard against his belly as the lamp began to dim. "Stop it! Stop it! *Stop it!*"

Even though.

She can help me. She's the only one in the world who can.

He had to make sure. He had to.

It'd taken him less than twelve hours to find her.

Lydia knew it was her caller from the day before, the one who didn't believe in ghosts, but who nevertheless was slowly walking toward the house. She watched him through the lace pattern on the front curtains. It was impossible for her to tell his age; he looked as gray and ageless as the line of weathered granite stones that designated their property line from the neighboring field. His jeans were wrinkled at the crotch and knees, and there was a ghost image of the seat belt across the front of his windbreaker.

Another ghost, Lydia thought, and was glad Keith had already left for work when she opened the door.

"Mrs. Terrell?" His voice sounded weaker in person than it had over the phone.

Lydia nodded, keeping the salt-laced threshold between them. "How did you find me?"

The man seemed to appreciate the straightforward approach. He smiled his thanks as he exhaled.

"The Internet," he said with a one-shoulder shrug, the smile widening. "Something called switchboard-dot-com. All you have to do is supply a phone number, and it gives you an address. Maps, too."

"Big Brother really is watching," she said, and chuckled when she realized that the man standing in front of her, the man who didn't believe in ghosts, was probably too young to know that the term had once been a rallying cry for her generation, and not just a reference to some book on a high school required reading list. "Sorry, I don't have much use for computers."

The man licked his lips and shifted from one foot to the other like a child who'd had too much sugar or had waited too long to ask to use the bathroom. Lydia gripped the doorknob a little harder and looked over his shoulder. Behind him, the rocks along the edge of the sidewalk shifted ever so slightly. Not much, not even enough to make a sound—but just enough to get her attention.

Sensing an interloper.

"Look, I really don't know why I'm here," he said, "but after we spoke I got the feeling that . . . *if* any of this was real, you could tell me what to do."

The stones shifted again, clicking softly. The man heard it and started to turn around.

Forcing herself to smile, Lydia stepped back to let

him enter. "I have fresh coffee and potato pancakes in the kitchen. Please come in. I'm Lydia."

"Mitchell," the man said, and didn't disturb so much as a grain of salt as he walked into her home.

The rocks tumbled over each other as she closed the door.

It was almost too incredible to believe it was really happening.

Here he was, three hours and almost two hundred miles away from everything he knew, or thought he knew, sitting in a stuffy, overheated kitchen with a woman he'd just met, a woman his mother's age, eating potato pancakes and talking about ghosts as if they were nothing more than stubborn laundry stains.

He couldn't remember ever being happier.

Lydia was an incredible woman.

"Another?" she asked, and although his stomach was frantically waving the white flag of surrender, he nodded and held out his plate. He'd eat until he burst if that's what she wanted.

Lydia was topping off both their coffee mugs as he forced another crisp forkful into his mouth.

"You either love potato pancakes or you're being incredibly gallant," she said as she set an old-fashioned burp-percolator down on the table between them. Mitchell studied her hands while she added milk and sugar to the blue stoneware mug on her side of the table. Her fingers were red and chapped, cold despite the room's stuffiness. It hurt him to see that and all he wanted to do was reach across the table and warm her hands.

But he didn't.

"They're great," he said instead and shoveled in another bite to prove it. "But I don't want to eat you out of house and home."

She laughed as she brought the mug to her lips.

"Believe me, you'd have to stay at least a week before that happened."

Mitchell's hand stopped halfway back to the plate, "What?"

"Nothing." Her smile lingered for a moment longer before fading. "I suppose you've already considered that the things happening in your house may be caused by natural phenomena. Houses settle and—"

"And old houses are notorious for having faulty wiring and air in the pipes, I know." Mitchell suddenly realized what he'd done and licked his lips, tasting salt and potatoes and cooking fat. "God, I'm sorry, I didn't mean for it to come out like that."

"Like what?" she asked, her smile once again obvious above the rim of her mug. He could see the beautiful young woman she'd been and grieved that he hadn't known her then.

"Insulting."

Mitchell held his breath until she shook her head. "You weren't, and it's good to be skeptical. In fact, sometimes it's the only thing that can save you. But you're right, old houses are full of sounds and troubles. This house you're sitting in has its share of sounds and thumps. It's been in my husband's family for seven generations, and there are so many loose timbers in the attic that when the wind comes out of the north you'd think you were standing in the middle of a Maine cornfield for all the rattling that goes on."

Mitchell chuckled politely even though he'd never been in Maine, let alone in a cornfield that he could remember.

"What about ghosts?" he asked, and immediately regretted it. She'd stopped laughing and age swept back over her face.

"You mean in the house?" He nodded. "No, there aren't any ghosts in the house. My husband doesn't believe in ghosts."

"Is that what keeps them out?"

Again, he'd meant it as a joke and, again, he failed. Her smile stayed hidden. She took one, two sips before lowering the mug, but she never moved her eyes away from the oily black-brown surface.

"No." She shook her head and a silver-brown curl danced across the top of one ear. He watched her hand as she brushed it back behind her ear. "But it helps, I think. My husband doesn't believe in anything that he can't see or taste or touch."

And this time Mitchell didn't stop himself. He reached out and took her hand, held it as if he was holding a tiny bird. She trembled once, but didn't pull away.

"It must be hard living with a man like that."

"No," she said, "it's very easy. In fact that's why I married him."

Mitchell shook his head. He didn't even know her husband's name, but he knew the man wasn't worthy of the woman sitting across from him.

"But doesn't he know what you do?"

"I don't *do* anything, Mitchell." She squeezed his hand and pulled away. "I walk into a house that's supposed to be haunted and then leave. There are no smoking mirrors, no incantations, no holy of holies recited."

"But in the interview you said—"

"I said I rid houses of ghosts, but that's not completely true. I don't get rid of ghosts, Mitchell, I collect souls and that's a very different thing, indeed."

It sounded as if she were confessing a terrible sin to him, and him alone. *God, why haven't I ever met a woman like her? Why haven't I met her before this? I can tell she feels comfortable with me.*

"I don't know why or how, but when I walk into a house that's supposed to be haunted, I attract the essence of whatever it is that remains when we die . . . the spirit or soul or . . ." She shrugged and folded her hands around her coffee mug. "A lot of the houses I *cleared* weren't haunted to begin with, but people believe what they want to believe, and see what they want to see. And some people, like you and my husband, don't believe in ghosts at all."

"No!" He suddenly didn't want to be anything like her husband. "I know that's what I said, but I was lying to myself.

"Please, Lydia. I believe in you."

Lydia tightened her grip on the mug, but it only made the small tremor in her hands worse. A drop of coffee sloshed over the rim. *It's started already.*

"Didn't you hear me, Mitchell? I don't exorcize ghosts. . . . I collect souls."

Her uncle's had been the first . . . at least, the first she'd been aware of.

It'd been the morning of her sixth birthday— Funny how she still could remember it. *Her mother had sent her out to the backyard to play while she baked the cake and finished decorating the house. Her mother had told her she wanted it to be a surprise, but Lydia—Liddie then—knew the real surprise was that her uncle Lydon was coming.*

She'd never met the man she was named for, but he was already a legend to her. Uncle Lydon was an "ambassador" and, as far back as Lydia could remember, his exploits and adventures had been her bedtime stories.

And he was coming to her birthday party.

Her friends, who also knew all about the time Brave Uncle Lydon had escaped a Bedouin horde by donning the robes of a humble shepherd, as well as the time Fearless Uncle Lydon had stayed in the embassy to answer the phones when everyone else had fled in terror after an earthquake destroyed most of the city. Lydia forgot the name of the city and what country it was in, but to her, Uncle Lydon was King Arthur, Zorro and Superman rolled into one.

And he was coming to her party!

Even though she wasn't supposed to know. And it was hard to pretend she didn't. But she tried, she really did.

Lydia was picking daisies to put around her cake when the screen door opened and a tall man in a sparkling white linen suit and bright red tie stepped out onto the patio. He was older than Lydia expected, and she was a little disappointed that he wasn't wearing shining armor or a cape, but she ran up to him, arms wide and hands filled with daisies to hug him fiercely around the knees.

"This is your uncle Lydon, Liddie," her mother said from the other side of the screen door. "Surprise."

Lydia squealed and giggled and pretended to be surprised. Until Uncle Lydon bent down and picked her up. And then she didn't have to act surprised. When their eyes met—his were dark like hers, almost the same shade of gray brown—he suddenly trembled and took a deep breath.

Uncle Lydon held his breath for a long time, so long that Lydia thought he'd gotten the hiccups and was hid-

*ing his breath to make them go away. Having a full work-
ing knowledge of hiccups and what did and didn't work,
Lydia was about tell him holding his breath would only
make the hiccups louder, when Uncle Lydon exhaled.*

*And Lydia felt his ghost leave his body and brush past
hers.*

*He was still alive, still holding her and smiling, but she
knew part of him had gone.*

*Lydia knew as much about ghosts as she did about hic-
cups, maybe more. Her daddy had told her about ghosts
when Bows, the cat that had been her companion since
forever, had woken up dead one morning. It'd been scary
to see him in his box, with his eyes wide open and not
breathing, but her daddy had told her that his soul was
up in Kitty Heaven and he was happy. A soul was that
part of a person or animal that you couldn't see, like a
ghost but not scary.*

*So Lydia hadn't been scared of ghosts. Until that mo-
ment, when she felt her uncle's ghost leave his body to
stand next to her.*

*And then she started to scream and kick and get as far
away from the empty eyes and hollow body as she could.*

*"I don't know what's the matter with her," her mother
said as she walked slowly across the patio, "she's usually
a joy."*

*"Oh, she still is," empty Uncle Lydon said as his ghost
shuffled up little dust devils in the dirt. Lydia howled at
the top of her lungs and squeezed her eyes shut. "She's
just not used to strangers, that's all it is. She's a love. A little love. And we're going to have wonderful times together. Don't cry, sweetheart. Don't cry, little angel."*

*"Yes, please don't cry, baby. Look, here's Daddy. If you
cry, you'll make Daddy sad, and you don't want that, do
you?"*

And, unfortunately, Lydia did as she was told and looked at her daddy.

He was holding a yellow HAPPY BIRTHDAY GIRL balloon in his hand and smiling at her through the screen door. His smile was the same as Uncle Lydon's. The same as her mother's. The same droopy half smile—like something, something important inside them had been taken away . . . or lost . . . or stolen.

"What's the matter with my baby?" her father asked.

His smile looked just like Uncle Lydon's. And her mother's. Empty and hollow.

Lydia stopped crying and went limp.

"There." Uncle Lydon laughed. "See, all she needed was a minute to get used to me. Well, now, shall we go in and see what your favorite uncle has brought the birthday girl all the way from Morocco?"

Lydia dropped the daisies and nodded. "That's my girl," her uncle said. "She's such a good girl," her mommy said. "Happy Birthday to you," her daddy sang as he opened the screen door to let them in.

All of them. Including the ghosts.

It'd taken a long time to figure out why she was so "special," and by then it was too late.

"Did you hear what I said?" she asked. "I collect souls."

He nodded, his eyes never leaving her face.

"And you don't care."

He shook his head.

"No," she said, grabbing the percolator as she stood up, "I don't suppose you would now. Well, I'll make more coffee, and you can tell me about your ghost."

He smiled.

It *was* already too late.

* * *

Mitchell told her everything while the steady *plop, plop* of percolating coffee played a soft counterbalance in the background. It was easier than he'd thought it'd be, or maybe it was just the way she'd said it—almost as if she were asking about children. *"Tell me about your children." "Tell me about your ghost."*

It was just so easy to tell her everything, this wonderful woman.

He knew he was falling in love with her long before the coffee stopped perking.

"It sounds like your home is occupied by the ghost of a woman," she said with a certainty that left no room for question, "probably a jealous young woman who sees your girlfriend as a rival for your affections. Does that sound possible?"

Mitchell nodded and watched her hands. He'd discovered she had a habit of twisting the plain gold wedding band she wore when she talked. *Plain gold, unadorned. Probably cheap, probably the only thing her husband could afford when they were married. That was wrong—she deserved more than just a simple gold band and I would have bought her diamonds, if I were her husband.*

She needs a man who believes in her.

"My guess," Lydia said, twisting her ring, "is that as long as you don't have a girlfriend, your house will be quiet."

She needs someone like me.

"So, it's either learn to live alone or—?"

Mitchell reached out and took her hand. "I don't want to live alone."

She needs me.

*   *   *

Lydia unplugged the percolator and carefully dumped the steaming grounds, knowing Keith would forget to do that when he plugged it back in when he got home. He was always forgetting to do that, and then wondering why the coffee tasted bitter.

She smiled, thinking about that, and scribbled a quick note to tell him where she was and to remind him to take the tuna casserole out of the refrigerator unless he wanted potato pancakes for supper. Again.

"How long a drive did you say it was to your place?"

When he didn't immediately answer, Lydia turned to find him staring at her. His eyes were round, like a child's who knew he was about to be abandoned.

"You—you aren't going to spend the night?"

"That won't be necessary, Mitchell."

"But I thought—we could celebrate afterwards."

She shook her head and watched tears begin to form in his eyes. *God, why didn't I try harder to get those damned videos taken off the market?* But it seemed as if for every two video clearing houses she found, another three would spring up. She'd been rediscovered by the newest wave of paranormal enthusiasts. Her following was expanding yearly.

God help them. And her.

"Please?"

"I'm sorry," she whispered, and then tapped the pencil against the piece of paper. "Let's see, you said it was three hours to your house?"

He nodded.

"And three hours back, plus traffic would make it—" Lydia counted the numbers on her fingers to make sure, "five o'clock. I'll tell my husband six, so he won't worry."

Lydia didn't look at him again until she stuck the note

to the refrigerator with the I ❤ YELLOWSTONE magnet Keith had found at a local garage sale. He wasn't big on traveling. Thank God.

Lydia looked straight ahead as she crossed the kitchen to take her coat down from the peg next to the door. Her car keys and wallet were in the left side pocket where they should be.

"All right," she said, opening the door, "shall we go?"

His body remained slumped at the table for a moment, but Lydia felt his spirit brush against her as it hovered at the door's threshold. When he finally stood up and stumbled out into the late morning, Lydia followed, carefully breaking the line of salt with the toe of her shoe so his spirit could follow.

Pretending to drop something, she mended the break and hoped it would be enough. She'd have to remember to fix it when she got home that night.

Keith looked up from his plate of potato pancakes as she stepped into the kitchen and he smiled.

"Hi! I made dinner."

Hanging up her coat, Lydia walked over to the refrigerator and took down the note, crumbling it into the trash before she got down the box of salt. She should have known he wouldn't see the note. He never did.

"Looks good," she said as she walked to the door. "Give me a minute, and I'll join you."

Keith grunted and slapped the bottom of the near-empty bottle of ketchup.

"You didn't go to the market, did you?" he asked.

"No, just visiting a friend."

"Oh. Hey, I got a call while you were out. Jack and Shirley's daughter Peggy just had a new baby."

"That's wonderful." Kneeling, Lydia pried open the metal spout and rebuilt the salt barrier across the doorway. "Is it a boy or girl?"

"Um."

She glanced at him over her shoulder. He shrugged. "Men. Did you at least ask the baby's name?"

"Terry? I think."

Lydia sighed and emptied out the rest of the salt.

"Ants, huh?"

"Yeah, thought I saw some this morning."

Keith smiled and lost interest. That was another thing she loved about him, his easy acceptance of everything she told him. If she'd suddenly decided to tell him the truth, that the salt was a protection against the souls that she'd stolen throughout the years, he would have believed her . . . and then asked if she wanted to rent the new Jackie Chan movie at Blockbuster.

But what she loved most was the fact that she couldn't harm him. He'd lost his soul in the jungles of Vietnam, long before he'd met her.

Mitchell had almost died of embarrassment when they got back to the house. Debra had taped a note to the front door for the whole neighborhood, and Lydia, to see:

CALL ME THE MINUTE YOU GET RID OF GHOST!
I LOVE YOU—D

There was a phone number, to her sister's place, that she'd underlined three times.

He would have crumpled it up and shoved it into his

pocket, forgetting it immediately, if Lydia hadn't commented about it. Told him, with a smile of infinite patience, that he was a very lucky young man.

He agreed with her, he said, but only because she was there with him.

And then her smile had gone away, and soon after that she did, too.

She stayed only a moment, no longer than it took to walk from the front door to the bottom of the staircase and back again, but she touched him on the cheek before she left and said, "I'm so sorry, Mitchell, but if it's any consolation, you won't feel any difference. The house is quiet now, dear. You can make that call now."

Mitchell had nodded, not hearing anything until she called him *dear*. Mitchell couldn't forget that or the touch of her hand against his cheek as he stood next to the phone in the quiet living room of the quiet house. The empty house. His house.

Mitchell twisted the note into a tight coil and used it to light the kindling in the fireplace.

Debra answered on the fourth ring. Breathless. Happy he'd called. Hopeful.

"Hi," he told her, "you can come home now. There's nothing here anymore."

While she yammered in his ear about how happy she was, Mitchell watched the flames curl the note to ash and touched the spot on his cheek where Lydia had touched him.

Lydia grabbed on to the doorjamb with her free hand, but she still heard her knees pop when she stood up. She was getting too old for this.

For *all* of this.

Holding the box of salt against the front of her sweater, Lydia took a deep breath and watched a leaf scurry across the path.

He pushed the others out of the way as she started to close the door. *Wait—don't go. Stay with me. Please.* And for a moment he thought she heard him. Just him, not any of the others who were all talking at once, trying to get her attention. Just him. Mitchell knew he was her favorite. He knew and she knew it, and that's all that mattered. *It's stupid . . . so stupid. Why don't the others go away and leave us alone?*

He would have made it to the porch before the door clicked shut, but he tripped.

And the stones moved.

Dennis L. McKiernan absolutely loves fantasy fiction—first novels were inspired by J. R. R. Tolkien, and his work in that vein continues to this day with such books as Once Upon a Winter's Night *and* Dragondoom.

The story that follows only solidifies his reputation as a modern master of fantasy fiction.

A Tower with No Doors

Dennis L. McKiernan

*When passed from mouth to mouth,
a simple truth oft falls victim.*

Once upon a time not so long ago—that is, if you are an immortal, but incredibly far back in the distant past if you happen to be a mayfly . . . and you, dear mayfly, flitting about as you are, I'll hurry my telling so that you might hear the end, too. Now let me see, where was I? Oh, yes, now I remember—there was a prince, a most handsome prince, who on a golden day went ahunting with his retinue, all of them splendidly arrayed in silks and satins and other such finery, and mounted upon high-stepping steeds, the most glorious of which was the prince's very own wonderful horse. With axes and lances and pearl-handled bows and gilded arrows fletched of peacock tail all glittering in the afternoon sun, toward the woodland they rode, some retainers with falcons awrist or other hooded hawking birds. And just as they entered the deep, dark forest, up jumped a snow-white hart.

" 'Tis mine," called the golden-haired prince, and sounding his silver-belled horn, he spurred swiftly after.

My lord!

My prince!

My liege! cried many, all leaping forward in pursuit as well. *'Ware, for white harts be enchanted!*

But the prince did not hear, and his horse was fleet, and soon the men hindward were lost arear.

But as fast as the prince did ride, the white hart was swifter still. And twisting and veering among the trees, the creature led the prince on a harrowing run. Over sunlit hill and through dimlit vale and up and down crystalline streams did the creature flee before the pursuit, and always just when the prince thought the hart was lost, a clear flash of white did he glimpse running among the dark trees. On they ran and on, and the sun did drift down the sky, until long shadows lay across the woodland as gathering evening drew nigh.

In the green distance behind, the retinue cast about quite 'wildered, for with the hart taking to stream upon stream and running up or down their lengths and emerging across rock ledges to come back among the trees, they had completely lost the track. And they were sore afraid, for men had been known to enter these darkling woods, never to be seen again. And whenever the hunt had run herein, they made certain to leave this sinister realm before twilight came on, and be back at the castle ere nightfall. "Come," said one of the noblemen, "let us return to the palace, for surely the prince is already there." And all the men did quickly agree to this course, saying it was exceedingly sensible. . . .

. . . Besides, it was getting dark.

As to the prince, at last the white hart was seen cresting a knoll to disappear beyond, and the prince reined his weary but wonderful horse to a halt along the bank of a clear-running stream. Dismounting, he let the steed take on water, while he himself drank, as well. And when he stood and looked about, nought did he recognize of the darkening 'scape. He was quite lost, his way back to the castle unknown. He set his silver-belled horn to his lips and blew a call to the air, yet only echoes sounded in response, to be swallowed in the leafy silence of the surround.

"Well, my friend," he said to his mount, "it seems we are fated to spend the night far from stable and bed." And he took up the reins and, afoot, led the horse up a long slope to camp upon high ground. Yet when he came to the crest of the knoll, there where the hart was last seen, what before him did he espy reaching skyward in the dying light of the day but a lone tower atop the next rise. Yet, what is this? On a golden rope up the side of the tower clambered a figure in black, striving to gain a candlelit window in the stonework high above.

"Come, old fellow," he said to his horse, "perchance our fortune has changed. Yon lies a refuge and mayhap a meal for each of us on this eve—oats for you and bread for me—and perhaps suitable quarters, as well. Rather would we beg shelter in a tower, secure from the beasts of the wood, than to lie in the open under night skies, with nought but a fire standing guard in the dark."

And so the prince took the reins of his steed and went down from the crest of the knoll and into the vale below, then up the long slope toward the base of the tower, twilight o'er the land. In mustering shadows as he neared the goal, he noted the golden rope was gone, perhaps drawn up to the candlelit window and in. Yet in its place a weeping drifted out and down, along with an argument in voice so low, he could not gather what was said, only that a conflict of wills was at hand. Yet when he reached the grey stone of the tower, one voice called out, "It is mine, not yours, and you must return it to me." And there followed a cruel laugh and additional weeping, but suddenly nothing more . . . and only mute silence reigned.

Around the base of the tower went the prince, leading his trusty mount, but no doors did he find whatsoever, and no other windows above. As he came full circle to the place where he began, he heard a scuttling among the boles of dark trees, and he just made out in the waning twilight the figure in black hieing down the slope and away from the tower with no doors. But, lo! the golden rope yet dangled, but it was now being drawn up.

The prince sprang forward and leapt as high as he could, and he just did catch the end, and up he clambered as the dark figure had done, his feet finding purchase as he went.

"Who's there?" called a lyrical voice, that of a lady, he was certain. "You cannot come back with your persistent demand unless you first set me free."

The prince did not answer as upward he scaled, to reach the window at last. And as he crossed the sill, his eyes did behold a creature most divine: 'twas a lady all unclothed, her hair as golden as his.

"Oh," she said, turning her back, and drawing her hair up and inward, for *that* was the golden rope he had climbed to reach this lofty place. Swiftly she unbraided the very long locks and loosened them afluff, and, covering herself in her own mane, at last she turned to the prince.

She was beautiful, incredibly beautiful, and the prince drew in a deep breath, trying to master his hammering heart, though he did wonder that he had a heart left, lost in her eyes as it was.

"My lord," she said, curtsying, the sweep of her hair parting here and there to reveal and then conceal, and she smiled quite knowingly.

"My lady," he responded, bowing, his quickening pulse in his ears, "I overheard: Are you trapped in this place? Mayhap I can set you free."

"Indeed I am trapped, by a magic spell, and I cannot hie from this tower. 'Twas most kind, your offer, but it simply cannot be."

Taken aback, the prince did frown, and he glanced at the window and said, "The one in black I saw climbing, is he at the root of your bane?"

" 'Tis a she," said the lady, "a terrible witch, who has set a geas 'pon me from which I cannot escape."

Reflexively the hand of the prince went to his belt, to rest on the pommel of his dagger, and he said, "Then mayhap I should slay her."

"Oh, no, my lord," cried the lady, falling to her knees, "you mustn't harm her at all, else I will be trapped evermore."

Quite distracted—for her hair had parted, revealing her plentiful charms—the prince cast about for aught to say, finally settling upon, "How came this to be?"

"Oh," she said, "oh," and paused, as if seeking a tale, and she settled back against the wall and smiled coyly up at him, with her snow-white legs slightly parted. After a moment when he made no move, she finally said, " 'Twas long ago when my mother was with child and she greatly desired the taste of parsley, and she begged my sire to gather some from the patch next door. Yet it was the garden of the witch, and when she caught him stealing the herb, she demanded the babe in return. He had no choice but to agree, and so when I was born I was given to the crone, and she placed me in this tower, and here I've been ever since, and if she should come to hurt, then here I'll ever remain."

"Then I'll discover another way to set you free," declared the prince, "mayhap destroy the tower."

" 'Tis magically warded," said the lady, standing and stepping toward the young man, her teeth a pearly white as she smiled. "Besides, let us not natter on about witches and freedom. Come and lie with me instead." And she took him in her embrace and thoroughly kissed him most deeply, and then began stripping him of his clothes.

A fire ran through his loins, and he did not resist, nor did he want to, but instead quickly wrenched off his spurred boots and doffed other garments, as well.

She looked at him admiringly, his desire apparent to the eye, and she reclined on the nearby bed and beckoned him to part her tresses and discover her treasures so hidden.

Revealed was a golden mound, and he quickly plunged himself within, and they both gasped in unbridled delight, their pleasure all-consuming, and she cast her locks over them both, and they coupled throughout the night, covered in a blanket of golden hair.

When dawn lay on the horizon, she took her gratification one last time, and, glowing, she said, "You must leave now, ere the witch comes again. But return on morrow eve, and once more we'll find joy in one another."

The prince donned his clothes as she braided her hair, and then he slid down her bound locks to the base of the grey stone tower, where he espied his steed quietly munching wild oats and tender green grass in the lush verdant dell below. As the prince wearily mounted up, he looked back at the edifice to catch a glimpse of the lady, but dark shutters now covered the window above, closing out the first rays of the sun. Sighing, he rode over the other knoll to come to the stream of the day before, and he and the horse took on deep draughts of clear water, and then set camp on the bank.

Exhausted, still the prince unsaddled the steed and curried him with twists of grass, then fell into a deep and dreamless sleep. When he awoke, 'twas midafternoon, and he was ravenously hungry. He took up his bow and stood along the bank and managed to impale a fish, and it was not more than half-cooked when he drew it from the small fire and consumed it whole.

Yet weary, he napped once more, and lavender twilight lay across the land when he wakened again. Taking a deep breath, he stood and saddled his steed and rode him back up the knoll, reaching the crown just in time to see the black-clad figure clambering once more up the side of the turret to the candlelit window above. Long did the prince pause, fingering his bow, thinking upon killing this evil being for trapping the lady in a stone tower with no doors.

Where he sat ahorse on the crest of the knoll, he once again could hear angry voices drifting out from the window and across the night air, yet what they said was not discernible, and it did not continue o'erlong. At last the black-clothed being slid down the golden braid to the ground below, and the prince then set an arrow to string and thought again that he should slay her. But then the words of the lady came back to him—*If she should come to hurt, then here I'll ever remain*—and he slipped the arrow back into his saddle quiver and unstrung his death-dealing bow.

When the crone was gone, the prince rode down

through the vale then up to the base of the grey stone tower, and there did dangle the plait. Up he scaled, finding the climb rather difficult, for he was yet weary—drained, some might say.

As before, the lady unbound her braid and loosened her lengthy tresses, and again they coupled relentlessly, all the while covered in a glorious blanket of beautiful golden hair.

In the paling of dawn, at her insistence they mated once more, and then she bade him to leave—"The witch, if she finds you here, I don't know what she might do."

And so, the prince slid down the golden rope and wearily rode away, while behind, the dark shutters were closed against the bright rays of the just-risen sun.

And the next night found an exhausted prince barely able to climb the braid. Yet again did the golden-haired lady spark irresistible desire, and covered in auric tresses, they once more coupled away. Yet when the light of dawn came on the heels of the night, he knew he had not the strength to clamber down. "I'll simply wait for the witch," he said, drawing his dagger with a trembling hand, "and force her to set you free." And that was the moment he saw his reflection in the gleaming steel: white-haired and wrinkled and skin and bones he was, and he reeled back in horror and dropped the blade. And the lady laughed cruelly, and filled with an energy not her own, she took him up and flung him out the window, where he landed in a great clump of briars, and thorns did pierce his eyes.

He lay all day, but barely alive, bleeding from a hundred small punctures. And when the sun set, he felt hands take hold and drag him free of the thorns. And someone did bind his wounds and give him a draught of cool water. Even so, he could not speak nor sit nor stand, for he had no strength whatsoever. And then he heard a person nearby calling out: "Edwig, Edwig, let down my hair."

There came a sneer from on high, followed by, "So that I may climb without a stair?"

The prince simply lay without moving, and he could hear feet scrabbling against the stone, and he knew that someone was climbing the braid, feet against the tower.

Surely it's not the witch who aided me so.

Moments later there began a noisy quarrel, words drifting down from above, only this time the prince could hear what was being said, so loud and shrill were the voices:

"You trapped another man!"

"What of it?"

'Murderer! Murderer! Below lies another whom you have drawn to your tower and drained of his life essence."

There came that same cruel laugh, and then the lady—for the prince did recognize her voice—said, "The white hart, a good illusion, eh? And this man was especially potent: he lasted a day longer than most."

"Edwig, I shall see that no more victims come to your tower and—" Of a sudden the speaker stopped, then said, "Edwig, I am pregnant."

"What?" demanded the lady, Edwig most certainly. "That cannot be."

"Ah, but it is," said the other, "for well do I know my own being even though I am apart from it, and did you not say yourself that this man was especially potent?"

"But I will lose all my power, should you be pregnant more than seven days. You must bring me the root of the—"

"Nay, I will not do so, Edwig. Instead, give me back my body, and the geas will be broken."

There came a shrill scream, and Edwig said, "But that means I will have to find another body, for you will not be a virgin if I give it back."

"So be it!" cried the one.

"So be it!" shouted Edwig, and there came a great lash of thunder, and then all fell into silence.

The prince lay without moving throughout the night, and the next day dawned and the sun rose on high, for he could feel it on his face. And as he lay in the warmth, he heard the sound of horns blowing, growing louder by the moment. He took hold of the strap on his own silver-belled horn and managed to bring the trump to his lips, and he blew a faint note, but he despaired, for it was so very weak. Yet it was enough, for within moments galloping horses drew near.

"Here's the prince's steed," a voice cried.

"And yon lies a body," shouted another.

The prince raised a hand.

"It's an old man," a third one called, "and he's alive."

Horses came nigh and someone dismounted, and the prince felt hands raising him to a sitting position. Water was pressed to his lips, and he drank thirstily.

"Where is my son, old man?"

It was his father's voice.

"Sire, it is I," said the prince, his words but a whisper, and he raised his hand so that his signet ring might be seen.

"You wear the sigil of my boy," said the king, "as well as his clothes, but you are an old man. You cannot be h—"

"Father, I have been bewitched by the lady of the tower."

"Tower? What tower?"

"The one at hand, Father."

"There is no tower at hand, only a barren knoll."

In that moment a great hunting hound came and lay down by the old man and licked his age-worn fingers, and all the king's retinue drew breaths in wonder, for well did they know that this hound loved no other than his very own master, the prince.

Too, the prince's magnificent horse nuzzled the oldster and softly whickered, and by this sign as well did all the men stir, for that splendid steed favored none else.

After long converse, with the prince reminding his father and the others of events in the past, at last they accepted him for who he was, though he was blind and aged. And they bore the frail old man back to the castle, bewitched though he might be.

When he recovered somewhat from his wounds, and had been fed substantial meals, he and his valet and his hunting hound and his noble set out to find the witch who had done this to him, for they would force her to reverse the spell and restore his drained-away youth.

They wandered the world for five years—an old blind man, a valet, a dog, and a most magnificent steed—seeking, but not finding.

Yet one eve, out in the waste, the prince heard a woman crooning a lullaby, and though he had not heard it in half a decade, he knew that it was the voice of the golden-haired lady.

"What is it you see?" he asked the valet.

Peering through the oncoming twilight, the valet replied, "A beautiful woman on a rug before a tent singing to two little golden-haired children."

"Take me to her," said the prince, and quickly it was done.

"My lady, do I know you? Did you once live in a tower?"

"Oh, my," she replied in the gathering dusk, "you must be him. Oh, you poor fellow, come to me, I have long-held in my body that which is rightfully yours."

And so he dismounted from his horse, and she bade him to lie down and place his head in her lap and, with her tears falling on his face, she said, "I have been saving this for you."

And she laid her right hand 'pon his brow and placed the left hand o'er his heart, and vigor flowed from her to him, as all the stolen vitality was restored. And, lo! his youth came back unto the prince in a burst of energy so intense that his eyes were healed and he could see again!

"You are not the one I met in the tower," said the prince, looking into her compassionate face.

"No," she replied. "I am the one whom you might have thought of as a dreadful crone, but that was *her* true form, not mine, for she stole my body from me."

"Ah then, it all comes clear," said the prince, and he sprang to his feet, renewed.

"My lady, you have made me that which I was. Could it be that you are a sorceress?"

"Nay, no mage am I, but a mere common girl."

"Then how did you trap the witch in the tower?"

"Ah, that," she said, nodding. "At the moment of exchange—my body for hers—then did some of her power become mine, and I had just enough to lay a geas on her from which she could not escape."

"She became a prisoner in her own tower," said the prince.

"Yes," said the lady. "And would remain so until I unto myself was restored."

"And when you changed back—?" asked the prince.

"I held on to your vitality and a bit of her power in case I would see you again . . . as has come about."

The prince smiled and settled back down at the side of the beautiful lady and took her hand in his, and he looked at the twin children, his hound licking the face of the laughing boy and his wonderful horse nuzzling the cooing girl.

"They are yours," the lady shyly said, when she saw where he did gaze.

He smiled back at her and they built a small fire and the valet brewed a fresh pot of tea and then discreetly withdrew. And the prince and the lady sat and sipped long into the night and spoke of all that had been.

And so ends my story of the tower with no doors, a story so distorted in the retelling by those who, unlike me, were not there, and so do not know the facts. And look at what has happened to the true tale: it has become a fable so entirely irrational that it makes no sense at all.

You, another immortal as am I, should be able to carry the genuine account forward and not inject too many errors in the retelling down through the years.

What of the pregnant mother and the yearning for parsley? Oh, that. Pfaa! It was a tale invented on the spot by the witch—a lamia, more like it, I deem—an outrageous fabrication to explain her presence in the tower, for the truth served not at all her ends. I ask you, what father and mother would ever agree to trade their newborn for a mere sprig of an herb? Oh, no. There was no parsley, nor the handing over of a babe by two nitwits. Instead, the lady's folks were common crofters who just happened to bear a beautiful, golden-haired daughter, who at sixteen caught the lamia's eye.

The hair? Though her own golden mane was quite magnificent, the lady herself did not have tresses that would reach from the window to the ground. Instead, that hair was brought about by a spell cast by the lamia, and she used it to get men up to her bed as well as to leech the vitality from them.

What's that? Oh, yes, the prince and the lady, they married and lived quite happily ever after.

What of the real witch, you ask? Well, I believe she is yet searching for a suitable virgin, but they are hard to come by these days.

Their names? Their human names? How should I know? Oh, "Edwig the Witch" I do remember, but as to the others—the lady, the prince? Pfaa! They all sound alike to me.

Oh my, but look, the mayfly is dead, though I told the tale in very little time. Ah me, such as the vagaries of extremely ephemeral lives. . . . Besides, 'twas his nature to land on my hide, and mine to swat him lifeless, as I did.

And now I must get back to my oats; I've gone some while without fare. Would you please place the feedbag over my nose? My hooves are *so* ill-suited to such a menial task.

The short-short story is a neat little creature: Every single word counts, and if done correctly, it's a polished gem. I really wanted one for this collection, and **Larry Niven** *of all people — author of bestselling vast landscapes such as* Ringworld *— came through.*

Recent work from Larry includes a new collection, Scatterbrain, *which contains short stories and excerpts from novels.*

BOOMERANG

Larry Niven

There have been a succession of last gods. When an entity too powerful to exist goes mythical, lesser entities pull themselves out of their hiding places and rule for a time.

Daramulum ruled in Australia and New Zealand. Being less energetic than most, he survived longer than most. The magic of the Outback abos did not chew deeply into his reserves of manna, but invaders were another matter. They brought their own religions. They knew farming, and they bred. Humans are natural wizards, and their numbers grew too great.

The first boomerang was his. Daramulum had brought it to men at the beginning of time. They tried to throw it away, repeatedly, until Daramulum showed them how it could knock a behemoth off its feet. Men used a smaller version to hunt marsupials. The first boomerang was scaled to Daramulum himself.

*   *   *

When he chose to become mythical, Daramulum went to the farthest ends of the Earth. He stood hundreds of manheights tall, with a stride to match. Where the ocean was too deep to wade, he borrowed the ocean's manna and grew taller. He took with him certain books whose knowledge should be destroyed, and he took the archetype of the boomerang.

At the far end of the Earth, Daramulum found himself armpit deep in a tall forest. Somehow he hadn't expected that.

He hurled the first boomerang away from him.

It circled the world many times, then, as boomerangs do, it came back. Circling more narrowly the point where Daramulum waited, it flew lower. It began to cut down trees. Before it reached Daramulum, it had leveled whole forests. The latest of last gods died in a titanic blast of light and heat.

So Daramulum went myth—leaving his own myth and mystery, a puzzle for the entire civilized world—in Tunguska in 1906 CE.

Elizabeth Hand, besides being a heck of a short-story writer (her two collections to date: Bibliomancy: Four Novellas *and* Last Summer at Mars Hill), *is also the author of seven novels, including her latest,* Mortal Love. *She lives on the coast of Maine.*

Here she writes about the nature of the beast: the beast, in this case, being the creative artist.

WONDERWALL

Elizabeth Hand

A long time ago, nearly thirty years now, I had a
friend who was waiting to be discovered. His name
was David Baldanders; we lived with two other
friends in one of the most disgusting places I've ever
seen, and certainly the worst that involved me signing a
lease.

Our apartment was a two-bedroom third-floor
walkup in Queenstown, a grim brick enclave just over
the District line in Hyattsville, Maryland. Queenstown
Apartments were inhabited mostly by drug dealers and
bikers who met their two-hundred-dollars-a-month
leases by processing speed and bad acid in their basement rooms; the upper floors were given over to wasted
welfare mothers from P. G. County and students from
the University of Maryland, Howard, and the University of the Archangels and Saint John the Divine.

The Divine, as students called it, was where I'd come
three years earlier to study acting. I wasn't actually ex-
pelled until the end of my junior year, but midway
through that term, my roommate, Marcella, and I were

kicked out of our campus dormitory, precipitating the move to Queenstown. Even for the mid-1970s, our behavior was excessive; I was only surprised the university officials waited so long before getting rid of us. Our parents were assessed for damages to our dorm room, which were extensive; among other things, I'd painted one wall floor-to-ceiling with the image from the cover of *Transformer*, surmounted by *JE SUIS DAMNÉ PAR L'ARC-EN-CIEL* scrawled in foot-high letters. Decades later, someone who'd lived in the room after I left told me that, year after year, Rimbaud's words would bleed through each successive layer of new paint. No one ever understood what they meant.

Our new apartment was at first an improvement on the dorm room, and Queenstown itself was an efficient example of a closed ecosystem. The bikers manufactured Black Beauties, which they sold to the students and welfare mothers upstairs, who would zigzag a few hundred feet across a wasteland of shattered glass and broken concrete to the Queenstown Restaurant, where I worked making pizzas that they would then cart back to their apartments. The pizza boxes piled up in the halls, drawing armies of roaches. My friend Oscar lived in the next building; whenever he visited our flat, he'd push open the door, pause, and then look over his shoulder dramatically.

"Listen—!" he'd whisper.

He'd stamp his foot, just once, and hold up his hand to command silence. Immediately we heard what sounded like surf washing over a gravel beach. In fact, it was the susurrus of hundreds of cockroaches clittering across the warped parquet floors in retreat.

There were better places to await discovery.

David Baldanders was my age, nineteen. He wasn't

much taller than me, with long thick black hair and a soft-featured face: round cheeks, full red lips between a downy black beard and mustache, slightly crooked teeth much yellowed from nicotine, small well-shaped hands. He wore an earring and a bandanna that he tied, pirate-style, over his head; filthy jeans, flannel shirts, filthy black Converse high-tops that flapped when he walked. His eyes were beautiful—indigo, black-lashed, soulful. When he laughed, people stopped in their tracks—he sounded like Herman Munster, that deep, goofy, foghorn voice at odds with his fey appearance.

We met in the Divine's Drama Department and immediately recognized each other as kindred spirits. Neither attractive nor talented enough to be in the center of the golden circle of aspiring actors that included most of our friends, we made ourselves indispensable by virtue of being flamboyant, unapologetic fuckups. People laughed when they saw us coming. They laughed even louder when we left. But David and I always made a point of laughing loudest of all.

"Can you fucking believe that?" A morning, it could have been any morning: I stood in the hall and stared in disbelief at the Department's sitting area. White walls, a few plastic chairs and tables overseen by the glass windows of the secretarial office. This was where the other students chain-smoked and waited, day after day, for news: casting announcements for Department plays; cattle calls for commercials, trade shows, summer reps. Above all else, the Department prided itself on graduating Working Actors—a really successful student might get called back for a walk-on in *Days of Our Lives*. My voice rose loud enough that heads turned. "It looks like a fucking *dentist's* office."

"Yeah, well, Roddy just got cast in a Trident commercial," David said, and we both fell against the wall, howling.

Rejection fed our disdain, but it was more than that. Within weeks of arriving at the Divine, I felt betrayed. I wanted—hungered for, thirsted for, craved like drink or drugs—High Art. So did David. We'd come to the Divine expecting Paris in the 1920s, Swinging London, Summer of Love in the Haight.

We were misinformed.

What we got was elocution taught by the Department head's wife; tryouts where tone-deaf students warbled numbers from *The Magic Show;* Advanced Speech classes where, week after week, the beefy Department head would declaim Macduff's speech—*All my pretty ones? Did you say all?*—never failing to move himself to tears.

And there was that sitting area. Just looking at it made me want to take a sledgehammer to the walls: all those smug faces above issues of *Variety* and *Theatre Arts;* all those sheets of white paper neatly taped to white cinder block with lists of names beneath: callbacks, cast lists, passing exam results. My name was never there. Nor was David's.

We never had a chance. We had no choice.

We took the sledgehammer to our heads.

Weekends my suitemate visited her parents, and while she was gone, David and I would break into her dorm room. We drank her vodka and listened to her copy of *David Live,* playing "Diamond Dogs" over and over as we clung to each other, smoking, dancing cheek to cheek. After midnight we'd cadge a ride down to Southwest, where abandoned warehouses had been turned into gay discos—the Lost and Found, Grand Central Station, Washington Square, Half Street. A solitary neon pentacle glowed atop the old *Washington Star* printing plant; we heard gunshots, sirens, the faint bass throb from funk bands at the Washington Coliseum, ceaseless boom and echo of trains uncoupling in the rail yards that extended from Union Station.

I wasn't a looker. My scalp was covered with henna-stiffened orange stubble that had been cut over three successive nights by a dozen friends. Marcella had pierced my ear with a cork and a needle and a bottle of Gordon's gin. David usually favored one long drop earring, and sometimes I'd wear its mate. Other times I'd shove a safety pin through my ear, then run a dog leash from the safety pin around my neck. I had two-inch-long black-varnished fingernails that caught fire when I lit my cigarettes from a Bic lighter. I kohled my eyes and lips, used Marcella's Chloé perfume, shoved myself into Marcella's expensive jeans even though they were too small for me.

But mostly I wore a white poet's blouse or frayed striped boatneck shirt, droopy black wool trousers, red sneakers, a red velvet beret my mother had given me for Christmas when I was seventeen. I chain-smoked Marlboros, three packs a day when I could afford them. For a while I smoked clay pipes and Borkum Riff tobacco. The pipes cost a dollar apiece at the tobacconist's in Georgetown. They broke easily, and club owners invariably hassled me, thinking I was getting high right under their noses. I was, but not from Borkum Riff. Occasionally I'd forgo makeup and wear army khakis and a boiled wool navy shirt I'd fished from a Dumpster. I used a mascara wand on my upper lip and wore my bashed-up old cowboy boots to make me look taller.

This fooled no one, but that didn't matter. In Southeast, I was invisible—or nearly so. I was a girl, white, not pretty enough to be either desirable or threatening. The burly leather-clad guys who stood guard over the entrances to the L & F were always nice to me, though there was a scary dyke bouncer whom I had to bribe, sometimes with cash, sometimes with rough foreplay behind the door.

Once inside, all that fell away. David and I stumbled to the bar and traded our drink tickets for vodka and orange juice. We drank fast, pushing upstairs through the crowd until we reached a vantage point above the dance floor. David would look around for someone he knew, someone he fancied, someone who might discover him. He'd give me a wet kiss, then stagger off; and I would stand, and drink, and watch.

The first time it happened, David and I were tripping. We were at the L & F, or maybe Washington Square. He'd gone into the men's room. I sat slumped just outside the door, trying to bore a hole through my hand with my eyes. A few people stepped on me; no one apologized, but no one swore at me, either. After a while I stumbled to my feet, lurched a few feet down the hallway, and turned.

The door to the men's room was painted gold. A shining film covered it, glistening with smeared rainbows like oil-scummed tarmac. The door opened with difficulty because of the number of people crammed inside. I had to keep moving so they could pass in and out. I leaned against the wall and stared at the floor for a few more minutes, then looked up again.

Across from me, the wall was gone. I could see men, pissing, talking, kneeling, crowding stalls, humping over urinals, cupping brown glass vials beneath their faces. I could see David in a crowd of men by the sinks. He stood with his back to me, in front of a long mirror framed with small round lightbulbs. His head was bowed. He was scooping water from the faucet and drinking it, so that his beard glittered red and silver. As I watched, he slowly lifted his face, until he was staring into the mirror. His reflected image stared back at me. I could see his pupils expand like drops of black ink in a glass of water, and his mouth fall open in pure panic.

"David," I murmured.

Beside him, a lanky boy with dirty-blond hair turned. He, too, was staring at me, but not with fear. His mouth split into a grin. He raised his hand and pointed at me, laughing.

"Poseur!"

"Shit—shit . . ." I looked up, and David stood there in the hall. He fumbled for a cigarette, his hand shaking, then sank onto the floor beside me. "Shit, you, you saw—you—"

I started to laugh. In a moment David did, too. We fell into each other's arms, shrieking, our faces slick with tears and dirt. I didn't even notice that his cigarette scorched a hole in my favorite shirt till later, or felt where it burned into my right palm, a penny-size wound that got infected and took weeks to heal. I bear the scar even now, the shape of an eye, shiny white tissue with a crimson pupil that seems to wink when I crease my hand.

It was about a month after this happened that we moved to Queenstown. Me, David, Marcy, a sweet spacy girl named Bunny Flitchins, all signed the lease. Two hundred bucks a month gave us a small living room, a bathroom, two small bedrooms, a kitchen squeezed into a corner overlooking a parking lot filled with busted

Buicks and shockshot Impalas. The place smelled of new paint and dry-cleaning fluid. The first time we opened the freezer, we found several plastic Ziploc bags filled with sheets of white paper. When we removed the paper and held it up to the light, we saw where rows of droplets had dried to faint grey smudges.

"Blotter acid," I said.

We discussed taking a hit. Marcy demurred. Bunny giggled, shaking her head. She didn't do drugs, and I would never have allowed her to: it would be like giving acid to your puppy.

"Give it to me," said David. He sat on the windowsill, smoking and dropping his ashes to the dirt three floors below. "I'll try it. Then we can cut them into tabs and sell them."

"That would be a *lot* of money," said Bunny delightedly. A tab of blotter went for a dollar back then, but you could sell them for a lot more at concerts, up to ten bucks a hit. She fanned out the sheets from one of the plastic bags. "We could make thousands and thousands of dollars."

"Millions," said Marcy.

I shook my head. "It could be poison. Strychnine. *I* wouldn't do it."

"Why not?" David scowled. "You do all kinds of shit."

"I wouldn't do it 'cause it's from *here*."

"Good point," said Bunny.

I grabbed the rest of the sheets from her, lit one of her gas jets on the stove, and held the paper above it. David cursed and yanked the bandanna from his head.

"What are you *doing?*"

But he quickly moved aside as I lunged to the window and tossed out the flaming pages. We watched them fall, delicate spirals of red and orange like tiger lilies corroding into black ash then grey then smoke.

"All gone," cried Bunny, and clapped.

We had hardly any furniture. Marcy had a bed and a desk in her room, nice Danish Modern stuff. I had a mattress on the other bedroom floor that I shared with David. Bunny slept in the living room. Every few days she'd drag a broken box spring up from the curb. After the fifth one appeared, the living room began to look like the interior of one of those pawnshops down on F Street that sold you an entire roomful of aluminum-tube furniture for fifty bucks, and we yelled at her to stop. Bunny slept on the box springs, a different one every night, but after a while she didn't stay over much. Her family lived in Northwest, but her father, a professor at the Divine, also had an apartment in Turkey Thicket, and Bunny started staying with him.

Marcy's family lived nearby, as well, in Alexandria. She was a slender, Slavic beauty with a waterfall of ice-blond hair and eyes like aqua headlamps, and the only one of us with a glamorous job—she worked as a model and receptionist at the most expensive beauty salon in Georgetown. But by early spring, she had pretty much moved back in with her parents, too.

This left me and David. He was still taking classes at the Divine, getting a ride with one of the other students who lived at Queenstown, or else catching a bus in front of Giant Food on Queens Chapel Road. Early in the semester he had switched his coursework: instead of theater, he now immersed himself in French language and literature.

I gave up all pretense of studying or attending classes. I worked a few shifts behind the counter at the Queenstown Restaurant, making pizzas and ringing up beer. I got most of my meals there, and when my friends came in to buy cases of Heineken, I never charged them. I made about sixty dollars a week, barely enough to pay the rent and keep me in cigarettes, but I got by. Bus fare was eighty cents to cross the District line; the newly opened subway was another fifty cents. I didn't eat much. I lived on popcorn and Reuben sandwiches from the restaurant, and there was a sympathetic waiter at the American Café in Georgetown who fed me ice cream sundaes when I was bumming around in the city. I saved enough for my cover at the discos and for the Atlantis, a club in the basement of a fleabag hotel at 930 F Street that had just started booking punk bands. The rest I spent on booze and Marlboros. Even if I was broke, someone would always spring me a drink and a smoke; if I had a full pack of cigarettes, I was ahead of the game. I stayed out all night, finally staggering out into some of the District's worst neighborhoods with a couple of bucks in my sneaker, if I was lucky. Usually I was broke.

Yet I really *was* lucky. Somehow I always managed to find my way home. At two or three or four a.m., I'd crash into my apartment, alone except for the cockroaches—David would have gone home with a pickup from the bars, and Marcy and Bunny had decamped to the suburbs. I'd be so drunk, I stuck to the mattress like a fly mashed against a window. Sometimes I'd sit cross-legged with the typewriter in front of me and write, naked because of the appalling heat, my damp skin grey with cigarette ash. I read *Tropic of Cancer,* reread *Dhalgen* and *A Fan's Notes* and a copy of *Illuminations* held together by a rubber band. I played Pere Ubu and Wire at the wrong speed, because I was too wasted to notice, and would finally pass out only to be ripped awake by the apocalyptic scream of the firehouse siren next door—I'd be standing in the middle of the room, screaming at the top of my lungs, before I realized I was no longer asleep. I saw people in my room, a lanky boy with dark-blond hair and clogs who pointed his finger at me and shouted *Poseur!* I heard voices. My dreams were of flames, of the walls around me exploding outward so that I could see the ruined city like a freshly tilled garden extending for miles and miles, burning cranes and skeletal buildings rising from the smoke to bloom, black and gold and red, against a topaz sky. I wanted to burn, too, tear through the wall that separated me from that other world, the *real* world, the one I glimpsed in books and music, the world I wanted to claim for myself.

But I didn't burn. I was just a fucked-up college student, and pretty soon I wasn't even that. That spring I flunked out of the Divine. All my other friends were still in school, getting boyfriends and girlfriends, getting cast in University productions of *An Inspector Calls* and *Arturo Roi*. Even David Baldanders managed to get good grades for his paper on Verlaine. Meanwhile I leaned out my third-floor window and smoked and watched the speed freaks stagger across the parking lot below. If I jumped, I could be with them: that was all it would take.

It was too beautiful for words, too terrifying to think this was what my life had shrunk to. In the mornings I made instant coffee and tried to read what I'd written the night before. Nice words but they made absolutely no sense. I cranked up Marcy's expensive stereo and played my records, compulsively transcribing song lyrics as though they might somehow bleed into something else, breed with my words and create a coherent storyline. I scrawled more words on the bedroom wall:

I HAVE BEEN DAMNED BY THE RAINBOW
I AM AN AMERICAN ARTIST, AND I HAVE NO CHAIRS

It had all started as an experiment. I held the blunt, unarticulated belief that meaning and transcendence could be shaken from the world, like unripe fruit from a tree; then consumed.

So I'd thrown my brain into the Waring blender along with vials of cheap acid and hashish, tobacco and speed and whatever alcohol was at hand. Now I wondered: Did I have the stomach to toss down the end result?

Whenever David showed up it was a huge relief.

"Come on," he said one afternoon. "Let's go to the movies."

We saw a double bill at the Biograph, *The Story of Adele H* and *Jules et Jim*. Torturously uncomfortable chairs, but only four bucks for four hours of air-conditioned bliss. David had seen *Adele H* six times already; he sat beside me, rapt, whispering the words to himself. I struggled with the French and mostly read the subtitles. Afterwards we stumbled blinking into the long ultraviolet D.C. twilight, the smell of honeysuckle and diesel, coke and lactic acid, our clothes crackling with heat like lightning and our skin electrified as the sugared air seeped into it like poison. We ran arm-in-arm up to the Café de Paris, sharing one of David's Gitanes. We had enough money for a bottle of red wine and a baguette. After a few hours, the waiter kicked us out, but we gave him a dollar anyway. That left us just enough for the Metro and the bus home.

It took us hours to get back. By the time we ran up the steps to our apartment, we'd sobered up again. It was not quite nine o'clock on a Friday night.

"Fuck!" said David. "What are we going to do now?"

No one was around. We got on the phone, but there were no parties, no one with a car to take us somewhere else. We riffled the apartment for a forgotten stash of beer or dope or money, turned our pockets inside out looking for stray seeds, Black Beauties, fragments of green dust.

Nada.

In Marcy's room we found about three dollars in change in one of her jeans pockets. Not enough to get drunk, not enough to get us back into the city.

"Damn," I said. "Not enough for shit."

From the parking lot came the low thunder of motorcycles, a baby crying, someone shouting.

"You fucking motherfucking fucker."

"That's a lot of fuckers," said David.

Then we heard a gunshot.

"Jesus!" yelled David, and yanked me to the floor. From the neighboring apartment echoed the *crack* of glass shattering. "They shot out a window!"

"I said, not enough money for *anything*." I pushed him away and sat up. "I'm not staying here all night."

"Okay, okay, wait . . ."

He crawled to the kitchen window, pulled himself onto the sill to peer out. "They *did* shoot out a window," he said admiringly. "Wow."

"Did they leave us any beer?"

David looked over his shoulder at me. "No. But I have an idea."

He crept back into the living room and emptied out his pockets beside me. "I think we have enough," he said after he counted his change for the third time. "Yeah. But we have to get there now—they close at nine."

"Who does?"

I followed him back downstairs and outside.

"Peoples Drug," said David. "Come on."

We crossed Queens Chapel Road, dodging Mustangs and blasted pickups. I watched wistfully as the 80 bus passed, heading back into the city. It was almost nine o'clock. Overhead the sky had that dusty gold-violet bloom it got in late spring. Cars raced by, music blaring; I could smell charcoal burning somewhere, hamburgers on a grill and the sweet far-off scent of apple blossom.

"Wait," I said.

I stopped in the middle of the road, arms spread, staring straight up into the sky and feeling what I imagined David must have felt when he leaned against the walls of Mr. P's and Grand Central Station: I was waiting, waiting, waiting for the world to fall on me like a hunting hawk.

"What the fuck are you *doing*?" shouted David as a car bore down and he dragged me to the far curb. "Come *on*."

"What are we getting?" I yelled as he dragged me into the drugstore.

"Triaminic."

I had thought there might be a law against selling four bottles of cough syrup to two messed-up looking kids. Apparently there wasn't, though I was embarrassed enough to stand back as David shamelessly counted pennies and nickels and quarters out onto the counter.

We went back to Queenstown. I had never done cough syrup before; not unless I had a cough. I thought we would dole it out a spoonful at a time, over the course of the evening. Instead David unscrewed the first bottle and knocked it back in one long swallow. I watched in amazed disgust, then shrugged and did the same.

"Aw, *fuck*."

I gagged and almost threw up, somehow kept it down. When I looked up, David was finishing off a second bottle, and I could see him eyeing the remaining one in front of me. I grabbed it and drank it, as well, then sprawled against the box spring. Someone lit a candle. David? Me? Someone put on a record, one of those Eno albums, *Another Green World*. Someone stared at me, a boy with long black hair unbound and eyes that blinked from blue to black and then shut down for the night.

"Wait," I said, trying to remember the words. "I. Want. You. To—"

Too late: David was out. My hand scrabbled across the floor, searching for the book I'd left there, a used New Directions paperback of Rimbaud's work. Even pages were in French; odd pages held their English translations.

I wanted David to read me "La lettre du voyant," Rimbaud's letter to his friend Paul Demeny; the letter of the seer. I knew it by heart in English and on the page but spoken French eluded me and always would. I opened the book, struggling to see through the scrim of cheap narcotic and nausea until at last I found it.

> *Je dis qu'il faut être voyant, se faire voyant.*

> *Le Poète se fait voyant par un long, immense et raisonné dérèglement de tous les sens. Toutes les formes d'amour, de souffrance, de folie; il cherche lui-même. . . .*

I say one must be a visionary, one must become a seer.

> The poet becomes a seer through a long, bound-
> less and systematic derangement of all the senses.
> All forms of love, of suffering, of madness; he seeks
> them within himself. . . .

As I read I began to laugh, then suddenly doubled
over. My mouth tasted sick, a second sweet skin sheath-
ing my tongue. I retched, and a bright-red clot exploded
onto the floor in front of me; I dipped my finger into it
then wrote across the warped parquet.

Dear Dav

I looked up. There was no light save the wavering
flame of a candle in a jar. Many candles, I saw now;
many flames. I blinked and ran my hand across my forehead. It felt damp. When I brought my finger to my lips,
I tasted sugar and blood. On the floor David sprawled,
snoring softly, his bandanna clenched in one hand. Behind him the walls reflected candles, endless candles;
though as I stared I saw they were not reflected light
after all but a line of flames, upright, swaying like figures dancing. I rubbed my eyes, a wave cresting inside
my head then breaking even as I felt something splinter
in my eye. I started to cry out but could not: I was
frozen, freezing. Someone had left the door open.

"Who's there?" I said thickly, and crawled across the
room. My foot nudged the candle; the jar toppled and
the flame went out.

But it wasn't dark. In the corridor outside our apartment door, a hundred-watt bulb dangled from a wire.
Beneath it, on the top step, sat the boy I'd seen in the
urinal beside David. His hair was the color of dirty
straw, his face sullen. He had muddy green-blue eyes,

bad teeth, fingernails bitten down to the skin; skeins of dried blood covered his fingertips like webbing. A filthy bandanna was knotted tightly around his throat.

"Hey," I said. I couldn't stand very well, so slumped against the wall, slid until I was sitting almost beside him. I fumbled in my pocket and found one of David's crumpled Gitanes, fumbled some more until I found a book of matches. I tried to light one, but it was damp; tried a second time and failed again.

Beside me, the blond boy swore. He grabbed the matches from me and lit one, turned to hold it cupped before my face. I brought the cigarette close and breathed in, watched the fingertip flare of crimson then blue as the match went out.

But the cigarette was lit. I took a drag, passed it to the boy. He smoked in silence, after a minute handed it back to me. The acrid smoke couldn't mask his oily smell, sweat and shit and urine; but also a faint odor of green hay and sunlight. When he turned his face to me, I saw that he was older than I had first thought, his skin dark-seamed by sun and exposure.

"Here," he said. His voice was harsh and difficult to understand. He held his hand out. I opened mine expectantly, but as he spread his fingers only a stream of sand fell onto my palm, gritty and stinking of piss. I drew back, cursing. As I did, he leaned forward and spat in my face.

"Poseur."

"You *fuck*," I yelled. I tried to get up, but he was already on his feet. His hand was tearing at his neck; an instant later something lashed across my face, slicing upward from cheek to brow. I shouted in pain and fell back, clutching my cheek. There was a red veil between me and the world; I blinked and for an instant saw through it. I glimpsed the young man running down the steps, his hoarse laughter echoing through the stairwell; heard the clang of the fire door swinging open then crashing shut; then silence.

"Shit," I groaned, and sank back to the floor. I tried to staunch the blood with my hand. My other hand rested on the floor. Something warm brushed against my fingers: I grabbed it and held it before me: a filthy bandanna, twisted tight as a noose, one whip-end black and wet with blood.

I saw him one more time. It was high summer by then, the school year over. Marcy and Bunny were gone till the fall, Marcy to Europe with her parents, Bunny to a private hospital in Kentucky. David would be leaving soon, to return to his family in Philadelphia. I had found another job in the city, a real job, a GS-1 position with the Smithsonian; the lowest-level job one could have in the government, but it was a paycheck. I worked three twelve-hour shifts in a row, three days a week, and wore a mustard-yellow polyester uniform with a photo ID that opened doors to all the museums on the Mall. Nights I sweated away with David at the bars or the Atlantis; days I spent at the newly opened East Wing of the National Gallery of Art, its vast open white-marble space an air-conditioned vivarium where I wandered stoned, struck senseless by huge moving shapes like sharks spun of metal and canvas: Calder's great mobile, Miro's tapestry, a line of somber Rothkos, darkly shimmering waterfalls in an upstairs gallery. Breakfast was a Black Beauty and a Snickers bar; dinner whatever I could find to drink.

We were at the Lost and Found, late night early August. David as usual had gone off on his own. I was, for once, relatively sober: I was in the middle of my three-day workweek—normally I wouldn't have gone out, but David was leaving the next morning. I was on the club's upper level, an area like the deck of an ocean liner, where you could lean on the rails and look down onto the dance floor below. The club was crowded, the music deafening. I was watching the men dance with each other, hundreds of them, maybe thousands, strobe-lit beneath mirrorballs and shifting layers of blue and grey smoke that would ignite suddenly with white blades of laser light, strafing the writhing forms below so they let out a sudden single-voiced shriek, punching the air with their fists and blasting at whistles. I rested my arms on the rounded metal rail and smoked, thinking how beautiful it all was, how strange, how alive. It was like watching the sea.

And as I gazed, slowly it changed; slowly something changed. One song bled into another, arms waved like tendrils, a shadow moved through the air above them. I looked up, startled, glanced aside and saw the blond young man standing there a few feet from me. His fingers grasped the railing; he stared at the dance floor with an expression at once hungry and disdainful and disbelieving. After a moment, he slowly lifted his head, turned and stared at me.

I said nothing. I touched my hand to my throat, where his bandanna was knotted there, loosely. It was stiff as rope beneath my fingers: I hadn't washed it. I stared back at him, his green-blue eyes hard and somehow dull—not stupid, but with the obdurate matte gleam of unpolished agate. I wanted to say something, but I was afraid of him; and before I could speak, he turned his head to stare back down at the floor below us.

"Cela s'est passé," he said, and shook his head.

I looked to where he was gazing. I saw that the dance floor was endless, eternal: the cinder-block warehouse walls had disappeared. Instead, the moving waves of bodies extended for miles and miles until they melted into the horizon. They were no longer bodies but flames, countless flickering lights like the candles I had seen in my apartment, flames like men dancing; and then they were not even flames but bodies consumed by flame, flesh and cloth burned away until only the bones remained and then not even bone but only the memory of motion, a shimmer of wind on the water then the water gone and only a vast and empty room, littered with refuse: glass vials, broken plastic whistles, plastic cups, dog collars, ash.

I blinked. A siren wailed. I began to scream, standing in the middle of my room, alone, clutching at a bandanna tied loosely around my neck. On the mattress on the floor David turned, groaning, and stared up at me with one bright blue eye.

"It's just the firehouse," he said, and reached to pull me back beside him. It was five a.m. He was still wearing the clothes he'd worn to the Lost and Found. So was I: I touched the bandanna at my throat and thought of the young man at the railing beside me. "C'mon, you've hardly slept yet," urged David. "You have to get a little sleep."

He left the next day. I never saw him again.

A few weeks later my mother came, ostensibly to visit her cousin in Chevy Chase, but really to check on me. She found me spread-eagled on my bare mattress, screenless windows open to let the summer's furnace heat pour like molten iron into the room. Around me were the posters I'd shredded and torn from the walls; on the walls were meaningless phrases, crushed remains of cockroaches and waterbugs, countless rust-colored handprints, bullet-shaped gouges where I'd dug my fingernails into the drywall.

"I think you should come home," my mother said gently. She stared at my hands, fingertips netted with dried blood, my knuckles raw and seeping red. "I don't think you really want to stay here. Do you? I think you should come home."

I was too exhausted to argue. I threw what remained of my belongings into a few cardboard boxes, gave notice at the Smithsonian, and went home.

It's thought that Rimbaud completed his entire body of work before his nineteenth birthday; the last prose poems, *Illuminations*, indicate he may have been profoundly moved by the time he spent in London in 1874. After that came journey and exile, years spent as an arms trader in Abyssinia until he came home to France to die, slowly and painfully, losing his right leg to syphilis, electrodes fastened to his nerveless arm in an attempt to regenerate life and motion. He died on the morning of November 10, 1891, at ten o'clock. In his delirium, he believed that he was back in Abyssinia, readying himself to depart upon a ship called *Aphinar*. He was thirty-seven years old.

I didn't live at home for long—about ten months. I got a job at a bookstore; my mother drove me there each day on her way to work and picked me up on her way home. Evenings I ate dinner with her and my two younger sisters. Weekends I went out with friends I'd gone to high school with. I picked up the threads of a few relationships begun and abandoned years earlier. I drank too much but not as much as before. I quit smoking.

I was nineteen. When Rimbaud was my age, he had already finished his life work. I hadn't even started yet. He had changed the world; I could barely change my socks. He had walked through the wall, but I had only smashed my head against it, fruitlessly, in anguish and despair. It had defeated me, and I hadn't even left a mark.

Eventually I returned to D.C. I got my old job back at the Smithsonian, squatted for a while with friends in Northeast, got an apartment, a boyfriend, a promotion. By the time I returned to the city, David had graduated from the Divine. We spoke on the phone a few times: he had a steady boyfriend now, an older man, a businessman from France. David was going to Paris with him to live. Marcy married well and moved to Aspen. Bunny got out of the hospital and was doing much better; over the next few decades, she would be my only real contact with that other life, the only one of us who kept in touch with everyone.

Slowly, slowly, I began to see things differently. Slowly I began to see that there were other ways to bring down a wall: that you could dismantle it, brick by brick, stone by stone, over years and years and years. The wall would always be there—at least for me it is—but sometimes I can see where I've made a mark in it, a chink where I can put my eye and look through to the other side. Only for a moment; but I know better now than to expect more than that.

I spoke to David only a few times over the years, and finally not at all. When we last spoke, maybe fifteen years ago, he told me that he was HIV positive. A few years after that, Bunny told me that the virus had gone into full-blown AIDS, and that he had gone home to live with his father in Pennsylvania. Then a few years after that she told me no, he was living in France again, she had heard from him and he seemed to be better.

Cela s'est passé, the young man had told me as we watched the men dancing in the L & F twenty-six years ago. *That is over.*

Yesterday I was at Waterloo Station, hurrying to catch the train to Basingstoke. I walked past the new Eurostar terminal, the sleek Paris-bound bullet trains like marine animals waiting to churn their way back through the Chunnel to the sea. Curved glass walls separated me from them; armed security patrols and British soldiers strode watchfully along the platform, checking passenger IDs and waving people towards the trains.

I was just turning towards the old station when I saw them. They were standing in front of a glass wall like an aquarium's: a middle-aged man in an expensive looking dark blue overcoat, his black hair still thick though greying at the temples, his hand resting on the shoulders of his companion. A slightly younger man, very thin, his face gaunt and ravaged, burned the color of new brick by the sun, his fair hair gone to grey. He was leaning on a cane; when the older man gestured he turned and began to walk, slowly, painstakingly down the platform. I stopped and watched: I wanted to call out, to see if they would turn and answer, but the blue-washed glass barrier would have muted any sound I made.

I turned, blinking in the light of midday, touched the bandanna at my throat and the notebook in my pocket, and hurried on. They would not have seen me anyway. They were already boarding the train. They were on their way to Paris.

Janny Wurts is a triple threat, two of which I'll mention here (the other, as you'll see, later): She's a heck of a writer as well as a heck of an artist. Quite a combination.

She's the best-selling author of Grand Conspiracy, *and* Peril's Gate *is a recent title in the huge* Wars of Light and Shadow *series.*

If you read fantasy, you've seen her artwork gracing many covers.

Enjoy the following.

BLOOD, OAK, IRON

Janny Wurts

The old King of Chaldir lay dying. Everyone knew. Scarcely anyone cared. He lay under quilts in a bed with gold posts and purple hangings, his waxy, cadaverous face throwing grotesque shadows by the guttering flare of the candles. Whole seconds passed, while his unsteady breath seemed to stop.

Such times the man who kept vigil at the bedside would lean close, a hand weathered brown from the bridle rein reaching out to clasp the skeletal wrist that rested limp on the coverlet. "I am here," he murmured softly. "I'll see you don't die in the dark."

More minutes would pass, while the candle flames bent in the drafts and the autumn winds rattled the casements. The trace scent of frost would knife through the close air, displacing its burden of unguents and tisanes, and the decayed must of age and sickness.

The old king never moved. His eggshell lids did not open.

Findlaire, who was the only legitimate royal son, would arise at measured intervals. Only lately aware

that he was a prince in line for Chaldir's succession, he
took no joy from the prospect. He was a tall man, long-
strided, clothed still in a forester's leather, and his face
wore the lines of a near-sighted squint. He replenished
the wicks as they flickered and drowned. Then he laced
patient knuckles in his salt-stranded hair and tried not
to think of the dark that hemmed the wavering circles
of light cast over the patterned carpet. The old king
might have been unloved, but his suite was no less than
lavish.

Throughout his long life, his attendants and councilors had served his needs out of fear. Now that he lay
dying, they waited and whispered of uncanny powers,
and the curse that held him in possession. Abroad in the
fields, simple country folk gathered the grain shocks for
threshing. The annual harvest would follow its rhythm,
despite the imminent change in succession. The lands of
Chaldir were reasonably prosperous. Its people were
submissive but not starving. Kings were crowned, and
kings passed away, but the shadow behind the power
that governed the realm had not changed for three
thousand years.

The ancient bargain with the fiend would prevail, folk
said. Never mind that Prince Findlaire had been raised
in lands far away, had never since he was a speechless
infant inhabited the realm that his birthright destined
him to inherit. Once the incumbent king died, and before the new one was crowned, the curse that burdened
the royal line would claim its uncanny due. The heir was
doomed to be claimed by the wraith, with the chancellor and the king's council of Chaldir left to keep what
peace they could, under the terms of a horrific bargain.

Another dawn paled the sky through the casement.
Crows soared across sunrise like scraps of black rag. They

perched on the battlements and raised raucous complaint on the hour that Findlaire arose. He snuffed out all but four of the candles. Then he moved in his woodsman's quiet to the doorway, where he raised word to summon the servants. He stayed as they unlocked and unbarred the oak panel. A lean shadow braced against the armoire, he watched, his hands crossed at his belt, beside the empty scabbard of the knife he no longer wore at his hip. If the course his own fate must take was prescribed, he could still insist that his dying liege was attended with kindness and decency.

When the sheets had been changed and the king's withered flesh was resettled under the blankets in comfort, Findlaire returned to the bedside. He kissed the cheek of the father he had never known, who was now too far gone to exchange any word with a son born after the curse had overwhelmed his last human awareness. Then Findlaire left, to spend the day in the palace library poring over record scrolls and dusty piles of books.

In the afternoon, his uncle Guriman found him asleep, his cheek and the knuckles of one strong hand pillowed on the pages of Chaldir's bygone history. With his broad, outdoorsman's shoulders, and his forearms tucked like a cat's, Findlaire seemed relaxed but never innocuous.

"You aren't going to find any answers," Guriman said, his fish-pale elegance clothed in ribboned velvets and his girlish lisp a disquieting affectation for a man more than five decades old.

Findlaire opened his eyes, which were limpid as slate in a streambed. He straightened up. Not a muscle in his rangy frame tightened, but the stillness about him acquired the poise of a fully drawn bow. He regarded the soft uncle whose mounted henchmen had run him to earth like an animal, one day a fortnight past. The wrists underneath his chamois cuffs were still raw from his struggles, as men-at-arms he did not know had bundled him into a carriage and borne him to Chaldir, trussed and furious. They had hauled him into the palace and offered him meat and a bed, and called him "Your Grace," and "Prince." His bonds had been cut, since. But he was kept as close as a prisoner, and liveried cross-bowmen flanked him wherever he went.

As they did now, in deferent quiet, one pair ranked at each end of the table. Others stood guard at the door-way. Their vigilance brightened like heat off stirred em-bers as Findlaire locked eyes with the uncle he had only just learned he possessed. Where another man might have railed or cursed, the forester preferred to say noth-ing. A lifetime of setting snares for shy animals had taught him unbreakable patience.

"Why trouble yourself?" Guriman ventured at last. He fingered a scroll with a pallid hand, his nails clean as a pampered woman's. "The king will die. As the closest male heir in line for the throne, the fiend of Chaldir will have you. Why waste your last days of awareness dig-ging in vain through old books? You have little time. While your mind's still your own, I could send you a vir-gin girl to give you an hour of pleasure."

"You could unlock the doors," Findlaire said.

"Oh, no. To let you go would be utterly wasteful." Gu-riman gave the scroll a contemptuous flick. The parch-ment rolled the width of the table, and bumped against the jumble of manuscripts already searched and dis-carded. "I spent too many years keeping track of your whereabouts. Damn your mother to the nethermost hell pit for thinking to spare you from your fate. You will not escape, or shirk your crown, or hide in the obscurity of a commoner's lifestyle."

Findlaire glanced down, once more absorbed by the pages he had been reading. His stilled face suggested that antagonistic uncles and poised men-at-arms and locked doors were of little more moment than dust to the waters of a creek. Yet in the pale sunlight warming the table, his hands had closed into fists.

As though that small sign of frustration scratched an itch, Guriman shifted his weight from one slippered foot to the other. "I could recite you the history you're seeking. The bad bargain struck by your ancestor has granted the fiend a new body for each generation, in perpetuity. Its wraith will enslave the closest male relative as each possessed sovereign departs. You are the king's son. Your lot is cast. There will be no reprieve. Why should you not savor the time you have left? Trust me in this, each one of your forebears has searched this library before you. Not one in a hundred doomed generations found any means to keep the fiend from its promised binding."

Findlaire refused answer.

In baiting that blank wall of resistance, even Guriman found little sport.

If the books held no clues, *this* prince made it plain: he would comb through their pages again. He had no use for wealth or a ruler's inheritance. The crossbowmen watched his deliberate calm and did not find him complacent. Findlaire did not rage at his straits. Whatever vile promise his progenitor had made, whatever the downfall that claimed each descendent, the fiend's displaced wraith would not take him willing.

"You'll succumb," Guriman insisted at length. "You'll find no help for yourself in the past, though you blind yourself reading old manuscripts."

And sundown approached, like spite itself. Persistence wrung no secret from the crumbling books. Findlaire stood up to the prod of his jailers, and stretched aching shoulders, and longed for the grace of his yew bow, and his hunter's quiver of arrows. He was a man accustomed to venison roasted over an outdoor spit. The rich supper Guriman's lackeys brought did nothing but sour his stomach. Tonight, he spurned the overcooked meal. On a servant's brown bread and a pitcher of water, he would stand the night's vigil alongside his dying father.

The hours of darkness descended again, marked and measured by the arrhythmic whisper of the failing king's breath. Findlaire paced to stay wakeful. He tended the candles and leaned on the wall by the tower's iron barred casement. He had no sharp object to free the jammed catch. A crack in the glass let in the outdoors. Drawing in the chill autumn air, Findlaire listened to the mournful chime of a cowbell, windborne from some crofter's pasture. From the turret below, he caught snatches of coarse laughter, or yells of triumph as one of the soldiers on watch won at knucklebones or dice. The gusts sifted dry leaves across the starlit bailey, while the frost etched its hoary fingerprint over the runners of ivy latched to the outside sill.

Findlaire rested his forehead upon his closed fist. Weariness sucked him too hollow for sleep. He suffered the enclosed suffocation of walls with senses that felt silted and dull. Yet the passion burned in him, bright as pain itself. Longing seared every nerve to rebellion. There was an indelible part of his spirit that would not accept his imprisonment. The heart that belonged to the open forest could not be resigned to the usage of Chaldir's wraith.

Absorbed by the clean, white rise of the moon, Findlaire almost forgot his surroundings. If not for the hideous, ongoing need to keep track of the dying king's breaths, he might not have noticed the muted rasp, as furtive fingers lifted the door latch.

The brush of changed air against his nape aroused all his woodsman's instincts. Spurred to reaction, he whirled about. His reach for his knife met an empty sheath, and frustration. Past salvage, his peril was upon him.

The assassin launched through the bank of lit candles. Through the winnowed streamers of flame, Findlaire saw his form as a hurtling shadow the instant before he struck. Then a muscled, panting body slammed into him, bent on choking his life with a garrote.

Findlaire entangled his fist in the string before it looped tight round his throat. Slammed backward, he struck the wall. A tapestry ripped from its looped rings. His grunt mingled with the killer's snarl of frustration. Their locked struggle toppled them both to the floor. Rolling and kicking, and gouging for purchase, they tumbled across the rucked wool. Their battering progress swept over the rug and smashed through table and basin and towel racks. A scatter of overset candles crashed in a flying spray of spilled wax. Findlaire closed his hand on a billet of split wood, then used that at need to belabor his opponent. He knew where to strike to stun a trapped lynx. To subdue a man the same way fairly sickened him.

The assailant dropped, limp but unhurt. Findlaire recoiled back to his feet. Bent double, retching, he rushed the breached door. There, his armed sentries were now lying senseless, most likely drugged with a potion. Yet before he won clear, his chance to seize freedom was torn from his grasp once again. More men arrived and charged over the threshold. These bore him down with battering fists. The matchstick of wood he had snatched for a weapon proved no use against mail and steel helmets. Findlaire fought as the fox set upon by the pack, beyond every rational hope. Yet numbers prevailed. Slammed dizzy and bleeding, he lay under the weight of his captors, breathing hard. A man with a sword stepped into the corridor and dispatched the incapable bowmen. The ugly sound of their dying reached Findlaire. He shouted his astonished protest, the more horrified as he realized the unconscious assassin would be just as callously executed.

"Shut up, you!"

When he shouted again, he found himself served with a kick in the belly. After that, Findlaire could do nothing at all but curl up and be wretchedly sick.

Later, propped up in a chair, with the abraded burns from the garrote a livid welt on his hand, he held his body tenderly still to quell the ache of his bruises. When Guriman arrived to inspect him and gloat, he had no inclination to speak. The smell of fresh death, and old incense, and medicine befouled the closed room, until he could wish to stop breathing.

On the bed, the dying king rasped, inhale to exhale, while beyond the barred glass, the stars slowly turned, serene in their timeless courses.

"Why did you not let the paid killer take you?" Guriman said, almost taunting. He approached in his beautiful brocade robe, careful to avoid the befouled carpet.

"The creature was hired by my bitterest rival, or did you not know?"

Findlaire's quiet awareness itself framed reply. He might be a stranger unused to court ways, and the poisonous whispers of intrigue. Men might lie to themselves, caught up by ambition and their secretive, grasping desires. Yet a huntsman could recognize the hierarchy of wolf packs. Greed and avarice showed in the glitter of men's eyes. Such bitter jealousies could be sensed, and the smoldering envy of those who coveted Guriman's power as chancellor: the dominance and control that would divide all the world into the strong and the weak, with the forceful set over the cowed and the frightened.

"Poor craven," mused Guriman. "Too soft, or too simple to let go when you're beaten. If you had died before the old king, the fiend would be left to claim your next of kin. By default, the curse would have fallen on me. Where is your regret? Your hour of contrition? Your end could have bought a crude victory."

"No victory that matters," Findlaire rasped, his throat sore. No more would he say, beyond that. Eyes shut, he dreamed of green foliage, and of the roe deer grazing snug in their moonlit glens.

Guriman grew bored. He departed before long, appointing more trustworthy men-at-arms to redouble their guard at the doorway. Barred inside, Findlaire was left to his solitary vigil alongside the dying king. There was no sense of peace in the bony, stilled face on the pillow. No thoughts, in that skull, worth expressing. No work, for the hands that lay childishly soft, but age-spotted against silken coverlets. The oblivion inflicted by Chaldir's fiend did not instill beauty with quietude. Life expended its vigor, robbed of its self-awareness and without the innate, purposeful dignity alive in the simplest tree.

Findlaire tried, and failed, to encompass a concept that escaped definition of loss. His hurts kept him wakeful without need to pace. Throughout the crawling hours of night, he nursed his thrashed flesh, and attended the damaged stubs of the candles. The flames he kept burning shone bright and ephemeral, no less short-lived than the stifled existence he refused out of hand to accept.

Yet when the stars paled, the old king was still breathing. As though human will, through no mind of its own, fought the wraith's passage to its next host through the blank urge of bodily reflex.

When the raw, crimson dawn streaked the sky past the casement, Findlaire pinched out the wicks, one by one. As morning arrived, servants came and relieved him, to endure through the day until sundown.

By now gritty-eyed and aching tired, and wasted from the aftermath of nausea, Findlaire could not face another hour indoors. If he must sleep, he would choose a place where Guriman's penchant for comfort would be most inconvenienced, if he came to gloat.

The battlements between the wind-raked keeps were chilly enough, but the guardsmen blocked Findlaire's access. They refused him passage to the outer wall, no matter which portal he tried.

"Can't let you jump," the armed captain said gruffly. "We've got orders. Your life's to be guarded."

The bailey proved to be off-limits, as well, as too open a venue for assassins.

"Last night's attempt won't happen again," puffed the bowman who tagged at his heels, not pleased to be led on a pointless chase up and down tower stairwells. "Why not accept what can never be changed?"

Another man added, "The greater good of the king-dom demands that the fiend must be given its victim."

Findlaire stopped. He turned his head, his gray eyes wide open. "I'm no man's puppet," he told them.

His guardsmen exchanged dour glances and shrugged. The future was nothing if not inevitable. The terms of the curse would not be thwarted. The fiend would de-vour Findlaire's awareness and inhabit the shell of his body, while Guriman ruled, secure in his post as king's chancellor.

"You know the old fox has planned this for years. He's learned the hard way how to keep the fiend in a state of sated stupor. Why care, in the end? Your mind will be gone. If young children die screaming to feed your damned flesh, why should their suffering matter? The countryside will not be scourged through another reign of terror. For the sacrifice of an innocent few, the fiend's hunger can be constrained. For all our sakes, should your subjects not have the semblance of their prosperity?"

"Paid for, at what cost?" Findlaire shook his head.

But the guards, to a man, looked on without pity. "You don't realize the horrific bloodbath your destined end will prevent."

"I do," Findlaire rebutted. He had read the records. Year upon year, the graphic account had been kept by Chaldir's historians, a sorrowful toll of red slaughter set down in lines of immutable ink.

Findlaire descended another steep staircase, while his armed wardens crowded at his heels.

After a long bout of pacing through corridors and try-ing numerous forbidden doors, he encountered the cramped courtyard which adjoined the queen's aban-doned apartments. The walled garden enclosed a cracked fountain, choked with the yellowed curls of willow leaves. Wind sifted a fine drizzle over the bent stems in the flower beds. Amid tangled weeds, a few hardy chrysanthemums raised blossoms of delicate purple. Half-smothered in snarls of bittersweet vine, the black stands of yew wore their poisonous yield of red berries.

While the men-at-arms grumbled and huddled under the arched portal to forestall the chance to escape, Findlaire walked the puddled pathways. He paused under the hulk of an ancient oak. The crabbed branches were tagged with bedraggled leaves, brown and sickened with galls. The scaled metal of a circular bench girdled the massive trunk. Time and age had expanded the tree's girth, until the collar of ornamental scrollwork had dug in like a shackle. The once graceful tracery of the wrought iron had been swallowed into the bulging, scabrous bark. Findlaire traced his straight fingers over the wound, moved to pity.

For how many generations had Chaldir's indifferent royal gardeners disregarded the tormented oak's plight?

"If I'd stood in my forefather's place with a chisel, I would have spared you this misery," Findlaire told the tree's hobbled spirit.

No remedy could lift the affliction now. The iron was too deeply embedded to excise without destroying the life of the tree.

A breeze ruffled through the leaves overhead. Droplets spilled down like cold tears. The morbid thought stirred within Findlaire's mind that his father suffered a similar blight. He had been throttled while still alive by the unnatural compulsions imposed by a fiend. Yet what axe in the world could cut through a binding curse, and what tool could rend the insubstantial blight of a wraith?

Distraught with sadness, Findlaire sat with his back braced against the wounded tree. For a helpless interval, he sought the illusion of oblivion behind his shuttered eyelids.

Exhaustion overcame him. He slept, while the rain fell and beaded his hair and slicked over his weathered features.

The dream came upon him unaware, its texture spun from the sorrowful thread that shaped his enclosed surroundings. He remained within the queen's ruined garden, amid the sere heads of dead flowers, while the drifts of dry-rotted leaves moldered under the tired oak. The rough bark rasped through the leathers on his back. His feet slowly chilled in his deer-hide boots, and his hands nestled loose in his lap.

Skin, bone, wood, and pith, he melted into the oak tree. The rusted bench kept its strangling grip on the bole, and gradually, over the passage of years, the metal artistry wrought by the smith came to fetter his ankles. He cried from the pain, perhaps as the tree had, voiceless and mute in its agony. None heard. No one came. His legs ached from the pressure. His shins gained weeping sores that scabbed over, transformed into welted scars that paralyzed tissue and tendon. Had he been a red-blooded animal, so deformed, a kind man would have dealt him a mercy stroke.

No such simple expedient was shown to the tree. Shackled in metal, impaired beyond healing, Findlaire ached beyond bearing for loss: the tree's and his own, for a natural freedom imprisoned and twisted by force.

Endurance remained. The tree had not died, though the iron bench girdled it.

For three thousand years, Chaldir's cursed royal line had bound over the lives of its sacrificed princes. Dreaming, Findlaire received the unfolding awareness: that the oak tree knew all their names. He shared the defeated vision of his predecessors, of strong men who had failed: of kings who had died by their own hand, and so condemned their sons, or their brothers. The kings who had tried blinding, or maiming a limb, on the chance that the wraith might reject a flawed vessel, and perhaps move on to roost elsewhere. He knew the fear of the desperately craven, and the seizing terror of others whose hearts had stopped, unable to withstand the uneasy nights of the vigil. He dreamed of men who had fled, and men who had killed their own fathers in ritual, seeking to destroy Chaldir's fiend. He knew the wise men, and their desperate seeking, reduced to vanquished despair. One after the next, Findlaire saw the sad ghosts whose joy and whose laughter had been robbed by the curse that hounded Chaldir's royal lineage.

"You will follow in our footsteps," they said, weeping the tears of the ages. "Like us, you will have no choice at the end. Your sire will die, and you will be left to suffer the next chapter of a blighted legacy."

Bound to the oak's memory, Findlaire saw the changing loom of the garden spin its tapestry of four seasons. Under spring moonlight, he watched generations of Chaldir's jeweled courtiers dance by torchlight or embrace as young lovers under the tree. Their lives seemed more fleeting than those of the moths, which circled the torch flames in blinded frenzy. He witnessed the night when his mother had given her promise to his lost father: that she would flee the realm and bear the king's child in secret, then foster him into a commoner's home to be raised in nameless obscurity.

"There is endurance in oak, and cold iron, and blood." The voice was a woman's, and faint as the whisper of leaves brushed by a passing breeze. "A seed's urge to grow is rooted and fixed. But a man is born gifted with movement and choice. Why has your lineage begotten its sons? Why has each one bequeathed a doomed child, one generation after another?"

"Hope," Findlaire murmured in dreaming reply. The one word contained all the treasure he knew: the green scent of balsam, which had infused the peace and boundless beauty that lived in the summer wood. He offered that grave like a flawless jewel, to the heart of the crippled tree.

Soon after that he opened his eyes to gray mist. His leathers had soaked in the icy drizzle. He felt gritty, used up, and the chill of the rainfall had sunk through to his bones. The neglected garden held nothing but puddles, each reflecting the moss-grown walls, the cracked stone of the fountain, and the tangle of weed-choked flower beds.

Yet standing, attuned to a forester's instincts, Findlaire sensed that he was no longer alone.

An oak leaf winnowed down and feathered his cheek like the brush of a withered finger.

He followed its spiraling flight toward the ground, then noticed the acorn he had missed before, on the flagstone next to his boot. He picked it up. Hope lay within its hardened shell: the unfulfilled promise of a fresh start, and the latent dream of a seedling that might sprout and grow without any hindrance or boundary. Findlaire tucked the acorn into his pocket.

While his uncle's vigilant guards barred the door, the withered leaf settled, trembling.

"The king will die tonight," Guriman said, while outside the glass casement, clouds banked and gathered, and lightning flared on the horizon. "The vigil has lasted for seven days, and the fiend has taken your measure. Are you certain you don't wish me to send you a woman? This may be the last chance you have in this world to savor a human comfort."

"No." Findlaire stood with his back to the wall while the candles around the king's bed were lit, one by one, by a liveried servant. "I will get you no heir." In his hardened fist, clenched over the acorn, he had all the comfort he wanted.

Guriman shrugged. "Such scruple you have! But the gesture is meaningless. I have sons aplenty. The unlucky eldest will inherit the curse. He, or one of his grandsons, will be alive to receive the fiend's wraith when you finally succumb to old age."

Findlaire had nothing to say.

"No last wishes?" prodded Guriman. "No bequests? No noble words for your subjects?" His lightless pale eyes flicked over the tall forester, who held his stilled ground in the corner. "Well, then. Suit yourself. Once the old king is dead and you are possessed, I will return with a living child. You won't be so calm or so reticent then, as you murder to satisfy the fiend's appetite."

Findlaire gripped the acorn. Unlike a man, an unquickened seed could not know the cruelty of anticipation. Its natural being did not encompass the concept of futility or abject despair. A man, trapped to face the descent of the dark, could do little but cling to the undefiled stillness of silence.

Soon enough, Guriman grew restless, and he left. Findlaire remained behind the locked door, with the dying king and the flames of the candles, and the wind-driven rain, beating the barred glass of the casements. Darkness descended, thick as a pall, while the storm gathered force and the gusts shrilled over the tower stonework.

Thunder growled and hammered the air, and lightning cracked over the battlements. Inside the locked chamber, like the hush of held breath, the dread hour approached, when the fiend would spin free of its housing of flesh and lay claim to its next hapless bearer. The release that drew nigh brought the old king no peace. He thrashed, moaning, and plucked at his sheets, as though fighting the wraith that had ravaged him. As though he knew his ending approached, with the spirit left holding its vile burden of murder and the cheated waste of a lifetime.

Findlaire moved, then. He could not ignore suffering. He collected the frail, icy hands of his father. Using the tone that had gentled hurt deer, he sat and spoke quiet reassurance.

"You are not alone. No matter how dreadful the evil inside, someone who cares sits beside you." With no decent shred of comfort to give, Findlaire closed his strong fingers over the old man's and abided. As he had for the tree, he offered up all he owned: the undying renewal that clothed the green glens, steeped in patience to outlast all strife.

In time, the king quieted. His raucous breaths slowed. The fidgeting tremors released his aged limbs. He lay like a figure of chalk on the pillows, while the rhythm of his labored heart missed its beat and finally wearied and stopped.

Findlaire looked up. He saw the glassy stare of dead eyes and understood that Chaldir's doom was upon him. He released the slack hands, stood up, then stepped back, while the jaw of the corpse gaped open. The last wisp of breath sighed out of slack lungs, disgorging the wraith of the fiend.

It emerged as a pallid, luminous mist, writhing like smoke through the darkness. Aware, all at once, that the candles had snuffed, Findlaire gave ground before it. He retreated until he slammed into the wall, as no doubt his victimized forebears had done, on countless nights before this one.

The wraith winnowed toward him. He watched it advance; his pulse raced with dread. Yet where others had shouted or screamed curses, or whimpered in paralyzed fear, his own lips stayed sealed. Findlaire made no sound. With every last fiber of will he possessed, he clung to determined silence.

The fiend came on, an animate, swirling mist that bridged the black air in between. Findlaire pressed against stone, as helpless as his predecessors, while the abhorrent coils snaked in to claim him.

The touch, when it came, was numbingly cold.

Here, many another royal victim had quieted. Battered past all resistance, a man might let go in surrender, grateful for the discovery that his defeat would be softly painless. The wraith's entry would sear out all feeling sensation and seal the mind in dreamless oblivion.

Others fought, hammering their fists bloody in useless rage that their struggle bought no last salvation.

Still others wept blinding tears of self-pity and cried out in wounded loss.

Findlaire held still, without fight, without sound. Yet his calm held no shred of acceptance. The denial he shaped as Chaldir's wraith enveloped him was not the outrage born of defeat. He held nothing else but the flame of his love: for life, for freedom, for the unassailable dignity wrapped up in his memory of balsam.

Eyes closed, lips shut, lungs clamped against the need

to inhale, he clasped the acorn and cherished its limitless promise of hope.

Yet a man can stop breathing for only so long. Wrung dizzy, sucked into the blank ebb toward faintness, Findlaire knew the urge to survive must eventually compel his starving lungs to seek air. When consciousness faltered and reflex resurged, the wraith of the fiend would seize entry. Its freezing draught would flow into his chest, then lace through his blood, and savage his heart.

This, a forester who lived by his traps understood. Like the constricted oak in the garden, he must honor life. He would pay the price of a twisted existence, but that ending would not be eternal. *There would be a seed sometime,* that would find new ground; a king's son who survived to win freedom.

Left nothing else, he must concede that his single failure did not bring defeat for all time. He hung his last thought on that chance for renewal: the heart's-peace of the wood, that did not own strife or acknowledge destruction as final.

While his mind dimmed and the wraith twined about him, and the storm cracked and slammed with unbridled fury, he remembered the maimed tree choked in the garden, and its fathomless strength of endurance.

Hope was an acorn, enclosed in his hand.

As his will broke and his burning chest shuddered, and the wraith's poisoned presence swirled in on the air drawn through his contorted throat, the oak tree gave him, like a perfect jewel, the rooted acceptance of its own being.

Man and tree melded. Human flesh acquired the staid hardiness of wood, and blood flowed, sap slow, thick as syrup. The girdling pain of cold iron-cased ankles that forgot every quickened sensation of movement. Thought froze, and awareness knew only itself, a spiraling force that flowed with the seasons, to grow, and to reach for the light.

The awareness of a tree did not know terror. It did not feel passion or rage or discontent. It tendered no coin but the gift of its ongoing right to existence.

There, the wraith found no pain to exploit, no raw nerve to torment, no desire to balk. However it groped, it encountered no restless need to haze into submission. Stuck fast, nailed still, encircled by life that stayed true to itself within a strangling ring of cold iron, the fiend's hunger could find no resistance to grapple. Man and tree joined for the space of one breath, no more than the gap between heartbeats. On that crystalline instant, the wraith was pinned down. It howled, imprisoned in calm. It battered against the unbreakable dignity held in the latent spark in an acorn.

Life for life's sake framed the only defense its destructive will could not breach.

Given nothing to dominate, the wraith that had fed upon Chaldir's princes lost its power and faded, and finally snuffed out of existence.

Outside the king's palace, the storm reached its peak. Lightning flickered and cracked. The darkness blazed white, seared across by the wild force of the elements. The shaft that spread down struck and split the old oak. Its untamed might splintered bark and limb and warped wood, and unleashed an explosion of blazing fragments. The iron bench glowed sullen red, and then steamed in the quench of the deluge.

Within the closed bedchamber, Findlaire collapsed. He sprawled motionless under the shadow of night, the acorn still cradled within the palm of his defiant hand.

He lay so, as dawn broke and the early light pierced

through the clouds and flooded the glass of the casements. Voices approached from the corridor outside, strident over the wails of a child.

Findlaire woke to that sound. He stirred and beheld the corpse of his father, settled at peace on the bed. Then the door was wrenched open. As Guriman strode through with the terrified offering to further his wicked alliance, the prince who was forester was up on his feet. Nor was he calm any longer.

Guriman quailed before the bared face of his rage. Cowering, he stepped back and hastily passed off the child to one of the guardsmen. "The fiend's wraith," he stammered. "Chaldir's curse on our lineage—"

"Broken!" snapped Findlaire, a man of few words. "You are left with your conscience and with a brother you owe the right of a decent funeral."

At Guriman's back, the henchman who was left clutching the child dropped, shaken, onto his knees. His submission was followed, shame-faced, by others, until not a guard was left standing. "Long live the king."

Findlaire stared at them, startled. Then he shook his head. "Choose someone else worthy. I've already worn the only crown that has any natural meaning."

While Guriman regarded him, speechlessly stupefied, Findlaire let go and laughed. Freed to walk out, he would leave for the forest and fulfill a promise by planting an acorn.

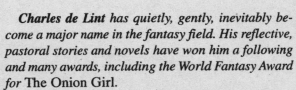

Charles de Lint has quietly, gently, inevitably become a major name in the fantasy field. His reflective, pastoral stories and novels have won him a following and many awards, including the World Fantasy Award for The Onion Girl.

For Flights, *he looks into a thing familiar to his fiction: the prism of human love.*

Riding Shotgun

Charles de Lint

I

I wasn't surprised to learn that my father had died. He would have been seventy-two this winter, and he'd always lived hard—I doubted that had changed after I left the farm. What surprised me was that I was in his will. We hadn't spoken in twenty-five years. I hadn't thought of him, except in passing, for maybe half that time. If you'd asked me, I would have said he'd leave his estate to a charity like MADD, considering how it was drunk driving that changed all of our lives.

I missed the funeral. There are a lot of Coes in the phone book, so it took the lawyers a while to track me down.

When they told me he'd left everything to me, I authorized them to put the farm up for sale, with the proceeds to be split between MADD and the local animal shelter. Dad never much cared for me, but he always did have a soft spot for strays.

I could have used the money. I'm a half-owner of a

vintage clothing and thrift shop in Lower Foxville, and there always seems to be more money going out than coming in. But I knew it wouldn't be right to keep this unexpected inheritance.

Alessandra was good about it. There are things we argue about, but how we deal with family isn't one of them.

We're not exactly a couple, but we don't see other people either. It's hard to explain. We met in AA, and we're good for each other. Neither of us has had a drink in fifteen years—sixteen for me, actually.

We have a pair of bachelor apartments in the same building as the store. Ours isn't a platonic relationship, but neither of us can sleep with someone else. Alessandra gets panic attacks if she wakes and there's someone in bed with her.

For me, it just makes the bad dreams worse.

2

We open late on Mondays, so one fall morning after the farm's sold but before the closing date, Alessandra and I drive out to have a look at the place. Alessandra wouldn't have come at all, but I don't drive anymore, and Newford's public transport system stops at the subdivisions that are still four or five miles south of the farm.

"I haven't been here in twenty-five years," I say as we pull into the lane.

I see the farmhouse ahead, surrounded by elms and maples in their fall colors. The barn and outbuildings lie behind the house, the fields yellow and brown, the hay tall. You know how they say you can never go back, or how everything looks smaller if you do?

As we drive up the lane, everything looks exactly the same.

"I hadn't spoken to him for that long either," I add. "To my father, I mean. Not once."

Alessandra nods. She knows. It's not like we haven't shared war stories a hundred times before. Late at night when the darkness closes in and a drink seems like the only thing that will let us sleep. Instead we talk.

She pulls up near the house and shuts off the engine.

"So what am I doing here?" I ask. "Why would he want me to have anything?"

"I wouldn't know, Marshall," she says. "I never met your father."

And wished she'd never met her own.

I nod. I wasn't really expecting an answer. The question had been pretty much rhetorical.

"Do you have the key for the house?" she asks.

That makes me smile. I'd forgotten about that. So some things have changed. Back when I lived here, I can't remember us ever locking our doors.

"I think I'll walk around a little outside first," I say.

"Sure. I'll wait in the car."

"I won't be long."

She touches the bag on the seat between us. "Don't worry. I've got a book."

She's always got a book. We pick them up by the boxful at garage and rummage sales, usually for free. You'd be surprised what people will just leave on the curb when the sale's done. Saves them carting it back inside the house and storing it, I guess.

At the rate we read, and considering our income,

these books are a real windfall. Reading's another way to go somewhere else and keep the past at bay.

"Don't . . . you know," she says as I'm getting out of the car.

Get all wound up in what you can't change. She doesn't have to say it.

"I'm okay," I tell her.

But I'm not. I don't realize how *not* until about ten minutes later.

If the old man's last will and testament surprised me, what I find behind the barn pretty much takes all the strength from my legs. I find it hard to breathe. It's all I can do just to stand there at the corner of the barn, staring, my hand up on the greying barn wood to keep my balance.

I don't see the rusted junker, sitting in the tall grass on its wheel rims, the tires rotted away, the grille and right fender smashed in, windshield a spiderweb of cracks, side windows gone. I see the car I'd bought in 1977: a 1965 Chevy Impala two-door hardtop, with a 253 V-8 under the hood and 48,000 original miles on it. Black interior, crocus-yellow exterior, whitewalls. That long sleek slope of the rear window.

I'm dizzy looking at it. The wreck it is, the beauty and freedom it represented to the seventeen-year-old who'd worked his ass off for a whole summer and winter to be able to afford it. I see them both for a long time—the car that's there and the one in my head—until it finally settles back into the junker it is and I can breathe again. I push away from the wall, no longer needing it for support.

I had no idea that the old man had retrieved the car after the accident. Or that he'd stored it back here.

I was in police custody for the funeral because there was no one to put up my bail. When I got out of prison after doing my time, the last place I wanted to come was the farm. I wouldn't have been welcome anyway.

I walk over to the car and try the door, but it's rusted shut. I make a trip into the barn and come back with a crowbar to pry the door open. I don't know what all's been nesting in it, but it doesn't smell too bad.

I get in, and my foot bangs against a beer bottle. I remember that bottle, and the other half-dozen just like it I drank that long-ago afternoon.

I sit and stare at the spiderweb cracks that turn the view through the windshield into something like a finished jigsaw puzzle. My chest tightens again. Up on the dash, there's a baseball cap, half-eaten—by mice, I guess. I can make out the insignia. The Newford Hawks, from back when the city had a ball team. I used to listen to the games on a little transistor radio while I was doing my chores.

I'd dream about my car, listen to the games.

After the accident, I had different dreams about this car. About that day. About how it could all have been different.

I still do.

"Let me drive," Billy had said.

"You want to go to the quarry, little brother, you're staying in the shotgun seat."

I'd let him drive before, but I was feeling ornery that day. Too many beers.

Funny.

Alcohol was the problem.

And afterwards, alcohol was the only thing that had let me forget, allowing me the sweet taste of temporary oblivion. But that wasn't until I'd done my time and was

back on the street again. When I was inside, I'd wake up
two, three times a night, that afternoon still as fresh in
my mind as when it happened.

I reach under my shirt and pull out a key on a string.
I can't tell you why I've kept it all these years. I went
through a lot of strings, lost pretty much all I ever had
before I turned my life around again, but I've hung on
to that key through the years.

We've got a jar of old keys in the store, and I've
thought of tossing it in with the rest, but I never do.

Keys are funny things. They can unlock the cage and
let you out, the way it was for me when I finally got that
car. And they can lock you up and stand guard so that
you'll never be free.

That key was both for me.

The string comes over my head easily, and that little
flat piece of metal with its cut edge fits into the ignition
just the way it's supposed to. I don't know why, but I put
my foot on the clutch and turn the key to the right.

Of course nothing happens. It wasn't like I was actually expecting it to start up. But when you have the key
that fits the lock, you have to try, right?

Then I turn it to the left. Backwards.

Nothing.

I smile to myself and start to turn it back, but it won't
budge. I give it a harder turn, then back and forth, trying to loosen it.

Something like an electric charge runs up my arm.

That arm, my whole right side goes numb. There's a
sharp pain in the center of my chest, radiating out. My
vision blurs.

I think:

I'm having a heart attack.

No wonder the old man left the place to me in his will, left this old car just waiting for me.

He knew.

He just *knew* this would happen.

Crazy idea, but I'm not exactly thinking straight. And then I realize the pain's on the wrong side of my body for a heart attack.

Then what—?

The sharp hurt doesn't go away, but my vision clears. Vertigo hits me, deep and sudden, but at the same time I'm disassociated from it. I feel like the world's falling away below me, only it doesn't seem to concern me. Everything stays in focus. Preternaturally sharp.

I watch the cracks in the windshield disappear. They recede, leaving behind clear, uncracked glass. Weirder still, the view beyond the windshield is a flickering dance of images. It's like watching time-lapse photography. Seasons change. Weeds and scrub trees come and ago. Clouds strobe in the sky, here one moment—thick and woolly, or thin and long, or dark and pregnant with rain—gone the next.

And that's when I know I'm dreaming.

Or having some kind of attack.

Heart attack ... panic attack ,,,

It all stops so suddenly, it's as if I've suddenly run up against a wall. The last time I felt like that was twenty-five years ago, when the car was just about to hit the tree. When I put my arm out to stop Billy's forward motion, but there was too much momentum. He just about tore my arm out of its socket with the force of his forward motion. Went crashing into the windshield. Cracking it. Spraying blood ...

The windshield's not cracked anymore.

There's a summer day on the other side of it, not the fall day that's supposed to be there.

"Al . . . aless . . ."

I can't get her name out.

"I'm definitely driving," a voice says from beside me. "You are totally wasted."

I turn so slowly, scared of what I'll see, scared of what I won't see. But he's there. My brother Billy.

Alive.

Alive!

I put out a hand to touch him. To see if he's real.

He can't be real.

He backs away from my hand.

"Whoa," he says. "What's with the groping, Marsh?"

And then I understand. Not how or why. I just understand that I've been given a second chance.

"Are you okay?" Billy asks. "You look a little like Patty Crawford, just before she puked all over the bleachers."

I let my hand drop.

"I . . . I'm okay," I tell him.

My voice sounds like a stranger's in my ears. Distant. No, it's just that it's from another time. Funny, I remember so much, a lot of it in painstaking detail, but not the sound of his voice. Not that mole, on his neck, right under his ear.

"I'm just feeling a little . . ."

"Out of it?" Billy finishes for me. "How many beers did you have, anyway?"

I look down at my feet. There's an empty bottle there. I don't see any others, but I remember I was starting in on my second half of a twelve-pack. I don't even know why. It's a beautiful summer's day. I'm alive. My *brother*'s alive. Why the hell would I be drinking?

"So can I drive?" Billy asks.

I need to explain something here. Billy was the golden boy in our family. The smart one who knew by the time he was fourteen that he was going to be a doctor. I, on the other hand, was unfocused. I liked cars. I liked girls. I liked to party. I had no idea what I wanted to do with my life beyond get off the farm.

The old man didn't get it—because it was different for his generation, I guess. You figured out what you wanted to be, what you *could* be, given your situation in life, and that's what you aimed for. He couldn't understand that not only did I not know, but I didn't care, either.

It was bad enough before Mom died. But after that, the friction between us got worse and worse. I could pretend that he favored my brother because Billy had Mom's blond hair, that his cherubic features reminded us of her, too. But the truth is, Billy was focused—something the old man could admire. He worked hard in school, aiming for scholarships. The money he got from his part-time jobs went into a college fund, not towards a car.

I couldn't begin to compete.

But the funny thing is, I never resented Billy for that. The old man, sure. But never Billy.

His dying was such a waste. See, that was the real heartbreak when he died. He was going to be somebody. A doctor. He was going to save lives.

I wasn't ever going to be anybody.

But I was the one who survived. The drunk driver. The one with nothing to lose.

Sitting here in my old Impala, looking at Billy, I know it doesn't have to be that way now. I can change what happened. I could just refuse to go anywhere, but Billy'd never let up. He was supposed to be meeting some girl at the quarry. So we have to go.

But so long as I'm not driving, it's not going to end the way it did the first time around.

"Sure," I say. "You can drive."

I open the driver's door and walk around the car while he scoots over to my seat. He grins at me when I get in, makes a show of putting on his seat belt. He wasn't wearing one the last time we did this. He takes off his ball cap and throws it onto the dashboard.

I fasten my seat belt, as well, and then we're off.

It's funny, considering how much I've thought of that moment, that day, but I can never remember what caused me to lose control of the car. I just know *where* it happened. I tense up as we start into the sharp turn on our local dead man's curve—more than one car's gone skidding off the gravel here. But Billy's got everything under control. He's driving fast, but not too fast.

And then it comes. Something, I still don't know what. A cat, a dog, a rabbit. It doesn't matter. Something small. Brown and fast.

Billy does the same thing I did—brakes—and the car starts to slide on the gravel. But he's not drunk, and he doesn't panic. He begins to straighten out, but we hit a pothole, and it startles him enough to momentarily lose his concentration. The back wheels skid on the gravel. He touches the brakes, remembers he shouldn't, and lifts his foot.

Too late.

We're going sideways.

He tries to straighten us again, touches the gas. The wheels catch on a bare patch of dirt along the side of the road. We shoot forward. Out of the curve, across the road.

We're going fast enough to clear the ditch.

We clear it.

I see the tree coming up. The same oak tree I hit.

We bottom out on the field—the shocks can't absorb this kind of an impact, but it doesn't slow our momentum.

Then we hit the tree, and the last thing I remember is my seat belt snapping and my face heading for the windshield.

3

"Hey, cowboy."

I blink at the unfamiliar voice. Open my eyes. The bright blue of the sky above me hurts too much to look at. It makes my eyes water, so I close them again and lie there for a long moment, trying to figure out where I am.

When it comes back to me, it's all in a rush: the crash. The same damn crash that killed Billy twenty-five years ago, repeating itself even though this time I wasn't driving.

And if I'm alive, then that means . . .

I sit up fast, and my head spins. I'm lying in tall, summer-green grass. The sky's clear above me; the sun's bright. I can hear the sound of bees and flies and June bugs. I don't hurt anywhere. I turn slowly, take in the big oak tree, the road. There's no car anywhere in sight. No Billy.

That's impossible. I'd think I was dreaming, but if I am, then I haven't stopped, because I'm not back in that old wrecked Impala of mine. I'm here, at the crash site, and it's still summer—not the autumn day when I pried open the Impala's door in back of the old man's barn.

Then I see the girl, the one whose voice brought me out of my blackout. She's standing on the side of the road, one hand on her hip. Her hair's so dark, it's black and she's wearing it pulled back in a ponytail. Her features are pretty, if a little hard. She's wearing bell-bottom jeans, fraying at the hems, and a white tube top. Cute little plastic see-through shoes.

"Welcome back to the world," she says. "Or what's left of it for us."

I realize I know her and dredge her name up from my memory. Ginny Burns. She used to live in the trailer park at the edge of town and ran away from home a couple of years ago—at least it was a couple of years ago if I'm still in the past. She was always a little wild, and her taking off like that didn't really surprise anybody.

Like about half the kids in school, I had a major crush on her, but she was unattainable. Three years older than me, and she didn't date kids.

I'm surprised she's come back.

"Ginny?" I say.

She studies me a little closer. "I know you," she says. "Marshall Coe—right? You've grown up some since the last time I saw you."

I may look like a kid, but I'm a middle-aged man inside this seventeen-year-old boy's body. Still, I feel a flush of pleasure at the thought of her actually knowing my name. I cover it up by standing and brushing the grass and dirt from my jeans.

"So when did you get back?" I ask, trying to be cool.

"What makes you think I ever left?"

"Well, you've been . . . gone."

She gives me a sad smile that softens her features and makes her look even prettier.

"Yeah," she says. "Just like you."

I'm confused for a minute. How could she know I left? Went to jail, moved to the city. That I had this whole life before I found myself back here in my seventeenth year, starting it over again.

"How—?" I start to ask her, but the next thing she says puts a stopper in my mouth that I can't talk around.

"Did I die?" she says. Her face goes hard again. "With a wire around my neck and some freak's dick up my ass."

"I . . ."

I don't know what to say. I'm focused on the word *die*. Then I remember her saying "just like you." And then . . .

"What . . . what do you mean? . . ."

She comes over to where I'm standing. "Sit down," she says, then lowers herself to the ground beside me, sitting cross-legged. "I forgot that it takes time for it all to sink in."

"What . . . seriously . . . what are you talking about?"

"The short of it," she says, "is we're dead. And I don't completely know the long of it."

"Dead? And my brother?"

She shrugs. "You're the only one who's been lying here."

"But we were together in the car. . . ."

"Look, I know it's confusing, but it gets easier. Just don't try to figure everything out at the same time—it's too much at first."

Easy for her to say.

"So I'm—we're dead."

She nods. "Yeah. It wasn't pretty for me, and I guess it wasn't for you either."

"What do you mean?"

"You've been lying here for a few days. Sometimes it takes the soul a while to wake up again—especially if they died hard."

I give a slow nod. "I guess I did. But all I really remember is that tree coming up on me . . . so fast. . . ."

"I wish I *didn't* remember," she says.

I think about the little she's already told me of how she died, and it's already too much. Time to change the subject.

"How do you know all this stuff?" I ask.

She shrugs. "Hanging around in boneyards. The dead have all kinds of things to tell you if you're willing to listen."

"So . . . this is it? This is what we get when we die?"

She shakes her head. "No. Most folks go on—don't ask me where, because I don't know and I haven't met anybody yet who can tell me."

"But these ghosts you've talked to—?"

"Well, like I said, most people go on. Then there's those you find in boneyards, or haunting the place they died. They won't accept that they're dead, so they just . . . linger. And finally there's the folks like us."

She paused a moment, but I don't say anything. I'm not so ready to be a part of her *us*. I don't know that I'm dead for sure. I don't know anything, really. For all I know, I'm still sitting in that junked-out car out behind my dad's barn, dreaming all this up. It would sure explain why I feel so damn calm.

But whether I believe or not, I find myself needing to know more.

"What about"—I still can't say *us,* so I settle for—"them?"

"We've still got unfinished business," she says. "We *can't* go on. Not till it's done."

I figure I know what her unfinished business is.

"You're waiting for your killer to be found," I say.

"Hell, no. I'm just waiting for somebody to find my body so that people know I'm dead."

I can't imagine that. Though I guess if I'm dreaming, I'm actually imagining *all* of this.

"I wonder why I'm still here?" I find myself saying.

"I couldn't tell you."

I give a slow nod. "I guess that's something we all have to work out for ourselves."

I look back at the oak tree, take in the fresh scars on its trunk. Ginny said I've been lying here in the field for days. I guess that explains why the car's not here. And why Billy's gone. I'm hoping it's because he got out of it okay. I'm also hoping that he's not going through what I did, but I don't see why he would. I was drunk, with a history of being picked up for one thing or another. Fighting, mostly, and drinking. But joyriding once. Vandalism a couple of times. By the time of the accident, the sheriff was looking for any excuse to put me away, and it's not like the old man ever stood up for me.

But Billy was about as clean-cut as they come. Dad would go pay his bail. He'd make sure Billy didn't spend an hour in jail, never mind the years in prison I did.

But I have to be sure.

"I need to see that he's all right," I say, and stand up.

"Your brother?"

"Yeah."

"Mind if I tag along? It gets lonesome sometimes."

"I don't mind," I say.

I start to walk down the road, back to the farm, and she falls into step beside me.

"So I guess you're stuck around here," I say.

She gives me a puzzled look, then smiles. "No, we can go anywhere we want. But I keep coming back, thinking there's some way I can get someone to notice me—you know, so I can steer them to my grave? People can see us, but not all the time, and not necessarily when we want them to. Pike says it's not impossible to interact with those we left behind, but that it's really hard. They have to be what he calls *sensitive*. The big problem is that, even if you do make contact, no one seems to get what you're trying to say—it comes out garbled, for some reason, or like a riddle—and it's not like you can write it out for them on a piece of paper, because the thing you can't do is have physical contact with the, you know, physical world."

"Because we're ghosts now."

She nods.

"Who's Pike?" I ask.

"John Pike," she says. "He lived at the end of Connell Road."

And then I remember. He was a real hermit, living in a tar-paper shack at the end of the road. Rumor was, he had a fortune in gold stashed away somewhere in that run-down excuse of a house of his, some kind of treasure, for sure. But he also had a couple of mean dogs and a shotgun loaded with salt that he wasn't afraid to use on trespassers. It did a bang-up job of keeping the curious away when he was alive.

"He died back in '75, '76," I say. "I was just a kid then."

"So was I. But I remember his picture in the paper."

I did, too. This scary wild man, long-haired and bearded. Kids used to dare each other to sneak into his place because everybody knew it was haunted.

"So he really was still hanging around," I say. "Like a ghost."

She nods. "At least he was when I died, and didn't that freak me out when I first met him. But he's gone on now."

She talks about it so easily, like still hanging around after you're dead is the most natural thing in the world. But the funny thing is, the longer we're walking along here, talking, the less unbelievable it seems. I mean, considering how this day's already gone for me ...

"So he said, if we try really hard, we can contact the people we left behind?"

"Yeah," she says. "But that it's also really hard. You need a pretty strong connection between yourself and the person you left behind. And like I said, the time's got to be right and there's no way to guess that moment, so all you can do is keep trying. The world's not real for us anymore. All we can do is look at it. We can't be part of it anymore."

"It feels pretty real to me."

I scuff my shoes against the gravel and send bits of it flying into the ditch.

"It just feels real because you expect it to," she says. "But nothing really moved, and no one can see you. You can't really *affect* anything."

"I just kicked that gravel."

I do it again.

She shakes her head. "No, it just seems like you can. You'll see."

4

"Want to hear a weird story?" I say after we've been walking for a while.

She laughs. "What's weirder than the afterlife?"

I think of what happened about fifteen minutes ago when she stepped in front of this pickup that went barreling by us. How the driver never saw her. How I tried to grab her. How the pickup went right through both of us.

It's taken me most of those fifteen minutes for my legs to stop feeling so rubbery. Except if I'm dead, how come it still feels like I have a body?

"Earth to Marshall," she says.

I blink and give her a confused look.

"You said you had a weird story," she says. "But now you're just being weird."

"Sorry."

So I tell her about it all, my old Impala, how when I was trying to get the key out of the ignition, I found myself here, back in the past.

There's a long silence before she finally asks, "Is this on the level?"

I nod.

"So you're really how old?"

"Forty-three."

"Forty-three," she repeats, and she gets a look in her eyes that I can't describe. "Imagine having all those years."

I kind of glossed over the jail time and the years on skid row, and I don't expand on them now, because I know what she means. I might have had some tough times—doesn't matter that I brought them on myself—but at least I had them.

"Anything you'd go back and change if you could?" I ask instead.

She nods. "For starters, I wouldn't have gotten in the car with the freak that killed me. You know I had a funny feeling as soon as I opened his door, but I so wanted that ride. I was *so* ready to get away from here."

She shakes her head, and I don't know what to say. And then we're at the lane leading up to my old man's farm, and I can't think of anything but Billy and my need to know that he's okay.

She trails along behind as we walk up the lane, the same lane I drove up with Alessandra this morning, except that morning hasn't even happened yet. And I guess the way things have turned out, it never will.

I'm not sure what I expected to find here, but it wasn't the old man sitting on the front porch when he should be out in the back forty with his tractor. He's dressed for work: coveralls over a T-shirt, work boots on his feet, John Deere hat on the table beside him. But he doesn't look like he's ready to go anywhere. He looks deflated—defeated—and I get scared. Not for me, but for Billy. Because I know now: I died in that crash, but so did my brother. There's no other way to explain the old man's grief.

I can barely look at him, sitting there in the rocker, holding a framed picture loosely against his chest, gaze staring right through me as I come onto the porch. Ginny takes a seat on the stairs and doesn't follow me up.

I stand there looking at him for a long time. There's an unfamiliar emotion swelling inside me—unfamiliar so far as it concerns my feelings for the old man. I feel bad. For letting him down. For being such a shit. For not trying to be the man he wanted me to be. But especially for killing the son he loved.

"I . . . I'm so sorry, Dad."

I say the words I never got to say before.

He doesn't hear me, but he shifts in his chair as

though he feels something. Then he lays the photo he's been holding against his chest down on his lap, and I find myself staring down at a school picture of my own seventeen-year-old self.

It's not Billy he's mourning.

It's me.

I back away and slowly make my way down the stairs until I'm sitting beside Ginny.

"What is it?" she says.

I shake my head. For a long time all I can do is stare out across the fields. Ginny puts a hand on my arm. Turns out we can touch each other. We just can't touch anything in the world we left behind.

"It's me," I finally say. "He's mourning me."

"Well, what did you expect? You're his son."

"No, you don't get it. He hated me. When . . . the other time . . . before I changed how it would turn out . . . when I got drunk and my brother died in the crash . . . he never spoke to me again. He never went my bail. He never tried to see me. He was never in the court-room. . . ."

My voice trails off. It's impossible to catalog the enormity of the distance that lay between us.

"So what?" Ginny asks. "Now he hates your brother?"

"I . . ."

I realize I don't know.

I go back up the stairs. The front door's open, but the screen door's closed. I reach for the handle, but I can't get a grip on it.

"Just walk through," Ginny says, coming up behind me. "Maybe we can't touch the world, but it can't touch us either. At least not"—she looks at my father, grieving—"physically."

I need to go inside, to find Billy, but the business with the door is freaking me badly. I can't imagine walking through the screen. But I just can't seem to grab hold of the handle.

Ginny steps by me and walks right through the door—screen, wooden crossbars and all. It's like earlier on the road, when the truck went through us both. She reaches a hand back to me, and I take it. I let her lead me inside.

"Which way?" she asks.

I nod down the hallway towards the kitchen and take the lead, ignoring the closed doors of the parlor and the front sitting room. They haven't been used since my mother died.

When we find the kitchen empty, I lead us up the back stairs. My relief is immediate when we find Billy in his room, sitting at his desk, reading a book. I stay in the doorway, content to look at him, to know he's alive, but Ginny slips past me and walks over to the desk.

"Eeuw," she says as she looks at his book.

I join her and see that he's studying graphic black-and-white pictures of an autopsy. He's had that book for a while, and it *is* gross—I know, I've flipped through it before, but I can never take more than a few pictures

"He's going to be a doctor," I tell Ginny. "He needs to know about this stuff."

"Yeah, but morbid much?"

I shrug. "He's always been interested in how people work. You know, muscle tissue and arteries and nerves and stuff."

Ginny nods. "All the things we don't have."

"I guess."

"He's a good-looking kid," she says.

"He takes after our mother."

I put my hand on Billy's head, trying to ruffle his hair, but my fingers go into his skull. I pull my hand back quickly.

It doesn't matter that I can't touch him, I tell myself. All that matters is that he's alive.

But I'd still like to give him a last hug before I go.

I settle for a look—drinking in the familiar sight of him, sitting at his desk and studying—then I leave the room.

"What was she like?" Ginny asks as she follows me out into the hall.

"Our mom? Everything the old man and I'm not: gentle, kind, thoughtful. And beautiful. She was like an angel, and now she's sleeping with them."

I want to hold that thought, but I can't. Not anymore.

"Unless she's like us," I add as we go down the stairs and step back through the screen door. "trapped in some kind of nonlife, able to see and hear the world go on around us, but unable to interact with it."

"Maybe heaven's where we end up when we go on," Ginny says.

"Maybe," I say, wanting to be convinced.

But Ginny lets my word hang, so if I'm going to believe Mom's safe and happy somewhere, I have to do my own convincing.

I give the old man a last glance before I step off the porch and head back up the lane. There's nothing left for me here now. I don't know what happens next, but at least I've accomplished this much: I've changed the past and made things right again.

But it's funny. I don't feel any better. Truth is, what I really want is a drink. Not a beer, like I was drinking before I died, but a stiff shot of whiskey.

I need some oblivion.

I almost ask Ginny if there's such a thing as ghost whiskey—maybe there's a reason another word for hard liquor is *spirits*—but I settle on stepping out of my own head and getting Ginny to talk about her life instead.

"What was your mother like?" I ask her.

She shrugs. "I don't know. She left us not long after I was born."

I don't remember that from what I knew of her before, but I guess it's not so surprising. The kids I hung with only ever talked about how hot she was.

"That can't have been easy," I say.

"I never knew it to be any different. My dad was good to me—you know, he did his best. But he wasn't equipped to raise a kid, especially not the girl I turned out to be."

I can guess what she means, but I ask her anyway.

"A girl with a reputation," she explains. She shakes her head. "It's not something I ever asked for or wanted, but I sure as hell had one all the same."

"But you—"

I stop myself from saying it, but she nods and gives me a sad smile.

"Put out all the time, right?"

"It's just . . . I heard . . ."

She cups her hands on her breasts. They're not disproportionately huge, but you can't ignore them, either. Not in that tight little tube top.

"I got these the summer I turned twelve," she says, "and by Christmastime, everybody thought I was a slut. I got tired of arguing about it, so after a while, I just started acting like the trailer trash everybody'd already decided I was. But I'll tell you this, I was still a virgin when I died." Her features cloud over. "Well, right up to those last few minutes, I guess."

"I don't understand. Why would all these guys—?"

"Oh, please. Derek Kirkwood was the one who started it—said I'd done it with him under the bleachers during a football game. Now, I *was* down there with him, but only having one of his beers. And maybe I let him kiss me and have a little grope, but we never did it."

"Then why didn't you say something when he started telling people you did?"

"I'd already stopped caring. I had a lot of 'boyfriends,' all right. I was happy to have people take me to dances, to drink their beer and smoke their joints, but the most any of them got was a hand job." She gives me a sassy grin that never reaches her eyes. "But none of them was going to admit they didn't score when Kirkwood supposedly had. They might not ask me out again, but hell. If I *had* put out, they still probably wouldn't have."

"Jesus."

"If I'd've had any brains, I'd've put a stop to that long before it got to that point. But it was kind of fun at first—flattering that all these guys wanted me. And then it was too late."

We've reached the end of the lane, but neither of us makes a move to step onto the road.

"So that's why I took off," she says. "I wanted a new start. I wanted to go someplace where I could be who I decided I was, instead of letting other people decide it for me." She shakes her head. "And you can see what a good plan that was."

"I feel like a shit," I say.

"Why? Because you wanted to get into my pants as much as those other guys?"

I nod.

"Well, don't. I probably flirted with you like I did with any guy. I had a rep to uphold and all."

"It doesn't seem fair."

She shakes her head. "Nope. And neither does what we've got now, but we're stuck with it all the same."

She looks back down the lane at the farmhouse, then turns to look at me.

"So what are you going to do now, Marshall Coe?" she asks.

"I don't know."

"Ever been to Tibet?"

"I've never been any farther than the city—not in this life or the other one I had."

"So let's do a little traveling. Seeing the sights is about the only option left to us at this point."

Now it's my turn to take a last look at the old farmhouse.

I don't understand how my father could be grieving for me, but it's too late now to find out why he is.

I changed the past so that Billy's alive. Instead of the waste of a life I had, he can go out there and help people, make it a better world. But I can't be a part of that world.

So there's nothing left for me here except for the question of why I didn't go on after I died. Thinking about it, I realize I don't really care.

"Sure," I say when I turn back to her. "Why not?"

5

I think time moves differently when you're dead. You don't eat and you don't sleep, but there's always a little hunger in you, that's maybe got nothing to do with food, and while you don't lie down and take a nap, there are holes in your awareness all the same. The days don't seem to follow one after the other so much as jump around. When they don't slide by in a confusing blur.

I guess what I'm trying to say is that I lose track of time. I lose track of everything—the life I had that ended when I tried to start up that old Impala of mine, and the half-day or so of the second one I got.

It all just goes away.

We really do go to Tibet. We go to a lot of different countries, spending most of our time in the wild places. It's not like the big cities aren't interesting—and just as wild in their own way—but it gets old fast when people and vehicles keep going through you because no one knows you're there. That doesn't happen to you in the big empty places. The mountains of Nepal. The Australian outback. Out on the Arctic tundra. Deep in the Amazon jungles. The red rock canyons of southern Utah. The Mongolian steppes. The mountains of Peru. The Sahara.

Sometimes we're noticed there—by people sensitive to the spirit world—but we can't communicate with them, and we don't try. The only conversations we have are with the other dead, and we don't spend a lot of time with them either. The ones who stayed here are mostly a bitter, self-centered group, unable to understand why the world still goes on after they've died. I know I'm generalizing here, but unless one has unfinished business, why stay?

But the people with unfinished business aren't usually such great company either. Most of them died hard and unhappy, and they don't seem as resilient as Ginny in how they deal with it. They're focused on their deaths, determined to get their business done and move on.

No, that's not true. Most of them are just focused on

She was way more than a girlfriend, but I'm not thinking about that right now. I'm thinking about how she was five years younger than me. How right now she'd be fifteen or sixteen, still living at home with her father—the drunk who used her as punching bag.

"I've got to see her," I say.

Ginny starts to say something, but I guess there's a look in my eyes that makes her just shrug instead.

"I'm proud of you, Billy," I tell my brother. "But what the hell are you doing fighting? You're going to be a doctor. You don't have time for crap like that."

He doesn't respond. Why should he? He can't hear me. He doesn't even know that we're here.

Then I lead the way out of his apartment, heading for where Alessandra is living at this time in her life.

"I guess you knew her for a long time," Ginny says when we're standing outside the brownstone where Alessandra and her father live.

I nod. "But not when she was a teenager."

"Then how'd you know to find this place?"

"She took me by here one time. Later, when we were together."

We stand on the pavement for a while, looking at the building. We're at the edge of the sidewalk where it meets the road so that we don't have people walking through us, but there's not much foot traffic anymore. It's almost dinnertime, and most people are home by now.

"So are we going in?" Ginny asks.

"I guess."

But I'm reluctant.

For one thing, I'm feeling this enormous guilt at having let all those years Alessandra and I were together just slip away out of my mind like they didn't mean anything. It was just the opposite. They meant everything. *She* meant everything.

For another, I'm nervous about what we'll find. If we've picked a time when her dad's drunk, it'll kill me to have to stand by, unable to step in and help.

"Marsh?" Ginny says.

I turn to look at her.

"You don't have to do this."

I shake my head. "Yeah, I do."

And I move forward, up the steps. Apartment 310, Alessandra told me. We walk through the front door and into the foyer—doing this has long since stopped bothering me—and head up to the third floor. We can hear yelling when we come out of the stairwell, and it gets louder as we go down the hall. Then there's the sound of breaking glass.

"Is her mother around?" Ginny asks, her voice hushed.

"No. She died when Alessandra was just a kid."

We step through the door, into the apartment. The noise is coming from down the hall, in the kitchen. I don't want to be here. I don't want to bear silent witness to Alessandra's terrors.

But I can't stop myself now.

Alessandra's stories were bad, but it's worse seeing it firsthand. She's lying on the floor, curled into a fetal position and bleeding from a cut on her head. Her father's standing over her, a broken bottle in his hand. That explains the cut.

Alessandra's crying—soundlessly, trying to be invisible. That's how she'd describe it to me. That all she was ever able to do was try to be invisible.

But it never helped.

Her father's yelling something, but I can't make out the words through the red rage that comes over me.

I've hated this man for a long, long time. In another, forgotten life, but it all comes back to me now in a rush. All those nights that Alessandra woke up crying. All those war stories she told, her voice flat, her eyes lost, looking off into the past.

Her father pulls back his foot, and I lose it.

I charge at him, hands flat in front of me.

I don't know what I'm thinking. What good will it do if I go running through him? But I can't do *nothing*.

And then the impossible happens.

My hands meet flesh. The force of my momentum knocks him backwards, off balance, and he goes down. The back of his head catches on the edge of the kitchen counter and makes an awful sound. A wet, *cracking* sound.

He twists as he falls. Lands on the floor. On his face.

And he doesn't move.

I stand there, stunned, then slowly step forward. I nudge him with my foot, but the toe of my shoe goes right through him.

I turn to Ginny. "What . . . what just happened? . . ."

She shakes her head, and we stand in the kitchen for what seems like a very long time. Staring at him, waiting for him to move.

He never does.

But Alessandra gets up. She holds her hand to her head, and blood seeps through her fingers. She shuffles over to him with the look of a scared dog, ready to bolt at a moment's notice. She does what I did, nudges him with a foot. Her shoe makes contact, but her father still doesn't move.

She stares at him, emotions playing across her features. Then she spits on him and slowly backs out of the kitchen.

I'm about to follow her—to do I don't know what—but Ginny grabs my arm.

"Marsh," she says, her voice strained.

I turn to see that the body on the floor has started to glow. Ginny and I exchange puzzled glances. When we look back, the glow is lifting from the body, separate from, but retaining the body's shape.

It's Alessandra's father. The *spirit* of her father. Sitting up.

Neither of us has ever seen somebody die before. We've never been right there when it happens. We don't know *what's* going to happen.

I'm thinking, I don't want to be here.

The spirit looks around, then pushes itself up from the floor until it's finally standing. Its face turns to us, but before I can tell if we register in its consciousness—if it even has a consciousness at this point—the spirit begins to diminish. I'm not quite sure how to describe it. It's as if there was a tiny pinprick hole in the fabric of the world, and the light that makes up the spirit just gets sucked away into it.

The last thing we see is that pinhole, shining a light so fierce that when it abruptly winks out, we have stars flashing in our gazes.

I clear my throat, then manage to say, "I guess it . . . went on."

Ginny gives a slow nod. "I guess."

I remember Alessandra, and we go looking for her, but she's left the apartment. I don't know if my killing her father is going to make things better or worse for her. If it's going to stop her slow descent into alcoholism that fol-

lowed her finally getting away from the man in the life
where I knew her, or if it's going to push her into a more
radical plunge into I don't know what.

I can only hope she'll be all right.

"Was this my unfinished business?" I say, thinking
aloud. "Helping Alessandra—maybe saving her life?"

"You're still here, aren't you?" Ginny says.

There's that.

I reach towards the nearest wall, and my hand goes
through it. Just like it always has since I died.

"How could I have been able to push him like that?"
I say. "I can't even pick up a pencil."

"I don't know. Maybe you just . . ."

"Just what?" I ask when she doesn't finish.

"Really needed to," she says. She seems reluctant.
"Maybe if we need to do it badly enough . . . we can. You
know, to help somebody or something like that."

I study her for a long moment.

"You've known this all along," I finally say. "Haven't
you?"

She nods. "But it's nothing I've ever been able to do.
Pike told me about it."

"Why didn't you tell *me*? Why were you so insistent
on my believing that we can't affect the real world?"

"I was scared."

"Scared of what?"

"That you'd leave me."

"I don't understand," I say. "You told me that when
we first met. You didn't even know me then."

She shrugs. "You just seemed so normal—and you
were, too. You are. I'd been so lonely for so long. . . ."

I'm beginning to understand.

"You know how to deal with your own unfinished
business, don't you?" I say.

She won't meet my gaze, but she nods.

"But you're scared to go on to . . . wherever it is we go next."

"I had so little time to be me," she says. "What happens when we cross over? Do we just disappear like your girlfriend's father did?"

"We don't know what happened to him. Where he went."

"I know. But I don't want to go yet. I'm not ready."

I can tell she hates saying it, because it groups her with all those losers hiding out in their graveyards, able to go on, but refusing to do so.

"Is there even such a thing as unfinished business?" I ask.

She nods.

"And when we do it—whatever it is—do we just get sucked away like Alessandra's old man did?"

"No. But, you know. You start feeling . . . thinner. Like there's nothing keeping you here anymore except your own need to stay."

"Did the graveyard ghosts tell you that?" I ask.

She shakes her head. "No, Pike did."

"Too bad he's not around anymore." I say. "I'd like to have asked him about all of this."

She told me he'd gone on, way back when we first met. But when I look at her now, I see from the expression on her face that that wasn't true either.

"He's still haunting that shack of his, isn't he?"

She nods.

We stand there for a while, neither of us speaking, uncomfortable with what's lying between us and too aware of the dead body in the kitchen, of what we both saw happen to the spirit that rose up from it.

I can't leave it like this.

"I won't leave you behind," I tell her. "When we go, we can go together."

"Promise?"

I nod.

But then everything changes again. Because when we go out looking for Alessandra, we find, instead, the ghost of a broken girl.

6

Her name's Sarah Hooper, and I recognize her from the picture in the newspaper that I saw earlier today. She's the third victim of whatever freak it is who's been going around killing young women over the past few weeks. She looks even smaller and frailer in person than she did in the photo. But she didn't go down easy.

"They say you shouldn't fight back," she tells us, "but I didn't care. I guess I knew he was going to kill me, and I just wanted to hurt him if I could. I hit him a few times—in the face, where I knew it'd show—but in the end, he was just . . . you know . . . too strong. . . ."

It's not too hard to figure out what her unfinished business is.

She was pretty messed up when we found her sitting on the ground in an alley not far from Alessandra's apartment, just staring at the brick wall across from her, but she's tougher than she looks.

"So I'm really dead," she says as we bring her up to speed on what she is now, why she's here. "I wasn't sure." She laughs, without any humor. "I know how that sounds, but you don't expect to still be around . . . after, you know? Not like this, where nothing seems any different except you can't touch anything. Nobody can hear or see you."

"Do you think you'd recognize the guy?" Ginny asks.

"Oh, yeah. We have—had a class together at the university. I never really talked to him except for this one time when he asked me out, but he caught me on a bad day and I just shot him down."

Ginny nods. "He gave you the creeps even then."

"Not really. He's just one of those guys with the choirboy good looks, and that's never appealed to me. But mostly I guess I was so hard on him because of the way he was always looking at me in class. He was, like, *always* watching me, it seemed."

"Do you know his name?" I ask.

"Coe," she says. "William Coe—don't try to call him Bill, or Billy. I called him Bill when I was turning him down, and he set me straight pretty quick."

Everything inside me goes still.

"Are . . . are you sure?" Ginny asks.

Sarah nods. "You don't forget the name of the guy who kills you." Her gaze goes from Ginny to me. "Do you know him?" she asks.

I give a slow nod. "He's my brother."

"Your brother. Jesus." She pauses for a heartbeat, then adds, "So did he kill you, too?"

I start to shake my head, but Ginny speaks up before I can.

"He was driving the car when Marsh died," she says.

I want to say he didn't do it on purpose, but I'm having too much trouble getting my head around the idea that Billy could be responsible for this woman's death. And at least two more.

Billy, who wanted to be a doctor. To help people.

Or mâybe just to find out how they work so he'd know the best way to hurt them. To prolong their pain.

Because I'm thinking of that book with all the autopsy photographs in it. Maybe . . . maybe those pictures made him feel good. . . .

The idea of it makes me sick.

"So," Sarah's saying, "I just need to find a way to . . . what? Bring him to justice? Get my revenge on him?"

"Something like that," Ginny says.

"And then what?"

"You go on."

"Go on where?"

Ginny shrugs. "We don't know. Nobody on this side does."

Sarah gives a slow nod of her head. "I've got to think about this."

"You don't have to be alone," Ginny says as Sarah starts to walk away.

"Yeah, I do," she says. "I really do."

We watch her walk away, down the alley. Neither of us makes a move to stop her.

"So that's where he got the black eye," I say.

Ginny nods. "I'm so sorry, Marsh."

"You had nothing to do with it."

"I know. But . . ."

"And that damn book of his. It should have been a clue."

"There's no way you could have known."

A deep sadness has settled inside me. But riding on top of it is the same anger I felt a few hours ago when Alessandra's father was beating her. I have that need to hit something, and I kick at the nearest garbage bag. It goes flying across the alley and breaks against the far wall, spilling its contents.

"Don't be mad at me," Ginny says.

I know what she's thinking. First she disappointed me, and now my brother's hurt me even worse.

But I'm not mad—not at her. She wasn't deliberately trying to hurt me. She didn't tell me everything only because she was so lonely.

Maybe if I really was the seventeen-year-old I look to be . . . maybe I wouldn't understand. But I've seen things that kid never has and never will. Prison, living on the streets, the life of an alcoholic. I know that people mess up and get messed up by what life hands them.

Ginny had a fucked-up life and a worse death. And then she spent two years as a ghost, unable or unwilling to touch or be touched by anything or anybody. Is it any wonder she's clung to the first person who came along and treated her the way everybody deserves to be treated?

"I'm not mad," I tell her.

"How can you not be mad? I've lied to you about everything."

I shake my head. "No, just about the one thing."

"But maybe you could have stopped your brother *before* he started killing those girls."

Girls who died the way she did, alone and hard.

I hadn't even thought of that. That I could have stopped him.

"Maybe," I say. "But probably not. I'd've had to follow him around every day, just to know he was doing it. I'd have to *suspect* him first, and why would I do that? He was my little brother. You don't suspect your little brother of being a freak. So I'd've had to catch him in the act—or heard about it the way we just did—to believe."

And maybe that's my unfinished business. I came

back and changed the way things were meant to be. Maybe my unfinished business is to fix this second mistake, because it looks like what I thought was my first mistake—drunk driving, killing my own brother—wasn't really a mistake at all.

Ginny's gaze goes to the garbage bag I kicked against the wall, then returns to me. I know what she's thinking. But she says it anyway.

"You have to kill him—like you did your girlfriend's dad."

Don't think I haven't already thought of that. But I shake my head.

"I don't know if I can just kill a person in cold blood," I say.

"What do you call what happened back in your old girlfriend's apartment?"

"An act of passion. Not something I planned to do like this would be." I sigh. "But it's not just that."

"Is it because he's your brother?"

I shake my head again, but I don't have any words for a while. I stare at the spill of garbage across the alley.

Ginny waits. Finally, I turn to look at her.

"I think I probably could do it," I say. "But I just can't stop thinking about the three girls that he's killed. How there might be even more—they just haven't found the other bodies yet."

"And if we don't do something now, he'll kill even more."

"I know. What I'm trying to figure out is a way to undo what I've done so that nobody ever got killed."

Understanding dawns in Ginny's eyes.

"You're going to try to get the car to bring you back again."

I nod.

"You're going to leave me."

I want to say, it's not like that. But we both know it is.

7

The old Impala's still out behind the barn. My dad saved it this time around, just as he did before. It's not in as bad shape as it was in my other life. The front end's still banged in, and the windshield's cracked. But it's still got all its windows, and it's not nearly as rusted out. There's not as much scrub and weeds growing around it either.

We get in the car and stare out through the cracks in the windshield. In this life I don't have a key hanging around my neck. But in this life there's a key still in the ignition.

I put my hand on it, but my fingers go right through.

I think about Billy, let the anger come back, but that doesn't help either.

"Maybe all I have to do is wake up," I say after about ten minutes of this. "Maybe all of this really is just a dream—right from when I first stuck that key in the ignition."

"Except I'm here," Ginny says.

I don't want to say, that doesn't make a difference. It could still be a dream.

"There's that," I tell her instead.

"You must be doing something wrong," she says.

Now that she's accepted that I'm doing this—or at least that I'm trying—she's been full of useful suggestions. Unfortunately, they aren't helping any more than my own efforts.

"What were you thinking about when it happened before?" she asks. "Were you really concentrating on the day of the crash . . . on your brother? . . ."

I shake my head, and her voice trails off.

"I wasn't thinking hard about anything," I say. "And for sure I wasn't looking for a way to live it all over again. I spent most of that other life of mine just trying to forget."

"Then I guess we need to go see Pike."

"I guess we do."

The funny thing is, this need of mine to stop Billy ... I'm not even sure that this is my unfinished business. If I believe that, then I have to believe that life is preordained, and I don't buy that. We make a difference in the world. For good or bad, whether we want to or not, we make a difference. And I think it's our choices that make the difference.

But I'm not really looking for a Frank Capra moment here, though I'd love to wake up from this.

Instead I find myself at what's left of John Pike's ruin of a shack with the crazy-looking old man himself sitting there on a rocker, the ghost of an old bluetick hound asleep at his feet.

"Been a while," he says to Ginny.

She nods. "I want you to meet my friend," she says, and introduces me.

I can't help myself. I have to ask about the treasure, if it really exists.

"Sure, it does," he says. "Have a look inside."

So I do, but there's nothing there. Just a big mess of moldering books and magazines, old newspapers yellowed and chewed up by mice.

"I don't see it," I say.

"It's right in front of you, boy. The books. The *learning*. You won't find a bigger treasure than that."

The kid I look to be would have been disappointed. And I do feel a little twinge of disappointment myself, because like everybody else, I half believed those stories. But I understand what he means. I learned the worth of books and knowledge over the years. Mind you, I didn't use them to learn so much as to occupy my mind so that I wouldn't think of other things—things I used to wipe out of my mind with alcohol before I went on the wagon.

"We need your advice," Ginny says when I come back out onto the porch.

And then we tell him the whole sorry tale.

"Can't be done," he says when we finish up. "I've got some ideas about how you did it in the first place, but without a body, you're not going to be able to do it again."

"You're sure about that?"

"Sure as I'm dead, and I'm plenty damn sure about that."

I try not to let my frustration show, and I look out across the scrub brush lot that fronts what's left of his cabin.

"But that doesn't mean there isn't a solution to this problem of yours," he goes on.

I turn back to look at him, trying not to feel too much hope.

"I've heard stories," he says, "of spirits who ride a living person—take them over and make them do the things that are so hard for us ghosts to do. *Physical* things."

"You mean like possess them?"

He nods. "You just slip into their heads and take over. It works best with someone who's empty—you know, he's got nothing going in his life, nothing to look forward to. They're just waiting for any damn thing to come along and fill them up."

I start to understand what he's telling me, but that won't work with Billy. He's got too much to look forward to. All these other girls he's going to kill . . .

"But it also works on someone you were close to when you were alive," Pike adds. "Works better, maybe."

"Like my brother."

He nods. "But the way I heard it, you get only the one shot at riding somebody. You can't just jump from person to person."

"I'd only need the one shot." I hesitate, then add, "Except how do I know I can get the car to take me back again? I don't even know how it worked in the first place."

"It's not the car that's doing it," Pike says. "I think it's the key."

"What do you mean?"

"Sometimes, if you touch something often enough for luck, all those touches gather up inside the thing to become a real charm, the way riverbanks get beaches when sand drifts up in the curve of the watercourse. It's not planned—it just happens. And not all at once, but slowly, over the years."

"You think I made a charm out of that key?"

"Have you got a better explanation?"

I didn't.

"So," Pike goes on, "you just have to hope the key sitting there in the ignition of that car is the same one that you carried around with you for all those years."

"It probably is," Ginny says, "because you didn't get to take it away with you this last time."

Because this last time I died.

"And if that's the case," Pike says, "it's probably the same key you brought back with you from that other life of yours."

If, if, if . . .

"There's only way you're going to find out," he tells me.

Taking over Billy's easier than I think it will be. He's sitting in class at the university, and I just sidle up to him and slip right in. Then I get up and walk out of the lecture hall, leaving his books behind. Ginny falls in step beside me, and I turn to look at her.

"I can still see you," I say.

"I guess once you know how, it doesn't go away."

"You had a funny look on your face just now."

She nods. "I wasn't sure who it was inside."

She reaches out a hand to touch my arm, but it goes right through.

"We better get going," I say. "Before Sarah shows up with her own revenge in mind."

When we get outside, I check Billy's wallet. There's enough money in there to take a cab out to the farm, so that's what we do.

The old man's out in the back forty—we can hear his tractor from here—so we know we won't be disturbed. I get in behind the wheel, but I look at Ginny sitting beside me before I touch the key.

"I don't mean to break my promise," I start to say.

She shakes her head. "It's okay. I'm already dead. Saving these girls is way more important."

"I wish I could go back and save you."

"I wouldn't have listened to you anyway. You'd be just this kid, talking weird."

"If this works, I'm going to look for you when I'm done."

She gives me a sad look.

"I won't know who you are," she says. "All these years that we've been together won't have happened. Not for me."

"I'll remind you."

"Don't make any more promises."

There's no blame in her voice, but it hurts all the same.

"I can't even kiss you good-bye," I say.

She smiles, the sadness deepening in her eyes.

"I wouldn't want you to," she says. "Not looking like . . . him."

I nod. I reach for the key and turn it, waiting. But nothing happens.

"Do whatever you did the last time," Ginny says.

I think about it until it comes back to me. I turn the key right, then left twice, then quickly back and forth, and damned if the electric charge doesn't come rushing up my arm and the world around me starts to do its rewind thing again.

"Good-bye, Marshall Coe," I hear Ginny say. "I'm going to miss you."

Then she's gone and I'm back in time again, Billy and me, sitting in the car on that long ago afternoon.

8

Here's the thing that none of us considered: If I'm riding Billy, who's going to be inside my body?

I find out pretty quick.

I don't come back to the same moment I did before,

where Billy was trying to convince me to let him drive. I come back to where he's already in the driver's seat, about to start up the car. I turn to look beside me and I'm sitting there—which, let me tell you, is freaky enough. But even freakier is, it's Billy looking out of my eyes.

"What the hell? . . ." he says.

His voice is slurred—from all the alcohol in my body that he's not used to, I guess—and he's totally confused. Well, who can blame him? But I don't give him time to adjust. I start up the car and pull out from behind the barn—my third time making this trip.

"Oh, Jesus," Billy says. "Stop the car, Marsh. I . . . I'm . . . something's wrong. . . ."

I just keep on driving.

He reaches out a hand to me, but I shove him against the passenger's door. Hard. His head bangs against the doorframe.

He's saying something else, voice rising in panic, but I tune him out because I need to work this through. I thought I'd go back to when I arrived the last time, before I let him get behind the wheel. I'd refuse to let him drive, and everything'd go back to the way it's supposed to be.

But obviously, I didn't.

It takes me a moment to figure out why I didn't. It's because when I worked the mojo this time, it was his body turning the key. This was the only point we could return to, when he had *his* hand on the key in the ignition.

What I have to do is figure out what happens next.

If the passenger always dies in the crash that's coming up, does that mean he'll die in my body? Or will we switch back and I'll die again?

I can't take that chance. It's not that I'm scared of dying—I've already been there. It's that I can't take the chance that *he'll* survive.

Then I realize what I have to do. I can't let the crash happen. I don't know how I'll stop him from becoming the killer he's going to be, but that's not something I should be trying to work out while driving this car.

On this road.

On this afternoon.

"Jesus Christ, Marsh!" he yells. "Stop the goddamn car!"

We're driving faster than I realized, but he's fumbling with the door handle anyway, trying to get it open. He's still got his seat belt on. But he could take it off. He could fall out. And at this speed, he could kill himself.

I keep one hand on the wheel, and grab at him.

Turn my gaze back to the road.

And realize we're already into the curve.

How'd we get here so fast?

Billy struggles in my grip. I stomp my foot on the brake but he pulls me at just that moment and I hit the gas pedal instead. I see the flash of the little animal darting out onto the road. I don't know if we run over it or not because right then we're leaving the road, heading straight for that damned oak tree again, and I realize I screwed it up this time, as well.

9

I get to go to the funeral this time.

My own funeral. In Billy's body. How weird is that?

Not half as weird as things are going to get, I guess. I have to deal with my father's grief. Then there's the whole business of being Billy, only I can't be Billy. I can't become the doctor he was going to be. I don't have it in me. I'm having enough trouble just *pretending* to be him these past few days.

To tell you the truth, I don't know how long I can deal with any of this. I mean, I can't even look in a mirror.

So I don't know what's going to happen, how long I'll last, but I know I have to hang on for a while because I still have some unfinished business. For one thing, there's a girl in the city who needs looking after. I have to get Alessandra away from her old man. But I can't just waltz in and sweep her away. She's only twelve or so at the moment.

Hell, I look to be only sixteen myself.

But there's something else I have to do before I deal with any of that.

After the funeral, I go back to the house with my father. He changes like he's going to work in the fields, but instead he takes down that photo of me and goes out and sits on the porch. Holding the photo. Staring across the fields.

I change, too. I walk around behind the barn to where my old Impala sits. I ask the old man why he had it towed here.

"It's all we've got left of him," he tells me.

There's no key in the ignition. I found it in my hand after the crash, and I put it in my pocket—just as I did the first time around. And just as in that other life, I'm wearing it on a string around my neck.

Don't ask me why. It just seems important.

I look at the car for a while longer, then walk away, across the fields alongside the house until I get to the country road. I follow it to the dead man's curve, leav-
　　the road when I reach the old oak tree.

Anybody seeing me here is going to think I'm mourning my brother, but I'm not. I'm waiting for Ginny to show up.

I've come each afternoon since the crash.

I don't know if I'll be able to see her, but I call her name, and I talk out loud, hoping she's around, that she can at least hear and see me, even if I can't see her. I tell the story of the first time we met, and I urge her to stop living a half-life. To finish her business here and go on.

I can't tell if she hears me. I can't tell if she follows my advice or not. So I come back each day and do it all over again.

Today's no different. I walk up to the oak tree and lay my hands on the fresh scars that mar its bark. I say Ginny's name. Once. Twice.

And this time a voice answers me.

"Who are you?"

I turn, and there she is, standing on the side of the road, the same way she was the first time I met her.

"You're here," I say.

And I smile. It's the first time I've smiled in three days. It's so good to see her again.

"You can see me," she says. "You're alive and you can see me."

"Yeah, I can."

"And you can hear me."

I nod. "Come down and sit with me, Ginny. We need to talk."

She studies me for a long moment, then slowly comes down from the road and sits down under the oak. She puts out a hand to touch me, but her fingers go through my arm.

"I thought maybe . . . ," she says, but she lets her voice trail off.

Something I can't read moves in her eyes, and she looks away. I wait, patient, until she turns back to me.

"I know you," she says. "You're Marshall Coe's little brother."

It's such a small thing, but I'm pleased that she remembers me—remembers *me* by name—and not Billy.

"Yeah. Well sort of."

"What do you mean, 'sort of'?"

"It's a long story," I tell her.

"The one thing I have a lot of is time," she says.

"I know."

"*How* do you know?"

So I start to tell her, right from the beginning, the way I've just told you.

A. A. Attanasio has authored nineteen novels, *which include* Radix, The Last Legends of Earth, The Moon's Wife: A Hystery, The Dragon and the Unicorn, *and a biker variation on the* Iliad, *written with Robert S. Henderson, titled* Silent.

He lives—and oh, how I envy him—in Hawaii.

DEMONS HIDE THEIR FACES

A. A. Attanasio

Winterset in Egypt beside the rotting canal at Sidi Bishr, with the little, ceramic hashish pipe in her freckled hand, a thin thread of palpitant smoke twisting in the air before her, the professor faced her student and informed him seriously and with hollow impersonality, "The most avid collectors of books are demons. But they want only the old texts. The *oldest* texts."

The student, with his generous innocence, didn't take her meaning literally. "Yeah, I've heard tell that a smuggler in the stalls of Portobello Road can get thirty thousand pounds for even a small tablet from the dynasty of Nippur." He was a young man, with the look of a young man. "Those prices would make anybody a devil." Rufous hair cropped close to a round head, alert, brown, lemuroid eyes, and a lanky frame gave him the winsome aspect of a youth who had flourished as an antelope in another life.

* * *

That memory of ignorance traveled with him wherever he wandered across the floor of the damned. He never tired of recollecting his evening in Sidi Bishr and touching the pain of the nescience that had delivered him to this eerie netherworld. He never tired at all—for in hell, no one sleeps.

"Texts are more than you think they are," said the professor, and the sweet smoke from her pipe puzzled the air between them. "It's not for the money that demons want those ancient artifacts."

Again, he assumed that by demons the professor meant immoral collectors, people who would stop at nothing to acquire the rare cuneiform tablets and cylinder seals that commanded the highest prices at auctions. His misunderstanding was natural, for the professor did not seem a woman inclined to supernatural fantasies. She was known among the wealthiest families in both hemispheres as an antiquary of the highest erudition with postings as a bonded codex agent for Christie's and Sotheby's, credentialed as a bibliopole at the Museum of Antiquities in Berlin, and tenured as professor of historiography on faculty at the Sculo Normale Superiore in Pisa, where the student had met her.

His quest began at the Horned Gates of Goetia. Footed upon a lakebed of jagged lava and grouted with human bones, a colossal time-stained wall extended to the bor-
d￼ f sight, wide as the worldrim. The improbable
￼ reared toward an indigo zenith and chimeric
￼es that ranged across the welkin with a dis-

dainful and seraphic likeness of floating pagodas and blue tabernacles.

A round gateway stood unguarded. Corroded iron palings, wrought intricate as Gothic heraldry for devils, told him nothing. Nor did he recognize, at first, yon cinderland.

"I don't think we're going to find any valuable artifacts here." The student watched gnats spinning in the humid air above the putrid canal, where children dived into the ooze for coins. No bookstalls existed among the sprawling hovels of oyster-colored brick. "Why are we here?"

"The oldest texts are puissant talismans against evil." The professor sucked placidly on her ceramic pipe and watched light bleed from the citron sky. "Do you believe in evil?"

He squinted to see if she were teasing him. On the crowded tram out of Alexandria, which had forced them together among Bedouin with their chickens and vegetable baskets and improvident Egyptian families on their way to the dense Attarine Quarter or their steep littoral villages outside El Iskandariya, she had offered nothing. "Does it matter what I think?"

Does it matter? Had he actually said that to her? He could no longer be certain if that fateful evening in Sidi Bishr stamped his mind with memory or imagination. Since entering Goetia, mongrel speculations prospered. The wind coughed like a lion in this gloomy world. Individual clouds hung low over slurry horizons and migrated lumberingly as herds of gray bison.

From out of the mists, a rider approached, a plum-blue African in a snowy turban. Upon the broken ground, his camel set down its large soft pads with serene elegance. The rider turned his flat profile toward the carbolic brink of the sky and spoke in Enochian, a language like the screaming of eagles.

"So, you cherish a modern sensibility?" Behind the professor, scarlet rays reached through clouds of mosquitoes and glimmered on the violet waterways and the goose-winged sails of dhows hurrying toward night. "You accept that we are infinitesimal creatures, our lives insignificant, our opinions of reality arbitrary and ultimately meaningless. Yes?"

"Reality itself is meaningless."

"Ah. Quite so." She laughed as abruptly as snapping a twig or plucking a flower. "Does that trouble you?"

"Should it?" The student felt annoyed. Love—or an alloy of carnal yearning and exotic allure that the student understood as love—had inspired him to follow her to Egypt on what she called a "book hunt." He had hoped that this trip would provide an opportunity for serious work by which he could demonstrate his skills and perhaps win her affection. But she seemed to be toying with his mind. And that stirred in him both gamey vexation and quirky arousal.

Was it the desperate moment of standing in a volcanic terrain the color of elephants—or the redolence of sandalwood lufting from the rider's black aba that inspired th͏ dent to take the large extended hand? No sooner ͏hoisted atop the camel than they hurtled into ͏͏og.

The crying wind seethed. Eyes bleared by mist and speed, he pressed his face into the rider's back, breathed deeply of tawny incense. The wind's tormented cries writhed louder. He couldn't stop his ears for holding on to the rider, clasping with all his might not to be thrown by the jaunting beast.

The wind, shrieking through the crannies of his brain, buckled into voices. Schizoid whispers and shouts assailed him. Vaporous calls and responses feathered into ghostly conversations. And the cloven wind, like a vast living thing, uttered intimacies and obscene endearments that pinned his soul like a rape victim.

The professor said with sad resignation, as if imparting a fact stolen from the dead and costing her soul, "The measure of a mind has no other gauge than the significance that the mind endows upon the world."

"Then, my measure is pretty close to zero," he answered, allowing himself to sound nettled, "because I don't think the world has any significance whatsoever."

"Zero—" She smiled without mirth. He had never before seen a woman of such farouche beauty, and her unhappy smile stirred in him a scary and parlous thrill. "Zero is a most remarkable cipher—a figure of wonder second only to infinity."

"I was never much for math."

"And yet, math is all there is. Ever ponder that fact?" Behind wisps of sun-crayoned hair, her broad face—with its faceted cheekbones, violently askew nose, and proud, Byronic jaw—surveyed reality through eyes ice green and recessed as a pugilist's, with no farded upper lid. "Ever wonder why mathematics so precisely maps reality?"

"Never gave it any thought."

* * *

Sunrays slashed the fog of Goetia to summer haze. The
camel bumped softly along a grassy hummock. Park-
land sprawled before them, replete with chestnut av-
enues, flowery hedgerows, and high, peaceful fields
tilted on slopes of emerald sward. The blue of the cu-
mulus sky cut his heart with bliss.

They stopped, and the turbaned rider reached
around, grabbed his passenger's arm, and deftly swung
him to the ground. "You understand me now," he said in
a chamois voice. "The wind has brought you to the
Enochian language."

"Who are you?"

"I am the messenger sent to deliver you from the
Goetic Gates." Behind him, a flock of doves flew into
the beautiful sky. "This is where we part, I to the up-
lands and you—you go down there." The blue-black
face gestured behind the traveler to a charred swamp of
haggard briar, a smoldering garden of tormented trees
hung with lichens and shag moss tattered and sere as
rotted cerements.

"Of course. You're a bibliophile, as am I." The professor's remorseless gaze frightened and thrilled him. She
looked simultaneously menacing and incomprehensibly
lovely. "Words are your passion, yes?"

"Yes."

"You realize, of course, that words began as numbers.
The ꜰ   lphabets are alphanumeric systems. To the an-
          y letter possesses a unique number value.
          quals the sum of the number values of that
          And every phrase, sentence, page, and

text exhibits an additive number value. Fundamentally, this ancient system constitutes a protoform of our own alphanumeric computers."

Watching her sitting in the vitreous light of day's end, her back against a rough thorn tree with Altair caught in the branches, he listened to the fluency of her voice without hearing her. When he realized that she had stopped and waited on his reply, he felt as though he was trying to retrieve a canceled dream. "I'm more interested in phonological studies in Akkadian."

In the Swamp of Goetia, the claggy mud pulled at each step and led him in a slow spiral among dolorous trees and rank weeds. At the center, he came to a black mere where nothing moved. Shawl moss hung still, gray as wizards' beards in the twisted cypresses. Cattails and reeds stood paralyzed. On a flat rock at the center of the glassy mere, the demon of the place sat.

He thought it was a turtle, head and limbs tucked out of sight. From inside its serried shell shaggy with green fungus, it addressed him in the Enochian tongue, "I am ancient proof alone, a voice not heard yet loved as the stillness in the black pearl. Who are you?"

"I am lost."

"You're not listening." The professor adjusted her silk puggaree scarf against the chill crepuscular wind. Night swelled quickly. The children who had been playing in the murky canal were gone. Above the fan palms, clear panels of starscapes glinted, and a few cirrus burned orange among the constellations. "The alphanumerics of writing originally served exclusively as a hieratic system."

"Hieratic—employed by priests. For what? To worship their gods?" He offered her a quiet smile. "Were Enku, Ani, and Ishtar big on ciphering?"

"The ciphering of writing manipulates the gods." She leaned forward with an almost deathly smirk. "The first texts are the software programs that direct the magic forces of the world. With them, the magic of Summer generated civilization—all the fundaments we take for granted: time defined in base sixty, agriculture, husbandry, architecture, cities—and, of course, money."

His attention had drifted into the smoky glitter of day's end among the closing fruit stands and the narrow shops crammed with clayware and lucky mirrors. "You or the hashish talking?"

From its craggy shell, the demon directed him—or banished him—out of the marsh, "You dreamcreature of a hotter world, come no closer. Turn your face of light toward the gleaming grass, and step away among amber horizon clouds. What you seek goes again shining into darkness, far from here. Begone, bright glance."

To his right, tule grass shimmered in a sudden breeze, glistening like fur. The windtrack swept toward a blighted horizon of bare trees in agonized poses. Beyond them, resinous clouds staggered low in the sky. He trudged toward them and at dusk mounted a scarp of poison ivy and clambered free of the leprous swamp.

The turtle in its painted shell awaited on a rock hob. "All things ended in their beginning end here."

The slant light leaning over his shoulder pierced the opaque murk he had traversed, and he glanced back as witness to mud-mired wraiths of miscarried life: clownish ruffles of condoms wavering like sea anemones in oily clouds of sperm, prawns of abortus, gilled gray clots, wrinkled death puppets roiling among small weightless skulls and quail-size briskets. In disgust, he yanked his attention away from that slithery soup. And the turtle chortled, "These kissed life on the mouth—and were eaten."

"Don't begrudge me my small pleasures." The professor drew languorously on her ceramic pipe and exhaled through her nostrils dragon jets of blue smoke. "Before the advent of writing—of spelling—there was no civilization. For over a hundred thousand years, humanity— people no different than you and I—wandered the surface of the earth as nomads, puny, dispossessed clans following wild herds and the seasons. Why did that change so abruptly? How have we come to find ourselves here in a world of jets and cell phones?" Her hard eyes softened to a suspiring gaze. "Magic."

"Right."

"Naturally, you're disinclined to believe me. But truth is not suspended because of your disbelief." She leaned back and averted her green gaze. A fire of carob-wood flapped on the strand, stirred by gusts from the dark sea on the other side of the canal, beyond slouching dunes. Silhouettes of robed figures passed before it. "The world we see around us is but a scrim to a vaster drama. Demons and the allies of life contend on a stage wide as all the universe, and the outcome of that conflict is entirely at hazard."

Beyond Goetia, tableland of scalloped salt glowed violet under starshine. He slogged all night toward crenulate mountains. At dawn, he toiled up a fuming esker and stood staring through mauve veils of blowing pumice at a mirage city. Thirst bulged in his thick face. He squinted against sundogs flaring from parabolic windows of art deco spires. Marble vaults and domes flamingo pink in early light, glittering steel cables, zeppelins big as August clouds moored to tower needles, and ribbon monorails hovered upon puma-hued sands.

Parched and haggard, he slumped into the Metropolis of Aethyrs. A fountain whose cubist segments smeared together in the blurry heat to an alabaster archer jetting prismatic water from her naked breasts slaked his thirst. Crowds coalesced out of the quaking air, their phantom forms sparkling like trout.

In the moil of the translucent crowd, he confronted an older doublegoer, an effigy of sadness, hair streaked with sun-pastels, and weathered countenance of immense world-weary serenity.

Himself?

"I brought you to Egypt to recruit you." The professor did not look at him as she spoke. She watched a kohl-limned moon rising, floating full in the dreamless gulf of night—newel bone ascending to the void above earth, to the celestial planes of the gods and the stairway of stars. "I myself was recruited long ago. I'm tired now. I want to live again in the quotidian world. But someone must take my place. Only in Egypt, where the magi built the most precise corridors into the demonworld, may we kindle a hope of retrieving the texts they are stealing. If we don't get them back, civilization will collapse."

"You realize how wack this sounds—professor?" It

could only have been a joke, and he inclined his head backward, anticipating her laughter.

"I'm counting on your not believing me." On her breath, the phosphorus night of a desert Egypt. Moonlight moved in her hair like a lustrous fluid. "Deception is out of the question. But incredulity will serve, as well—as it did with me. So long ago."

"Well, okay." He waited till she looked at him, and in her fainéant eyes he fathomed she was not joking. "You've got my incredulity. What do you want to do with it?"

Above the Metropolis of Aethyrs, storm clouds towered like a cathedral. Before he could question his older self, a tornado of flies descended from those thunderheads and assailed the plaza. The ghost crowds stampeded down the boulevards, waving fists above their heads.

A frenzied horde of mounted lancers and archers, faces veiled with black head scarves, charged out of the maelstrom of flies. Robes bedighted with mirror shards and red tinsel, they rode standing, headlong horses eyes rolling, snarling and slavering, wild manes jet flames. He fled. The nightmare riders slashed through the vaporous denizens of the mirage city and bore down on him, yammering in Enochian voices high and far-carrying, "The dreaming fire! Stamp it out!"

Among purple billows of flies, he fled.

The student left behind the greasy canal at Sidi Bishr. Snagged in an invisible weave of curiosity, fantasy, and obdurate desire, he obeyed the odd instructions of his professor. "The demons have stolen a cuneiform tablet from the ancient dynasty of Sargon—the powerful *Lugal Zuqi-qi-pum Maqatum—Kings Thrown to the Scorpions*." Her face was tired and yet ferocious. Hard bits of moonlight shone in her eyes as though some prodigious activity in her brain had squeezed her thoughts to diamonds. "You'll find it in one of the 'prophets' tombs'—the first cave in the sea cliffs west of the canal. When you bring it back, you will have established your career, because the *Thrown Kings* has yet to be discovered. Hurry, though. Access is possible only on that final day of winter when the full moon rises. And watch your step. There'll be the usual litter of beer bottles underfoot."

Beneath the screaming horses, he fell. The trampling hooves pounded him flat, to a slant of three o'clock in the afternoon sunlight. Uncanny memories of boredom, soul ache, driftless solitude beyond rescue possessed him: weed precincts of railyards, gray rain leaning on windows, dangling husks in a spider's web, fronds of peeling wallpaper, neon shadows flickering onto cracked ceilings, aimless pollen dust bound for limbo across a vacant farmyard. This oppressive miscellany so saturated him with desuetude, he wanted to die.

Lugal Zuqi-qi-pum Maqatum stashed in a sea cave? He felt like a fool as he crossed the cobbled beach where the sponge-fleet harbored. The burnished faces of the crew glowed like copperware in the driftwood fires, watching him. Through zinc moonlight, he found his way past corrugated iron wharves and an irrigation trough from the canal choked with bramble. He breathed the windflung brine below the sea cliffs and the brassy kiss of nearby factories. A path of coral marl crunched under his shoes and led him to a gaunt cave.

The mournful horn of a barge sliding along the canal turned his attention to the distant sparkling skyline, coruscating minarets and skyscrapers beyond a dark headland and terraces of date palms with Betelgeuse peeking through. That the professor refused to accompany him, that she preferred the indolence of her ceramic pipe, assured him this was all a gruesome joke. But to what end?

He poked his head in the narrow opening. By reflected surf-glow, he spied the promised litter of beer bottles and fast-food cardboard, footprints in the sandspits at the cave entry, and names and dates scrawled in Arabic script upon the wall.

"Let her have her joke," he mumbled, and shoved into the cramped space, intending to turn about quickly and find her laughing in the moonlight under the pectoral curve of a dune.

Brisk sunlight and a bad smell crazed over him from the Horned Gates of Goetia. And his heart coughed with fear.

He wanted to die. Yet, something viscous and sticky in him cleaved to the world's brink. Not love, for all love's fabled glory. Nor hope, the soul's shuddering sickness. Willpower was a thing in a jar.

Rage alone upheld him. Fury at the absurdity. *Demons?* He violently rejected the idea that watchers in the dark could molest him with—what? Sadness? Desolation? The idea choked him with ire. He would not be squashed by ogres and monsters.

He would not let go. Like the stone refusal of Christ in the pietà's arms of Mary, like mountains welded to the planet's rim, he clung to life. With indomitable anger, his entire being quivered. And he rose up from the floor of creation.

He rose up through the scalloped salt flats. The barren pan wove shimmering illusions with the horizon's hot, blue thread. Platinum towers, glass high-rises, and office buildings with dirigibles moored to their steeples stood on planes of heat divorced from the ground. He turned his back upon the Metropolis of Aethyrs, contemptuous of its apparitions, and scanned the white expanse for the whirlwind of flies and the masked horsemen. The dry lake ranged empty under the fierce sun.

"Where am I?" he asked the fiery dream. "What's happened to me?" Throttled with dismay, he bawled a grotesque cry.

Days later, filthy and ragged, he shambled out of the desert. Swollen shapeless in a horror of agony, he shuffled into a magnolia forest. He collapsed among aloe spears crowding a pool of water clear as air, and he drank.

Gradually, sight returned. He sat up with a start. With stupefied brain, he squinted at the pool that had refreshed him and saw submerged bodies bloated and pale as dough. Their hair spread like smoke across the pebbly pond bed.

"Suicides," someone spoke in Enochian—a woman in maroon pajamas and black veil. She sat drenched in sunlight on the porphyry steps of a small temple. Onyx columns and copula of green chalcedony enclosed a marble pedestal. Atop the pedestal, a statue's gypsum head lay on its side wearing an ancient, enigmatic smile—and his face.

Spellbound, he stood and uttered in a voice hoarse with wonder, "You know me."

"Of course." The eyes above the veil, soft with dreams, susurrant as an addict's, were black honey. "You are a factory for the manufacture of excrement. You are a pylorus of endless hunger. I know you, you world of multiplying bacteria. Awe of maggots."

"Demons!" He groused and angrily departed the Temple of Himself. "Hell!" he spat derisively, finally accepting the absurd truth of his predicament. "Hell and demons! Damn it all!"

Behind him, the priestess from his temple yelled, "You will drink rats' tears! Do you hear me? You bile duct! You sphincter!"

"Yeah, yeah."

At the sandy verge of the magnolia forest, he paused. Inversions of heat stood the sky's tranquil lake upon the silicate plain of noon. Far off, he glimpsed the Metropolis of Aethyrs. But he was not bound there. His own ghost in that city had confided a longer journey and only silent speculation where he might retrieve the tutelary *Lugal Zuqi-qi-pum Maqatum.*

"The dreaming fire—" That was the name given him by the demon horsemen whose hooves could not kill him. *Dreaming this fiery hell . . . and dunes like slouching lions . . . an evil dream.*

Yet, a dream from which there was no waking—for

he never slept. He felt his mind slip along fault lines of madness.

More deviltry ...

He stared at a rock warped by heat until it disappeared. He provoked wind-feathered clouds out of sapphire emptiness. He inked night and stenciled the void with stars.

For the first time in hell, he smiled.

A hoarded mass of bougainvillea, palms, and giant ferns interrupted the magnetic haze of the wasteland. Morning sun spangled among mango trees isolated in an oasis backed by a salt lake and its further forevers of desert.

He breathed the jasmine air and strolled into the magnificent grove. A pool where he knelt to drink reflected how his wanderings as a dreamcreature in the netherworld had reconfigured his hot atoms upon some grittier imagination deep in his psyche: sun-hued hair, curly as a heifer's, weathered face hollowed as an elk's, a taurine neck, and eyes, once reminiscent of a gazelle's, now tapered to the thin, pitiless gaze of a jinni.

At a watering trough shaded by acacia and sycamore, camels gnarred. Their dismounted riders, cowled figures in crimson robes trimmed in tinsel, loitered in a courtyard beyond large folding doors with pistol bolts and inscribed panels of sphinxes and griffins. They sat together on the raked sand of a rock garden and motioned for him to approach.

"Lugal Zuqi-qi-pum Maqatum," an iron voice spoke. In the corrugated sand before them stood a clay tablet incised with cuneal scratchings. "Take it."

*   *   *

Over a carafe of date wine, he conversed with the demons in the rock garden. They wanted empathy. "We are part of each other," they explained in their basso-profundo voices. "You and we belong to the same universe, albeit at far extremes. And now that you know you are a dreaming fire, you can annoy us, but you cannot thwart us. You are too small. Try to understand. Here, at the dark limits of our expanding cosmos—in the googolth year of what you call time—each *atom* of our world is as large as the entire universe of your lifetime. Our reality is inherited from yours. Can you blame us for tinkering with our past—your world—to shape the contours of our experience?"

Butterflies, red as firecracker confetti, jittered around the sweet fumes of the carafe. "Why does your happiness require you to inflict suffering on my world?"

"We don't think that way, anymore than your carpenters think they are inflicting suffering on the forest when they carve a tree into a house."

"I've seen evil."

"Dreamcreature, you see what you dream. You see with human eyes. We sympathize. Our positron brains, like your carbon brains, perceive reality in selective ways. Truth is a fiction. Reality unknowable."

He peered into the darkness of their hooded faces with mutinous eyes. "I will return the *Thrown Kings* to my world. That magic will hold you at bay."

"You shall thwart only a portion of our efforts to design our own truth. We shall steal other texts."

"And I will return here and take them back."

"Some, yes. Others, no. You shall tire. Hot and compact as you are, as dazzling to us in your power as you are, your energy is finite."

"Others will join me."

"*Others?* No. You are alone, doomed to defend one small segment of time in your world. The texts you retrieve will preserve your civilization only for a while. We will steal them again. You will retrieve them again. We will steal and you retrieve. Again and again you will attack us and then circle back to that small tract of years that is yours and yours alone to protect, like a vicious guard dog—on a short leash."

The demons' words made his brain feel like a strange machine whose function eluded him. "I will tell others. Many will join me."

"The laws of information and entropy do not permit that."

"I don't understand."

"Of course not, else you would not speak such foolishness. The more information you spread, the greater the chaos you create. The more chaos you create, the easier for us to topple your civilization the way a lumberjack fells a tree for the sawmill. You will help us enormously if you do not hold this secret very close indeed."

Terror smoldered in him. "What are you saying?"

"Think of a house of cards. The information necessary to define the coordinates in space of those precisely ordered cards is much less by far than the information required to define the coordinates of those same cards scattered randomly. The greater the chaos, the more information. And *vice versa*." The burly voice smote him.

"The more people who know of us—or the more information you share with that one person who will replace you when you finally weary of this perpetual task—the greater the chaos by far—and the more material available for us to do our work."

Crushed breathless by this hopeless revelation, he could barely ask, "Why are you telling me this?"

They bellowed the answer in satanic chorus, "This is *information,* you benighted fool! The more you know, the greater the chaos that—"

He snatched the *Kings Thrown to the Scorpions* and ran wailing from the garden of demons, wailing as loud as he could to drown out those voices damning him with their hideous secrets.

A winged viper, tarry feathers a blur, eyes like fireflies, guided him across the badlands of hell to the Goetic Gates. Stepping past those slanderous iron palings, he found himself again in the sea cave at Sidi Bishr among strewn litter of empty bottles, of used condoms.

By some demonic temporal parallax, he had been returned to a time prior to his departure, antecedent even to his birth. *The demons' tight leash.* For weeks to come, he felt as one does in dreams. Imbrued with salty bereavement for the mundane reality departed from him forever, he proceeded in a daze. He carried heavily the silence inflicted on him and bridled in his heart the horror of madness.

As predicted by the professor who had damned him, *Lugal Zuqi-qi-pum Maqatum* earned him recognition in academic circles. He accepted a lecturer's chair in Sumerology at Trondheim in Norway, as far from Egypt as he could arrange. Yet, within a year, there appeared in the classroom a serenely tall man of blue-black skin wearing a black aba and white turban.

Among the sand cliffs and monument rocks of Egypt, secret corridors delivered him joylorn to the demon-world whenever the taciturn messenger summoned. He came and went frequently to that hallucinary demesne upon the universe's dark rim, recovering texts the demons stole. Each journey wore him closer to madness.

At last, he could take no more. In that sanctuary of memory anterior to aught of demons and their darkness beyond the crumbling stars, he recalled the professor who had recruited him. She would be of an age.

Winterset in Egypt at the opulent Shiraz teahouse, sitting under mirrored birdcages on a thistle-soft Baluchistan carpet, Hejaz incense twisting soft iridescent braids in the air behind him, the professor faced his student and informed her with a gentle, knowing smile. "The most avid collectors of books are demons. But they want only the old texts. The *oldest* texts."

Nina Kiriki Hoffman *has been writing SF and fantasy for more than twenty years, and selling a heck of a lot of it. Her works have been finalists for the World Fantasy and Endeavor Awards.*

Novels include A Fistful of Sky *and* The Silent Strength of Stone; *her third short-story collection,* Time Travelers, Ghosts, and Other Visitors, *was published last year.*

Nina works in a bookstore, teaches writing, and sometimes carries tiny strange toys around in her bag.

Relations

Nina Kiriki Hoffman

Why did people always break?

Just when Sarah had them tenderized and sweet, trained to be just what she wanted, delicious and only the slightest bit resistant, the tiny tussle of kitten claws that excited her, something went wrong inside them and they broke.

This one, Jill, with her mountain cabin in the Idaho Sawtooths, her elegant ownership of a fantastic view and beautiful furniture, lovely music and imported foods, this one was a favorite, the best Sarah had found in a long time. Jill had lasted longer than the others, had kept her fighting spirit alive for quite a while. Sarah had loved Jill for months, and Jill had eventually loved Sarah. But now Jill's gray-green eyes were dead.

Sarah closed her eyes and kissed Jill. Jill still tasted sweet, and her lips responded to the kiss. Almost, Sarah could pretend they were at the beginning of capitulation, her favorite part of the relationship, where the other recognized that Sarah was powerful enough to force things, but didn't realize how powerful, how completely impossible to resist. That training was what Sarah loved. The tiny steps and occasional big ones toward the other's recognition that the other had no escape and no resources and no hope.

It was now, when the realization was complete, that Sarah lost interest.

She hugged Jill and stepped back, stared into Jill's eyes, looking for some last glimmer of fight to stamp out. All fight was gone. Jill stood silent, haunted, waiting.

"I won't be back," Sarah said. She touched Jill's lips with her first two fingers, watched Jill's pupils dilate, turned away before she saw anything that would hold her here. It was time to hunt for someone else.

Sarah loved the hunt.

There were rules to the hunting and ownership of humans. If she were going to bring someone home, where there were other people who had powers, some of them stronger than Sarah, she would have to follow the rules.

The new rule was: No more slaves. So, really, she couldn't bring anyone home anymore. At first she had fretted and raged, but then she realized she could own people away from home. Once she figured that out, she realized she need not follow any of the other rules, either, the ones about never take a person on their home ground, take only those who won't be missed or needed, only take another if you are in dire need of help. Life got much more interesting after Sarah threw out the rules, though she spent most of her time away from home now, and did the minimum amount of service for Family she could get away with.

She found Alonzo in a field.

She found him from above. Air was her sign, and air lifted her whenever she asked it to, carried her, even rendered her invisible as she desired. She hunted from air.

From above, Alonzo's dark red hair flamed in the sun, a weave of copper glints. His shirtless shoulders were wide. Sarah drifted down to look from the side, and she liked what she saw. He was young but full grown, dark from sun, strong with the slidy muscles of work, tall and perfect, focused on what he was doing. She even liked his face, with its deep-set brown eyes and long jaw.

She touched down in shadow, on a big rock under a maple tree at the edge of the field, then let air reveal her. She sat on the rock and watched Alonzo walk the furrows of the field. He was rangy and self-confident, stooping now and then to shift a clod of earth sideways, tamping down elsewhere. He was wearing wash-whitened jeans, but his feet were bare. What was he doing?

Singing.

Sarah cupped hands to her ears as Alonzo walked away from her. He was singing, but so softly she almost couldn't hear it. The tune almost sounded familiar. He stooped and touched the earth, smoothed something, patted something, sang, and wandered away. Presently he reached the far end of the field and turned back, walking another row, singing and stooping and working his way to her.

She waited. When he reached the near end of his row, five feet from her, she sent a breeze toward him. He glanced up.

"Oh," he said, in a rising tone, his voice warm and pleasant and low. "Who're you? How long you been there?"

"I'm Sarah."

"How'd you get way out here away from everything?"

She smiled at him and shrugged.

"I mean, this part of the farm isn't even on the road. Whatcha doing out here?"

"Watching you."

He rose and straightened, edged his shoulders back. He smiled at her.

She loved his eyes, deep under thick copper brows, their shadowed brown lightened by a few gold flecks. She loved his mouth. His smile stretched it wide. His full lower lip looked luscious.

"Why?" he asked.

"You're beautiful."

"Oh." Color flooded his face, and he turned away. "Don't you say that."

"Why not? It's true." She slid down the rock to stand before him. He was a head taller than she, his skin shades darker, sunbrowned, his chest lightly forested with red hair. His skin glistened with a sheen of perspiration. He smelled sweaty, and his hands were sheathed in dirt damped by sweat.

"Girls are beautiful. Men are handsome," he said, then in a lower voice, "You're beautiful."

Almost, she left. If he were an idiot, he wouldn't amuse her for long, no matter how fine his physical attributes were.

But she was here, face-to-face. Might as well give him a couple of other chances to impress her. "I introduced myself. Who are you?"

"Alonzo," he said.

"What were you doing, Alonzo?"

"Singing to the seeds."

A breeze brushed the back of her neck, raised prickles even in the hot, hot day. Seed singing? She remembered something about that. Something, but what? Nobody had brought it up in the course of normal events. There was a working farm at Chapel Hollow, but she left all that plant stuff to the others. For community service, she disciplined people and hunted and gathered.

"Bet that sounds funny, huh? Not many as does it anymore, but we always get a better crop when I do it."

"What song are you singing?" She stepped closer to him, and he smiled again, engaging and sweet. He smelled lovely, musky and male.

"Don't know, exactly. Nonsense, I s'pose. Whatever I think they need to hear."

"May I listen too?"

"Sure." He held out his hand, and she slid hers into it, wondering how long it had been since some trusting child had reached out to her, unafraid, unknowing. Fifteen years? Twenty? Not since she came into her gifts and talents, surely.

Alonzo was delicious. His hand was hard and hot in hers, callused and strong, though his grip was gentle. "Got three more rows to do," he said. He turned and tugged her with him along a furrow, and then his voice rose, eerie and strange, soft and stirring. "Time to wake, time to grow, time to change, time to send, find the water, find the sun, find the work your center holds," he sang. Knelt, touched ground, plunged a finger down into it, crooned something that made Sarah's cinnamon hair rise on its roots. *"Silla krella kalypta, miksash kooly tashypta."*

Her fingers clenched his. "What?" she whispered. "What? What are you saying?"

"Huh? I dunno. Probably something Mama sang to me when I was little."

She had never heard the lyrics before, but after she got over the shock of hearing her family language from this stranger—a language only used at home for rituals and curses—she worked out what he said. *Find your fertility, and I will protect you.*

"Where'd your mother come from?"

"Right here. Four generations we've worked this land. Put down roots, Mama said." Alonzo laughed.

"Four generations?" Sarah's family had been at Chapel Hollow for seven generations. Maybe this was some discarded offshoot of her family, or a tiny branch of the Southwater Clan, their split so long ago, she hadn't even heard rumors.

Family.

That was an added complication she hadn't anticipated. One could mistreat family in all kinds of ways, but one wasn't allowed to own them. On the other hand, if the waters were diluted enough, maybe Alonzo and his family had lost the powers that set Sarah and her family apart. Maybe they had different rules. Maybe she could own him anyway no matter what the rules were: So long as she overpowered him, how could he stop her?

What if she didn't overpower him? What if he had powers of his own?

Wouldn't that be terrific? She hadn't had a good fight in way too long.

"Four generations," Alonzo repeated. "We're not going anywhere. That's why I'm glad you came here." He tugged gently on her hand, and she went with him up the row as he sang to the things in the ground about sprouting, growing, strengthening, producing flowers and pollen and seed and fruit, ultimately providing and dying. Half the time he sang in English, and half in Ilmonish. Sarah fell into a light daze as she walked the earth with him. Something about his songs charmed and calmed her, made her think nothing mattered besides the sun on their heads, the scents of turned earth and nearby trees, the soft, rich soil under their feet, and the connection of their clasped hands. It was pleasant to walk along sweating with a boy. Every once in a while she summoned a breeze to breathe across their damp foreheads and the burning backs of their necks, tease their hair and brush over their arms. Alonzo smiled at her. Nice teeth.

She woke after they had walked the rest of the field, and the sun was straight above them. "You thirsty?" Alonzo asked.

Sarah licked her lips. What had she been thinking? She'd wasted an hour or two walking along beside this gentle idiot while he crooned to plants. Maybe she should get out of here, find someone more interesting to work on. Even if Alonzo *was* Family, that didn't make him automatically interesting.

"Actually, I'm *very* thirsty," Sarah said. She surprised herself. Usually if she was thirsty, she drank. Her throat was parched now. How had she come to this state without noticing?

"Come on up to the house, I'll get you some lemonade."

Go to his home place? No, that wasn't a good idea, not unless he lived alone. "Who else is at the house?"

"Everybody who's not out doing a job or at school. The three younger kids are off to school right now, but they'll be home after a bit. Mama's baking today, and Grandma is repairing. Grandpa's in the basement. He's always in the basement. Dad's plowing over in the east field, and my older brother Jacob, he's off with the cattle for the day."

Supposing any of them had powers, she'd rather not encounter several at once. First she needed to find out what Alonzo's skills were. "How about if I wait here and you go get the lemonade," Sarah said.

"Shy, are you?"

She smiled at him.

"That's so cute," he said. "Okay. You wait here. Don't you go away!"

When Sarah pulled her hand away from Alonzo's, it came slowly, which alarmed her. Had he been binding her to him? Those songs—

He leaned over and planted a kiss on her cheek, then ran across the field away from her. The kiss sizzled against her skin, a pleasant burn in the heat of the day. Her mouth tasted sweet now, a taste like the blood of bitten clover stems. She wandered back to the boulder under the maple where she had first watched Alonzo. She sat in the shade and brooded at her toes.

He was spelling her. Was he really spelling her? How could that be, without her noticing?

She muttered the chant for "Things Seen and Unseen," and saw that a downy blanket of green vines wrapped around her. She couldn't feel them or touch them. She didn't know what they were doing to her. But she knew she hadn't donned them on purpose, so they must be Alonzo's doing.

Oh, no. She said a prayer to air. Wind sprang up and blew the vines off her, and she woke up. Trapping her! Spelling her! Alonzo was hunting *her!* How dare he? Did he even know who she was? Well, she could show him. This *was* a fight, but he didn't fight fair.

Then again, neither did she.

The vines were easy to dispel. Once they were gone, and the mental fog that had calmed her with them, she said "Things Seen and Unseen" again, and realized that lines like thick, twisted ropes went from the soles of her feet to the earth below. She lifted her feet and felt the bottoms. She could see the ropes for the duration of the spell, but she couldn't feel them or break them. She raised her arms and asked air to lift her. It tugged her up into the sky, but before she got very high, the ropes on her feet stopped her. She tried going sideways and again was stopped.

What had he said about putting down roots?

She tried cutting spells, transforming spells, destroying spells. Nothing even nicked the ropes.

This couldn't be right. That dumb boy couldn't have trapped her this way. Or maybe he could. It might take major work to get out of this one.

Alonzo walked toward her across the field, carrying a wooden tray with a bottle, two glasses, and a plate of pastries on it. "Hey," he said. "You all right?"

He didn't know what she was. Best keep it that way as long as possible. Feign ignorance. "Thirsty," she said.

"Got your lemonade right here. You hungry? Mama sent along some brownies too. She wins prizes with these brownies at the county fair every year. She's looking forward to meeting you."

"Alonzo, I don't want to meet your mother."

"Sure you do. I bet she'll like you. You're way prettier than the girl Jacob got."

"What happened to the girl Jacob got?"

"Sissy? She's home now, waiting to have her first baby. Grandma's training her up in repairing work." He set the tray on the rock beside her, poured a tall glass of lemonade, and handed it to her.

The glass was cool and sweating in her hand. Sarah's mouth hungered for the lemonade. Her throat was so dry, just breathing hurt a little. What if this was another way he was binding her to this place, though? "Lemonade makes me thirsty," she whispered. "Can I have some water?"

"Well, sure. Wait here just a sec. There's a stream off a little ways. I'll get you a glassful." Alonzo took the empty glass and struck off into the forest.

Sarah set the glass of lemonade on the tray and rose to her feet. She couldn't transform the ropes at her soles into anything else, but what if she changed herself? She turned her face skyward and let herself melt into air, a transformation she feared, to utterly abandon herself to her element. She had had to demonstrate mastery in this skill before her great-aunt and teacher would lead her further into the dark disciplines, but she had never grown comfortable with it.

She had not tried it in years, but found that she still had this power. She became air and lifted free of the trap Alonzo had laid for her. Aahhhh. Good.

"Sarah?" Alonzo returned, calling her: she could feel his voice all through her. "Sarah, where'd you go? I got your water. Sarah?"

Now. Let's leave this place. Disperse utterly and go away, re-collect ourself somewhere else. She flung herself wide.

"Stop it," Alonzo said. He set down the glass of water, held out his hands, clenched them into fists.

Something flexed and jerked Sarah back into a person-sized and person-shaped package. She stood on the rock, suddenly herself again, terrified and shivering.

Alonzo leapt up onto the rock beside her and put his arms around her. "I'm sorry. I didn't mean to scare you.

I don't ever want to hurt you. But you're mine now, Sarah, and I don't want you all misty."

"I'm yours?"

"Didn't you give yourself to me? You came here and found me and walked with me while I was seed singing. Our earth knows you now. You're mine."

Her tears surprised her. He stroked her hair, then stooped and got the glass of water, held it to her lips. Little sobs shook her. She took the glass from his hand and sipped. The water was cool and sweet. She felt it in her mouth, her throat, her stomach, spreading out through her body, claiming her, another binding to this place, but she couldn't stop drinking, she was so thirsty. "I'm yours," she whispered. This stupid sweet boy had spelled her down tight. Set a trap for a sparrow, and caught a vulture. He didn't know yet.

He would learn.

"Let's have babies together." He took the empty glass from her hand, set it on the tray, held her and kissed her gently.

"No," she whispered. A baby. She had longed for a baby all her life. Ever since she was born, she had been told the greatest thing she could ever do was have a baby, but she had tried every spell she knew, every remedy, even ridiculous ones, and her womb had never quickened, no matter who she slept with. "We can't, Alonzo." Maybe he would free her now. She thought of little cinnamon-haired children with Alonzo-brown eyes, children who would love her just the way she was. If only.

She remembered when she was six and her youngest sister was born. She had loved holding the baby. She had even sought out other people's babies to hold and care for. She had grown, confident that someday she'd get her own baby and nobody would be able to take it away.

She had made rules: Even when it cried, she wouldn't hit it. She would just hug it. She would always feed it when it was hungry. She would change it the instant it needed a new diaper. She would have the happiest baby in the world.

Then when she was twelve, her teacher, her great-aunt, did a foretelling, found she was barren. Something had soured in her then. She had tried to defy the fore-telling. Later she had accepted it.

"We can't?" Alonzo asked. "Why not?"

"Something's wrong with me."

"No," he said. "You're perfect." He sat down on the rock and tugged her down too, pulled her into his lap. She relaxed into his embrace, wondering. He had already trapped her, when she hadn't known anyone could. What if he knew stronger spells than she did?

He set his hand on her stomach and closed his eyes. She felt warm power seep from his palm and into her like sunshine, strange and comforting, and then a blossom of heat inside her, spirals of heat in her breasts, a rising itch and readiness. "Perfect," he whispered.

She pulled his mouth to hers, tore his pants off, lifted her dress, sucked him inside.

The sun had gone west, the light changed to gold, the shadows lengthened, when she finally let him go. Her back itched and burned from the rough rock. She felt swollen and sore and strangely contented. Alonzo, scratched and bruised, was asleep now, facedown on the rocks beside her, his mouth half-open, his breathing quiet. He looked pale and exhausted. He didn't snore. Good. One thing she wouldn't have to fix.

She sat up, placed her hands over her stomach, sought inside herself, felt something she had given up hope she would ever feel. Tiny sparks.

Sparks. A future.

She set her palm on the rock. *How did you fix me?*

That is our skill, mine and Alonzo's, to make things ripe and ready, whispered the spirit of the place. *It was born in him, one in a long line of such people. It's one of the things this family has taught me.*

Thank you, Sarah thought, and then, *Am I trapped here forever?*

Do you want to leave?

For a moment she thought of her own branch of Family. She owed them duty, but would they really miss her? Probably not. Most of them hated her. Besides, technically, she was still with Family.

A fierce longing for open sky and infinite possibilities, the freedom of any direction, any new person she chose to play with, any possible next rose up in her, flooded her with regrets and frustrations.

She touched her stomach. It would be all right.

She could make her own people now.

ABOUT THE EDITOR

Al Sarrantonio, the author of numerous books, is a winner of the Bram Stoker Award and has been a finalist for the World Fantasy Award and the British Fantasy Award. He is the editor of several books, including the highly acclaimed anthologies *Redshift: Extreme Visions of Speculative Fiction* and *999: New Stories of Horror and Suspense.* His short stories have appeared in magazines such as *Heavy Metal, Asimov's Science Fiction, Realms of Fantasy, Analog, Fantastic,* and *Amazing,* as well as in anthologies such as *The Year's Best Horror Stories, Visions of Fantasy: Tales from the Masters, Great Ghost Stories,* and *The Best of Shadows.*

COPYRIGHTS

"The Sorcerer's Apprentice" copyright © 2004 by Agberg, Ltd.

"Perpetua" copyright © 2004 by Kit Reed

"The Edges of Never-Haven" copyright © 2004 by Catherine Asaro

"Pat Moore" copyright © 2004 by Tim Powers

" ▓▒▒▓▒ : Six Hypotheses" copyright © 2004 by *The Ontario Review*

"The Silver Dragon" copyright © 2004 by Elizabeth A. Lynn

"Fallen Angel" copyright © 2004 by L. E. Modesitt, Jr.

"The Following" copyright © 2004 by P. D. Cacek

"A Tower with No Doors" copyright © 2004 by Dennis L. McKiernan

"Boomerang" copyright © 2004 by Larry Niven

"Wonderwall" copyright © 2004 by Elizabeth Hand

"Blood, Oak, Iron" copyright © 2004 by Janny Wurts

"Riding Shotgun," copyright © 2004 by Charles de Lint

"Demons Hide Their Faces" copyright © 2004 by A. A. Attanasio

"Relations" copyright © 2004 by Nina Kiriki Hoffman

Tales of Mithgar as told by Dennis L. McKiernan

THE EYE OF THE HUNTER
0-451-45268-2

The comet known as the Eye of the Hunter is riding
through Mithgar's skies again, bringing with it
destruction and the much dreaded master, Baron Stoke.
Only a small band of worthies, united in their quest,
can save Mithgar in its hour of need.

VOYAGE OF THE FOX RIDER
0-451-45411-1

An unexpected visitor, troubled by a mysterious
vanishing, and a prescient nightmare, enlists the help of
Mage Alamar. In a quest for her missing beloved, Mage
and Foxrider, Man, Elf, and Dwarf oppose a master of
evil bent on opening a path through which a
terrifying, dark power might come to the world
of Mithgar.

THE DRAGONSTONE
0-451-45456-1

A terrifying conflagration is coming to engulf
Mithgar—unless Arin can solve a mysterious riddle
which instructs her to seek the cat, the one eye, the
peacock, the ferret, and the keeper, for they alone will
aid her in her quest for the fearsome Dragonstone.

Available wherever books are sold or at
penguin.com

R417